WESTERN

Rugged men looking for love...

A Temporary Texas Arrangement
Cathy Gillen Thacker

Grace And The Cowboy
Mary Anne Wilson

MILLS & BOON

A TEMPORARY TEXAS ARRANGEMENT
© 2023 by Cathy Gillen Thacker
Philippine Copyright 2023
Australian Copyright 2023
New Zealand Copyright 2023

First Published 2023
First Australian Paperback Edition 2023
ISBN 978 1 867 29820 5

GRACE AND THE COWBOY
© 2023 by Mary Anne Wilson
Philippine Copyright 2023
Australian Copyright 2023
New Zealand Copyright 2023

First Published 2023
First Australian Paperback Edition 2023
ISBN 978 1 867 29820 5

® and ™ (apart from those relating to FSC®) are trademarks of Harlequin Enterprises
(Australia) Pty Limited or its corporate affiliates. Trademarks indicated with ® are
registered in Australia, New Zealand and in other countries.
Contact admin_legal@Harlequin.ca for details.

This is a work of fiction. Names, characters, places, and incidents are either the
product of the author's imagination or are used fictitiously, and any resemblance to
actual persons, living or dead, business establishments, events, or locales is entirely
coincidental.

Published by
Harlequin Mills & Boon
An imprint of Harlequin Enterprises (Australia) Pty Limited
(ABN 47 001 180 918), a subsidiary of HarperCollins
Publishers Australia Pty Limited
(ABN 36 009 913 517)
Level 19, 201 Elizabeth Street
SYDNEY NSW 2000 AUSTRALIA

MIX
Paper | Supporting
responsible forestry
FSC® C001695

Cover art used by arrangement with Harlequin Books S.A.. All rights reserved.

Printed and bound in Australia by McPherson's Printing Group

A Temporary Texas Arrangement
Cathy Gillen Thacker

MILLS & BOON

Cathy Gillen Thacker is a married mother of three. She and her husband reside in North Carolina. Her stories have made numerous appearances on bestseller lists, but her best reward is knowing one of her books made someone's day a little brighter. A popular Harlequin author, she loves telling passionate stories with happy endings and thinks nothing beats a good romance and a hot cup of tea! Visit her at cathygillenthacker.com for information on her books, recipes and a list of her favourite things.

Visit the Author Profile page
at millsandboon.com.au for more titles.

Dear Reader,

During our marriage, my husband and I have moved cross-country four times and locally five. What do I hate about it? Packing and unpacking. What do I love? The excitement of finding a new place to live and the joy of making it ours.

Veterinarian Tess Gardner is moving to Laramie, Texas, the place where her family is rooted. She has an exciting new job. And she's inherited a house that is a bit more than what she expected.

Enter CEO Noah Lockhart. He has also moved back to Laramie, in the wake of his wife's death several years before, to be near his family. Life for him and his girls is finally settling down and getting back to normal. Or it will, he is certain, once the latest member of the ranch menagerie is born.

All Noah wants from Tess is help getting through the birth and the first week or two of their new pet's life. In exchange, he will give her a private guest suite and a place to live, rent free, while her house is renovated.

He doesn't expect to get close to her. She doesn't expect to fall for him. But you know what they say about love—it's what happens when you are busy making other plans.

I hope you enjoy this last book in the Lockharts Lost & Found series. If you have missed any of the seven other novels, there is information on Facebook and on my website, cathygillenthacker.com.

Thanks for reading! You, dear readers, are what make all the hard work, creating every fictional family and their stories, worthwhile!

Cathy Gillen Thacker

DEDICATION

This book is dedicated to Ryan, our gorgeous
sock-and-mischief-loving yellow Labrador retriever.
Thanks for always bringing us our shoes and
putting them on our lap when it's time to go for a walk.
Don't know what we would do without you, sunshine.

CHAPTER ONE

"YOU'RE REALLY GOING to go in there. Alone. Just before dark?" The low, masculine voice came from somewhere behind her.

With the brisk January wind cutting through her clothes, Tess Gardner paused, house key in hand, and turned toward the Laramie, Texas, street. Senses tingling, she watched as the man stepped out of a charcoal-gray Expedition, now parked at the curb. He wasn't the shearling coat-wearing cowboy she had expected to see in this rural southwestern town she was about to call home. Rather, he appeared to be an executive type, in business-casual wool slacks, dress shirt and loosened tie. An expensive down jacket covered his broad shoulders and hung open, revealing taut, muscular abs. Shiny dress boots covered his feet.

Had it been any other day, any other time in her recently upended life, she might have responded favorably to this tall, commanding man striding casually up the sidewalk in the dwindling daylight. But after the long drive from Denver, all she wanted was to get a first look at the home she had inherited from her late uncle. Then crash.

The interloper, however, had other plans. He strode closer, all indomitable male.

Tess drew a bolstering breath. She let her gaze drift over his short, dark hair and ruggedly chiseled features before returning to his midnight blue eyes. Damn, he was handsome.

Trying not to shiver in the cold, damp air, she regarded him cautiously. Drawing on the careful wariness she had learned from growing up in the city, she countered, "And who are you exactly?"

His smile was even more compelling than his voice. "Noah Lockhart." He reached into his shirt pocket for a business card.

Disappointment swept through her. She sighed. "Let me guess. Another Realtor." A half dozen had already contacted her, eager to know if she wanted to sell.

He shook his head. "No." He came halfway up the cement porch steps of the century-old Craftsman bungalow and handed over his card, inundating her with the brisk, woodsy fragrance of his cologne. Their fingers touched briefly and another tingle of awareness shot through her. "I own a software company," he said.

Now she really didn't understand why he had stopped by, offering unsolicited advice. Was he flirting with her? His cordial attitude said *yes*, but the warning in his low voice when he had first approached her, and had seen that she was about to enter the house, said *no*.

He sobered, his gaze lasering into hers. "I've been trying to get ahold of you through the Laramie Veterinary Clinic," he added.

So he was *what*? Tess wondered, feeling all the more confused. A pet owner in need of veterinary care? A potential business associate? Certainly not one of the county's many successful, eligible men who, she had been teasingly informed by Sara, her new coworker/boss, would be lining up to date her as soon as she arrived.

Curious, she scanned his card.

In bold print on the first line, it said:

Noah Lockhart, CEO and Founder

Okay, she thought, so his name was vaguely familiar. Below that, it said:

Lockhart Solutions. "An app for every need."

The company logo of intertwining diamonds was beside that.

Recognition turned swiftly to admiration. She was pretty sure the weather app she used had been designed by Lockhart Solutions. The restaurant finder, too. And the CEO of the company, who looked to be in his mid-thirties, was standing right in front of her. In Laramie, Texas, of all places.

"But even though I've left half a dozen messages, I haven't gotten any calls back," he continued in frustration.

Tess imagined that wasn't typical for someone of his importance. That was just too darn bad.

Struggling not to feel the full impact of his disarming, masculine presence, Tess returned his frown with a deliberate one of her own. She didn't know if she was relieved or disappointed he wasn't there to ask her out. She did know she hated being pressured into anything. Especially when the coercion came from a place of entitlement. She propped her hands on her hips, the mixture of fatigue and temper warming her from the inside out. "First of all, I haven't even started working there yet."

His expression remained determined. "I know."

"There are four other veterinarians working at the animal clinic."

"None with your expertise," he stated.

Somehow, Tess doubted that. If her new boss and managing partner, Sara Anderson McCabe, had thought that Tess was the only one qualified to handle Noah's problem—whatever it was—she would have called Tess to discuss the situation, and then asked Tess to consult on the case. Sara hadn't done that. Which led Tess to believe this wasn't the vital issue or 'emergency' Noah deemed it to be.

More likely, someone as successful as Noah Lockhart was simply not accustomed to waiting on anyone or anything. That wasn't her problem. Setting professional boundaries was. She shifted the bag higher on her shoulder, then said firmly, "You can make an appointment for next week."

After she had taken the weekend to get settled.

Judging by the downward curve of his sensual lips, her suggestion did not please, nor would, in any way, deter him. His gaze sifted over her face, and he sent another deeply persuasive look her way. "I was hoping I could talk you into making a house call, before that." He followed his statement with a hopeful smile. The kind he apparently did not expect would be denied.

Tess let out a breath. *Great*. Sara had been wrong about him. Noah Lockhart was just another rich, entitled person. Just like the ridiculously demanding clients she had been trying to escape when she left her position in Denver. Not to mention the memories of the ex-fiancé who had broken her heart...

Determined not to make the same mistakes twice, however, she said coolly, "You're still going to have to go through the clinic."

He shoved a hand through his hair and exhaled. Unhappiness simmered between them. Broad shoulders flexing, he said, "Normally, I'd be happy to do that—"

And here they went. "Let me guess," she scoffed. "You don't have time for that?"

Another grimace. "Actually, no, I—we—likely don't."

"Well, that makes two of us," Tess huffed, figuring this conversation had come to an end. "Now, if you will excuse me…" Hoping he'd finally get the hint, she turned back to the front door of the Craftsman bungalow, slid the key into the lock, turned it and heard it open with a satisfying click.

Aware that Noah Lockhart was still standing behind her, despite the fact he had been summarily dismissed, she pushed the door open. Head held high, she marched across the threshold. And strode face-first into the biggest, stickiest spiderweb she had ever encountered in her life!

At the same time, she felt something gross and scary drop onto the top of her head. "Aggghhh!" she screamed, dropping her bag and backing up, frantically batting away whatever it was crawling through her thick, curly hair…

THIS, NOAH THOUGHT RUEFULLY, was exactly what Tess Gardner's new boss had feared. Sara Anderson McCabe had worried if Tess had seen the interior of the house she had inherited from her late uncle, before she toured the clinic and met the staff she was going to be working with, she might change her mind and head right back to Denver and the fancy veterinary practice she had come from.

Not that anyone had expected her to crash headfirst into a spiderweb worthy of a horror movie.

He covered the distance between them in two swift steps, reaching her just as she backed perilously toward the edge of the porch, still screaming and batting at her hair. With good reason. The large, gray spider was still moving across her scalp, crawling from her crown toward her face.

Noah grabbed Tess protectively by the shoulders with one hand, and used his other to flick the pest away.

It landed on the porch and scurried into the bushes while Tess continued to shudder violently.

"You're okay," he told her soothingly, able to feel her shaking through the thick layer of her winter jacket. She smelled good, too, her perfume a mix of citrus and pa-tchouli. "I got it off of you."

She sagged in relief. And reluctantly, he let her go, watching as she brushed at the soft cashmere sweater clinging to her midriff, then slid her hand down her jean-clad legs, grimacing every time she encountered more of the sticky web.

Damn, she was beautiful, with long, wildly curly blond hair and long-lashed, sage-green eyes. Around five foot eight, to his own six foot three inches, she was the perfect weight for her slender frame, with curves in all the right places, and she had the face of an angel.

Not that she seemed to realize just how incredibly be-guiling she was. It was a fact that probably drove all the guys, including him, crazy.

Oblivious to the ardent nature of his thoughts, she shot him a sidelong glance. Took another deep breath. Straight-ened. "Was it a spider?"

Noah had never been one to push his way into anyone else's business, but glad he had been there to help her out, he said, "Yes."

Her pretty eyes narrowed. "A brown recluse or black widow?"

He shook his head. "A wolf spider."

"Pregnant with about a million babies?"

He chuckled. "Aren't they always?"

She muttered something beneath her breath that he was pretty sure wasn't in the least bit ladylike. Then, pointing at the ceiling several feet beyond the still open front door, where much of the web was still dangling precariously, she turned back to regard him suspiciously. "Did you know it was there? Is that why you told me not to go in alone?"

He held her gaze intently. He hadn't been this aware of a woman since he'd lost his wife, but there was something about Tess that captured—and held—his attention. A latent vulnerability, maybe. "It never would have occurred to me that was what you would have encountered when you opened the door."

Squinting, she propped her hands on her hips. "Then why the warning about not going in alone?"

Good question. Since he had never been known to chase after damsels in distress. Or offer help indiscriminately. He had always figured if someone wanted his aid, that person would let him know, and then he would render it in a very trustworthy fashion. Otherwise, he stayed out of it. Tonight, though, he hadn't. Which was…interesting… given how many problems of his own he had to manage.

She was still waiting for his answer.

He shrugged, focusing on the facts. "Waylon hadn't been here for at least a year, before he passed four months ago, and he was never known for his domestic skills." So he honestly hadn't known what she would be walking into.

She scanned the neat front yard. Although it was only a little past five o'clock in the afternoon, the sun was already setting in the wintry gray sky. "But the lawn and the exterior of the house are perfectly maintained!"

"The neighbors do that as a courtesy for him."

"But not the interior?" she persisted.

"Waylon didn't want to trouble folks, so he never gave anyone a key."

Tess turned her gaze to the shadowy interior. All the window blinds were closed. Because it was turning dusk, the inside of the home was getting darker by the minute. And the mangled cobweb was still dangling in the doorway.

Noah knew it was none of his business. That she was an adult, free to do as she chose. Yet, he had to offer the kind of help he knew he would want anyone in his family to receive, in a similar situation.

"Sure you want to stay here alone?" Noah asked.

ACTUALLY, NOW THAT she knew what she was facing, Tess most definitely did *not* want to stay here tonight. "I don't have a choice," she admitted with grim resignation. "I don't have a hotel room. Everything in the vicinity is booked. I guess I waited too long to make a reservation."

He nodded, seemingly not surprised.

"The Lake Laramie Lodge and the Laramie Inn are always booked well in advance. During the week, it's business conferences and company retreats."

"And the weekends?" she queried.

"On Saturdays and Sundays it tends to be filled with guests in town for a wedding or family reunion, or hobby aficionados of some sort. This weekend I think there's a ham-radio conference... Next week, scrapbooking, maybe? You can look it up online or just read the signs posted around town, if you want to learn more."

"Good to know. Anyway..." Tess pulled her cell phone from her pocket and punched the flashlight button. Bright light poured out. "I'm sure I can handle it. Especially if we turn on the lights..."

She reached for the switches just inside the door. To her surprise, neither brought any illumination.

Noah glanced at the fixture on the ceiling inside the house, then the porch light. "Maybe the bulbs are just burned out," he said.

Stepping past the dangling web, he went on inside, to a table lamp. She watched as he tried it. Nothing.

Still wary of being attacked by another spider, she lingered just inside the portal, her hands shoved inside the pockets of her winter jacket. The air coming out of the interior of the house seemed even colder than the below-freezing temperature outside. Which meant the furnace wasn't on, either. Although that could be fixed.

Noah went to another lamp. Again, nothing happened when he turned the switch. "You think all the bulbs could be burned out?" Tess asked hopefully, knowing that at least that would be an easy fix.

"Or…" He strode through the main room to the kitchen, which was located at the rear of the two-story brick home. She followed him, careful to avoid plowing through another web, then watched as he pushed down the lever on the toaster. Peering inside the small appliance, he frowned.

Anxiety swirled through Tess, as she wondered what she had gotten herself into. "Not working, either?"

"No." Noah moved purposefully over to the sink and tried the faucet. When no water came out, he hunkered down and looked inside the cabinet below. Tried something else, but to no avail. As he straightened, three small mice scampered out, running past him, then disappeared behind the pantry door. Tess managed not to shriek while he grimaced, and concluded, "Both the electricity and water are turned off."

Which meant the mice and the spiders weren't the worst of her problems. "You're *kidding*!" After rushing to join him at the sink, she tried the ancient faucet herself. Again…nothing.

Noah reached for the cords next to the window above the sink and opened the dark wooden blinds. They were covered with a thick film of dust. As was, Tess noted in discouragement, everything else in sight.

Plus, the spiders had had a field day.

There were big cobwebs in every corner, stretched across the ceiling and the tops of the window blinds, and strewn over the beat-up furniture. Worse, when she looked closely, she could see mice droppings trailing across much of the floor. Which could mean she had more than the three rodent guests she had already encountered. *Ugh*.

"Seen enough for right now?" Noah asked.

Tess shook her head in dismay. She'd had such dreams for this place. Hoped it would give her the kind of permanent home and sense of belonging she had always yearned for. But while she was certainly taken aback by what they had discovered here tonight, she wasn't going to let it scare her off. Besides, in addition to the property, her late uncle had left her the proceeds of his life-insurance policy, with the expectation she would use the funds to fix up the house. "Maybe the upstairs will be better…"

Unfortunately, it wasn't. The single bathroom looked as if it hadn't had a good scrubbing in years. Two of the bedrooms were filled with piles of fishing and camping equipment. The third held a sagging bed, and heaps of clothes suitable for an oil roughneck who spent most of his time on ocean rigs.

On a whim, she checked out the light switch, and the sink in the bathroom, too. Neither worked.

Noah was gazing at her from a short distance away. "Well, that settles it, you can't stay here," he said.

Tess had already come to the same conclusion.

Although, after two very long days in her SUV, she wasn't looking forward to the two-hour drive to San Antonio for an available hotel room.

He met her gaze equably. "You can come home with me."

CHAPTER TWO

Noah may as well have suggested they run away together, given the astonished look on Tess Gardner's pretty face. Then, without another word, she brushed by him and headed down the staircase, still using her cell-phone flashlight to lead the way.

Noah followed, giving her plenty of space. He had an idea what she was feeling. He had been orphaned as a kid and had lived in three different foster homes, over a two-year period, before finally being reunited with his seven siblings and adopted by Robert and Carol Lockhart. So he knew firsthand what it was like to be alone, in unfamiliar circumstances, with those around you offering help you weren't sure it was safe to take.

If he wanted to help her, and he did, he would have to make sure she knew his intentions were honorable.

Being careful to avoid cobwebs, she walked out of the numbing cold inside the house, and onto the front porch, breathing deeply of the brisk air. Slender shoulders squared, she swung back to him. "Why would you want to do that for me?"

It wasn't lost on him that for a fiercely independent woman like her, an offer like this probably wasn't the norm. But for someone like him—who had finished growing up here—it was. Patiently, he explained, "Because this is Laramie County, and neighbors help neighbors out here all the time. Plus—" he winked, teasing, as if this was his only motive "—maybe it will give me an in with the new vet. But if you want, you could always call Sara Anderson McCabe—" their only mutual acquaintance, that he knew of, anyway "—for a character reference."

The mention of the other Laramie County veterinarian had Tess relaxing slightly. "First, I already did Face-Time with her earlier today. Both her kids are sick with strep throat. And on top of that, between the construction for the new addition on her house, the extra work at the veterinary clinic since the founding partner retired five weeks ago and the fact she is seven months pregnant, she is completely wiped out. I'm not about to add anything to her already full slate."

Noah admired Tess's compassion. That she was willing and able to put others first, even when her own situation was far less than ideal, spoke volumes about this newcomer. Perhaps Sara had been right. Even though the two of them had kind of gotten off on the wrong foot, his gut told him that Tess was going to fit right into this rural community.

She studied him even more closely, then after a pause, admitted wearily, "And second, it's not necessary. I already know what Sara's going to say when it comes to your character. Since you were first on the list of eligible men she thought I should meet."

Noah frowned. His old friend had already been matchmaking? This was news to him. But perhaps not such an unexpected occurrence for the gorgeous woman standing opposite him.

He studied the guileless look in Tess's light green eyes.

"Initially, I sort of assumed that was why you were here," she continued dryly, with a provoking lift of her brow. "To get a jump on the competition?"

Glad to know he wasn't the only one who routinely tried

to find the irony or humor in every situation, Noah stifled his embarrassment and scrubbed a hand over his face.

As long as they were going to talk candidly…

He met her casually probing gaze. "Ah, no." Romance had most definitely *not* been on his mind when he had stopped by the house on a whim, to see if she had arrived or if there was anything he could do for the town's newest resident. "Since my wife passed a couple of years ago, I've had my hands full with my three little girls. And I don't see that changing anytime soon."

Her eyes widening in obvious surprise, she stepped toward him. Up and down the block, the time-activated streetlamps suddenly switched on, spreading yellow light through the increasing winter gloom and enabling her to peer at him even more closely. She tilted her head up to his. "So, you're *not* interested in dating?"

He shook his head. A woman like this…well, she could make him forget his new, more cautious approach to life. And that was something he just couldn't risk.

She sighed in obvious relief and stepped back.

He watched the color come into her high, sculpted cheeks. "And you?" Noah asked.

"No," she said emphatically. "I'm definitely not on the market."

Their eyes locked.

"Although I am interested in meeting new people…" she said, then paused. "Making friends," she added eventually.

Noah exhaled. "Can never have enough of those," he said, meaning it. It was his friends and family who had helped him through the past few tumultuous years.

And would continue to help him.

Because as rough as it had been to weather the emotional impact of losing the first and only love of his life, it was even harder to face life as a single dad.

"So about that offer to bunk at your place tonight…" Tess said, pacing the length of the porch, squinting to evaluate. "It really wouldn't be an inconvenience?"

Wanting to give her the kind of small-town Texas welcome his friends Sara and Matt McCabe had wanted for her, Noah shook his head. "Nah. I've got a big house with a nice guest suite. But if you get there and you're not comfortable with the setup for any reason, you could always take refuge at my folks' ranch house just down the road. They are babysitting my three girls this evening, so you'll have a chance to meet them, too." He released a breath. "And if you're *still* not comfortable with that option, my mom is a social worker for Laramie County, so it's possible she might be able to pull some strings and find you a place to bunk for the night."

Tess pursed her lips. "Like where?"

"Uh… I honestly don't know," he admitted. "Maybe there's an on-call room at the hospital that's not being used?"

She ran a hand through her thick mane of curly hair. "This is getting ridiculously complicated."

"You're right. And it doesn't have to be. So what do you say?" he asked her gruffly. "How about you lock up here, and we head out to my place?"

When she still looked a little hesitant, he added, "You can follow in your Tahoe. Check out the accommodations. And we can take it from there."

FORTUNATELY, THE DRIVE was an easy one. And fifteen minutes later, Noah was turning his charcoal-gray Expedition onto a paved driveway off the country road they'd been traveling on, winding his way past the mailbox. Tess was right behind him, in her red SUV.

The black wrought-iron archway over the entrance proclaimed the property to be the Welcome Ranch. Which was ironically appropriate, given the circumstances, Tess couldn't help but think.

Neat fences surrounded the manicured property. In the distance, a sprawling home could be seen. The impressive two-story abode featured California architecture, with an ivory stucco exterior. There were plenty of windows, and the first floor was all lit up. In the distance she could also see a grassy paddock and a big, elegant barn that looked as if it had been recently built.

She didn't notice any livestock grazing in the moonlit pastures. But she supposed there could be horses stabled in the barn.

Noah parked next to an extended-cab pickup that was in front of the four-car garage. Tess took the space next to that. As they got out, the front door opened, and a handsome couple in their midfifties stepped out and stood beneath the shelter of the portico.

He fell into step beside her. "My folks," he explained as he ushered her toward them. "Mom, Dad, this is Tess Gardner, the new veterinarian at the Laramie clinic. Tess, my parents, Robert and Carol Lockhart."

"Oh, you're here to see Miss Coco!" Carol Lockhart exclaimed, making an incorrect assumption. A slender woman with short dark hair and vivid green eyes, she was dressed in a cashmere turtleneck, tailored wool slacks and comfortable-looking winter boots.

Her tall, dark-haired husband had the year-round tan and fit appearance of someone who spent his life working outdoors. He nodded at Tess in approval. "Mighty nice of you."

Noah shifted closer to Tess and lifted a halting palm, before any further assumptions could be made. "That's not happening tonight," he said definitively, looking chagrined at the way his parents were jumping to conclusions. "Tess isn't starting work at the clinic until Monday, and she has had a really long day. Or actually, probably a couple of very long days."

He was right about that. Tess's muscles ached from the two-day, 800-plus-mile drive from Denver to Laramie County. Some of it over mountain roads. Much of it in inclement weather. Still, she didn't want anyone making decisions about what she was or wasn't up to. Curious, she turned back to his mother. "Who is Miss Coco?"

Carol explained, "Noah and the girls' miniature donkey. Noah's been worrying nonstop about her the last few weeks. So when he heard you had cared for a lot of mules back in Colorado during your fellowship, and were considered quite the expert, he was ecstatic."

Noah exhaled. He sent his mother a look that said he did not appreciate Carol speaking for him. "I wouldn't say ecstatic, exactly."

"Relieved, maybe?" his dad suggested.

"Something like that," Noah murmured.

Frowning in confusion, his mom turned back to him. "So if Tess isn't here to see Miss Coco tonight, then…?"

"I'm afraid I didn't plan my arrival very well," Tess admitted, chagrined. "I thought the house I inherited from my uncle would be clean and empty. It was neither. There's also no electricity or water."

Noah added matter-of-factly, "Unfortunately, as you know, the offices that can turn the utilities back on won't be open until Monday. All the lodging in the area is booked. So I offered to let her bunk here temporarily."

Carol and Robert both smiled, understanding. Before they could say anything else, he asked, "Were the girls well-behaved for you?"

His parents nodded. "They went to bed at eight o'clock and went right to sleep," his dad said.

The interior of the house did seem quiet.

A lethargic chocolate-brown Labrador retriever ambled out on the porch. Recognizing an animal lover when he saw one, he went straight for Tess. She kneeled to greet him, letting him sniff her while she scratched him behind the ears. With a blissful huff, he sat down next to her, leaning his body against her legs.

"You know…we could stay a few more minutes if you all want to walk out to the barn, just for a minute," Carol suggested hopefully.

Tess had the idea that the older woman was worried about the miniature donkey, too. Although no one had yet said exactly why…

Her fatigue fading, the way it always did when there was an animal in need of care, she turned back to Noah. A little embarrassed she hadn't been more helpful when he had tried to talk to her earlier, she asked, "Is that where Miss Coco is housed?"

Noah nodded.

"We could stay with the girls until you're back from the barn," Carol offered. "And I know Noah would feel better if you just took a quick peek at Miss Coco."

So would Tess. Appreciating the unexpectedly warm welcome from both Noah and his folks, she smiled. "Just let me get my medical bag out of my SUV."

"You really don't have to do this," Noah said as they took off across the lawn, toward a big slate-gray barn that looked as new as the house.

He paused to slide open the door and turn on the overhead lighting. The floor was concrete and there were a half-dozen stalls made of beautiful wood, and a heater was circulating warm air. He motioned for her to come inside.

Aware how comfortable she already felt with him, Tess smiled. "The least I can do, given how truly hospitable you have been."

Their eyes met. With a brief businesslike nod in her direction, he pulled the door shut, to keep in the heat, and led the way forward.

Tess had to quicken her steps to keep up with him. As she neared him, she caught another whiff of his woodsy scent, and something else, maybe the soap or shampoo he used, that was brisk and masculine.

A tingle of awareness surged through her. She pushed it away. She had mixed work and pleasure once, to a heartbreaking result. She couldn't allow herself to react similarly here. Especially to a man whose heart was ultimately as closed off as her ex's had been. "So what has you so concerned?" She forced herself to get back to business. "Can you give me a little history...?"

He paused and placed one hand over the top of the middle stall on the right. "Eight months ago, I went to the local 4-H adoption fair with my oldest daughter, Lucy." He eased open the stall door, gazing tenderly down at the miniature jennet curled up sleepily on fresh hay. "She fell in love with Miss Coco the minute she saw her..."

Tess gazed down at her new patient, entranced. "I can see why. Oh, Noah. She is beautiful!" With a light brown coat the color of powdered cocoa, a white stripe that went from her ears down her face, to the base of her throat, and white socks and tail, Tess figured the miniature donkey measured about two and a half feet tall. Her eyes were big and dark, and she was watching them carefully.

"Luckily, she has a personality to match. The problem is, I didn't know she was gestating when we adopted her.

I just assumed her belly was a little swollen from lack of care. By the time I found out it wasn't an issue of malnutrition or lack of exercise, Lucy—my oldest—was already very attached."

Tess kneeled next to Coco, petting her. "And you don't want two donkeys." She opened up her bag.

"It's not really that. As you can see, I obviously have space for them. It's my three-year-old twins I am worried about. Lucy's eight. She can follow directions and understands there is no negotiation when it comes to the safety and welfare of animals in our care. The rules are the rules. Period."

Tess examined Coco's belly and the area around the birth canal, finding everything just as it should be. She reached for her stethoscope, pausing to listen to the strong, steady beat of Coco's heart, the breath going in and out of her lungs. Then she listened to the foal nestled inside. All was great.

She removed the earbuds and turned back to Noah. "And the twins...?"

"Are still at an excitable age. Angelica is sweet and mellow most of the time. A follower. Avery, on the other hand, has a real mind of her own. When she sets out on a mission, whatever it is, it can be hard to rein her in."

Tess laid the stethoscope around her neck and resumed petting Coco. She gazed up at Noah, who was still standing with his back to the side of the stall, the edges of his jacket open, his arms folded in front of him. He had the kind of take-charge, yet inherently kind, aura she admired. And if she were emotionally available, she'd be a goner. "Are you worried the twins will be too rough with the foal and that the baby's mama might be too protective and hurt them?"

He nodded with no hesitation. "Both—if the twins get too wound up. But I heard about something called imprint training, where you teach an animal from the moment they are born to trust and love the human touch. Which really gentles them. Sara said you gave classes in it, back in Colorado."

The ambient lighting in the stable made him look even more handsome. Which was definitely something she did not need to be noticing. Any more than how good he smelled. Or how strong and fit his body looked in business-casual clothing.

Fighting the shiver of sensual awareness sliding through her, she forced herself to smile back at him. "I did."

His gaze sifted over her, igniting tiny sparks of electricity everywhere he looked. "And you plan to give them here?"

Tess nodded. "When I get settled in, yes."

His expression fell in disappointment.

"But I could help show you what to do, in the meantime, so you will be prepared."

He cocked an eyebrow, his good humor returning. "Private lessons?"

One lesson, maybe. Ignoring the potent masculinity and charisma radiating from him, she returned dryly, "I don't think it will take you all that long to get the hang of what to do. In the meantime, Miss Coco and her baby are doing fine. Everything is as it should be."

"Any idea when she will go into labor and deliver?" he asked, concerned.

She studied the conflicted expression on his face. "I'm guessing you heard that a miniature jennet's gestation period can last anywhere from eleven to fourteen months."

He nodded.

"Right now, I'm guessing it will be another one to two weeks." Tess put her stethoscope back in her vet bag and closed the clasp. She rose to her feet. When her shearling lined boots unexpectedly slid a little on the crushed hay, Noah put out a hand to steady her, the warmth of his hand encircling her wrist. His gentle, protective touch sent another storm of sensations through her. She worked to hold back a flush.

Gallantly, he waited until he was sure she had her footing, then let her go slowly. He stepped back, folding his arms across his chest once again. The warmth inside her surged even more as he looked her in the eye. "How will I know when it's time?" he asked.

She replied in the same serious tone. "A number of things will happen. The foal will turn and move into the birth canal. Miss Coco'll be restless and may even look thinner. And she'll be holding her tail away from her body to one side. At that point, she will need to be closely monitored twenty-four seven."

Noah began to look overwhelmed again.

Together, they walked out. "What about being here when Miss Coco's foal is born?" He paused just outside the barn doors. "Will you do that for us, to make sure everything goes all right?"

Tess nodded. "Be happy to," she promised with a reassuring smile. Ushering new life into the world was the best part of her job.

As they reached the porch, the fatigue hit her, hard. Noah went to get her two bags out of her Tahoe, while Carol showed her where to wash up and poured her a hot cup of tea. By the time he'd returned, his parents were already half out the door.

He regarded her sympathetically. "What else can I get you?"

Her hands gripping the mug, Tess shook her head. "Nothing. Thanks. All I want is a hot shower, and a bed. Time to sleep."

He gave her an understanding look. "I'll show you the guest suite."

She followed Noah as he led the way up the stairs, then past two rooms, where his three daughters could be seen snuggled cozily in their beds, sleeping in the glow of their night-lights.

Tess couldn't help but think how lucky he was, to have such a beautiful family and nice home, as the two of them moved silently past his girls, to the very end of the hall.

Oblivious to her quiet envy, he showed her the nicely outfitted guest suite with a private bath, chaise lounge just right for reading and comfortable-looking queen-size bed. He set her bags down just inside the door, in full host mode. "If there is anything you need that's not in the bathroom, let me know." He stepped back into the hall, and as their eyes met, a new warmth spiraled through her. He continued in a low, husky voice calibrated not to wake his daughters. "The kitchen is fully stocked, so make yourself at home there, too."

"Thank you," Tess returned, just as softly, marveling at his kindness, even as she reminded herself he had already stated that, just like her, he was not emotionally available. For anything more than a casual friendship, anyway. "I will."

"Well..." He cleared his throat, suddenly looking as reluctant to part company as she was. Which made her wonder if the latent physical attraction went both ways.

Giving no clue as to what he was thinking, he nodded at her. "See you in the morning."

A distracting shiver swept through her once again.

Working to slow her racing pulse, she responded with an inner casualness she couldn't begin to feel. "Sure, see you then." She smiled as he turned to walk away. And just like that, she was on her own for the rest of the night.

CHAPTER THREE

HOURS LATER, NOAH was awakened from a deep sleep. "Daddy, there was a pretty lady in the kitchen, and she said to give you this when you waked up," Lucy said importantly. She and her twin sisters climbed onto his bed, the twins on one side, Lucy perched on the other.

Damn. He'd overslept. Noah scrubbed a hand over his face. *Not exactly the way he wanted to start the day.*

"Are you awake now?" Avery asked. "'Cause we want to know what the letter says. And Lucy still has trouble reading cursive."

"Okay." Noah sat up. A piece of paper was pushed into his hand. "'Noah,'" he began, reading out loud. "'Thanks so much for all your help and hospitality last night. Tess Gardner.'"

Nothing about seeing each other again.

Noah felt a wave of disappointment move through him. He couldn't say why exactly, but he had expected a little more. Something warmer or more personal. But then, she'd said she wasn't looking for anything more than friendship. Same as him. And she did have a lot on her slate.

A lot of which she was still going to need help with.

He thought about the look on her face when she'd run into that giant spiderweb, how it had felt to step in to rescue her, and feel her brush up against him, for one long incredible moment. He swallowed, pushing aside another wave of unexpected yearning.

He hadn't been close to anyone since Shelby had died. Hadn't wanted to be. Initially, it had been because he was still grieving and couldn't imagine anyone ever taking her place. Later, because he didn't want to risk the pain that came with a loss like that. He'd also known he hadn't the time or energy to try and incorporate someone special into his life. Never mind worry about how his girls would react if he did ever start dating again. So to feel fiercely attracted to Tess now was…well, unexpected, at the very least.

Feeling like the worst host ever, he swallowed. "Did she leave?" *Please tell me she hasn't gone yet.*

"Uh-huh. But she said to tell you that she looked in on Miss Coco and she's fine this morning, too. And also she took Tank out to the barn with her, so he probably won't need to go out for a while, although he will need to be fed. She gave him fresh water."

Pleased by the unexpected help, he smiled, ruminating softly. "That was nice of her…"

"Who is *she*?" Lucy queried, looking protective. She flung her long, tangly hair out of her eyes. Hair she did not brush nearly enough. Unlike her twin sisters, who were always brushing and styling each other's hair. "And why was she in *our house*? And why didn't we ever see her before this morning?"

Unable to get out of bed with the girls perched on either side of him, and unwilling to make them move just yet, Noah pushed up, so he was sitting against the headboard. He figured this was as good a time as any to have this conversation. "The nice lady's Dr. Tess Gardner. The new veterinarian I was telling you girls about. The one who knows a whole lot about taking care of miniature donkeys and their foals. She just moved here yesterday, and she came by last night to check out Miss Coco for us." At least that was what had ended up happening. Which was a good thing. It had given them a chance to get to know each other a little better, and see each other in a different light.

As he had watched Tess care for their miniature donkeys, it was easy to see why Sara had been so determined to get Tess to accept a position at the vet clinic in town. Tess was a very skilled clinician. Gentle. Thorough. Kind. And professional.

All were traits he considered essential.

In a veterinarian.

In a friend…

And of course she was very beautiful, and sexy in that breezy girl-next-door way, too.

Not that he should be noticing…

Exhaling, Noah continued, "Dr. Tess checked on Miss Coco's baby foal, too. And it was all good. Both were healthy as could be."

His three daughters readily accepted his explanation, for why Tess had been in their kitchen so early in the morning.

Although, Lucy gave it more thought, and her eyes widened. "She watched over Miss Coco *all night*? In the stable?"

Noah shook his head. "She slept in the house."

"Why?" Lucy's scowl deepened.

Patiently, Noah explained, "There was an unexpected mess-up with Dr. Tess's plans. Her house didn't have any power or water. The hotels were full, and she needed a place to sleep, so I offered her our guest room."

His eight-year-old folded her arms in front of her, and her lower lip slid out, into a pout. "Only our grandma and grandpa sleep in the guest room," she reminded him archly. "Or our aunts and uncles."

"Well, last night it was Dr. Tess."

Lucy continued to mull over that fact, not necessarily

happily. Since all seven of his siblings had found love and gotten married recently, she had made it clear on numerous occasions that she was worried he would do the same. While she liked the attention of adult women, and the feminine, maternal perspective they brought, she didn't want anyone taking her late mother's place.

Initially, he hadn't, either.

But lately…seeing the rest of his family all paired up and so happy, he had begun to realize just how lonely he was. Having kids was great.

It was even better when you had someone to share them with.

But the woman who took his late wife's place in their lives was not going to be just anyone.

She'd have to be full of life and love. Independent. Kind. Giving.

Sort of like… Tess Gardner. Hold on! Where in the hell had *that* thought come from?

Lucy was frowning. "Hmm."

Figuring a change of subject was in order, Noah motioned for the girls to move. As soon as they hopped off the bed, he threw back the covers and swung his legs over the edge. "Who wants to go with me to give Tank his breakfast and then run down to the barn and check on Miss Coco?"

"Me!" all three girls squealed in unison.

"Then get your barn boots on," he said, shoving aside all thoughts of Tess and the impact she'd had on him in only a few glorious hours. "And I'll meet you in the kitchen."

"WELL, WHAT DO you think?" Sara Anderson McCabe asked, after she had shown Tess around the veterinary clinic, and introduced her to all the staff before weekend office hours started at nine o'clock on Saturday morning.

The effervescent managing partner walked Tess into the

small room with a desk that would serve as Tess's private office. With its polished linoleum floor, and standard office desk and chair, it was nothing like the luxurious office at her job in Denver. Yet, somehow, it was so much warmer.

"Are you going to be able to be happy here?" Sara asked, squinting at her.

Tess nodded. "I'm sure I will be." Everyone was just so darn nice. Including, and especially, Noah Lockhart. Not that she should be thinking of him…

Sara rested her palm on her pregnant belly. "Did you find a hotel to stay in until the movers get your belongings here from Denver? Or were you going to just go ahead and move into the house you inherited, as is?"

"Well, there was a slight problem with that." Briefly, she explained about the lack of utilities, and abundance of spiders and mice.

"Oh, no."

Oh, *yes*…

Sara shook her head, not looking all that surprised, now that she'd had a moment to think about it. "Well, Waylon wasn't known for his housekeeping. Not that he was ever home for long. When he came in off the oil rigs, all he ever wanted to do was go fishing until it was time to head back to the Gulf." She sighed. "But I had no idea he turned all his home's utilities off during his absences. Although I suppose it makes sense. Financially, anyway." She gave Tess another thoughtful squint. "So what did you do?"

"Um…"

This was a rural county. Sara was bound to find out, anyway. Not that it had been a secret.

Tess swallowed. "Noah Lockhart offered to put me up last night, at the Welcome Ranch."

Sara did a double take, unable to completely contain her pleased look. "You met Noah?"

"Yeah. He stopped by while I was looking at my uncle Waylon's house." *And gallantly saved me from more than a few spiders.*

The woman's eyes lit up hopefully. "What did you think?"

That she had never met anyone who could take her breath away with just a look, the way he could.

Aware Sara was still waiting for her reaction, Tess shook her head, struggling for something she *could* say. Finally, she sobered and managed a response. "He's, um, very tall." About six foot three inches to her own five foot eight. *And handsome.* "And, uh, helpful." Oh, Lord, what was this? When had she ever been so tongue-tied? Or felt like such a teenager? One with a secret crush?

Sara laughed. She lifted a halting palm. "Okay, I won't pry. Moving on. So what's your plan now?"

That was the problem. Tess didn't really have one. Yet. "Well, I can't get the power and water turned on until their offices open on Monday. But I have an exterminator meeting me at the house this afternoon. And I'm going to spend the rest of the day just getting my bearings and figuring out what I need."

Concern radiated from Sara. "Do you have a place to stay in the meantime?"

Tess nodded. "I made a reservation at a River Walk hotel in San Antonio for the next two nights." Although she was hoping not to need to drive all that way if she could get her new home clean enough to camp out in for the next few days.

"Somewhere with spa services, I hope?" the other woman teased.

Tess chuckled in response, then grabbed her purse and keys. "Anyway, I better get going."

Sara walked her as far as the employees' entrance. "Let

me know if you do need anything. Including a place to stay. Matt and the kids and I can always make room."

Tess knew that. She just didn't like depending on others for anything. It was always much better when she could handle things on her own. Which was exactly what she planned to do.

SEVERAL HOURS LATER, Tess had everything she needed for the cleanup of her new home to begin. She headed for Spring Street. No sooner had she parked, than a now-familiar charcoal-gray Expedition pulled up behind her.

Noah stepped out.

Unlike the evening before, when he'd been garbed in business-casual, he was dressed in a pair of old jeans and a flannel shirt, as well as a thick fleece vest and construction-style work boots.

He looked so good he made her mouth water.

Pushing away the unwanted desire, she met him at the tailgate of her Tahoe. Despite herself, she was glad he had come to her rescue again. She tilted her head back to look into his eyes. "Seriously, cowboy, we have to stop meeting like this."

He grinned at her droll tone. His midnight blue eyes took on the sexy glint she was beginning to know so well. "I figured you were going to need help."

He had figured right. What she hadn't decided was if it was a good idea or a bad idea to allow herself to depend on him. Especially because she had been down this road before, only to have it end disastrously.

Pushing all thoughts of her ex and their failed relationship away, she opened up her tailgate. Determined now to focus on the gargantuan task at hand.

He saw the big box. "A wet-dry vac. Good idea."

His approval warmed her. Why, she didn't know. She

inhaled the masculine scent of his soap and shampoo. "It will be when I finally get electricity on Monday."

At least she *hoped* it would be on Monday.

Out here in the country, there was no guarantee they offered same-day service, for an extra fee, the way they did in the city.

Grateful for his lack of recrimination or judgment, with regard to her lack of proper planning, Tess let Noah help her slide the bulky box onto the ground. He smiled genially, as relaxed as she was stressed.

Nonsensically, she chattered on. "I figured it was the fastest way to get up all the crud inside and dispose of it."

He scanned her work clothes and equally no-nonsense boots. Her own quarter-zip fleece jacket.

"In the meantime," she sighed, lifting out the rest of her purchases, "there's the old-fashioned way, of broom, dustpan and trash bag."

Noah stepped closer, inundating her with the heat and strength of his big masculine body. Then he rubbed his hand across his closely shaven jaw, before dropping it once again. "Actually—" he let his gaze drift over her face before returning to her eyes "—we could use your shop vac today. If you don't mind borrowing some electrical power from a neighbor."

He really knew how to tempt her. But… "I can't ask someone I don't know."

He chuckled, a deep rumbling low in his throat. "Sure, you can," he drawled, surveying her as if he found her completely irresistible. Another shimmer of tension floated between them and she felt her breath catch in her throat. What was it about this man that drove her to distraction? "Neighbors help each other out around here. Remember? But I can understand your reluctance to ask for a favor, when you meet the new neighbors for the first time. So if you want—" he placed a reassuring hand on her shoulder, the warmth of his touch emanating through her clothes "—I can rustle up some outdoor extension cords, go next door and set that up for you. As well as help you put the wet-dry vac together."

The part of her that wanted to keep her heart under lock and key responded with a resounding *No!* The temptation to lean on Noah Lockhart was too strong as it was. But the more practical part of her felt differently. She had to be at work at her new job, seeing patients, forty-eight hours from now. And right now, like it or not, the house she had inherited was definitely not livable.

She drew in a deep, enervating breath and dared to meet his eyes, trying not to think how attracted she was to him. She swallowed hard. "Sure." She forced herself to sound casual. As if she was used to such random kindness in her life. She took out the rest of the cleaning products and microfiber cloths, and shut the SUV tailgate. "Thanks... I would really appreciate that."

He picked up the bulky box and easily carried it up the front steps to the porch. "Now we're talking."

She followed with the bags. When they were face-to-face again, she tilted her head at him, curious. "Not that I'm not grateful for the help, but don't you have responsibilities of your own to tend to?"

He came near enough that she could feel his hot breath fanning against her skin. "My girls are on a play date with their cousins, over at my parents' ranch."

He whipped out his cell phone, punched a button on the screen and began typing. To whom, she didn't know.

"I'm supposed to join them at six this evening, for dinner," he explained.

But until then, the implication was, he was free to do whatever he felt like doing.

"Nice." She set down her things, then fished around in the front pocket of her jeans for her keys. Unable to help herself, she added with an appreciative smile, "Your daughters were very cute, by the way."

The proud, affectionate look on Noah's face told her he knew he had hit the jackpot when it came to his kids. She could not help but agree.

Wistfully, once again, she wished she had a few of her own just like them. In fact, as far as timing went, she had thought she would be married, with at least one child by now. But she had fallen in love with someone who ultimately hadn't felt the same, so…

He finished texting. Glancing up, his eyes scanned her face, his expression serious now. "I hope they were polite to you this morning."

Tess reflected on the three pajama-clad little girls, with their pink cheeks and tousled hair. The three-year-old twins had their daddy's deep blue eyes. Their big sister, Lucy, was lovely, too. Albeit observant and intuitive. Guarded. Aware he was waiting on her reply, she said finally, "I think they were more shocked than anything."

He lifted an eyebrow. Urging…no, more like demanding that she go on.

Tess cleared her throat. "Lucy made it clear women did not spend the night at the Welcome Ranch, unless they were family." *Which I am definitely not.*

"Ah, well…" He slid his phone into his pocket. "As I said, I'm not looking for a new woman in my life."

Which should be reassuring.

It had been yesterday.

Now, that knowledge just left her feeling off-kilter. The way she always did when she allowed herself to want something that was not likely to happen. Like she had with her ex. Thinking that time—and increasing intimacy—and a more settled lifestyle after the super demanding years of vet school and residency—would ease them into a blissful future. And give them both the lifelong commitment and family that she had yearned for.

Unfortunately, her ex had other ideas. And priorities.

Noah's phone tinged, signaling an incoming text. He pulled it out and looked at the screen. Smiled, as he announced, "My brother Gabe lives a few blocks over. He's got a few outdoor extension cords we can borrow. He's going to bring them right over."

Another pleasant surprise. She could so get used to this. "That's nice of him."

"Yeah."

Tess unlocked the front door and carefully led the way inside. It was as icy cold and musty-smelling as the day before. To the point that all she could think was *ugh*.

Eminently calm, Noah looked up. "The spiders were busy."

The cowboy standing beside her was right. New webs were everywhere. Tess sighed. She hoped this wasn't an omen. "They certainly were."

CHAPTER FOUR

"WANT TO TAKE a break?" Noah asked, an hour later.

Looking even more overwhelmed than she had when they had first walked in, Tess nodded. She sighed, completely vulnerable now as she met his gaze, seeming on the verge of tears.

It was easy to see why she was so demoralized, Noah thought. While the exterior of the brick home was pristine, the interior of the house looked like something out of an episode of *Hoarders*. And though they had been knocking webs down from the ceiling and windows with the broom, and vacuuming up dirt and debris, there was still so much to do.

Tess shoved a hand through her wild butterscotch-blond curls. Her elegant features were tinged an emotional pink. He moved close enough to see the frustration glimmering in her eyes. "I mean it helps to have some of the dust and gunk gone," she said, flashing him a grateful half smile, "but I still kind of feel like all we're doing at the moment is rearranging the deck chairs on the *Titanic*."

"Yeah. I can see that analogy." He stepped nearer. It was all he could do not to take her in his arms and comfort her. But he knew that could lead to trouble with a capital *T*. "Do you think it would help if we cleared out a room or two? Just made some space?"

Her teeth raked her plump lower lip. "Probably, yeah." A look of relief flashed on her face.

Next question.

Savoring her nearness and the pleasure that came from being alone with her like this, he asked, "Is it going to be difficult for you to sort through this stuff?"

She shoved her hands in the pockets of her jeans. The take-charge veterinarian was back. "No. There are only two things I'm keeping. The first is that rusted-out cast-iron skillet in the kitchen that I'm pretty sure belonged to my grandmother. The second are the fishing lures my uncle made, and one of his tackle boxes to keep them in. Everything else that can be donated will be. The stuff that can't will be trashed."

He liked her decisiveness. "What is your timetable for getting this all done?"

Another shadow crossed her face. Their eyes locked, providing another wave of unbidden heat between them. "Ah, yesterday," she joked, running her hands through her hair again.

He noticed how the midday sunshine, which was flooding in through the grimy windows, caught the shimmer of gold in her blond hair.

He reached over and took her hand in his, wondering what it would take to make her feel as crazy with longing and giddy with desire as he did at this moment. "What would you say if I could make that happen?"

She peered at him, the corners of her luscious lips turning up slightly. *"Are you serious?"*

Pushing aside the primal urge to kiss her, he took a deep, calming breath and watched her retreat into scrupulous politeness. "Well, not the yesterday part. I haven't mastered time travel yet," he quipped, letting go of her hand and once again giving her the physical space she seemed to require. He curtailed his own rising emotions. "But I *could* probably get this place cleared out for you today."

"How?" She folded her arms against her middle, the action pushing up the soft curves of her breasts. "Do you have trash haulers and charity pickup on speed dial?"

He had been ready for this kind of reticence, given how high she had her guard up. "Close. Six of my seven siblings live in Laramie County. And the sister who doesn't is visiting with her husband and twins this weekend. So they're at my parents' ranch."

"Still—" another beleaguered sigh "—it's pretty last-moment."

He wondered what it would take to begin to tear down the walls around her heart. And allow his own to come tumbling down in the process. "Let me guess. You don't want to impose."

She winced, looking uncomfortable again. "I really don't."

He locked eyes with her. "How about this then? I'll send out a Lockhart family text, asking for volunteers. And we'll see what happens."

"Un-be-liev-able!" Tess said five hours later. She waved at the pest-control associate, who was backing out of her driveway. Then turned to Noah, unable to help but smile, as the two of them walked back inside the house. The rooms had been completely cleared out of all debris and swept clean. She went from room to room, amazed at how spacious the house seemed, now that the rooms were empty. "I can't believe this was done in just five hours!"

"I know." Noah glanced around appreciatively, too. "Isn't my family fantastic?"

"They certainly are." They'd started showing up minutes after he'd sent out his SOS text. His sister-in-law Allison, a lifestyle blogger, had instinctively known what could be repurposed and what could not. His brother-in-law Zach had brought his Callahan Custom Carpentry delivery truck. Others had pickups and SUVs. The women sorted stuff inside, and the men carried things out. All of them talking and joking, and warmly welcoming her to the community.

For the first time in her life, Tess had a glimpse of what it would be like to be part of a big, loving family. To have people you could count on to be there for you, even on short notice. Growing up the only child of a single mom, with her only other blood relatives—the uncle and grandmother she never really knew—in Texas, Tess'd had to learn to rely mostly on herself, and her mom, when her mom was around. After her mom had died, she'd had her ex. But since she and Carlton had split, she had only her casual friends, who were just as caught up in their busy lives, as she had been. To suddenly be surrounded by so many warm and generous people was a revelation.

And in Laramie County, Texas, apparently the norm.

Achingly aware of how cozy and enticing this all was, she took a seat next to him on the staircase steps. Somehow, they managed not to touch, but barely, given how big and manly Noah's tall frame was. They each held chilled bottles of water that had been donated by one of his sibs. "But you're not really surprised at the quick way they accomplished this, are you?"

He turned to her, his brawny shoulder nudging hers in the process. "They did the same for us, when the girls and I moved back from California, a few years ago. They had us all unpacked and everything organized and put away, in less than a day. So—" he shrugged amiably, pausing to take another long, deep drink "—I knew if we all worked together we could get it done. Even if my available siblings and or their spouses only came in for an hour or two each."

"Do they still help you, too?" Tess asked. Aware she had

met all of his siblings except Mackenzie, who had been helping his mom with preparations for the family dinner scheduled for that evening.

"Yeah. We all help each other, although I think, at least for now," he frowned, "with me the only parent on scene for my three little girls, I'm doing more taking than giving." He exhaled, his expression turning more optimistic. "Although in time, I think that will change, and I'll be able to pay them back for all the help they give me, every week."

She studied his handsome profile. "What sort of things do they do?"

"My brothers help with any chore that requires more than one person—like putting up outside Christmas decorations or hauling hay for the barn. My sisters assist with clothes shopping. Which," he made a rueful face, "can be a hysterical mess if the girls think I don't understand what is pretty and what is not!" He tossed his head in mock, kid-drama.

She laughed at his comically indignant tone.

Having met his three girls, she could see each of them doing just that.

Resisting the urge to take his hand in hers, she prodded softly, "What else?"

"Oh. Well. They all carpool with me so I don't have to go into town twice daily on weekdays. My parents and sibs also take turns making an extra casserole or dinner, and drop one off with me, for our dinner. They have the girls over for sleepovers or playdates. Stuff like that."

"It sounds wonderful."

He nodded. "It is."

Feeling very glad he was there with her, despite herself, she got to her feet once again. Still tingling with awareness and something else—some other soul-deep yearning she chose not to identify—she began to pace. "Well, I'm going to have to figure out a way to thank them all."

He moved lazily to his feet. Tossed the empty bottle into the box earmarked for temporary recycling. Then, rocking forward on his toes, he hooked his thumbs into the loops on either side of his fly. "They don't expect anything in return except maybe a word of thanks, which you already said to each of them."

Tess knew that. She also knew she would feel better if she did more than that… But there was no time to figure that out now.

"So what's next?" Noah said.

It was five o'clock. Which reminded her… Tess dragged in a breath and retrieved her phone. "I need to cancel my hotel reservations in San Antonio." She pulled up the website and let them know she wouldn't be coming. "Done!"

He looked at her as if he could read her mind. Then quirked an eyebrow. "You're going to stay here tonight?"

Tess walked over to the fireplace and kneeled in front of it. She didn't have any wood, but she knew where the firewood-sales stand was. Her self-sufficient nature came back full-force. "That's the plan." She reached around for the handle that would open the flue. It seemed to be…stuck.

"Here. Let me." Noah kneeled beside her and easily managed what she had been unable to. The damper opened with a rusty screech.

Tess winced. "That doesn't sound good."

"No kidding." Still hunkered down on the hearth, he pulled out his phone, turned on the flashlight and aimed it up the chimney. A loud fluttering sound and several chirps followed. They both ducked in response. But fortunately, whatever bird, or *birds*, that had been there went up, not down into the house. Probably because the down exit had been blocked, and they likely assumed it still was.

"Come take a look," he said.

Curious, Tess leaned toward him and followed the beam of his light. "Oh, no. A nest." It looked as if the visitors had really made themselves at home for some time now.

"Yep." Noah aimed the beam across the interior walls. "And quite a bit of soot, too." He frowned in concern. "You're going to need to get a chimney sweep out here to clean it before you can safely build a fire in this."

Sitting back on her heels, Tess moaned and buried her face in her hands.

There went one of the most important parts of her plan.

He gave her a curious sidelong glance, and shut the flue. Moving smoothly to his feet, he chivalrously offered her a hand up.

Tess accepted his help, only because it would have been awkward not to, after all they had been through. Ignoring the sparks that started in her fingertips and spread outward through her entire body, she disengaged their grip, then took a big gulp of air. "Well, maybe I won't need to make a fire in there tonight," she mused, trying to look on the bright side, "if I can find a warm enough sleeping bag at the super store."

Somehow, he wasn't surprised to see her thinking about roughing it until she could get all the utilities turned on, and her belongings sent down from Denver.

"Or," he said, regarding her amiably, "you could stay with us again until your place is livable and all your stuff gets here."

He had no idea how tempting that idea sounded. Especially given the kindness of her host.

He winked at her playfully. "Unless the Welcome Ranch is too 'California' for your taste. And you need accommodations that are more Texan."

Tess rolled her eyes at his teasing. "You know it's not that," she drawled right back.

True, the style of his home was unexpected for this neck of the woods, where southwestern and Southern decor reigned. But it was beautiful and quite comfortable nevertheless.

She bit her lip and let out a long-suffering sigh. "I just don't want to impose."

"So—" he spread his hands wide "—we'll barter, to make things even. *You* check on Miss Coco and her foal, two times every day, until her little one is born and doing well. And the girls and I'll give you the shelter you need and all the privacy you want."

She chewed her lip, deliberating. The last thing she wanted was to be an imposition, and this arrangement he'd proposed was hardly a fair exchange. But there was no denying that it would be wonderful not to have to worry about making the house livable while simultaneously starting her new job.

Tess studied him intently, aware that they had known each other just twenty-four hours now and she already felt closer to him than most people she had known all her life. "You know, of course, that you are likely talking several weeks?" Which was a long time for a houseguest, especially one who was still a relative stranger.

He tilted his head, his seductive lips curving up in an inviting smile. "At least."

Oh, this could be trouble.

So much trouble, if she ever gave in to the attraction simmering between them and did something really crazy like kiss him…or let him kiss her.

And yet, with so few options, could she really afford to quibble? They were both adults, responsible ones at that. She could handle this. They both could.

"Well…?" he implored softly.

Her heartbeat kicked into high gear. "You really wouldn't mind?"

He sobered, then responded quietly, "I wouldn't offer if I did."

Silently, she went through all the rest of the reasons why and why not. Found, in the end, she was still leaning toward staying with him and his three adorable little girls. "And you really think that would be an even trade for several weeks of lodging…?"

He chuckled. "Given how nervous I am about birthing my first and probably only miniature donkey?" he said in a low, deadpan tone. "I sure as heck do."

She couldn't help but laugh at his comically feigned look of terror. She held up a palm. "Okay, I accept. But we do our own thing. You carry on as normal with your family and I will try not to get in the way."

He paused, as if trying to figure out how to phrase something. "That sounds fine," he said eventually. "In the meantime," he continued matter-of-factly, "you have been invited to my folks' ranch for dinner with the family. Most of whom you have already met."

The part of Tess who had become acquainted with most of his siblings and their spouses, and knew how nice they all were, wanted to accept the invitation. However, the other part of her, that needed to take a breath, knew what a bad idea it was.

She'd gotten romantically attached to a guy before, because she had found herself in a challenging situation and needed emotional support. Same as him.

While their relationship had continued through vet school, residency, and into their first jobs after graduation, their engagement had not ended well.

She had no intention of making the same mistake.

"Thank you, but I have a lot to do this evening. Laundry and a few other chores…so if that's okay I'll pass on the offer." Then she realized she was being a little presumptuous. "But, um, if you'd rather I not use your washer and dryer, I saw a Laundromat in town. I could easily stop there…"

"Don't be silly. When I said make yourself at home, I meant it."

"DADDY, YOU ARE *not* being fair!"

Uh-oh, Tess thought as the shrill voice came her way.

Lucy stomped closer, bypassing the laundry room, where Tess had been working, through the back hallway, and into the kitchen, where she was now seated. Checking her email, on her laptop computer. "My bedtime is *always* a half hour later than the twins!"

"Under normal circumstances, yes," Noah returned calmly as he shut the back door behind them and ushered the weary-looking twins forward. He had a backpack slung over his shoulder, and a big foil-wrapped package in his hands that she guessed was dinner leftovers.

Avery and Angelica turned and gazed up. Their dad was so tall they had to tilt their heads way back to see his face. "Do we have to get a bath tonight?" Avery asked.

Noah set the platter on the kitchen island, then came back to the twins. "Do you want one?"

The three-year-olds looked at each other, deliberating. Avery stifled a yawn. "No. I just want to wash my face and brush my teeth and get in my pajamas."

"I want to do that, too," Angelica said, following her twin's lead.

Meanwhile, Lucy was storming the back hallway, her arms crossed in front of her. She was so worked up that steam was practically coming out of her ears.

Noah looked at Tess. "Sorry," he mouthed.

She gave him a smile and a nod, letting him know it was okay. Then watched as he pulled out a computer tablet from the *Family* backpack of all their stuff. "All right, Lucy, you can have twenty minutes of screen time. But then you're going upstairs and going to bed with no more argument. Understand?"

Rather than looking appeased, Lucy's sulky expression deepened. "Yes."

He pointed her in the direction of the great room. Sent another apologetic look at Tess and disappeared with the twins.

Trying not to imagine what it would be like to be part of a family like this, instead of coming home every day to a solitude that often seemed far too lonely, Tess returned to the laundry room. She continued pulling her clothes out of the dryer, then proceeded to deposit them in the wicker basket. She was just going to be here for a short while, she reminded herself. And she and Noah had agreed they would each do their own thing, without getting in each other's way. So there was no reason to offer to help him with anything. Except...

Lucy was back. Standing in the doorway. Tablet in her arms. In that moment, she looked very much like her take-charge daddy. "Aren't you coming?" she demanded.

Tess stood. She settled the basket on her hip, doing her best to exude the kind of casual tranquility she was pretty sure Lucy needed in this moment. "You want me to sit with you?" she asked as if it was no big deal. When it felt like a big deal to her. After all, what did she know about caring for kids?

"Well, duh."

"Um, sure." Making certain to give the child her space, Tess followed her to the big U-shaped sectional. She sat on one end. Still looking mighty unhappy, Lucy settled on the other, making no move to turn on her tablet.

Tess was surprised by the girl's attitude. She had been as welcoming as her two sisters, when they'd encountered her in the Welcome Ranch kitchen that morning. What had changed to make her resent Tess so? The fact that she was back? Intending to stay for a few weeks, at Noah's request? He had to have told them something. None of them had seemed shocked to see her there, sitting in front of her computer. Or doing her laundry.

Then again, maybe it's not about me. Maybe it has to do with someone or something else.

Tess favored Lucy with a gentle smile. "Did you have fun at the Circle L?"

She received another resentful scowl in return. Lucy peered at her suspiciously. "How do *you* know where we were?"

"Your dad told me."

Lucy got up and went over to a table in the foyer. She came back with two framed pictures. The first was a wedding photo of Noah and his late wife. Noah looked about a decade or so younger. His wife seemed to be about the same age. The other was of their family of five, when her mom had still been alive, and Lucy looked to have been around four or five, while the twins were still at the age where they weren't yet walking.

"This is my mommy," Lucy declared. "Her name is Shelby. She loved us very much. Especially my daddy."

"I bet she did. She looks very beautiful." So beautiful in fact, it would be hard for any woman to compete with that.

"Yes. Which is why you should leave," Lucy continued.

"Lucy!" Noah's voice sounded from the top of the stairs. He came down swiftly. "You know better than to be rude to our guests."

Lucy sighed and stood. "Tess needs to go home, Daddy. 'Cause it is really late."

"Past your bedtime, certainly," Noah agreed sternly. He held out his hand to his oldest daughter. "Let's go."

She shuffled to obey. "What about the twins?"

"They are already tucked in. Now what do you say to our guest?"

"Sorry."

She clearly did not mean it.

But to Tess's relief, her dad let it go.

The two moved back up the stairs. Her heart went out to the petulant child. It couldn't have been easy, losing her mother at such a young age. Lucy probably still missed Shelby terribly, just as Tess still missed her own mother, close to a decade after her mom's death. The last thing Tess wanted was to somehow make things worse for Lucy. If her presence here was going to be a problem for the grieving child, she knew she would have to find other accommodation. But in the meantime, there were still chores to be done. Tess finished folding her laundry, and then went into the kitchen to check on the cast iron skillet she'd put in the oven. To her delight, the re-seasoning process was finished and it was ready. She pulled out the baking sheet that the heavy skillet was sitting on and set it on the stove.

Once again, Noah was back, looking embarrassed. "Sorry about what happened earlier," he said gruffly.

This time, Tess's heart went out to them both. Not sure whether or not he wanted to talk about it further, she lifted a hand and said, "Totally understandable—no apology necessary."

Not surprisingly, he still seemed to think there was. Noah let out what might have been a sigh, then scrubbed a hand over his face, before once again meeting Tess's eyes. "I'd like to say it's just because she is overtired tonight," he said candidly, "but the truth is," Noah paused and frowned again, "Lucy can be pretty mercurial."

Was that a warning of more temper tantrums to come? Tess wasn't sure. She did need to ask. "Is my being here going to make things more difficult for her—or you? Because if it is…" Tess paused sincerely. "I'm sure I can find somewhere else to bunk while still checking in on Miss Coco, twice daily, like we agreed."

Noah vetoed that idea with a shake of his head. "That won't be necessary," he told her gruffly. "Lucy knows very well that no matter how grumpy or out of sorts she might be feeling, she still has to treat others kindly and use her manners, and I promise you, even if I have to gently remind her at times, that she will."

His weary expression had her feeling empathy for him, all over again. Struggling against the need to comfort him with a touch, she gave him her most understanding smile. "And I promise you, I won't take offense. I know she is just a kid, and she's doing the best she can, the way we all are."

He nodded and drew another breath. "Thanks."

Tingling from the near contact, Tess turned back to the stove. Suddenly wondering, she asked, "Is it okay if I leave this skillet here on the stove until it cools? It's going to take a while."

"Sure."

Noah followed her gaze to the gleaming black cast-iron skillet. Then his eyes widened in surprise. "That can't be the one you rescued from Waylon's home."

It had been such a sentimental find for her, refurbishing it had been at the top of her list of chores. Tess smiled, relieved to have something a little easier to talk about. "It is, actually."

The awkwardness between them faded as he surveyed

the pan from all angles, clearly impressed. "I can't believe it. It looks brand-new."

"Doesn't it?" Tess said proudly.

He moved closer, inspecting it with interest. His tall body radiated both heat and strength. He sent her an approving sidelong glance before moving away once again. "How did you get all the rust off?"

She watched him go with just a tinge of disappointment. "I used table salt and steel wool, and a lot of elbow grease. Then I seasoned it with oil and put it in the oven to cure."

Looking finally ready to hang out and take a breath, he sprawled in a kitchen chair, long legs stretched out in front of him. "Amazing."

Trying not to think how sexy he looked, even doing practically nothing, she tilted her head at him. Refusing to notice how attracted she was to him, she asked, "You've never cooked in cast iron?"

"No." He lifted his arms over his head, stretched languidly. "My mom and sisters do, but I never knew how they cleaned them up." Lazily, he dropped his arms to his sides. Smiled. "You obviously do."

Tess roamed the large state-of-the-art space restlessly, not sure what she should do now that he and the girls were home again. Hide in her room? Or stay downstairs and finish her laundry? Because she still had a load in the dryer…

Figuring the best thing to do was just play it casual, too, she continued, "My mom was an executive chef for some of the best restaurants in Denver. Mostly French cuisine. All very chichi. But when she was home, which wasn't all that often, she often talked about the food she'd eaten, growing up, that her mother had prepared in her cast-iron skillet."

Noah tilted his head in the direction of the stove top. "You think that's the one?"

"I do. I just think it hadn't been cared for properly or

used in a very long time. Which is a shame." Hence, she had needed to bring it back to life, ASAP, as a way of honoring both her grandmother and her mother.

He pushed out of his chair, sauntered over to the fridge and pulled out a beer. Wordlessly, he offered her one. She shook her head. He shut the door behind him and twisted off the cap. Lounging against the counter, he asked, "So you know how to cook in it, then?"

"Oh, yeah. My mom had a whole set of cast iron, and a nice set of stainless-steel cookware, too. Plus, chef's knives, and so on. I inherited it all when she died of pneumonia, my first year of vet school." A lump rose in Tess's throat. Tears stung the back of her eyes. Funny, how things could still hurt. Even nearly a decade later.

He put his drink aside and moved to give her a comforting hug. "Sorry." He squeezed her shoulders companionably, then admitted thickly, "I know firsthand how hard it is to suffer a loss like that. I lost both my parents, too."

It took a moment for what he had said to sink in. Tess did a double take.

He picked up his drink and took another sip. "My sibs and I are all adopted. Our biological parents perished in a fire, after lightning struck our home in the middle of the night, when I was about Lucy's age."

And she thought *she'd* had it bad. She gave in to impulse and hugged him, too, just for a moment. "That sounds really traumatic," she murmured, stepping back.

He nodded in confirmation, then continued reluctantly, "My parents got us all out, to safety, but then went back in for a few things after the rain put the fire out...or so they thought. A spark ignited the gas water heater, which was in the attic. The whole place exploded. They were killed instantly."

"Oh, my God, Noah, I am so sorry."

He moved out of touching range, took another long sip of beer. "It was a long time ago."

"Still, it must have been really tough."

Sorrow came and went in his eyes. Replaced by cool acceptance. "You're right. It was." His expression became even more bleak. "All of us kids were split up into different foster homes, and it was a few years before Carol and Robert were able to get permission from the court to adopt us all."

He shook off his low mood and straightened. "Anyway, that's one reason I don't ever like to put off until tomorrow anything that could be done today. Like," he said, his expression turning warm and welcoming once again, "ensuring you're comfortable. So what else do you need to really settle in? Dinner? Because my mom sent a huge plate of leftovers in case you hadn't eaten."

It was going to be really hard to keep her guard up, if he was so generous and helpful all the time. She reminded herself this was a short-term arrangement. Meant to be kept businesslike. So why was it feeling like it could be something *more*?

She flashed a smile. "Thanks. That was nice of her. But I'm good. I stopped for a sandwich on my way out of town."

Without warning, his brow furrowed. "Did you have a chance to check on Miss Coco?"

His concern for the animal was laudable. "Yes. She's doing fine."

His eyes turned a mesmerizing blue. "Looking any closer to…?"

Tess cut off his question with a definitive shake of her head. "I still think what I did last night, that it will be another week or two. Possibly even a little more. We will just have to wait and see."

Noah, who was so calm and competent in all other situations, abruptly looked tense and ill-at-ease. Knowing he was as out of his element birthing pets, as she was caring for kids, she touched his arm, her fingers curling around his bicep. "It really is going to be okay," she soothed.

He leaned into her grip. "Promise me?" he rasped.

Trying not to imagine what it would be like to have those strong arms wrapped around her, Tess said, "I promise."

CHAPTER FIVE

THE VOW HUNG in the air between them. Fragile. Unexpected. Connecting…

The closeness they'd felt all day turned into a wave of white-hot heat. Tess felt herself moving inevitably toward him at the same time he moved toward her. The next thing she knew, his head was lowering. His lips captured hers. A powerful current swept through her, filling her with warmth and need.

It had been so long since she had been held like this. So long since she had felt so wanted and needed. So desired. She opened her lips to the insistent pressure of his. The masculine taste of him overwhelmed her. With a soft moan, she wreathed her arms around his neck. In turn, he wrapped his arms around her and pulled her so close they were one. Her breasts molded to the hardness of his chest, and she succumbed to the erotic sweep of his tongue. Wanting more, until their hearts beat in tandem. Lower still, there was a building pressure and a tingling that stole her breath. And still the tender yet erotic kiss continued, magically showing her what could be, if only she could find the courage to open up her heart…

Noah hadn't meant to put the moves on Tess. They had an agreement, after all. Neither one of them was looking for a relationship. Their lives were full enough already. Yet, the time he'd spent with her over the last two days, the ease with which she'd slipped into his life, the soft surrender of her body and tenderness of her lips as they melted against him left him wondering. Was his lack of regret over this embrace a sign that he was beginning to feel ready to move on from Shelby? To be physically and emotionally close to a woman again? All he knew for certain was that Tess felt so good, so right, in his arms. Their kiss so hot and enticing.

And that was, of course, when she moaned again, this time in trepidation, and placed her palms against his chest.

Abruptly glad one of them had some common sense, he lifted his head. Moved back on a short exhalation of breath, and she did the same.

He read the regret on her pretty face. A tinge of disappointment swept through him.

Her hand flew to her mouth. Pink color filled her cheeks. "I'm sorry," she said.

Strangely enough, Noah wasn't. He might not be quite ready to go all-in with this woman, but their encounter had felt all kinds of fantastic.

Tess shook her head as if that would clear it. She pressed her fingertips to her damp, kiss-swollen lips. A mixture of remorse and wonder shone in her sage-green eyes. "I don't know what came over me!" She turned away as if they hadn't just shared an embrace that had rocked his world. "I guess it's just all the emotion of the past week or so," she said, as if explaining to a gullible newbie. "It caught up with me. And—and…"

She was so distressed, he had to help her out. Even if what he was going to say to soothe her embarrassment wasn't quite true. It was all he could do not to take her all the way back in his arms and kiss her again, just to prove their heated reaction to each other hadn't been an anomaly. "Left you unexpectedly wanting some comfort?" he guessed kindly. Knowing even if she didn't, this was not as calamitous as she was making it out to be.

Tess blinked. "Yes…that must be it! In any case, it will never happen again." She ran both hands through her hair. Her chest rose and fell with each agitated breath she drew. She huffed in embarrassment. "So how about we just pretend this never happened?"

Not sure how that was going to work, Noah watched her whirl away from him and march back to the mudroom, retrieve her folded laundry and dart up the stairs. Moments later, the guest-room door shut quietly. And that was the last he saw of her that evening.

"How's that?" Noah's brother Travis asked, the following afternoon.

Noah studied the black-and-white image on his phone. "Maybe a little farther back."

Travis nodded in understanding.

A handyman and cowboy, he was the go-to sibling for any domestic conundrum. Although neither of them had ever done anything like this before, Noah thought.

Travis moved the ladder, climbed back up and held the nanny cam against the stall wall.

Suddenly, Noah could see everything he needed to see. "Perfect," he said.

In quick order, Travis whipped the drill out of his tool belt and finished putting it up. While he removed the ladder, Noah went across the aisle to get Miss Coco, who had been temporarily housed in another stall.

The miniature donkey looked unhappy. The way she always did when there were loud, unfamiliar noises.

He paused to pet her, then led her back to her normal stall.

"She looks uncomfortable," Travis noted.

Her pregnant belly was awfully big, Noah thought, sympathizing. "Yeah, I think she wants to get this over with as much as we do."

His brother teased, "*We* meaning you and the girls... or you and Tess?"

He'd had enough of this at his parents' the evening before. Everyone in his family wanted to see him paired up again. Irritation grew. "Don't start."

"Hey." Travis collapsed the ladder. "You can't deny there are sparks between you and the lovely new vet. We all saw them when we were clearing out her house yesterday. Plus, you arranged to put her up here for the next few weeks or so."

Yes, he had. And it seemed like a fine idea. Until he had ended up kissing her, she had kissed him back and then run away. Only to exit the ranch early this morning again, this time before any of them had gotten up.

She had left him a note, though. Documenting their donkey's continued good health. "That's for Miss Coco's sake."

Travis chuckled with the ease of a happily married man. "Keep telling yourself that."

They walked out of the barn together. Travis put the construction ladder back on his truck while Noah shut the door behind them. The winter day was sunny and surprisingly warm, for January. In the distance, they could see his three girls playing with his sister Jillian's three triplet daughters, with Jillian supervising.

Noah figured it might not be a bad idea to get some feedback. Up 'til now, he'd had zero interest in even spending time with a woman, one-on-one, never mind getting close to her. Feeling incredibly blessed to have the help of two of his siblings today, Noah turned back to Travis. "And, anyway," he huffed, "she's not interested." Which was probably good, since it had been several years since he had been on a date and was more than a little rusty.

Travis raised an eyebrow. "Didn't look that way to any of us," he countered mildly.

Noah ran a hand over his forehead, wishing he hadn't given in to the unexpected wave of desire and chased her away. He grimaced, reviewing the depth of his mistake. "Yeah, well, I tested the waters yesterday." Once again, moving way too recklessly, way too soon. Just as he had since he was a kid and his whole world had gone to ashes in a single moment.

"Tested the waters," Travis echoed, his brow furrowed. "In what way?"

Ruefully, Noah recalled, "We kissed."

Travis mulled over that statement. "You kissed her? Or she kissed you?"

"Both." And it had been fantastic, for as long as it lasted, anyway. Which, in retrospect, seemed not nearly long enough.

Travis shrugged. "Sounds promising to me."

It had been. Until reality sunk in. And it was reality he had to deal with now, like it or not. Noah grimaced, then admitted, "She apologized. And said we should just forget it ever happened."

Travis clapped a reassuring hand on Noah's shoulder. "But you can't," his brother noted happily.

Worse. He didn't *want* to forget it.

Tess had made him feel alive. Their kiss had brought him joy. Made him want to burst out of his self-imposed shell.

They continued on across the lawn, toward Jillian and the six little girls, who were all rowdy as could be. Why couldn't his life be that simple, Noah wondered, as he watched them race around the lawn. "Want my opinion?" Travis asked.

Noah squinted, considering. Travis had hit the lottery with his wife, Skye, and their son, Robbie. "Maybe."

"You've always been one to follow your instincts, which are pretty damn good, by the way. You've also never been one to sit around and wait for things to happen to you. So if something in you wants to explore the sparks between you and Tess Gardner, then I say go for it."

"It's not that simple, bro. I've got the girls to consider." Their feelings had to count in this, too.

Travis nodded solemnly. "I get that, believe me. And I know Lucy, Avery and Angelica will always be your first priority. But why not give the pursuit everything you've got and see where things lead?" He exhaled slowly, giving Noah a look full of sad remembrance. "Because our family knows better than most how life can change in an instant. And there's nothing worse than looking back, thinking, if only I'd done what I should or could have done...and didn't."

ON SUNDAY AFTERNOON, Tess spent an hour walking the property with the husband-and-wife contractor team recommended to her. "So how long do you think it will take?" she asked when they had returned to the first floor, which, despite the warmer weather outside, was still as cold as a tomb.

Molly looked at Chance. Then the extensive notes she had made. She did most of the design work and scouting of materials. Her husband handled the general contracting. "Three weeks, if everything goes according to plan," she predicted finally.

"Four, if it doesn't," Chance said. "And even then...we should be able to get you in comfortably."

The attractive thirtysomething couple seemed very capable. "That's great!" Tess said, relieved. She smiled at the duo, ready to get going. "Where do I sign?"

Casually, Molly slid her clipboard back into her bag. "I'll email you the contract with the written bid later this evening. You can docu-sign it, and we'll get our crew started."

They left and Tess glanced at her watch. It was barely three o'clock. She still had two errands to do, and then she really needed to head back to the Welcome Ranch and face Noah. Yes, they had kissed…impulsively…and it had been a reckless mistake. One she foolishly kept reliving in her way-too-romantic heart.

She still had to face him sometime. Find a way to move their acquaintance permanently to the friendship phase. Because the last thing she wanted was another failed romance with a man who'd told her from the very beginning what he was, and wasn't, interested in. And while she now realized maybe she wasn't as immune to romance as she had thought, Noah still had no room in his life for anything but his work and his kids.

Yes, there were sparks between them. Powerful sparks. But it would be foolish to pursue that chemistry, since up to now, anyway, she had never been able to make love, without first being in love.

Hence the safe path was the one she and Noah had started out on—the one that would keep them strictly platonic friends.

Resolved, Tess turned her attention to the errands, still waiting to be done. Both took a little longer than expected.

An hour and a half later, Tess turned her Tahoe into the lane leading up to the ranch. Noah's Expedition was parked next to the house. She parked on the other side of him, then got out and walked over to the barn. By the time she had finished checking on Miss Coco and returned to her SUV, Noah was coming out of the back of the house.

He looked good. *Too good* really, in jeans, boots, a casual sweater and open down jacket that made the most of his broad shoulders and muscular chest.

Suddenly, all she could think about was the kiss they had shared last night, and how much she wanted to do it again.

He was watching her curiously, as if trying to read her mind, while she worked to keep her emotions at bay. "Did you have a good day?"

"Yeah." Finding his steady regard a little unnerving, Tess turned away. She got her carryall out of her SUV and walked around the back to the cargo area. Then she pushed the button to activate the lift gate. "I wanted to spend some time at the clinic, acquainting myself with their computer systems. Rather than do it tomorrow. So I spent the bulk of the day doing that."

"Makes sense."

"And then I met with contractors and had a little shopping to do."

"Wow, you have been busy."

Unfortunately, the near constant activity had not kept him, or the sizzling hot kiss they had shared, entirely off her mind.

The back of her car opened.

Oblivious to the wistful nature of her thoughts, he looked at the paper grocery sacks stashed inside. "Need some help with any of that?"

"Sure." Tess smiled with a casualness she couldn't begin to feel. "If you're offering."

He took the heavier ones. She carried the bread and eggs. "What's all this for?" he asked mildly, matching his strides to hers.

"As long as I'm staying here, I want to pitch in with some of the food costs. Help out financially in any way I can, to earn my keep, so to speak." They had agreed to each do their own thing, while she was under his roof. But it didn't mean she wanted to freeload off his groceries, day after day. Worse, have things in the fridge taking up space that were off-limits to everyone else. Which was why she had also purchased kid-and-family-friendly items.

"You don't have to do that," he told her solemnly, his tall frame radiating barely leashed energy. Together, they mounted the steps that led to the mudroom entrance, close to the driveway. "But, sure…whatever you like."

Happy he hadn't taken offense, Tess released a long, slow breath. She always felt better when she was at her most independent. "Thank you." She waited while he transferred the bags to one arm and opened the back door. He held the door for her, inherently gallant as ever.

She caught a whiff of his soap and man scent as she passed. Trying not to think about the way he looked at her—as if she was the most fascinating woman on the planet—she carried her things to the island and set them down.

Tess shrugged out of her coat, and at the same time he ditched his. Figuring this was the best time to ask, she looked over at him, surprised at how happy she already felt, even though she was in a new town, with a currently unlivable house, about to start a new job. She traded relaxed glances with him. "In the meantime, I wondered if it would be okay, later tonight, when the girls are in bed and you're done in the kitchen for the night, if I baked a few things to take to work in the morning. Just as an I'm-glad-to-be-here gift for the staff?"

He watched her unload her groceries. "I'm sure your

new coworkers would appreciate it." He took the empty bags, efficiently folding them for later repurposing. "And, of course, it's okay for you to use the kitchen."

"Thanks." Still wondering if she was going to eventually end up feeling as much of a nuisance here as she had in other places, in her past, she asked, "Where are the girls, by the way?" It was awfully quiet around here.

He turned, nodding at the living area adjacent to the kitchen. She followed his glance and saw the girls sprawled out over the sectional sofa in the living room. The twins were cuddled up together. Lucy was snuggled next to Tank. All were sound asleep.

"Oh, gosh," she whispered in chagrin. "You should have told me. I wouldn't have been speaking so loudly."

Noah shook his head and continued in a normal tone. "I want them to start waking up. If they sleep much longer, there will be no getting them to bed tonight. And they've all got to get up early tomorrow. The twins go to preschool. Lucy attends the elementary school in town."

Just like the two of them both had work. And would need to get their rest, too. "Ah. Right."

Abruptly, she noticed everything else she had missed, given how focused she had been on the tall, ruggedly handsome man at her side. Noah's computer was on, all four of his big displays lit up. The fragrance of fresh-brewed coffee hung in the air. A mug was on his desk. He'd clearly been working on something, while his daughters slept.

Once again, Tess felt like she was intruding.

She hated feeling that way.

And there was only one way to feel like less of an added burden to his already full life. "Actually, I was going to go down to the stable and check on Miss Coco and then go upstairs to catch up on some veterinary journal articles I've been meaning to read."

He looked relieved. Tess slipped out the back door, vet bag in hand.

THREE HECTIC HOURS LATER, after the kids were in bed, and Tess was finally able to come downstairs without feeling that she was likely to be in the way, she reflected on what a marathon it had been.

"Are your evenings always like that?" she asked Noah curiously, getting out the things she needed to make her baked goods.

Though she hadn't been there to see the high-spirited activity, she had certainly overheard it. From the time they woke up, cranky and out of sorts from a too-late-in-the-day nap, to the wild, out-of-control giggles and jumping on the beds, when it was time for them to be tucked in, the three girls had been going nonstop.

She couldn't imagine how Noah did it all alone, on top of running the company he'd founded. While still maintaining the patience of a saint.

He paused to gather up three insulated lunch bags from the pantry. "Sometimes it's calm."

She'd never seen a man quite so gentle. And loving. She imagined he had been the same way with his late wife. "But not tonight."

He shrugged his broad shoulders affably, then went to the fridge and got out cheese, fruit and bread. "They've had an unusually hectic four days. Starting Thursday after school, when my parents came over to stay with them so I could go to Fort Worth to meet with a trucking company that wants us to design a cloud-based asset-management platform that will track all their inventory plus shipments, vehicles, drivers, deliveries and so forth in real time. When finished, it will be installed as an app on everyone's phones."

"Sounds…complicated." Impressively so.

He nodded in satisfaction. "It is definitely a new direction for us. One that I think will give Lockhart Solutions much more potential for growth. Although we still plan to keep designing apps that improve everyday life."

"Is that what that is—" Tess gestured at the four monitors in his work area, with what appeared to be computer coding flashing on the screens "—all about?"

He stopped making sandwiches. "No. That's another project I have going. I'll show you." Tess followed as he went over to the desktop, typed in a command and pulled up a security-camera shot of Miss Coco's stall, then got out his cell phone. Another few clicks and the same photo appeared on that.

"Travis was here this afternoon and he helped me install cameras and motion detectors with ambient lighting. So whenever Miss Coco is up and around, I'll get a message and know. And can check on her."

"It looks like Miss Coco is sleeping peacefully now." The miniature donkey had also been fine when Tess had gone out to the stable to check on her. She wondered if there was something that had happened to precipitate this. Something Noah hadn't told her about yet. "Was there a problem earlier?"

He tilted his head to one side and gave her an easy grin. "Just in how we set it up."

As he came closer, she noticed he smelled like kids' bubble bath and shampoo. Patches of his shirt were damp, too, from where the kids had splashed him.

She had never imagined a single dad could be so sexy. Yet, here he was. Looking completely worse for wear. And all she wanted to do was haul him close and kiss him again.

Even more passionately this time. She swallowed around the parched feeling in her throat. "I don't understand."

"The alert on my phone goes off every time Miss Coco moves or rolls over or gets up to get a drink, which is a lot more often than I knew. Anyway, I need to put a timer on the app I wrote for this, so it will only alert me if she's up for five minutes or more at a time—"

Tess interrupted, "Make it ten."

The intensity in his dark blue eyes deepened.

Knowing that if she stood there next to him like that for much longer, they'd end up kissing again, she went back to the kitchen.

Squinting, he stayed where he was, phone still cradled in his big hand. "Are you sure?"

Aware she was tingling again, with yearning this time, Tess went back to grating icy cold butter into small chunks.

Scones.

She was making scones...

And they needed to turn out right.

Which meant she had to focus on what she was doing, not him.

"I'm positive." Glad for the physical distance between them, she looked over at him again, to make her point. "Unless you want to drive yourself absolutely crazy."

Judging by the depth of his scowl, he did not.

"Okay, well that's easily doable." Oblivious to the way she was still admiring everything about him, he sat down in front of the computer and made several changes on screen. Then stood with a satisfied exhalation of breath. "Done."

He strode back into the kitchen to join her and went back to assembling school lunches for the girls.

She was working at the opposite end of the island, to

make sure they each had plenty of personal space. "So what are you making?" he asked.

Happy to have something to concentrate on besides the attractive single dad opposite her, Tess began folding the grated butter into the flour mixture. "Scones. Vanilla, blueberry, apricot and peach."

With heavy lidded eyes, he watched her add vanilla and cream, then knead it in with her hands. His gaze drifted over her contemplatively before returning with slow deliberation to her eyes. "Smells good." He gave her a panty-melting smile. "And they aren't even in the oven yet."

Reminded of what a sensual activity cooking together could be, Tess let out a pent-up breath. She could tell he was remembering their kiss. Maybe even longing for another one. There was no way they were going to end up in each other's arms again. *No way.*

Determined to keep her boundaries firmly in place, she avoided looking at him directly and reassured him cheerfully, "Not to worry." She patted the crumbly dough into a round circle, then cut it into eighths. "I planned to leave a sampling of the four different types for you and the girls."

She reached for the parchment-lined baking sheets, irritated he was making her feel all kinds of things she most certainly did not want to experience right now. Like the absence of love and family and joy in her life. She was a vet, for heaven's sake! Shouldn't she at least have a pet?

With a huff, she added, "If they like scones, that is."

The compassion in his regard sent another thrill racing through her. "I am sure they will," he told her.

Beginning to realize she was going to have to keep herself very physically busy to avoid more moments like this, moments that could tempt them into intimacy, Tess slid the first pan of scones into the oven.

Resolved, she swung back to face him. "You know, I

don't have to limit my contribution to caring for animals and buying groceries while I'm bunking here. I could pitch in with household chores, fold laundry, even cook a little, too, if it would help out." Ease his burden a little bit. And give him more time to simply enjoy spending time with his three adorable little girls. Instead of juggling everything all at once.

CHAPTER SIX

NOAH REGARDED TESS SILENTLY, not sure how to respond to her offer to help out even further. The interested side of him was all in. But the widowed single dad? He knew it was never going to be that easy. Especially with Lucy still running hot and cold. She was okay with Tess being there one moment, then indifferent and or resentful the next.

Trying hard not to think about what he would really like to do, which was forget about everything but the two of them, wrap her in his arms and kiss her until dawn, he tamped down his desire with effort and met her eyes. Then he asked casually, "What happened to the idea we would each do our own thing?"

Which would have eliminated this problem entirely. And made life a whole lot more boring.

Oblivious to his thoughts, and already back on task, Tess was chopping up fruit for the next batch of scones. She had twisted her hair into a loose sexy knot on the back of her head when she'd begun to cook. The butterscotch curls spilled out over the butterfly clip. Loose strands brushed her cheeks and the nape of her neck. She did not seem to have any idea how sexy she looked, but he did. Boy, did he ever.

Ignoring the pressure building at the front of his jeans, he went back to making school lunches. With a shrug, she continued, "It probably would've worked great if it were just the two of us." Her delicate hands moved with laudable expertise as she completed each culinary task, making him wonder how those same skilled fingers would feel on him.

She leaned toward him slightly. "But it's not, Noah." She drew a conflicted breath and went on matter-of-factly, making her case. "And with all that needs to get done around here, it seems selfish and self-centered of me to hide out in the guest suite when I am on the ranch. Instead of coming down here and pitching in and helping out."

Damn, she was generous. And kind. And smart. And pretty. Plus, all the things he yearned for in a woman, and expected to never have again, after Shelby passed. Yet, here he was, feeling like maybe it was time for him to open up his heart again. Even as the cautious side of him said things were fine as they were. And resolutely warned against bringing a new woman into their midst.

Noticing she was still waiting for his response, he cleared his throat, said carefully, "I see your point."

The color in her cheeks deepened—as if she sensed his rejection coming. She went back to shredding cold butter on the box grater. "Then…?"

He pushed aside his desire to get even closer to her, close enough to make love and share confidences, and said kindly instead, "I wish it was that simple, Tess—but it's not. Nothing is when it comes to my girls." And me. "So," he told her regretfully, "I'd like to stick to our original agreement and keep things as casual and separate as possible."

Tess's hands stilled. He couldn't tell if she was disappointed or relieved. Her feelings were definitely hurt. As he had half suspected they would be when he turned down her offer. Wanting her to understand where he was coming from, he continued, "We had a nanny in California. We hired her when Shelby first got sick and kept her on even after she finished her cancer treatment, because frankly we really needed the help." He exhaled, his lips compressing as he recollected sorrowfully, "Carrie stayed with us that first year after Shelby died, and it really helped because she was able to bring a woman's touch into the household and fill the void that my wife's death left." Noah sighed. "But she didn't want to move to Texas with us because her fiancé and all her family were in California." He shook his head, recalling grimly. "The girls were really distraught. In a sense it was like losing Shelby all over again and they cried for weeks. And I don't want them to get too attached to anyone outside the family again."

Tess's slender body relaxed. She nodded sympathetically, understanding.

He watched her fold wet ingredients into dry with the same easy skill she seemed to do everything else. He could only imagine how that dexterity would transmit to lovemaking.

Forcing himself to get back on track, he closed up the reusable lunch sacks and admitted wearily, "I also don't want Lucy jumping to any conclusions."

Her delicate brow pleated. Her gaze drifted over him. "Because Lucy is opposed to you dating anyone?"

Worse. With brutal honesty, he explained how deep the hurt in him and his girls went. Not a one of them wanted to love and lose again. "Because Lucy wants her mom back and that can't happen. And anything that points that out to her again is painful to her," Noah concluded gruffly.

Which made it painful for the rest of them, too.

TESS WAS IN her office at the vet clinic late Monday afternoon, making notes on the patients she had seen that day, when Sara stopped in. The rest of the staff had already left, so the building was quiet, with the dark of midwinter descending outside.

"Everything go okay for you today?" the managing partner asked.

Tess nodded happily. "It was a great first day on the job, thanks."

Sara eased into a chair, resting a hand on her pregnant belly. "How's the rest of your situation going?"

Tess explained the deal she had made with Noah over the weekend. To keep watch over the donkey, until the birth, whenever that happened. And then stay on for as long as needed until momma and baby were doing well, the imprint training completed and he was sure he could handle them on his own.

Sara did some quick calculations. "So you'll likely be living at Welcome Ranch until mid-February?"

Tess nodded. "Thereabouts. At least that's the plan. I just hope the renovation gets done in four weeks, as promised…" She talked about her meeting with the married contractors she had hired, who were reputedly the very best in the area. Especially when it came to kitchen and bathroom design.

"Not to worry. Molly and Chance don't make promises they can't keep. They will finish on schedule. Meanwhile, we both need to lock up and get out of here."

Knowing her coworker was right, Tess stood.

Sara walked her out. "The scones were delicious, by the way. Everyone loved them."

Recalling the culinary lessons she had received in her youth, Tess admitted, "My mom used to say food made with love is the ultimate icebreaker."

Sara's smile bloomed. "Your mom was right. Speaking of which, my husband, Matt, is making his famous chili and cornbread tomorrow evening. You want to come for dinner with us and the kids? See our ranch?"

"Love to." She needed more friends in Laramie County,

so she wouldn't be constantly feeling the need to lean on Noah, for all things, big and small.

Tess got in her Tahoe and drove out to the Welcome Ranch. Noah was pacing the porch, on what appeared to be some sort of business call. He gave her a curt nod, and turned his back, continuing to grimly troubleshoot some problem. Inside, dinner prep appeared to be temporarily halted. The girls were close to a meltdown.

"We're hungry!" Angelica said.

Her twin Avery nodded. "Super hungry."

Lucy scowled. "Whenever Daddy gets that look on his face, it's going to be forever before he gets off the phone."

Tess took off her coat and ventured another glance outside. Noah did indeed look completely wrapped up in whatever was going on.

Not willing to just stand around and do nothing when the kids needed to be fed, she headed into the kitchen. She turned the flame on under the big pot of water. "So what were you going to have?"

"Spaghetti with butter and parm for the twins and spaghetti with red sauce and meatballs for me and Daddy," Lucy said.

The latter appeared to have been simmering on the back burner, but had been turned off. She adjusted the flame back to simmer.

All three girls climbed up on the stools at the island, to watch. "Do you know how to cook?" Avery asked.

Tess nodded, acutely aware this was not part of the deal she had made with Noah just the night before. "I do. My mom was an executive chef, and she taught me how when I was a kid. It was the only way we could spend a lot of time together."

"'Cause she worked a lot, just like our daddy?" Angelica murmured.

"That's right. But that's what parents have to do, you know—work so they can take care of their families." Especially single parents, like her mom and Noah. Like it or not, they had a lot to juggle.

And sometimes, despite their best efforts, they needed help.

Even if it wasn't from a big, extended, loving family, but the relative stranger/houseguest who just happened to be there.

Lucy studied her with open curiosity. "I used to cook with my mommy."

"We didn't," Avery announced with a beleaguered sigh. "We were too little."

"Just babies," Angelica said.

Tess smiled at the trio of girls, who were no longer fussing with each other and complaining. She could really get used to coming home nightly to this eager little fan club. "Do you-all cook with your dad?"

They shook their heads in disappointment. "Not really," Lucy said. "He's too impatient and he says he's not good at explaining things in the kitchen."

Tess understood.

Teaching one child to cook was one thing.

Monitoring all three of his lively little girls with their differing skill sets, probably another.

"I can help you tonight, though," Lucy said. "Just like I used to help my mommy."

"We're big enough, too, now," Avery claimed.

"Yes, we are," Angelica agreed.

Tess looked over at their eager expressions.

Oh boy, she was really getting into it, pushing past boundaries now, but Noah was still outside pacing and talking on the phone. And honestly, dinner did have to get made, the kids kept entertained so they wouldn't be interrupting him.

"You know what?" She looked at the ingredients on the counter. "I think that we could all make a salad together. You up for that?" she asked.

"Yes!" all three girls said in unison.

Tess rinsed the greens and then showed them how to tear up the romaine leaves into little pieces and put them in individual wooden salad bowls.

They were just adding croutons and shavings of parmesan cheese when Noah came back in.

He was off the phone. And when he saw what they were doing, he did not look happy. Not at all.

NOAH KNEW, EVEN as his temper flared, that he was overreacting to the sight of Tess making dinner with his kids. It wasn't as if she was vying for the position of their mom, or his next wife.

Far from it.

Yet the sight of her, still in her vet-clinic scrubs, looking so pretty as she charmed and entertained his daughters, hit him square in the solar plexus.

He'd thought he was doing fine on his own.

But it wasn't true, he admitted ruefully. Because if it was, Avery, Angelica and Lucy would look this happy all the time. They didn't. Which meant he still had work to do. And an example to set.

Fortunately, the deeply ingrained manners instilled in him as a kid made it easy to invite her to join them and make small talk throughout the meal. Most of which was focused on the kids and their days at school.

Not surprisingly, Tess avoided direct eye contact with him and made herself scarce after dinner, staying only long enough to help him clear the dishes before heading down to the stable to check on Miss Coco.

Figuring they would talk this out later, he took the girls upstairs, shepherded them through the bath and bedtime routines and read them their stories. When he finally finished around eight o'clock, and went to find her, the door to the guest suite stood open. The room was dark and empty.

Downstairs, there was no sign of Tess, either. He went to the security monitor and checked the stable. She wasn't there, either.

Tank was curled up by the back door, as if guarding it. Noah noticed that the back porch lights were on. Tess was sitting outside in her coat, with a small wool blanket drawn across her lap, and was studying a stack of book-marked magazines.

Knowing he was entitled to be ticked off, yet feeling a little remorseful for his grumpy mood, he walked out onto the back deck. Stepping closer, he exhaled his exasperation.

She slid him a surprised glance.

"What are you doing?" The words were out before he could halt them.

Lips set stubbornly, she went back to the glossy pictures in front of her. "I'm looking over some design possibilities Molly wanted me to peruse. And enjoying my evening."

Enjoying? Really? He surveyed her wind-chapped cheeks and tousled hair. "It's too cold to be sitting outside."

She took a tube of ChapStick out of her pocket and rubbed it across her lips. "Maybe for a native Texan," she quipped.

He returned her challenging look. "Ha! Funny!"

She decided to make a second pass over her soft, luscious lips. "It's thirty-two degrees, cowboy. Which is *nothing* in a Denver winter."

So she was a little ticked off at him, too. For initially behaving like a jerk.

Luckily, he had reined his temper and resentment in.

And hadn't.

He cleared his throat, thinking this discussion would go better inside. "Still…" He stopped, then tried again. "Tess…"

She slid the tube back in her pocket and stood, squaring off with him resolutely. "Look, I know I overstepped my bounds. Continuing to prepare the dinner you started, interacting with your three girls and just generally being in the way of your normal routine."

So she intuitively understood how jarring it had been for him to walk in and see her doing all the things that Shelby would have been doing.

She stomped a little closer, tilting her head up. "But I have to tell you that I will *always* err on the side of doing what is best for children, and they were hungry and tired and needed to eat. Which they did as soon as I could get it all ready."

He saw how deeply he had insulted her. He lifted both palms in surrender. The last thing he wanted was to fight with her. He'd had way too much of that in his marriage. "I never said…"

She sent him a withering glare. "You don't have to! My dad died in a motorcycle accident before I was even born. So I was the only child of a single mom."

Tess lifted a hand, refusing to let him offer condolences.

Stonily, she continued, "I grew up being foisted on one family friend after another, on the nights when my mom worked as a chef and couldn't get a sitter." Her eyes shone with turbulent emotion. "She usually didn't get by to pick me up until well after midnight. Which meant," Tess continued grimly, "I either had to stay on someone's sofa, or go to sleep on a cot in the restaurant office. Only to be woken up to go home with her."

He thought he'd had a rough childhood. But this… His heart went out to her. "Sounds…awful."

She shrugged away his empathy. "Some of it was. Some of it wasn't."

He watched her drop the magazine she'd been reading on the stack on the deck table. "What was nice?"

Tess paused, her expression turning sentimental as she recalled with soft reluctance, "Sometimes on the weekends, my mom made us a special midnight dinner at the restaurant, after closing."

That sounded better.

She ran her hands through her hair, pushing the unruly blond strands off her face. "We would talk about our weeks." She released a shuddering breath. "That was always really special."

He watched her pace to the railing and back. "And what wasn't so great?"

She gave him an aggravated look, but to his surprise, answered him, anyway, her low voice roughened with pain. "Me, thinking about spending my entire life wondering if I would ever be important enough to anyone." The edge of her teeth raked her trembling lower lip. "Me—" tears glistened in her eyes "—trying to be patient. To not feel like I was perpetually, always and forever, in someone's way."

Then the tears flowed, flooding her beautiful face. As if it was all suddenly too much for her. Noah knew it was too much for him. He took her in his arms, bringing her against him, and held her close. Suddenly, they were kissing. *Passionately.* Her arms went around his neck. And this lip-lock was even more incredible than their first had been.

With a low moan of appreciation, she pushed against him, going up on tiptoe, better fitting the heat of her slender body against his. Heart racing, he drank in the scent of her, appreciating the sweet, tempting taste of her mouth and lips. She curled against him with a quiet moan, and the kiss turned tender, then feisty, as their bodies heated, and pulsed, and tender again.

Threading his hands through her hair, he kissed her long and hard and deep. She kissed him back, just as fervently, her hands skimming over his shoulders, down his back.

With a soft murmur of acquiescence, she arched against him. Wanting—demanding—more.

His own body hardened.

He could feel her vulnerability, the need that was as intense as his.

What were they doing?

Suddenly feeling like he was taking unfair advantage, he broke off the kiss and lifted his head. She stepped back, looking as emotionally shaken as he felt.

Once again, her defenses were up.

Which was understandable, since neither of them had meant for this to happen.

Guilt flowing through him, he released a breath. Tried to ease the situation with a little humor. "I know, that wasn't in our deal, either," he said wryly.

"Nor should it be." Tess ran a hand through her hair. "The deal we made last night was a smart one. I think we should go back to it."

If he didn't want to end up hurting her, the way he apparently just had, she was probably right. And yet…somehow it felt wrong to pretend nothing was happening, when it clearly was.

He locked gazes with her. Doing his best to give her what she wanted, said, "So each of us should just stick to doing our own thing?"

"Yes. As much as possible," she said stoically.

"Okay," he said, and nodded, even though right now he was selfishly thinking that wasn't what he wanted after all.

While there was no denying he had emotional baggage of his own, what he wanted was to be even closer to her. To see where things might lead…if they allowed the spark between them to fully ignite.

But clearly, she didn't feel the same way.

As if to prove his point, she grabbed her stack of magazines and held them in front of her like a shield, then brushed by him. "Luckily, tomorrow it won't be a problem." She tossed the parting words over her shoulder. "I'm having dinner with Sara and Matt. I won't be home until late, way after your kids are in bed for the night."

NOAH WAS JUST finishing up another phone call at noon the following day, when he saw his sister Jillian's Lockhart Antique Roses van pull up next to his house.

He and Tank walked out to greet her.

Smiling, she gave him a hug. "I come bearing gifts, as always."

He followed her around to the tailgate. "Food, I hope." The kids loved all the Lockhart women's cooking better than his. And his sisters and mom were always conspiring to make sure he had three or four dinners delivered for him and the kids every week. Things that only had to be put in the oven, or heated on the stove. "So what do we have?" he asked, smiling.

"Chicken tinga in little phyllo cups." She unhooked the latched carrying top on the baking dish to show him. "Heat this in the oven for ten minutes. Then sprinkle lightly with grated cheese and put the tray back in just until the cheese melts. Which will only take another minute or two." She handed him the chicken dish and pulled out a second covered tray. "There's also a veggie-and-fruit tray with ranch and yogurt for dipping."

"Wow. You really went all out."

"Yeah." She tilted her head to study him. "You sounded a little down this morning."

She had called to let him know she had prepared dinner for both their families that night. Because she and her husband, Cooper, had young triplet daughters, their weeknight meals were usually geared for kid palates. If they wanted to do something more gourmet, they always cooked it on the weekends, after the girls were in bed. "A lot of issues at work." Which was true.

Problem was, there were issues at home, too.

And in his romantic life…

And that was new.

Since he hadn't ever figured he would be in a relationship again, he hadn't expected to have to deal with those kinds of issues again. Like the lingering tension that could follow an emotional exchange. Or the frustration that came with the fact they weren't of the same mind. And might not ever really be.

It had been easier to just be a single dad, than worry about perpetually disappointing the woman in his life again.

Until he had met Tess Gardner, anyway…

Jillian made a face that reminded him she had not only started her own business from scratch, but also taken on the emergency guardianship of Cooper's three toddler nieces as well. Only to later adopt them and marry him. And together, they made one hell of a happy family.

She gave him a consoling pat on the arm. "Work comes with issues. For everyone, every day."

She accompanied him into the house, Tank lagging behind them. She paused to hand him her tray and shut the door. "It wasn't that."

Noah carried the meal into the kitchen and slid it all into the fridge. He figured if anyone would understand, it would be Jillian. He added more water to Tank's bowl. "I think I screwed things up with Tess."

His sister took off her coat and got comfortable. She settled on a stool and leaned forward, both arms on the kitchen island. "Tank and I are all ears."

Noah caught her eyeing his electric kettle. He put it on, then got out two mugs and a box of green-tea bags. Hard to explain how Tess had affected him. From the first moment he had laid eyes on her, he had felt an attraction that just would not go away. Instead, it seemed to get more intense every time he saw her.

Aware Jillian was waiting, he tilted his head and said, "Well, things started out a bit rocky."

Her gaze gentled with sisterly understanding. "In what sense?"

"I was trying to be helpful. She didn't trust it. Or me. But then she kind of needed my assistance getting her house cleared out. Finding a place to stay temporarily."

"That hasn't been going well?" she asked.

He paused as he got out the milk and sugar, not sure how much he wanted to reveal. Yet, knowing he had to confide in someone. *"It was."*

Jillian grinned, then guessed, "You kissed her?"

Noah nodded, recalling the lightning bolt of desire that first kiss had sent through him. "More than once, actually."

His sister paused in the act of opening up her tea bag and sliding it into her still-empty mug. "She kiss you back?"

Noah recalled the soft silkiness of Tess's lips, the sweet taste of her mouth. "Ah…yeah."

Jillian sobered, but couldn't quite make her grin disappear. She added a tea bag to his mug, too. "Then I don't see the problem."

Noah brought over the kettle and filled both mugs with steaming water. *There wouldn't have been one if I hadn't panicked.*

He shoved a hand through his hair. In retrospect, he wished he had reacted in any way but the way he had. Swallowing around the knot of remorse in his throat, he admitted, "I told her we should take a step back and avoid getting too involved, because I didn't want the kids to get the wrong idea about us."

Or maybe us to get the wrong idea about us.

"And think that Tess was going to be a permanent part of our family, the way they once thought Carrie, their nanny back in California, was going to be."

Jillian stirred her tea. Was concerned now. "And why would you do that?" she asked kindly. "Given that Tess isn't a nanny or trying to be?"

Noah straightened. "Because the twins really, really like her," he replied, defending himself. "And although her emotions are all over the place, as usual, Lucy's really warming up to her, too."

His sister lifted her mug and sipped. "And you consider that a problem? Especially considering how protective your eldest is?"

Noah tightened his hands around his mug. "Potentially." Because he wasn't the only one who would get hurt in this situation if he screwed up again. The way he had in his marriage when it became clear that he and Shelby did not want the same kind of lifestyle, and the two of them couldn't seem to get along. Unless, of course, Shelby did get exactly what she wanted, when she wanted it. Then she was incredible. Charming. Cheerful. So sweet and giving and attentive to him and the girls and Tank.

Had it not been for her fierce belief in him, there was no way that he would be where he was, professionally, today.

Seeming to know what he was thinking about, Jillian reached over to touch his forearm. "Want my advice?"

He looked at her, nodding.

"I know you've always been a fast-moving kind of guy, who could drop out of college and start his own company at age nineteen. But try not to get so far ahead of yourself this time. Or go borrowing trouble where none may exist."

It was certainly a tempting notion. Noah clinked mugs with her. "Live in the moment?"

Jillian smiled. "Right now, for you, there is no other way."

CHAPTER SEVEN

THE KIDS WERE long in bed, and Noah was on another work phone call Tuesday evening, when Tess returned to Welcome Ranch around 10:00 p.m. He saw her get out of her Tahoe and head for the stable, vet bag in hand. She was in there for about ten or fifteen minutes then walked back over to the house.

She slipped in the door, gave him a thumbs-up and headed straight to the guest suite upstairs, while he tried to formulate a reply to his colleague that didn't sound anywhere near as distracted as he felt.

The next morning, she slipped back out to the stables, just as he was leaving to take the girls to school. When he returned from town, some thirty minutes later, he was surprised to see her red Tahoe still parked next to the house.

Concerned, he went to the stable. Miss Coco lifted a drowsy head to look at him, then nestled right back down in the hay and went back to sleep.

So all was fine there.

Was it fine with Tess?

Worried, he hurried on over to the house. The kitchen was as he had left it, rife with the got-to-get-out-the-door-on-a-school day mess. Tank was upstairs, parked outside her closed bedroom door. Apparently guarding. As if he, too, knew something was out of the ordinary.

Noah stood there, debating.

Going up to see if she was okay would be intruding.

On the other hand, she was normally at the clinic by the time it opened. And it had opened a good hour and a half before. Which meant she wasn't just going in late. She wasn't going in. On day three of her new employment?

Resolved, he went up the stairs. Knocked.

Seconds later, he heard movement on the other side. She swung open the door. She was dressed in worn jeans and a pink-and-blue plaid flannel shirt, her thick curly hair drawn up in a bouncy ponytail at the back of her head. Her fair skin was flawless, save for the pink flush highlighting her sculpted cheeks.

She huffed out an irritated breath. "Yes?"

Okay, so she wasn't glad to see him. But he was determined to stay the course. "I wanted to see if everything was all right."

She slapped her hands on the sexy curves of her hips. Angled her chin at him. And stared at him with her usual fiery pride. "Why wouldn't it be?"

"You didn't go to work."

Tess squared her slender shoulders and took a deep breath. "I'm working from noon to nine today."

Suddenly it all made sense. Feeling like a fool, he said, "Evening office hours." Which were held four times a week. He knew that because Tank and Miss Coco got their veterinary care there. Although usually someone came out to his ranch, to see Miss Coco.

"Yes." She angled her thumb at the center of her chest, inadvertently drawing his attention to the open vee of her shirt and the soft curves of her breasts. "And I'm the vet seeing patients this evening. So…" She lifted a censuring eyebrow at him. "If that's all…" She started to shut the door.

It wasn't. Still hoping a truce might be possible, if she

would just give him a moment, he caught the door with the palm of his hand. "It's not."

She lifted her delicate brow. Another silence fell. They regarded each other warily.

He tried to make amends. "I'm sorry about what happened the other night."

"The kiss, or the immediate brush-off afterward?" she countered coolly.

He remained in the portal, wedged between the door and the frame. "I know what I said came out all wrong."

She continued watching him steadily, an emotion he could not decipher in her expression. "You think?"

Still holding her eyes, he stepped back out of the doorway. Lifting both palms in an age-old gesture of surrender, he offered a contrite nod. "I'd like to start fresh."

She moved away from him. Back ramrod-straight, she sat down on the padded chaise. Then picked up one of her cowgirl boots and held it in her hand. The firestorm of emotion she had been holding back since they had last spoken suddenly sparked in her eyes. "The thing is, Noah, I am not sure that is such a good idea."

Glad she was at least speaking to him again, he said, "Why not?"

That earned him another long, assessing look. Her eyes taking on an unexpected sheen of vulnerability, she pulled on one boot, then the other. With a sigh, she got to her feet once again. Then claimed with a weariness that seemed to come straight from her soul, "Because you are putting me in the same situation I was in with my ex."

Hoping to learn more about what she had loathed about her past, and wanted in her future, he challenged her mildly. "In what way?"

With a shrug, she admitted in a low, pain-edged voice, "Carlton set all the boundaries. Everything had to be done his way. My feelings weren't important. And unless I wanted to fight nonstop, it was just easier to go along with him."

Noah could understand the not-wanting-to-fight part. He hated disagreements, too. Especially the ones he'd had with Shelby that had gone on and on. Completely unnecessarily.

He watched her pace to the window and back, her hips swaying gently. "I find it hard to believe you were ever a pushover," he countered.

She swung back, gaze narrowed. "Well, believe it." She shook her head regretfully. "Part of it was that he had such a forceful personality. We were in vet school together. He was great at organizing vast quantities of material. Whereas I was better at the nuances. So he did all the big-picture stuff, and I worked on the details. It wasn't long before that process slipped into our dating life, too."

Realizing all over again how incredibly gorgeous she was, Noah stepped closer. "When did it start to become a problem?"

She lounged against the bureau, ankles crossed, arms folded in front of her. Hurt mixed with humiliation. "From the beginning." She bit her lip. "I just didn't want to admit it because there was already so much stress, just trying to excel in the rigorous curriculum. I needed someone strong on my team, and he was definitely that. And then when my mother died unexpectedly, of complications of pneumonia, well suffice it to say I needed him more than ever."

His heart going out to her, Noah took up the place next to her. "Did you live together?"

She shook her head, inundating him with her citrus-and-patchouli fragrance. "Not until the end of our last year of residency. Until then, he insisted we each keep our separate places, even though it would have been a lot easier, financially, to share space, since one of us was always sleeping at the other person's place."

He let his gaze drift over the delicately sculpted lines of her face before returning to her sage-green eyes. "What changed?"

"Carlton knew I wanted more of a commitment. He wasn't ready for marriage just yet, so he offered up living together—just as a trial, mind you—along with a proposal and an engagement ring, and I accepted."

"How did it work?"

Tess lifted her slender shoulders in a dismissive shrug. "Fine, I guess. Even though he was opposed to even talking about a wedding date."

"That didn't bother you?"

Sadness came and went in her expression. She sighed. "It did, but…back then, we had been together for well over six years and I was still laboring under the illusion that we would marry one day. We just needed to wait until the time was right." She released a heavy sigh. "But when we both got really nice job offers in different places, I began to see it didn't matter how patient I was. His needs—his *career*—would always take priority over us as a couple. He thought I should do the same. That for both of us, our careers had to come first. We had worked too hard and too long for them not to take precedence."

"So you broke up?"

More regret filled her expression. "We tried to make the long-distance thing work for about six months. But all that did was drive us further apart emotionally. So we called it quits."

He studied the soul-deep weariness reflected on her face. "Which was when?"

She sighed. "About two years ago."

With effort, he tamped down the need to pull her into his arms and kiss her again. "Anyone since?"

She rubbed idly at the denim stretched across her thigh. "I've been concentrating on my career."

"Protecting your heart."

She lifted her gaze to his. The flush in her cheeks deepened. "If that were all I were doing here, cowboy, maybe it wouldn't be so bad."

She was talking about the two of them again. But not in the positive way he hoped. "What else are you doing?"

"The same thing I did in the beginning with my ex. Going all out to make sure you're okay with literally everything going on between us, instead of tending to my own needs."

He knew he'd been running hot and cold with her. He was sorry about that. Sorry he'd let anything interfere with the friendship they had started to forge from that first night.

He also knew this situation they were in was spurred by both their issues. She needed to know that, too. He gazed into her eyes. Seeking forgiveness, peace. "And why would you be doing that?"

With a huff, she pushed away from the bureau. "That's the hell of it. I don't know."

He caught her before she could run away. "I think you do. I think you're doing that for the same reason I went dashing up the stairs when I got back from town, to make sure you weren't sick or something. Because like it or not, whether we *want* it or not, Tess, there is something between us."

Tess knew, as much as she loathed to admit it, that Noah was right. There was something special and electric and compelling between them. But that didn't necessarily mean they should give in to it. She whirled away from him, putting enough distance between them so they were no longer invading each other's personal space. "Yeah, and here's the part where you kiss me again," she taunted, daring him to make a pass at her again.

His grin widened, as if warning her he was more than eager to accept her challenge. Before she had a chance to back away, he wrapped his arms around her and brought her close enough to feel the heavy thudding of his heart.

She threw up her arms between them, splaying her palms against his chest, picking up steam with every second. Her heart in turmoil, she lifted her chin. "Don't. You. Dare."

His eyes glinted. "Hey, you are the one who brought it up."

Okay, so she had known it was a mistake to throw down the gauntlet with Noah, just as it had been a mistake to have any conversation at all with him when she was this upset. She should be concentrating only on her new job, the house she had inherited. Which meant she should already be looking for another place to stay in the interim. Even if it was in the stable. Because this—being so close to Noah—wasn't working. All it was doing was reminding her of her own loneliness and, worse, conjuring up feelings of unbidden longing and lust. Tempting her to throw caution to the wind and fall for him.

But it had been *so long* since anyone had looked at her the way he was looking at her now. As if she was the most beautiful woman on earth. As if the best thing for either of them right now would be a temporary fling.

"Well, I didn't mean it."

He tunneled his hands through her hair. "Didn't you?" he countered softly, tilting her face up to his. "Because I could have sworn you did…"

He was so on target with his observation she felt her knees wobble, just a tad. Determined not to let him know how much he was arousing her, Tess huffed, "We've already tested the waters twice. There's no need to test them again."

Noah delivered a slow, heart-stopping smile. "Kiss me again," he demanded, lowering his lips to hers, "and I'll consider it three strikes and I'm out."

Before she could draw a breath, he delivered the most evocative, tantalizing kiss she had ever experienced in her life. She hadn't been prepared for that and shuddered as he deepened the connection, pressing his body up against hers, mingling his tongue with hers. The pleasurable caress wreaked havoc with her carefully built defenses.

She hadn't realized until this moment just how much she needed to be physically touched, loved.

He broke off the kiss and regarded her closely, his eyes darkened and unwavering on hers. He rubbed his thumb across her lower lip. "Tell me to stop," he growled. "And I will never put the moves on you again."

This was her chance to walk away, to end it now. She couldn't. Even though she knew this was crazy. That it could never last. Not when his life was so complicated. Not when the ghost of Shelby loomed between them.

She also knew she wasn't going to be able to just walk away, not with his passion roaring through her, as sudden and fierce as a winter storm. She wanted him as much as he wanted her. She had to get this out of her system.

"Go," she said instead.

His sexy grin widened. She trembled at the raw tenderness in his gaze. "Go?"

She went up on tiptoe, winding her arms about his neck. "Give it all you've got."

"Well, all right then…" Not wasting a single moment, he

lowered his mouth to hers and kissed her again. Sensations swept through her, more potently than before. Suddenly, everything she wanted rose to the surface, and everything she'd held back came pouring forth. And what she wanted most was Noah Lockhart. Right here. Right now.

Rising to the challenge, he slid his palms down her spine, rested them on her hips, pressing her lower half to his. She felt the depth of his desire. And still, they kissed. And kissed. Until their hearts pounded in unison and she couldn't think of any place she would rather be. He was hot and hard and male. She wanted him to fill her up and end the aching loneliness deep inside her. To help her live again, *really* live. And if this one interlude was what it took to make it happen, so be it.

NOAH HADN'T EXPECTED Tess would take him up on his offer. But now that she was kissing him back, ardently, he was all in, too. Kissing her again, hot and hard and wet and deep. Until she moved restlessly against him, wanting still more. Raging need sweeping through him, he slipped off her shirt and her bra, removed her boots and unsnapped her jeans. She quivered as denim and panties slid down her silky-smooth thighs. Her hands rested on his broad shoulders while he helped her step out of them.

"So beautiful," he rasped, his thumbs tracing the curves of her breasts, caressing her pink, pouting nipples.

Still kneeling, he savored the sight of her. Then he parted her thighs, felt her with his fingertips and kissed her and stroked her until she was on the brink. Shuddering. Gone.

Unable to wait any longer, he left her side just long enough to retrieve a condom. When he returned, she was already in the bed, waiting. He stripped down, joined her. She watched, mesmerized, as he rolled it on. Then settled between her thighs. Her legs wrapped around his hips and a shaky breath escaped her. And then they were kissing again. She was wet and open. He was hot and pulsing. He took her slowly, allowing her the time to adjust to the weight and size of him, then going deeper still. Her muscles trembled, tensed. She let her hand slide down his spine to his hips, bringing him inside her more intimately. And then, there was no more waiting, no more wondering. Only feeling, and the inevitable buildup of passion and sensations that ended with her falling apart in his arms, and him following. Together, they hung together suspended in incredible pleasure.

Eventually, their breathing slowed. For several long, tender minutes, they clung together, enjoying the aftershocks.

He kissed the top of her head. "That was amazing," he said.

Her lips curved upward. "For me, too." She drew another deep satisfied breath. Shaking her head in mystification, she moved to look deep into his eyes. "I never imagined I could enjoy sex on a whim, just for pleasure. So this," she flattened her hand over his chest, confessing sincerely, "...this was a revelation."

To him, too.

He had married so young. For him sex, and love and commitment had always been inextricably combined. And once Shelby had passed, grief had shut down his desire. Until Tess had come into his life, anyway.

Unexpected hope rose. "Does this mean you're open to more?" he asked, before he could stop himself.

She bit her lip. Suddenly wavering. "This morning?"

God, he wanted to make love to her all over again. And again. He mimicked her almost-too-casual tone. "Today. Whenever." He held her eyes, hoping she would give him the answer he needed and wanted to hear. So he could finally move past the ghost of Shelby, move on…to a full life. One that included more than just familial love.

Tess paused in uncertainty. Even before Noah's phone started buzzing.

The interruption was all they needed to bring them back to reality.

Tess extricated herself from him, the bliss from their lovemaking fading fast. He felt like they had gone from zero to sixty, and then back to zero again, landing with a grinding halt. Which wasn't surprising, given how high the barbed wire had been around her heart when they met. And to be fair, he'd had his share of reservations, about ever moving on, romantically, too.

"What's wrong?" he said. He knew she had enjoyed the interlude as much as he had. She had said so.

With an offhanded shrug, Tess looked around for her clothes. Emanating a nonchalant attitude, he sensed she didn't begin to feel, any more than he did right now, she flashed him a deadpan smile. "You mean besides the fact the morning is nearly gone, and I have to be at the clinic at noon?"

Knowing the key to not having this end here and now was keeping this as informal as she seemed to need it to be, he caught her wrist and pulled her onto the bed, next to him. "Besides that."

She held her bundled clothes in front of her. Gazed down as if trying to figure out how to explain. "I thought I could handle a fling," she said mildly.

He sat quietly beside her, ignoring the instinctive need to haul her back in his arms and kiss her senseless. "And now?" he asked gently, sensing it would be a mistake to push her on this.

She raked her teeth across her lower lip. "It's just been a few minutes and I'm already second-guessing the wisdom of all this. Which is probably why—" Sobering slightly, she looked over at him. "Up to now, the only time I've been intimate with someone, we were in a committed relationship."

"Same here."

Swallowing, she continued, "Most of the time I'm too busy and frankly just not interested in even *going on a date*."

He had to ask. What had happened this morning? "So what's different now?"

You, he thought she was going to say. *Us*. But the moment passed. Her guard remained in place. She eased away from him slightly.

"Nothing, really. Which is why this can't happen again," she said.

Knowing it had to happen again, if they were ever going to take things to the next level, he let his gaze drift over her once again.

The question was…should he argue? Or be a gentleman and let her have her way?

Her voice quavered and he could see the uncertainty in her eyes. "I'm not an impulsive person, Noah. I can't let my emotions push me into doing things that aren't good for either of us in the long term."

Trying to hide his disappointment, he turned his back to let her dress, while he pulled on his boxer briefs and jeans. Shoving his arms through his shirt sleeves, he turned back to face her. Found her looking so damn sexy in her socks and undies. "What are you emotional about?"

She disappeared into the walk-in closet. "The stress of moving. Taking on a new job."

He sat down to put on his boots. "What else?"

She emerged in clinic scrubs. The stubborn set of her

chin superseded the vulnerable sheen in her green eyes. "The house I inherited from Waylon." She offered a cordial smile. "I thought it would give me answers, and instead all it's done is present me with more questions."

He moved to help her make the bed. "Like?"

She shrugged, making no effort to mask her confusion. "Why was my mother so determined to leave Laramie when she was only eighteen? I mean, I get it. She didn't want to be a short-order cook in a small-town diner, like her mom. But to never come back, even after I was born... so she could introduce me to her mom before her mom passed. Why didn't she do that?" Tess asked, hurt vibrating in her low voice. "Why did my mother and grandmother remain estranged until my grandmother passed, of an un-diagnosed heart ailment, when I was five?"

This time, Noah did take her in his arms. He pulled her comfortingly close. "Maybe they thought they still had time to work things out. That it would be easier for them if they waited."

Tess nodded, as if hoping that had been the situation. Drawing a breath, she eased from his arms.

"In any case," he continued, consoling her the best way he knew how, "the house clearly meant something to Waylon. He might not have had a clue how to properly take care of it, but he came back to Laramie every chance he got. And then left that house to you. Probably because it *was* a link to the family."

"I know, right? He wanted me to have this tie to the past." Tess picked up a brush.

Knowing there was more, Noah waited.

She turned, her gaze locking intimately with his, then inhaled. "I thought by coming here and taking charge of the house that I would somehow feel closer to my mom, my grandfather and grandmother, and my uncle." She brushed her hair. "But they are as much strangers to me as they have always been."

"And that's frustrating."

A nod. "As well as disappointing."

Tess stepped in front of the mirror.

He lounged in the open doorway, watching her make up her face. "You don't have to keep the house. You could fix it up and sell it, or simply sell it as is, and buy another property here in Laramie. Start fresh."

Tess shook her head. She dropped her lipstick into her cosmetics bag. "That would feel disloyal. Even if it isn't giving me the connection to family that I had hoped it would."

He stepped back to let her pass. "Maybe that will come, when you renovate it and live there for a while. It's how it was here. I mean, I built the exact same house here we had in California for the girls and it still took months to feel like it was home."

"Really? The exact same house?"

"I didn't change a thing. Everything was exactly the way Shelby picked it out the first time. Right down to the tile." Too late, he realized this was probably not the time to be talking about his late wife. Not that Tess seemed to mind hearing about any of it.

She looked around admiringly. "Well, she had great taste, because your house is beautiful."

"Yeah." Noah exhaled in relief. "And it certainly made life easier for a time, because I had zero decisions to make when it came to overall design, materials, etc."

Brush still in hand, Tess glanced out the window. "What about the stable?" She swung back to him, curiosity lighting her eyes. "Did you have one in California, too?"

"No. Our house was in a small town outside of San Francisco. So, no one had any livestock. Or stables. Or paddocks."

Tess grinned, triumphant. "So, then, you did choose something."

"Not really. My dad helped me figure out all the specifications of that. Which I needed."

She picked up a hair clip from her bedside table. "Because your dad is a rancher?"

"Because the girls were having a hard time adjusting from the California lifestyle to the Texas."

She paused in surprise. "They really noticed the difference?"

"Well, not so much the twins, but Lucy? Yeah. She didn't understand why there were so many pick-up trucks on the road, or why everyone had a favorite pair of western boots. And it especially ticked her off that the tacos tasted weird to her."

Tess walked back over to the bathroom mirror. "Because California Mexican food is different than Tex-Mex. Or even Colorado Mexican."

"Right." He followed her lazily. "Plus, the weather was very different. It was really hot here that first summer. Lucy was used to a more mild climate, year round. Being able to go to the beach and take off her shoes and walk in the sand. Plus, we were just a couple of hours from the ski slopes, so we were able to take a couple of winter vacays she remembered, too."

"Let me guess." Tess frowned as she twisted her hair into a sleek knot, on the back of her head. "No snow here yet."

"Actually, last year there was a big ice storm, but the kids couldn't go out and play in it, so…no, that did not qualify in my girls' estimation."

Unhappy with the knot, which did seem to be listing slightly on one side, she released her curls, smoothed her hair with her fingertips, and began again. "Colorado has a lot of great skiing."

Noah caught her eyes in the mirror. "Do you know how?"

Her smile bloomed. "Oh yes. It was one of the first things I did when I got to college. Go on the school sponsored trips and learn to ski." She paused to look him over. "What about you?" she asked.

For reasons he didn't understand, he wanted to impress her. "Not black diamond, but yeah, I can ski."

Their glances meshed, held. For a moment he imagined what it would be like to take a trip like that with her.

Spectacular, probably.

It wasn't clear what she was thinking in that moment, but something positive…

Relieved the discomfiture that had followed their impulsive lovemaking had faded, he shrugged and said, "Something else we have in common then."

She secured her hair in place. Perfectly this time. "And that would be?" she matched his light, playful tone.

"A love of the winter vacay."

Tess sent him a rueful look before moving by him and disappearing into the closet again. Then she came out wearing the sneakers she wore to the clinic. "You know, cowboy, it would be a lot easier for me to keep my distance from you if you weren't so darn appealing."

He knew exactly what she meant.

"Right back at you, darlin'." He wanted to know so much more about her, too.

An awkward silence fell.

He moved forward and took her hands, loving the silky softness of her skin. "I have a proposal. We got off on the wrong foot. Mostly because once I saw you on Waylon's porch, ready to step into that mess, I couldn't mind my own business."

She gave him a look that said, *You think?*

"I had to try and rescue you."

Mischief twinkled in her eyes. "You do that a lot?"

"Never," he joked. "It gives women the wrong idea."

She smiled with wry humor.

Serious now, he went on with the recitation of his mistakes. Of which there were many. "Then we connected. And I got scared and I blew it. And put up all the wrong boundaries. Then I regretted it and couldn't stay away and now here we are."

"Here we are." Tess let out a tremulous breath.

With him hosting a woman in his home who wasn't his wife, an employee, or family member, and instead of being annoyed or indifferent, he was liking it. Way too much. Which was why he'd made love to her.

Her expression turned wary. "Not sure what to do next…" she murmured.

He thought about the advice his sister had given him the day before. Advice that had worked wonders for her and Cooper and their adopted triplets.

He took her hands in his. "How about we forget all the previous stipulations we made and just take it one day, one *moment*, at a time?"

Tess regarded him cautiously. Tempted, yet… "I still don't want the girls hurt by any false assumptions on their part and I know you don't, either."

He shrugged. "So we'll keep things very light and casual and nonromantic around them."

"No long glances," she warned.

"Not a one," Noah promised, just as solemnly.

"Agreed," she said softly.

But even as he made this vow, Noah knew deep down it would be one that would be very hard to keep.

CHAPTER EIGHT

"ARE YOU FIGHTING?" Lucy asked Thursday evening, shortly after Tess came in from work.

Seven o'clock, and the girls were already in their pajamas. They were all sitting at the kitchen table, working on what appeared to be some sort of school project or homework, while Noah was rinsing the dinner dishes.

Noah and Tess turned to each other in surprise. They hadn't spent any time together since she'd left for work, the day before.

The time apart hadn't really eased the sexual sparks. She still felt them every time she looked his way. Which was why she was doing her best to be super casual, the way they had promised each other they would be, in the wake of their recent lovemaking.

Noah caught her eye, then turned back to Lucy. "Why would you think that, sweetheart?" he asked.

Lucy rested her chin on her upraised hand, still squinting at both of them. "Because you don't talk the way you usually do and you're not looking at each other. And when you and Mommy were mad at each other, she always gave you the silent treatment, so you didn't talk to her, either."

Wow, Tess thought. Nothing got by Noah's oldest daughter. She turned to face Lucy, too. "I'm not giving your dad the silent treatment, Lucy. I've just had two very long days at the vet clinic, and I guess I'm a little talked out."

"Are a lot of animals sick?" the eight-year-old asked in immediate concern.

Impressed by her empathy, Tess returned, "Some were. Others needed their yearly checkup or shots. And—" she paused for maximum dramatic effect "—there were a few really cute puppies, too."

The girls' eyes lit up. Tess pulled her phone from her pocket and brought up the clinic website's "Star Turn" page, where all the new pets photographs were. She walked over to show the girls, who oohed and aahed over each new pet.

"I wish I had your job," Lucy said.

"I want to grow lots of roses like Aunt Jillian," Avery interjected.

"Me, too," Angelica agreed dreamily.

"All good options," Noah said.

His phone buzzed. He checked caller ID. "I have to take this," he told them.

Lucy groaned. She buried her face in her hands. "Now I'll never get my practice spelling test done."

"We're making cards for our friend Danielle, who just had her tonsils out," Avery explained.

"So *we* can finish." Angelica colored all the more vigorously.

Tess made herself a cup of peppermint tea. Glad that she and Noah now had an agreement to take things one moment at a time, and would play it by ear, she took a seat at the table, too. Close by, Noah sat at his workstation and talked in serious tones. Clearly, this was a situation where he did need some assistance, if only for the length of the phone call.

"Can I help?" she asked Lucy.

"Do you know how to give a practice test?" the child asked warily.

Tess nodded.

Huffing out a breath, Lucy reluctantly handed over the words, her pencil poised over the blank page in front of her.

Tess asked her if she was ready to begin. She was. So Tess read the first word on the list. "Exercise."

Lucy sat there, staring at her. Perplexed at first, then clearly irritated.

Not sure she had pronounced it clearly, Tess said it again, as clearly as possible. "The first word on the list is *exercise*."

Lucy sighed and rolled her eyes, in full drama mode now. "Tess. You have to say it, and then use it in a sentence, and then repeat it, and then I write it down," she explained impatiently.

"Oh, right." Tess recalled her teachers doing just that. "Exercise," she said. "It's good for all adults and children to get exercise every day. Exercise…"

Satisfied, Lucy wrote her answer.

And so it went.

When they had finished all ten words, the twins were done with their get-well-soon cards, and Noah was off the phone. Lucy snatched up her paper. "You grade it, Daddy."

Noah looked it over. "Good job, Lucy. They're all correct."

Clearly not surprised she had aced it, Lucy glared at her dad and grumbled, "Tess makes up better sentences than you do."

Tess wasn't sure how to handle getting a compliment that also insulted someone else. Luckily, she didn't have to figure it out. Noah was shepherding the girls toward the stairs. Before they headed up for their bedtime routine, the twins dashed over to give Tess a good-night hug. Lucy offered only a beleaguered half smile and a sigh. "Thanks for helping me with my spelling test, Tess."

"You're welcome," she replied. Truth was, she had enjoyed it. Maybe too much.

After Noah and his daughters disappeared from view, Tess looked at Tank. He appeared as bone-tired as she felt. The security monitor showed Miss Coco was still sleeping, just the way she had been when Tess had looked in on her when she got home.

She paused to pet the dog, then, her stomach growling, she went to the fridge and got out one of the already prepared chicken Caesar salads she had picked up at the grocery store a few days earlier. She sat down at the island.

Noah came down the stairs. Looking *way* too good.

She watched as he strode into the kitchen and sat down on a stool beside her. He was wearing a business-casual shirt and slacks, which probably meant he'd had Zoom meetings and needed to dress accordingly. The sleeves were rolled up to his elbows, revealing sinewy forearms, with a dusting of dark hair. As always at this time of evening, he had damp splotches on his clothes and he smelled of kid shampoo and soap.

Which shouldn't have been all that sexy, but it was. She was beginning to realize she really liked seeing him in dad mode. It brought out a whole new side of him.

He rested his head on his elbow and looked over at her. "Guess you and I are going to need a new plan," he said, referring to the comments that had started off her evening, the moment she had returned to the ranch.

Wishing she could do what she really wanted to do, and take him by the hand and lead him right back up to her bed for another rollicking roll in the sheets, she worked off the clear plastic top on her store-bought salad. "Besides being super casual with each other?"

He held out a palm for her trash, then leaned over to

throw it away in the can. "Lucy is perceptive. She always has been."

Tess paused while she put the dressing over the top of the salad, then figured she had to ask. After all, if she and Noah were going to be friends, or even more than that, she had to know what she was getting into. She cut up her salad with a fork and knife. "It upset Lucy when you and Shelby argued?"

One corner of Noah's lip curled up. "Everything upsets Lucy one way or another, in case you didn't notice. But to answer your question, yes, she wanted absolute peace in the household one hundred percent of the time."

"And it wasn't that way?" she asked quietly.

Noah went back to the dinner dishes he'd abandoned. He took a moment to choose his words carefully. "Shelby and I were alike in that we each wanted what we wanted when we wanted it. When we were on the same page, that was great."

Tess could imagine.

He slid plates into the dishwasher, one by one. Then glasses and silverware. "When we weren't, it was problematic."

Tess continued to eat. "What did you fight about?" she asked, before she could stop herself.

Luckily, Noah didn't seem to mind.

He shrugged. "Early on, our quarrels were usually about how much time I was spending trying to get the business off the ground." His frown deepened. He got out the spray cleaner and some paper towels to clean the countertops, leaning over as he worked. "Later, it was money…mostly." The muscles in his shoulders and arms bunched. "I wanted to put as much cash as possible back in the business, to keep growing it, and she wanted to enjoy the fruits of all my labor, ASAP. Which she did, when she wanted something specific, like a chocolate Lab puppy."

Tess looked down at Tank, who was curled at her feet. She mimed shock. "You didn't want this gorgeous fella?"

Seeming to know he was being talked about, he gazed up at her affectionately and thumped his tail.

Noah scoffed. Finished with the cleanup, he came back and settled beside her at the island. "Of course, I fell in love with him the moment I set eyes on him. The problem was, it wasn't a good time. She had just found out she was pregnant, and she already had Lucy to care for."

Which would have been a lot.

"I thought it was all going to be too much even before we found out she was having twins. But Lucy—who at four and a half wasn't thrilled about the idea of having to share the spotlight with two new siblings—was already incredibly emotionally attached to Tank. So he became a part of the family." Noah leaned over to pet the Lab.

Tess watched the free-flowing affection between the two. She speared another bite of the cold, delicious dinner salad. "It seems to have worked out."

Noah sobered. "Yeah, he was a huge comfort to Lucy when Shelby was diagnosed with breast cancer a few months after the twins were born and had to have a lumpectomy and then go through twelve weeks of chemotherapy."

"That must have been really hard."

"It was. And before you ask, no, I did not deny Shelby *anything* after that. No matter what the ask." His tone turned gravelly. Eyes glistening, he glanced away. "I just wanted her to stay with us."

Tess realized she didn't know how he had lost his wife. "So what happened?" she asked gently, touching his arm. "Did the cancer come back?"

Noah shook his head. "No, she was in remission when she died."

"Then…?" Sensing her touch wasn't helping, Tess dropped her hand and sat back.

"It was an accident." His lips compressed into a thin line. "Shelby was trying to get her strength back and she went out running every morning with her friends, and she tripped and fell and struck her head on the curb. She was gone by the time the paramedics got her to the hospital."

"Oh, Noah…"

Head bent forward, almost as if in prayer, he clasped his hands tightly in front of him. "After that, all I could think of was the time we had wasted, not getting along, or just appreciating every moment for the gift it was, you know…?"

"I do. I felt the same way when I lost my mom."

Another silence fell. This time it was one of remembered grief, intimacy and connection.

Noah cleared his throat, looking ready to move on. "Anyway, sorry about Lucy jumping to conclusions earlier, about us being angry with each other," he told her sincerely. "I know it made you uncomfortable."

"She was right to speak up if something was on her mind."

He studied her, his heart suddenly on his sleeve. "I'm glad you feel that way, too," he said softly.

Yet another connection that was forging between them.

She wasn't sure what any of this meant, if anything. So the logical thing to do was ask. She rested her chin on her upraised fist, hoping what had happened between them before wasn't just a winter fling, that their newfound camaraderie wouldn't fade away. Summoning her courage, she did her best to pretend an insouciance she couldn't really begin to feel.

"So, um, Noah?"

"Yeah?" he asked, waiting patiently for her to continue.

"Do you think it would be okay if the kids knew I was becoming a family friend of you-all?" she asked before she could stop herself.

Clearly, they were going to have to tell them something. Especially Lucy.

"Absolutely, we should mention that." Desire that matched her own flared in his eyes. He sat back in his chair, his broad shoulders flexing against the starched fabric of his dress shirt. Gruffly, he continued, "As well as good friends to each other."

Good friends.

She realized that was not quite what she wanted, but it would do for now.

TESS WORKED LATE again Friday evening, delivering a Shetland pony on the other side of the county. By the time she got back to the Welcome Ranch around midnight, everyone but Noah was fast asleep.

He heated up a dinner plate of leftover lasagna for her, and they shared a glass of wine and talked about their days while she ate.

"I think Lucy actually missed you this evening," Noah confided.

Tess thought about the hot-and-cold reception she often got from his eldest daughter. Wanting to believe they were getting closer, she regarded him hopefully. She needed to know what lay ahead. Would their passion remain a one-off? Or build into something stronger? She knew for certain he and his girls were a package deal. As they should be.

So for anything real or lasting to happen between the two of them, all three of his daughters would have to be fully on board.

Tess sipped her wine. "You're not just saying that?" she asked anxiously.

His smile reached his eyes. He leaned in close, inundating her with the brisk, woodsy scent of his cologne and the deeper, inherently masculine fragrance of his skin. He traced the inside of her wrist with the tip of his index finger. "She wanted you to know she got a one hundred on her spelling test."

Tingles spread outward, moving up her arm to the center of her chest. Heat gathered low in Tess's middle. Wishing they could make love, yet knowing they wouldn't—not here, not now, with his kids in the house—she contented herself with the fact he had waited up for her, so they could spend this time alone together. "I have a feeling she gets one hundreds quite frequently."

"True." He drew back just far enough to peer into her eyes. "But this time she credited you and your help."

They exchanged happy grins.

"The twins wanted to see you, too."

Aware she hadn't been this relaxed or felt this free in a long time, she surveyed him, too, drinking in his handsome features and the scruff of beard on his jaw. Heart skittering in her chest, she asked, "You're not worried about them getting too used to having me around?" she asked quietly, aware she was on the verge of a happiness and a sense of belonging unlike anything she had ever felt before.

"Not anymore." Noah leaned closer and this time his lips did brush her brow. Briefly, he held her close. "Not when your presence is bringing us all so much joy."

"DADDY, DID YOU ask Tess yet?" Lucy asked pointedly as Tess was getting ready to go to work Saturday morning.

"Ask me what?" She finished filling her travel mug with fresh, hot coffee.

"To go to dinner tonight at the Circle L!" Avery said.

"All the cousins get to play while the moms have a bake-a-thon with Gramma this afternoon and then we're all going to eat dinner together!" Angelica explained.

Already starting to feel a little overwhelmed, like this was a test she most definitely did not want to fail, Tess asked, "What time does it start?"

Noah joined her next to the coffee maker. "Around midafternoon. My siblings and their spouses will start showing up when their little ones wake up from their naps."

Things were moving both too fast and too slow with her and Noah. She wanted to know a lot more about him. Yet, at the same time, she wasn't sure she was ready to go to a big family dinner with him, where she was most likely going to be the only newbie. Even though she had briefly met a lot of the Lockharts before, when they had helped her clear out her house, it seemed like a lot of pressure.

Especially for someone like her, who had grown up an only child of a single mom.

"Hmm." Tess eased on her coat, trying to figure out if she should delay this kind of gathering until she at least knew Noah and his girls a lot better. "Can I let you know when I get done at the clinic?"

Noah's regard remained maddeningly inscrutable. "Sure. No pressure."

Appeased, she said goodbye to the girls, who were already headed off to the playroom upstairs.

Noah walked her as far as the door. Then grabbed his coat and whistled for Tank. "Need to go out, buddy?"

Tail wagging, the chocolate Lab followed them outside.

Noah fell into step beside her, keeping an appropriate distance, in case Lucy was watching from an upstairs window. Which, as it turned out, the little sleuth was. Hands shoved in the pockets of his jacket, he remained several feet away and watched as she put her vet bag and thermos in the Tahoe. With a casual grin, he asked, "Anything I can say to convince you it'd be a *great* idea for you to join us at my folks' today?"

Wow, he had a one-track mind. When he wanted something, he went right after it.

Tess paused, her hand on the car door. "Not sure." This was the second invitation she had fielded from Carol and Robert Lockhart in a week. She swallowed around the dryness of her throat. "Will your parents keep asking until I go?"

Mischief lit his eyes. "Most likely."

So then, how to mitigate any potential faux pas? She squinted at him thoughtfully. "Could I just show up in time for dinner? And not participate in the bake-a-thon?"

He exhaled, evidently still playing it casual. "If you want to avoid disappointing the ladies, probably not."

He caught her confused look, then explained, "My sister Jillian was here earlier in the week and had one of the scones you made. She hasn't stopped raving about it."

"Oh." That was nice, wasn't it?

"The ladies were all hoping you would share some tips with them. Unless—" he paused to give her a lazy once-over that set her to tingling anew "—you are one of those people who keep their recipes secret?"

She scoffed at the ridiculousness of the idea. "No, of course not." Food was for sharing and bringing people together, not driving them apart!

His dark eyebrows lifted. "Then...?"

Realizing she needed all the protection she could get, she said, "Will everyone be aware I'm just coming as your friend?"

From his immediate response, she could tell that he not only got her resistance to romantic meddling, but also shared it. "And temporary houseguest. You bet." He waited until she got in her vehicle. "I'll send out a group text and make sure that is crystal clear to them." He shut the driver door for her.

Which meant it would all be fine, Tess thought with a measure of relief, as she drove away from him. Wouldn't it?

CHAPTER NINE

TESS WAS BARELY in the Circle L ranch-house door before she was surrounded by a group of female family members. Thanks to the way they had all pitched in during the marathon clean-out of her home, she knew all but one.

The effervescent blonde radiated warmth and sophistication. "Hi, Tess."

Before she could do more than draw a breath, she was enveloped in an easy hug that spoke volumes about the generosity and warmth of the Lockhart clan.

Drawing back, her host said, "I'm Mackenzie, Noah's sister from Fort Worth."

"The one who's married to Griff and has twin toddlers, Jenny and Jake? And a Bernese mountain dog named Bliss?"

"Right. Wow…you must have a great memory."

About pets and their owners, yes, she did. "Noah was updating me on the way over," she explained.

Mackenzie shot an affectionate glance at her brother, who was engulfed in his own series of greetings and hugs.

More followed for Tess, too.

"Sounds just like him," Mackenzie said affectionately.

Finally, she was escorted to the big, homey ranch-house kitchen, where over a half a dozen baking stations were already set up.

"Ready to part with all your scone-making secrets?"

Noah's sister Faith asked with a smile. Newly married to her adopted son's biological father, she radiated joy.

"I am." Tess put on the apron handed to her. "I just hope I don't disappoint."

Fortunately, her audience was as patient as they were serious about learning all the tricks her professional chef mother had taught her. From using supercold shaved butter and heavy cream to not overmixing the dough.

Each woman added a different ingredient to their concoction, everything from chopped fresh fruit to nuts and dark chocolate. When all the scones were rotating in and out of Carol's two large wall ovens, the women worked together to clean up.

And that was, of course, when the questions started.

"Was it hard for you leaving Denver?" Faith queried.

"You grew up and went to school there, right?" Gabe's wife, Susannah, asked right after.

"Yes. My first thirty years were all spent in Colorado. I grew up in Denver, went to Colorado State University for undergrad and vet school. That's in Fort Collins. And then I moved back to the Denver area, for my first job as a veterinarian."

"Did you relocate here just because of the house you inherited from Waylon?" Jillian asked.

Carol sent her daughter a look, seeming to warn her not to be too nosy. Even if she was Noah's closest female sibling.

"Or were you looking for adventure or even a fresh start?" Cade's wife, Allison, asked.

Probably trying to help divert attention away from Noah, Tess thought. Because, surely, those inquiries were coming soon. Tess sent Allison—who had already helped her find married local contractors Molly and Chance to do her house renovation—a grateful glance. "I've always been interested in Texas. And wanted to know more about my family who lived here."

Noah's mother cleared her throat.

Mackenzie shrugged. "Maybe she has someone special set to join her soon."

Everyone turned in curiosity. Tess felt herself flush, not sure what to say. "I, uh, was in a long-term relationship until a couple of years ago. Since, I've concentrated on my career."

"So you're open to someone new?" Travis's wife, Skye, a registered nurse, asked. "Because it's never good to spend too long alone…"

THE KIDS WERE bursting with energy, and the day was sunny and clear, so Noah and the rest of the men took them all outside to play in the big, fenced backyard, which had a playset and a sandbox. While they stood around and supervised the children, there was a lot of guy talk. First, predictions about the current football playoffs and upcoming Super Bowl. College basketball and the ever-popular March Madness was next. Then cattle. Horses. Schools. And finally, the latest "romance" in the family.

Gabe, the oldest, asked, "Is Tess your date?"

Yes, Noah thought, but remembering his promise to her, he said, "No."

Mackenzie's husband, Griff, an attorney never shy about giving advice, said, "Well, she should be."

His retired professional-baseball-playing brother, the former ladies' man of the bunch, elbowed him in the side. "You snooze, you lose," Cade teased.

The idea that he would let any guy cut in line ahead of him rankled. Noah turned, and reminded Cade, "Hey. She's living with me." What would they call that? If not getting his bid for attention in. And staking his claim. Every. Single. Day.

Eyebrows raised all around.

Noah bit down on a curse.

Damn, he was rusty with all this.

He'd really forgotten the finer points of dating a woman. If he had ever really known them, that was. Since he had gone straight from high school to freshman year of college to marriage.

Aware he was getting that look—the one that said he needed to up his game—Noah cleared his throat and tried again. "I mean staying with me," he corrected with as much gentlemanly ease as possible. "Temporarily."

Travis, the most recently married, chuckled. He rubbed a hand across his jaw. "Yeah, and I bet you wish those repairs on her house will never get done."

Actually, Noah thought, there was some truth to that. He liked sharing space with her. Trading confidences. Making love…

"Speaking of Tess…" his dad interrupted kindly. He inclined his head in the direction of the kitchen's big bay window. "Don't look now, but looks like she's getting the third degree."

Noah glanced over. The women were gathered around Tess, the way the guys had just been gathered around him. And his gut told him it wasn't because they were currently having a cooking lesson. He grimaced. He had promised Tess this wouldn't happen. "Excuse me." He turned on his heel. "I've got a rescue to undertake."

He slipped in the back door. Then sauntered into the kitchen, cheerfully disrupting whatever conversation had been going on.

Tess remained where she was, giving him a mild look. But he could feel her gratitude surging in his direction.

To make sure it didn't happen again, he stayed close by her the rest of the day. And begged off early, after dinner, to go back to Welcome Ranch to check on Miss Coco. They took the girls down to the barn with them.

Tess opened up her vet bag and examined the pregnant jennet while the girls watched. "Is she going to have her baby soon?" Lucy asked.

"I think it's still going to be at least another week," Tess replied, palpitating the donkey's midsection and checking out the position of the foal.

"How will you know for sure?" Angelica murmured curiously, hunkering down next to Tess. Her twin did the same.

Noah kneeled, too. Wanting to make sure that Tess had enough room to maneuver, he brought both twins onto his lap, while Lucy hung back a little, watching.

"Because Miss Coco will know her baby is ready to come out, and she'll let me know," Tess explained. She gave Noah a look, as if hoping the girls didn't need more specific information.

But he knew if they did, and he gave permission, which he would, that she would answer their questions as kindly and carefully as possible, making sure not to upset them.

Luckily, they took the lack of absolute due date in stride. Probably because they had already been waiting months for the foal to arrive.

Avery turned to Noah. "Daddy, after this baby is born, will Miss Coco have another foal?"

Another? Noah's brow furrowed. He wasn't sure what she was trying to ask. "You mean like twins?"

"No," Angelica inserted, picking up where her twin sister left off. "Like next year."

Thank heaven they had no male donkeys around. Noah

shook his head, sure about this much. "No. Two donkeys is enough for us," he said.

Angelica looked at Tess. "What about you?" Noah's three-year-old asked. "Do *you* have any babies?"

TESS HAD THOUGHT the inquisition from Noah's sisters was intrusive, in that well-meant, protective family way. But she hadn't expected *this*.

Trying not to wonder what Noah thought about her having a baby—with anyone—she smiled and said, "No, I don't, honey."

Lucy finally moved away from the stall door. Arms folded in front of her, she stared Tess down. "Do you want some?"

Did she?

Up to now, she had pretty much ruled it out. Mainly because she didn't want to parent alone, while juggling a demanding career and being sole financial support of the family, the way her mom had.

But now, being around Noah and his kids and his big, extended family, she was beginning to see it as a real possibility. Even if the only man she could currently see taking on the starring role in her daydream was the man opposite her. The man who had vowed never to marry again.

She supposed that also meant never having any more kids.

And that would be disappointing, she realized without warning. Gut-wrenchingly so.

Aware everyone was still waiting for her answer, she said, "Maybe someday. But I'd need to get married first. Now—" she put one earpiece of her stethoscope in her ear and held out the other for a willing volunteer "—who else wants to hear Miss Coco's heartbeat?"

AN HOUR LATER, Tess was sitting on the porch steps, watching Tank explore the yard, when the front door eased open and then quietly closed.

Noah sat down beside her, his thigh touching hers. "I'm aware you have every right to be irritated with me."

It helped, knowing he was sensitive to how difficult that Lockhart family shindig had been for her. She leaned into his touch for one millisecond before pulling away. "Your sisters were just being protective. Your mother tried to stop them."

"To no avail, apparently."

His droll tone brought a rueful smile to her face. She turned to face him. As their eyes met and held, she felt a shimmer of tension arc between them.

Man-woman tension.

Doing her best to maintain a poker face, Tess shrugged. "Lockharts are stubborn, when they get on a mission, I'm beginning to see."

He reached up and tucked a strand of hair behind her ear. "No kidding. But don't discount my mother. She's matchmaking, too."

Tess bit her lip. "Hence the two dinner invitations in one week." Only one of which had been accepted. Would today have been less stressful if she had gone to his folks' home both times?

Tess was unable to say.

Noticing she was shivering in a too-light fleece, Noah took off his jacket and draped it over her shoulders. Just like that, she was inundated with the warmth of his body and the woodsy scent of his cologne.

He leaned closer, whispering in her ear. "Well, she *is* a social worker…"

"And she thinks I need…work?" Tess said, unable to hold back the quip.

He laughed and shook his head. "No. But she does think a closed heart can get stuck shut."

Interesting. Tess snuggled deeper into the warmth of his coat. "Hmm." It was so nice on the porch steps, with the velvety black sky overhead, sprinkled with stars and a golden quarter moon. They were both going to be too cold sitting out here. She knew that. Yet, she wasn't quite ready to leave the peace and quiet of a Texas night in January.

Figuring the least she could do was share a little body heat, Tess scooted a little closer, until they were touching from hip to ankle, shoulder to waist. She gazed out over the ranch. Thinking *Welcome* was exactly the right name. She certainly felt at home here.

She just hoped her heart didn't get stuck shut. The way Carol Lockhart seemed to fear…

"Maybe that's what happened to my mom and grandmother." With a shrug, Tess mused quietly, "They walled off their feelings for each other, and then didn't know how to open up to each other once again."

He caught her hand in his and clasped it tightly. "I'm sorry about that."

She pulled their entwined fingers onto her lap. "Me, too. But it's in the past, and nothing can be done about it now, so—" she squared her shoulders and sat up straighter "—I need to stop dwelling on it, and move forward."

With a sexy half smile, he regarded her with admiration. "To…?"

"Getting a family like yours. And all the ones your siblings and parents enjoy."

That was ultimately what was going to make her happy. She knew that now. She wanted someone to share life's ups and downs with.

He continued holding her hand. "You mean that?"

Aware he was truly trying to understand her, she drew a breath. "I do."

As their eyes met, and held, she felt warmed through and through. "The thing is," he said softly, "we've got time to figure this out."

That's what Carlton had said, from the time they started dating, until they broke up: *We don't have to rush into anything...*

But Noah wasn't her ex.

He understood there was more to life than ambition, goals and a successful career.

He also seemed to appreciate the importance of sharing one's thoughts and feelings. Shaking his head ruefully, he continued, "Maybe it's because of the way my birth parents died, so suddenly, but it seems like I've been in a hurry my whole life. With Shelby. My work. I even tried to rush through the grieving process, after Shelby passed."

"Did that work for you?" Tess couldn't help but ask.

He paused, considering. "Yes and no. I mean I know I will always be sad about the loss, but I realize now that I am ready to move on, too."

Joy unfurled slowly inside Tess.

She was ready to embrace a new future, too.

"Which is why," Noah continued sincerely, squeezing her hand in his, "for the first time, I want to slow down and really enjoy each moment of my life. Take my time, getting to know you. See where whatever this is between us is going to take us."

Tess knew what a huge admission this was for him. "I'd like to get to know you a whole lot better, too," she said quietly. Except she wanted to do it a whole lot *faster*. Which was ironic, because for the first time in her life, she found herself wanting to not be as incredibly patient as she had been taught to be for so many years, but to rush in where fools feared to tread.

Who would have figured that?

CHAPTER TEN

"So what do you think?" Molly asked Tess, during their midjob walk-through Tuesday evening, after she'd finished work at the clinic.

Tess gazed at the interior of her home, in wonder. Joy flowed through her. "I can't believe you've only been working on this renovation for nine days!"

Molly grinned. "Chance and I told you we'd get it done on time."

They had definitely said that.

And right now, Tess believed they would. The mess of a house she'd inherited was no longer visible. A light neutral color adorned all the walls. The plumbing and electric had been redone, the new HVAC keeping the interior cozy, and a gas fireplace insert had been installed.

True, the newly sanded wood floors still needed to be stained and sealed, the bathroom upstairs finished and a new half bath put in the first floor, next to the expanded laundry room.

But recessed lighting throughout the first floor made it bright and cheerful against the wintry darkness outside.

Molly walked with Tess back into the kitchen, which remained a blank slate. She spread the plans for the kitchen across a piece of plywood on two sawhorses. Then opened up the folder that held the materials that would be used to finish it out. Creamy ivory cabinets, a farmhouse sink. Room for a French door refrigerator/freezer and dishwasher. Molly sobered. "I want to make sure you want a four-burner gas stove, not an ultradeluxe chef's model."

Tess shot her a curious look.

The contractor explained, "Word of your culinary talent is getting out, among the community. So I wanted to make sure you would be happy with the standard model you picked out."

Ah…small towns. Where everyone knew everyone. Pleased to have Molly watching out for her, too, Tess said, "My mom definitely would have gone for the higher-end model, with the six burners, center griddle and double ovens. As an executive chef, she wouldn't have been happy with anything less. But honestly, I only cook for myself, and that's when I'm off."

The other woman nodded, listening intently, giving her all the time she needed to consider.

Tess told herself not to second-guess her decision. "If I had a family—" like Noah and the girls "—it would be different, of course."

Molly's expression gentled. "You don't think that will happen?"

It hadn't yet.

And wishes weren't reality.

Better not to talk about what she was beginning to want in the worst way. For the first time in her life.

Tess exhaled. "No."

Molly's face lit up. An intuitive woman, she touched Tess's arm empathetically. "That's what I said before Chance and I got together. And look at us now. Happily married parents to two! So you never know…"

No, you didn't. Although Tess had been working hard to keep from thinking too far ahead. Yes, she and Noah and the girls were getting along splendidly, and she felt more at home with them every day. Noah had kept to his promise from the previous week, about going slow.

While she privately kept yearning for more.

Which wasn't good, she knew.

Especially if it turned out their friendship/one-time fling was one based in convenience. Nothing deeper...

Molly asked a few more questions regarding the quartz countertops and backsplash, the size of the island she was going to put in. "When do you expect your belongings to get here?" she asked.

Tess hesitated. "I'm not sure. Everything is still in storage. I have to let the movers know when I want them to get it on the truck. Once I do, they said it would take a couple of weeks to get it here."

"You probably should do that now, then," Molly said.

"I will," Tess promised.

Excitement flooded through her. It was *happening*. She was finally going to have a home of her own, renovated exactly to her specifications. Whatever else happened, she could be happy about that.

Molly gathered up the samples. "Well, I need to get home for dinner," she said.

"I need to get going, too," Tess murmured. She needed to check on Miss Coco. Plus, Noah or the girls might need help with something.

They walked around, turning off the interior lights.

"How is it going at the Welcome Ranch?" Molly asked.

Good question. One she was going to have difficulty answering candidly. "Mmm... Noah's been great. Very kind."

Molly paused to slip on her coat. "How about Lucy and the twins?"

"I'm half family friend, half houseguest to them. So they don't want to eat dinner without me, because 'that is rude if you are having guests.' But they also know there are times when I have to work late, or go out on a house or ranch call, before I head 'home' for the night, so…"

"Yeah, I can see how that could feel a little awkward at times."

Awkward and too cozy and a legion of other things…

Tess checked her phone to make sure there were no messages, then put on her coat, too. "Anyway, when I can, I try to do dishes or help with dinner or fold laundry as a way to repay Noah for putting me up."

Molly smiled in understanding. "I'm sure he appreciates whatever you do. I was a single parent to one, until Braden was almost five, and it was hard. I can't imagine how Noah has managed with three…"

Admirably well, Tess thought. She had no doubt he would go back to coping on his own just fine. It was herself, going back to a life alone, she was beginning to worry about.

"How did the walk-through go?" Noah asked Tess, twenty minutes later.

"Fine." Vet bag in hand, she strode into the stable, where it seemed his entire family was gathered. Including their chocolate Labrador retriever, Tank. "What's going on?"

"We can't get Tank to come back to the house," Avery explained.

"And we don't know why he doesn't want to come with us," Lucy said, looking upset. "He *always* comes when it's about dinnertime."

"Maybe he's just not hungry," Angelica mused.

Tess could see Tank hanging out in the aisleway, in the middle of the barn, across from Miss Coco's stall.

"He's been like this all day," Noah said. "Every time I let him out he makes a beeline for the stable. And won't leave until he goes inside and checks on Miss Coco. I have to snap a leash on him to get him to go back to the house."

Tess walked over to Tank and petted him on the head. "Sounds like you're doing a great job of guarding today, buddy."

She opened the wooden half door and went in to see the miniature donkey. Swiftly spotting the reason, she looked at Noah. "The foal is starting to turn." Which was one of the first signs of impending birth.

"What is that?" Lucy asked curiously.

Noah gave a barely perceptible nod, letting her know it was okay to continue.

Tess surveyed the girls gently, making eye contact with each. "Miss Coco is getting ready to have her baby donkey."

"Now?" Angelica and Avery clapped their hands and jumped up and down excitedly, squealing.

Noah put his finger to his lips. "Shhh!" He whispered sternly, "You don't want to scare our pets."

They settled immediately, somewhat chagrined. "Sorry, Daddy," the twins murmured in unison.

"It takes a while for the mama donkey to get ready to give birth, so it's not going to happen right away," Tess cautioned.

"When do you think?" His handsome face etched with concern, Noah echoed his eldest daughter's query.

Once again, she tried not to think how intimate this all felt. "Maybe by the weekend."

Lucy crossed her arms. Recalcitrant once again. "That can't happen. We are going to Fort Worth to see Aunt Mackenzie and Uncle Griff and *their* twins, with all the rest of our cousins." Hands on her hips, she swung back to Noah. "Daddy, tell Tess to tell Miss Coco she has to wait!"

Noah put a gentle hand on her shoulder. He looked

down at her, and patiently soothed, "It doesn't work that way, honey."

Lucy became even more defiant. She stomped her rubber-boot-clad foot. "But I want to see the baby donkey be born!"

"So do I!" chimed the twins, continuing to squeal loudly in excitement.

Noah shushed them all once again. "That's not a good idea."

Lucy's lower lip trembled. "Why not?" she demanded.

Sensing it was time for a little medical expertise, Tess interjected, "Because it is a very private and special time for a mama donkey, and she needs to have quiet, so she can't have a lot of people around while she is trying to give birth. It's too distracting. And it makes her very nervous and unhappy during what should be a very special, joyful time for her and her new foal."

Lucy considered that, her inherent kindness coming to the fore once again. "Are you going to be there?" she asked Tess.

Happy to see Noah's eldest was calm again, she replied, "Yes."

"Are you?" Lucy's eyes swung toward her dad.

"Yes, I am," he said.

"Then I want to be there, too," the eight-year-old insisted.

Noah frowned. "Even if it makes it harder for Miss Coco and her new baby donkey?" he returned.

Lucy fell silent. Torn between what she selfishly wanted, and what she knew was right.

"How about this?" Tess intervened gently once again. "How about your dad and I make a video of it, so we can show you later."

That had all three girls' attention—and approval.

"Can I see the baby donkey after it is born?" Lucy asked.

"Absolutely," Tess said while, beside her, Noah nodded his consent, too. She looked his oldest daughter in the eye. "I will introduce you and your sisters to the new foal. We'll do it one person at a time, so Miss Coco and her baby won't feel overwhelmed. And I will teach you how to touch them and talk to them, and care for them, too." Because imprint training should include the entire family to be truly successful.

Lucy exhaled in satisfaction. "Okay," she said, finally relenting. "But Miss Coco still has to wait until we get back from Fort Worth. Do you hear that, Miss Coco?" she scolded affectionately, before she left, giving their pet donkey a final loving stroke across her brow. "You need to wait to have your foal, until we get back on Sunday!"

"ARE YOU GOING to Fort Worth with the girls?" Tess asked later that evening, after the kids were all asleep. Noah set down an armload of firewood, next to the hearth.

His shoulders flexed as he shrugged out of his winter jacket and went to hang it up. "Normally, yes, I would." He walked back, his strides purposeful. Slanting her a glance over his shoulder, he added in a low, reassuring tone that sent tingles pouring through her, "But not with Miss Coco about to deliver."

Tess settled on the sofa with a basket of mismatched children's socks she had offered to sort. Anything to keep her hands and mind busy. And off the building desire to be intimate with him again.

She swallowed around the tightness in her throat. "I could get some help from the vet clinic if you like."

Noah hunkered down to build the fire. Denim stretched across his muscular legs and butt. Her body heated in response. "No. I want to be here." He reached to the left, and the same thing happened with the fabric of his shirt. It molded to his buff upper body and strong arms, reminding Tess what a fine body he had. "And, by the way, thanks for helping explain to the girls why they can't witness the birth."

She found two pink-and-white polka-dot wool socks and rolled them into a ball. "I agree with you. It'd be a bad idea."

Noah frowned over at her. "You say that like you're speaking from experience."

Tess nodded, deciding to be forthright, so he would know in advance what a worst-case scenario could look like. "When I was working at my previous job, I had a family that wanted to watch the birth of their miniature donkey's foal. The kids were all pretty young. I worried they would be too excited or maybe even scared by what they were going to see but—" she inhaled deeply, forcing herself to go on "—I was overruled."

Noah stuffed paper into the open spaces in the set logs. He sat back and reached for the long matches. "What happened?"

Tess shut her eyes briefly and continued sorrowfully. "There was a complication." She forced herself to meet Noah's eyes. Watched while he lit the fire, then rose and came back to sit beside her. "The foal came out with the cord wrapped around her neck."

He settled nearer, draping an arm along the back of the sofa, close enough to warm her shoulders. "Oh, no."

Horrifyingly, yes. "The parents saw and became hysterical that we were going to lose the foal. The kids followed suit." Tess shook her head, recalling the crying and screaming and panicked shouting. "I got everyone out of the way and saved both jennet and foal, but needless to say, there were some really tense moments."

He drew her closer still. "I can imagine."

"The kids were traumatized to the point the vet clinic waived the family's entire bill and I had to apologize to them. The thing was—" she paused to lick her lips "—I knew it was a bad idea, but I had no say."

His gaze roved her face. Commiserating. "Now you do?"

"Oh, yes, I made sure of that before I signed on with the clinic here."

He was looking at her like he wanted to kiss her again. But she knew if they started, they wouldn't want to stop. And with the kids right upstairs… It made more sense to wait until the next morning, when the girls were at school, and she didn't have to be at work until noon.

The unmasked longing in his eyes indicated he was thinking the same thing.

He touched a strand of her hair, rubbing it between his fingertips. "So…" He waggled his eyebrows at her, letting her know he still yearned to be with her as much as she yearned to be with him. "If you decided to kick me out of the stable when it's time…?"

"I could."

Their gazes meshed. Lingered. They exchanged knowing smiles.

Without warning, Tess knew morning couldn't come soon enough. "But I won't. We had a deal, remember?" She bent her head and went back to sorting socks. "I'm going to teach you how to imprint-train your family's new foal." With a flirtatious gaze aimed back at him, she murmured, "Plus, having grown up on a ranch, I imagine you saw this kind of thing all the time."

His sensual lips curved into an inviting smile. "I did. I even helped out a time or two." He suddenly sobered. "But I feel like this is going to be *different*."

Tess thought so, too.

Part of it was professional pride. She wanted things to go smoothly. The rest had to do with the time she and Noah would spend together, bringing new life into the world, helping the baby donkey draw his or her first breath. It was the kind of intimate activity that would bring them closer.

But was it the kind of closeness that would endure?

Only time would give her the answer to that.

CHAPTER ELEVEN

"NO SCHOOL TODAY?" Tess remarked in surprise on Friday morning. She was usually the first out the door during the weekdays, with Noah following an hour later, girls in tow. However, this morning, the three girls were already dressed in matching pink cords and sweaters. Their wheeled suitcases were next to the front door, along with their backpacks.

"It's a teacher workday, so we get the day off!" Lucy said importantly.

"Which is why we get to go to Fort Worth with Gramma and Grandpa early!" Avery announced.

"Ah." Tess grinned. "Now it all makes sense." She'd thought the girls were leaving at the end of the day. Not the beginning.

"We get to go to the zoo this afternoon," Angelica added.

"And the science museum tomorrow." Avery handed Tess a hairbrush. "Can you put my hair in a ponytail?" She had an elastic around her wrist.

"Sure." Tess smiled.

"Mine, too," Angelica said.

Tess fixed both girls hair. Lucy had done her own ponytail, but now she undid it. And walked over silently to Tess, handing over her elastic.

Happy to be included, Tess did as asked, while Noah watched silently, a quietly affectionate look on his face.

She understood the depth of his emotion.

She was falling in love with his kids, too.

"Can we go down and say goodbye to Miss Coco before we leave?" Lucy asked.

"Sure." Noah handed out coats. Together, they walked outside and trooped across the lawn, Tank beside them.

Miss Coco was sitting half-upright when they walked in, panting slightly. Her belly was protruding more than ever. "Do you think she's uncomfortable?" Lucy asked Tess worriedly. Tenderly, she stroked her pet's head.

"Yes. But most mamas are when they get to the end stages of their pregnancy," Tess said. "But not to worry. I think Miss Coco knows that is a good thing. It means her baby foal is getting ready to be born."

"But not 'til we get back from Aunt Mackenzie and Uncle Griff's house, right, Daddy?" Angelica reminded him.

Avery kneeled down to stroke Miss Coco'a soft brown tail. "We want to be here with her."

"I am sure Miss Coco knows how you feel," Noah said gently.

The sound of a vehicle approaching had him going to the door. "Kids, say goodbye now. Your ride is here!"

They scrambled to get ready. In their excitement, they embraced their dad and then impulsively stopped to give Tess hugs, too.

She held each of the girls in turn. Aware all over again how wonderful it would be to have a family like this, of her own. Or even to remain part of this one, in some way…

Tess walked to the door, waving at Carol and Robert. She turned to Noah. "I've got a few things I want to check out."

"No problem. I'll see them off and be right back."

When he returned, Tess was kneeling in the straw next to Miss Coco, who had decided to lie down again.

"More signs?" Noah asked.

Tess nodded, showing him. "The teats are all the way enlarged and they've developed a waxy cap on the ends." Tess ran her hands over the top of the jennet's body. "See these grooves on either side of Miss Coco's spine, near the tail? That means her pelvic ligaments are softening in preparation. Plus, the area around the opening of her birth canal is elongated and loose and soft."

"So… Soon?"

"I'm thinking maybe late tonight."

Briefly, Noah looked a little panicked. "What should I do?"

"Just keep an eye on her through the security camera. Check on her every hour or so. And let me know if she gets restless."

Tess could see he was still anxious. The way she would be if she was in his position. She sent him a reassuring smile. "I can be here in fifteen minutes, if you need me. All you have to do is call or text. I'm seeing patients at the clinic, but I'll have my phone on me all day."

Noah turned to the pregnant jennet. He kneeled down beside her and stroked her head gently, looking deep into the miniature donkey's soft, dark eyes. "You hear that, Miss Coco? There's nothing for you to worry about. You're not going through this alone. Tess and I will both be here," he promised.

NOAH SENT TESS updates through the day, brief texts that indicated what she expected to hear…that everything was the same.

She was just walking out to her Tahoe when the phone rang. She glanced at the caller ID. Instantly alert. "Noah?"

"All of a sudden, she's really restless," he informed her gravely. "I think it's time."

"Hang on. I'll be right there," Tess promised. "And, in the meantime, maybe you should set up the video camera so we can edit a movie of the birth for the kids."

"Already done."

"Great. See you shortly."

The drive went quickly.

Instead of parking next to the house and walking down, she left her SUV next to the stable and headed in. Noah was standing in the aisleway, arms crossed, concern etching deep grooves in his handsome face. She joined him where he stood.

"See that?" He pointed to Miss Coco's swollen genitals, flush with the hindquarters.

"Definitely getting ready to give birth," Tess said, glad he had called when he had. "But judging by the position of the foal, it's still going to be a few hours."

He lifted an eyebrow.

Not sure whether he considered that good news or bad, she set down her vet bag. "In the meantime, we have a few things to do."

He let out a rough exhalation of breath. "Like…?"

"Sterilize and put fresh hay, water and feed in a nearby stall, so we can move them after the foal is born. We don't want to expose the foal to contamination."

"On it," Noah said. "In fact, I'll set up two stalls, just in case we need 'em."

Anything, Tess thought, *to keep him busy, and calm*. Short of sending him out to boil water, anyway.

She handed him a pair of veterinary coveralls, and a box of sterile birthing gloves. Then told him to put the coveralls on, and wait on the shoulder-length gloves until the time came when she did need his veterinary assistance.

"Were you there to witness the births of your girls?" she asked eventually.

Noah set up bales of hay against the stable walls, to act as seats for them. "Yes."

The muscles in his shoulders flexed as he worked. Aware this was a new side of him, Tess took in his handsome profile and smiled. "Were you nervous?"

He chuckled. "Yeah. Especially the first time." He shook his head ruefully, remembering. "I drove Shelby all the way to the hospital, then realized I left her suitcase in the front hall. I had to call a friend of ours to go by the house and get it. But that was the only snafu in labor and delivery. Lucy came out, feisty as ever."

Tess could imagine. She studied the tenderness etched on his face. "What about with the twins?"

His brows drew together. "It was a little easier, since I had been through the whole birth process once. But it was more stressful, in another sense, because we knew Shelby was having twins. And we didn't know how that would go."

"But it went fine," Tess guessed.

"Yep." He nodded, smiling. "Although it was a whole lot faster. It required twelve hours of labor for Lucy to come into the world. The twins were both here two hours after Shelby's water broke, so…we barely made it to the hospital."

Tess imagined what that must have been like. "Sounds exciting."

Noah smiled. "It was. To the point…" he went on, then suddenly stopped.

"What were you going to say?" Whatever it was, Tess noticed, it seemed to have surprised him.

He shrugged and turned to her. Serious, happy now. "That I wouldn't mind doing it all again."

KNOWING NOAH WAS open to having another child, was spirit lifting to say the least. Watching him worry over Miss Coco, as her labor progressed, was a lot more difficult.

"I've never heard her sound like that," Noah said an hour and a half later as the donkey brayed in pain. She had been pacing, but now she was lying back down again, on her side, her tail held back away from her body.

"That's because her baby is coming..." Birthing gloves on, Tess kneeled next to Miss Coco. She could see the tip of one sac-covered hoof, then part of one leg, coming through the opening. And...*oh, no!*

"What is it?" Noah asked in alarm, reading her expression.

"Both feet need to come out before the head, in what's called diving position. Right now, we've only got one. Get on the other side of her and keep her calm while I..." Tess gently nudged the baby donkey's nose back inside the mama, then reached around until she found the other front leg, and brought it out, too.

Her sides heaving with the force of her contractions, Miss Coco brayed all the louder. And then the foal's head began to emerge. Tess guided it out.

The rest of the foal's body followed swiftly. It was covered in a bluish gray membrane, filled with fluid. Tess broke the sack, pulling placental membranes off the newborn donkey's nostrils and muzzle. She checked for obstruction, relieved to find nothing that would hamper breathing, and rubbed the chest wall to encourage better air intake. As she peeled away the rest of the neonatal sack, she noted in relief that all was as it should be. "Confirmation is perfect," she told Noah happily. The thick-coated twenty-pound foal was the same cocoa color as her mother, with a white streak down the middle of her face, and white socks on all four legs.

Noah's broad shoulders sagged in relief. "That's great." He gazed down tenderly at the newly born animal. "How can I help?" he asked.

"Get her used to the sound of your voice, and your touch." Her heart filled to bursting by the miracle of birth, she nodded at the stack of clean, soft towels. "And use those to gently wipe her down."

Grinning, Noah kneeled beside Tess, who was tending to Miss Coco, and cared for the newborn donkey. "The girls are going to be thrilled to find out we have another female on the Welcome Ranch."

Tess caught the placenta and put it into a plastic basin, for later examination. "Definitely seems to be the trend," she said wryly. "You and Tank are outnumbered."

Noah chuckled.

Miss Coco lumbered to her feet, the action breaking the umbilical cord. While Noah doused the stump with a syringe of chlorhexidine solution, Tess cleaned Miss Coco's hindquarters and mammary glands with mild soap and water. Finished, they moved both animals to the already prepared stall across the aisleway.

An exhausted Miss Coco collapsed on the soft clean hay. They settled her baby next to her, within reach of a teat. Blinking in confusion, the baby turned away.

"Is that supposed to happen?" Noah asked.

"Not to worry. We can help her get the hang of nursing." While Noah continued imprinting the newborn with his soothing touch and low, encouraging voice, Tess grabbed what she needed from her bag of supplies. "First, we have to milk out two to four ounces and give her some colostrum from a bottle. The latter of which I'll let you do..."

Minutes later, Noah was sitting next to the mama's head,

with his back against the stall wall, feeding the baby donkey with the expertise of a natural cowboy and veteran dad. Miss Coco looked on with a mix of contentment and fatigue. When the baby'd had her fill, they put the new jennet in the curve of her mama's body, to help them bond and keep the baby donkey warm. The two snuggled happily.

Tess tilted her head in the direction of the video camera Noah had mounted above the stall, to capture it all. "Your girls are going to love this."

Noah grinned, agreeing. "It'll be some home movie. Once we edit out all the goop, of course."

"And the scary sounds."

"Yep."

While Noah cleaned and disinfected the birth stall, Tess gathered up all her vet gear.

She and Noah both stripped off their shoulder-length gloves and coveralls, put them into a large trash bag for later disposal and faced off in the aisleway. Aware they made a pretty good team, even in as potentially stressful a situation as this, she pushed aside the sudden fierce desire to bring him all the way into her arms and kiss him passionately.

"So now what?" he asked softly, looking handsome and strong in his dark plaid flannel shirt and jeans. Like he wanted to kiss her, too.

Aware how hard it would be to stop, once they opened the door to something like that, she drew a bracing breath. Focused on what still lay ahead. "We wait to make sure the foal is strong enough to stand and nurse."

"Then we might as well get comfortable," Noah said. He got another six-foot-wide bale of hay and set it in the corner of the big roomy horse stall, where the donkeys were now quartered. Then left again briefly, returning with two cold electrolyte drinks. Their fingers brushed, then their bodies as they settled on the bale, their backs to the wall in the heated stable.

"Thanks," Tess said.

Noah nudged her arm, snuggling comfortably against her, too. "So tell me, Doc," he murmured softly. "What was it like, the first time you did this…?"

FOR THE NEXT hour or so, Noah and Tess traded animal husbandry stories—Tess's warm, womanly presence and soft voice was like a balm to his soul.

He talked about things he had seen on the Circle L. Albeit he'd been more of a watcher from a distance than a hands-on guy, until tonight. She told him about some of her most challenging cases. "Although I think this might be my most joyful," she said.

An hour after that, the newborn stood on wobbly legs and nosed her mama. With a muted groan, Miss Coco stood, and the baby attempted—unsuccessfully—to latch on to a teat. Only to fall onto the soft hay.

Noah leaned forward to jump to the rescue. But Tess held him back. "Let them try to work it out first."

Miss Coco licked her newborn gently. The baby donkey stood again, wobbling mightily as she headed for a teat. This time Miss Coco adjusted toward her body, too.

Only to have the foal fail and fall again.

Noah groaned. "This is torture," he said.

Tess remained confident. "They'll get it."

And sure enough, the next time they did. The little one latched on and began to nurse. The thirsty, suckling sounds filled the stable. And for long moments, all Noah and Tess could do was hold on to each other and take in the beauty and wonder of it all.

AROUND MIDNIGHT, NOAH went back to the house and returned with a big thermos of coffee and sandwiches for the two of them. Miss Coco and her baby had both lied down to rest, with the little one curled up against her mama's chest. The snuggling was greeting-card cute. Tess couldn't stop smiling, watching them.

He couldn't stop smiling, either, watching *her*. He nudged her thigh with his bent knee. "Is this the reason why you became a vet?"

She finished her sandwich and put the wadded-up wrapper back in the insulated bag. "One of them."

He leaned in close enough to track the luscious softness of her lips. "But I'm guessing this is one of your favorite parts?"

For a moment, he thought she wouldn't answer, then she shrugged, a flash of hurt in her expression. "Recently, I've come to accept that bringing animals into the world is the closest I will ever come to being a mom."

He paused, not sure what she was trying to tell him. Was there a health issue? Did she think that would affect how he saw her...?

Reading his mind, she lifted a hand. "There's no physical reason why not. Not that I know of, anyway. But..." She breathed in deeply, frowning. "I know how hard it was for my mom to bring me up on her own, how lonely it was for me. And maybe it's selfish. Or foolish. But I don't think I ever want to go that route." She raked her teeth across her lower lip. "If I had a family, it would have to be because I was married, and it was what my husband wanted, too."

He caught her hand in his. "I get it. And you're right. It's damn hard to parent on your own, even with a zillion family members nearby, ready and willing to help. Not to mention, offer advice."

Recalling the romantic coaching he had recently received from his sister Jillian, he winced.

Tess grinned, as always, sharing his sense of humor. "I hadn't thought about it that way." She clasped his hand tightly in return. "Maybe being an only child had its perks, too."

He loved the way her eyes lit up when she smiled. "You never had to fight over the last cookie," he pointed out.

"Or wait forever for my turn in the bathroom. Still—" she released her palm from his and went back to sipping her coffee "—being an only kid was lonely so I think if I ever were to embark on motherhood, I'd definitely want to have at least three or four kids."

And I've always wanted a son. Plus, I have three daughters who would really like to have a mother again, and possibly another sibling, too.

Not that if he had another baby, it would have to be a boy. A girl would be great, too. He turned to Tess, easily imagining how beautiful she would be with child. *His* child.

Was it too much, too soon, to even be thinking about? Noah couldn't say. All he knew for sure was that sitting there next to her, in the quiet of the stable, he was finally ready to put the loss of Shelby behind him. Move on to a fuller life. As well as tempted to volunteer to help Tess achieve her dreams. To give her reason for staying on at the Welcome Ranch with them, and becoming more and more a part of their lives.

CHAPTER TWELVE

TESS AND NOAH spent the night in the stable, keeping watch over mama and baby donkey. They talked about everything and nothing, exactly as they would have had they been on a date. Or two. Or three. And even as the hours passed, they never ran out of anything to say.

Shortly after dawn, the baby donkey finished nursing again. Satisfied both mama and baby were doing well, and no longer needed constant monitoring, Tess went back to the house to shower and get some sleep. Noah set out feed and water for Miss Coco, then mucked out the stall and headed back to the house, too.

The house was so quiet he figured she was already asleep. A little disappointed their intimate time together had come to an end, he headed for the shower, too. While he was getting dressed, the scent of something delicious filled the air.

Curious, he went downstairs. Tess was in the kitchen, looking gorgeous as could be in a soft flannel shirt, jeans and shearling lined ankle boots. Her curly hair was damp and swept into an unruly mass on the back of her head. She wasn't wearing any makeup. But she didn't need any.

He peered over her shoulder, drinking in the scent of her citrus perfume. "Either you made enough for two or you're hungry as a lumberjack," he murmured, as if her cooking for him like this was no big deal, when in fact it was a *very* big deal.

Her smile bloomed. "Ha ha, cowboy. Of course, I cooked for you, too."

He moved in, eying the sheet pan full of golden-brown toast, topped with thin slices of ham, mounds of grated gruyere cheese and béchamel sauce. "Croque madame?" he guessed, recalling her mother's expertise in French cuisine.

She topped each sandwich with another piece of toast, added more ham, gruyere and béchamel, then slid the sheet pan into the oven, to broil.

"Mmm-hmm." She swirled butter into the skillet on the stove, and added eggs with the skill of an experienced cook. "It's the perfect dish to eat any time of day."

He let his glance drift over her admiringly. Hands braced on her hips, he brought her against him. "Anything you cook would be perfect to eat any time of day."

Tess splayed her palms across his chest, and tipped her face up to his. She sighed contentedly, looking as happy and relaxed as he felt. "Flattery will get you a post doing dishes."

"Gratefully, darlin'." He tipped an imaginary hat at her. As ready to eat what she had prepared for them, as he was to make love with her again.

Tess nodded at the lightly dressed greens in a bowl. "Want to carry that to the table for me?"

Noah nodded, touched by all she had done. "Love to." *Love you*...he almost said.

AN UNEXPECTED SILENCE hung out between them. Tess wasn't sure what was wrong. She only knew that something in Noah came to a full stop. With a shake of his head, as if that would clear it, he turned away. Deep in thought, he finished setting the table.

Telling herself it was nothing—that he was probably

just as tired as she was, after their very long night—she finished off the entrée and brought the plates over, too.

"Damn, this is good," he said after taking the first bite.

She returned his grin. "Thanks."

His gaze turned tender. "Thank you for doing this for us."

A thrill swept through Tess. Was that more than gratitude in his eyes? Or was she just hoping to see what she wanted to see there? Affection? Connection? The possibility of more? All she knew for certain was that she secretly wanted all of those things from him. And more.

That did not mean, however, they were on the same page.

With effort, she pushed aside her romantic musings, and went back to the conversation, and the fact he was surprised she had gone to so much trouble for him. When the truth was, she was stunned to realize how much she had wanted to cook just for him, too. Because it was the kind of thing a wife did? Or because it would deepen the man-woman intimacy between them? Which it already had.

Noticing how quiet it was without the kids, she said, "I kind of owed you after the way you helped me in the stable all last night."

The camaraderie between them deepening all the more, he toasted orange-juice glasses with her. "They're our family donkeys."

She sipped her juice. "Still…a lot of guys would have left it to the vet."

He shook his head, his deep blue eyes still locked with hers. "Not me," he told her huskily. "I wanted to stay."

A surge of awareness flowed through her. She realized just how close she was to falling all the way in love with him. "I'm glad you did."

THEY WERE QUIET for a while after that. But it was the good kind of silence. The type that came when two people were so comfortable with each other that they didn't feel the need to fill up every moment with endless polite chatter.

Finished, Noah sat back in his chair. Tess leaned back in hers, too. He looked around, as if trying to figure out what he could do for her now. "Coffee?" he asked finally.

His low, husky voice sent curls of longing through her midriff. She knew she should get up and start the dishes, but she was too comfy right where she was, and she did not want this moment between them to end with something as mundane as daily chores. "No. I've still got too much adrenaline as it is."

"Yeah." He stretched out his long legs, his knee nudging hers beneath the table. "I know what you mean." He shifted again. They were no longer touching. "I feel like I should be sleeping…"

"But you can't. Not yet."

"Right."

They fell silent once again.

She gazed around.

He reached across the table and covered her hand with his. "What are you thinking?"

How much I adore your touch. Your kiss. Your…everything.

Aware she might be pushing the envelope, since all they had agreed upon up to now was a secret no-strings fling— making love only on the previous two Wednesdays, when the kids were at school and she had the morning off… Yes, they had spent time together off and on, but there had been no mention of taking it further. Only taking it slow, and letting the situation evolve day by day.

Aware he was still waiting for her to explain what she'd been thinking, she pushed aside her forbidden feelings, and cleared her throat, and talked about the other thing on her mind. The thing that struck her every time she stepped in his house. "About how much I love your home. It's so cozy and warm and welcoming." She gestured at the big, modern living area, with the floor-to-ceiling windows. The modern fireplace, and even more state-of-the-art kitchen. Even his work area, with the big L-shaped desk and all the computer monitors, was somehow comforting. Maybe because it seemed to signify that even when he was working, he was always still right there, for whatever his girls, his pets, even her...needed.

He took her other hand in his, too. Clasping both warmly, he made a funny face at her. "Well, it is the Welcome Ranch."

She rolled her eyes. She could so get used to his bad jokes. His easy ability to make her smile. Just like she could so get used to staying here, with him, and his kids...

She frowned. He noticed.

"And that's a problem because...?" He let go of her and sat back.

Tess gestured vaguely. "I'm not sure if mine will ever be that way, even after all the work is done." She forced herself to stand, before she gave away even more of her private insecurities. "A few throws and the right pillows can only do so much..."

She knew animals.

She did *not* know families, or how to navigate them. Never mind one as complex as Noah's...

He joined her at the sink as they started to do their dishes. She scraped and rinsed. He loaded them into the dishwasher.

Once again, they were working like two halves of a whole—his strong, masculine presence a balm to her troubled soul.

His shoulder nudged hers, sending a frisson of warmth

down her arm. "First of all, I have faith your home will be a lot like you," he told her in the kind, comforting tone she loved. "Which means it will be wonderful, inviting, the kind of place where people are going to want to come and hang out with you."

Listening intently, she gazed over at him. Happy to have someone to talk to who was so understanding.

"Second, once your home is done, and you move out of here, it's not going to be like you are locked in there, alone." He shut the dishwasher door with his knee. As they turned to face each other, they dried their hands on the same towel.

He made an inclusive gesture. "You can invite people like me and the kids over, or sometimes just me." His lips curved in amorous invitation. "And you can come here any time you want as well. To be with us."

He caught her wrists and reeled her in, not stopping until she was flush against him. "Because in case you haven't noticed—" he slid a hand down her spine and back up again "—there is a guest room with your name on it." He paused to tuck a strand of hair behind her ear. "And we love having you here, so you will always be welcome here," he told her gruffly.

She smiled despite herself. "You really mean that, don't you?"

His eyes glinted happily. "With all my heart, yeah, I do, darlin'."

The next thing Tess knew, his mouth was lowering toward hers. Their lips met in an explosion of heat and need. One kiss turned into another, and then another. And they were headed upstairs, bypassing her bedroom for his.

NOAH KNEW HE wasn't playing fair. Using this time alone to show her how much their attraction for each other could change things. For both of them. If they would both open their minds and hearts up to the possibilities, that was.

He shut the door behind them and, his lips still fused to hers, trapped her against the wall. Gasping, she laughed in surprise as he kissed his way from her cheek, to the lobe of her ear, to the open vee of her button-up flannel.

She gasped again, trembling now. "Noah…"

He drew back, to look into her eyes. Wanting to make sure she was fully on board. "I want you in my bed."

"Then what are you waiting for…?" She took his head in her hands, sifting her hands through his hair, and slowly, effortlessly brought their mouths back together.

His body roared to life.

Lower still, where she surged against him, trembling with need, he felt the soft, sweet bliss of her surrender. The first contact of their lips sent another jolt to his system. The way she was pressing against him let him know that she was already as turned on as he was.

Excitement coursing through him, he unbuttoned her shirt and undid the front clasp of her bra. Her breasts came tumbling out, and he caught them with his hands, rubbing the soft globes and taut nipples with the flat of his palms.

She moaned in response. "Two can play at this game, cowboy," she purred. Her hands gripped the bottom of his sweater and she pulled it up over his head. His T-shirt went the same way. Then her shirt and bra.

Naked from the waist up, he brought her closer still, so they were skin-to-skin. The unyielding surface of the wall still behind them.

"You are so sexy," she murmured, running her hands across his shoulders, down his back.

The caution that had been in her eyes from the start was not there now. "You think so?"

"Mmm…"

That was all the encouragement it took. He covered her jutting nipples with his hands, felt them press into his palms as he lowered his mouth to hers. This time, she was more than ready for him, her lips opening to the pressure of his. She went up on tiptoe, arching wantonly, giving even as she took. Causing him to shudder in response.

Needing more, he dropped his hands and wrapped his arms around her, fusing her with heat. She let out a soft, acquiescent sigh, at the friction of her bare breasts rubbing against his chest.

Impatient, she found the buckle on his belt.

He found hers.

Laughing, they kept going until they were both free of any impediment. Her delicate hands found and claimed him. He throbbed beneath her tender touch.

"Tess…"

He caught her to him and, still kissing her, danced her backward to the bed. Then he swept back the covers with one hand, and they tumbled down onto the sheets. He lay beside her, making his own demands now, stroking the insides of her thighs, the rounded curves of her buttocks and the sweet femininity of her lower abdomen. She whimpered as he slid his hand over her mound, tracing the flowering petals, exploring inside and out. Again and then again. Until they were both on the precipice of making this fantasy come true.

He found the protection they needed. She strained against him. He lifted her hips, and then they were one.

She was climaxing, opening herself up, inviting him deeper, deeper still. Until there was no more waiting, only feeling, only wanting her to be his. That swiftly, he followed her over the edge.

TESS CAUGHT HER breath and collapsed against Noah's chest, her body still throbbing with the force of her orgasm. She felt sated behind her most erotic dreams and yet she already wanted him again. How wild was that?

No more outrageous than the notion that they might be on the verge of falling in love with each other.

Except…she couldn't let herself think like that.

Noah had already been married. Had a wife. And now three kids and a very busy life.

Right now, it was easy to see each other, because she was living with him.

Soon, it wouldn't be.

At least not the way it was now…she thought with a frown, trying not to sigh.

"I've got three requests," Noah murmured, stroking a hand through her hair.

"Three!" Tess echoed, peering at him from beneath her lashes. Tamping down the yearning welling inside her heart, she returned his coaxing grin with a playful smile of her own. "That's *a lot*."

He chuckled, as if to say, guilty as charged. "Mmm-hmm. My first ask is we stop pretending that we don't have something pretty special going on here."

She drew back to look at him, not ready to agree to anything until she knew the rest of what he wanted from her. She splayed her hands across his chest, her body still aching for more. More kisses. More lovemaking. More unbelievable pleasure. "And the second?"

"I want us to spend this evening and all of tomorrow morning together, since the kids aren't here. And we don't have to worry about them seeing us in a compromising position. Third, I want you in my bed with me all night long."

She pursed her lips. "Those are some pretty big asks, cowboy."

"To match what we've got going on."

He was right. This would either bring them closer, or show them they weren't right for anything more than a fling, after all.

"Okay," she returned softly, then decided to make one more stipulation. "I'll do everything you ask, providing if whatever this is between us doesn't work out the way we both think it might, that we find a way to take a step back and be friends."

For a moment, she thought he might argue with her, insist they were meant for more, so a fall-back plan would not be necessary. But then he relaxed. "Friends forever, I promise."

"Me, too." Tess slid back into his arms, aware he was as ready to make love again as she was. She didn't know what the future held, only the present. And for now, she thought as they came together with hot, burning passion, the present was enough.

THE NEXT TWENTY-FOUR hours passed blissfully. With them treasuring every second alone together. Just before noon, Noah received a call from his mom. "They're about ten minutes away." He grabbed his jacket, then handed her hers. "I suggested they meet us at the stable." Tank followed them out the door.

Tess fell into step behind him. The morning was sunny and clear and cold. All in all, a beautiful winter day. Struggling to go back to a more casual reality after a romantic weekend alone, she asked, "Do your folks know about the baby donkey's birth?"

"Yeah, I texted them Friday night. Asked them not to

say anything because we wanted it to be a surprise for the girls."

"Speaking of things not to be shared…" She tucked her hand in his. "What happened…" she began nervously.

Noah gave her a solemn smile, guessing where she was going with this. "Is just between the two of us."

She released a relieved breath. She didn't want to risk anything happening to wreck the intimacy they'd found. Too much outside scrutiny, too soon, just might. "Yes."

Noah looked at her gently. "Don't worry. I don't want to share this with anyone, either."

He opened up the stable door, ducked inside with her and paused to kiss her sweetly. Outside, Tank gave a little woof. They heard the sound of his parents' SUV. They quickly drew apart and headed back outside, in plain view, standing a casual distance apart.

As soon as the car was parked, the girls came tumbling out. "We're home!" Lucy, Avery and Angelica shouted in unison. They raced to greet both Tess and Noah, hugging them both. Tess hugged the girls back, enjoying their exuberance.

The kids continued all talking at once. "We went to the zoo!" Avery declared.

"And the science museum!" Lucy put in.

"And had *two* sleepovers, too!" Angelica said.

Noah beamed. "Sounds like you had a great time. What do you say to your grandparents?"

A round of happy thank-yous followed.

"We'll leave their things in the house, and then get going," Robert said.

Noah looked at his dad. "You don't want to stay?"

His mom smiled, speaking in code. "We know you have a lot to do, and we do, too. So we'll visit later in the week."

More hugs followed. Carol and Robert drove off.

The girls looked at him and Tess, suddenly realizing something different was going on here, although they hadn't figured out what yet.

"We have a special surprise for you," Noah said.

Lucy gasped. Her initial scowl at having been left out turned to an expression of delight. "Miss Coco had her baby?"

"She did," Noah confirmed. He held out his hand to Lucy, giving Tess a look that asked her to do the same, so she took charge of the twins. "And Tess and I are going to take you into the stable to see them."

CHAPTER THIRTEEN

Noah paused just inside the stable doors, to make eye contact with each of his three daughters. "Remember, girls, we don't want to upset Miss Coco or scare the baby donkey, so we have to be super quiet and careful. Okay?"

All three of them nodded.

As discussed, they went into the stall with Tess, one at a time, and petted first Coco, then her little one, gently and tenderly. When they had finished, and stepped back into the aisleway to observe a little longer, the little one stood and began to nurse.

"Oh, Daddy, the baby is so pretty," Lucy whispered, already completely in love with their newest pet.

"And fluffy," Avery admired wonderingly.

"And the same color as her mama," Angelica gushed.

Lucy turned to Tess. Her brow furrowed. "I forgot to ask. Is it a boy or girl donkey?"

"It's a female."

"What's her name?" the eight-year-old asked.

"We were waiting for you to help with that," Noah said.

Less patiently, Lucy demanded, "Well, what have you been calling her?"

"Baby..." Noah replied, very softly. He put his index finger against his lips, reminding them to keep their voices low and soothing, too.

Lucy broke out in a triumphant grin, before dropping

her voice back to a stage whisper. "Then that's what we should name her!"

"Yes! *Baby!*" the twins echoed gleefully, whispering, too.

For a moment, Noah looked gobsmacked. Tess thought the idea was as cute as the three little girls. Finally, he rubbed his hand across his jaw and drawled, "Well, we can talk about it a little more—"

"Nope," Lucy interrupted importantly. She sent her sisters a bolstering glance. "*Baby* is what we want to call her."

Her sisters nodded in agreement.

Seeming to realize, as Tess did in that moment, just how rarely the girls came to terms on anything, right out of the gate, Noah exchanged a glance with her, then gave in. "It's settled then. Her name is Baby."

Lucy started to clap, then remembering the need to be quiet while the foal nursed, put her hands on her hips instead.

For a while, they all watched the wonder of mother and baby, and the free-flowing love between them. The miracle of life never failed to astound Tess.

She was pleased to see the girls and Noah were similarly affected.

Finally, Baby walked a short distance away and lied down on the hay. Miss Coco stretched out next to her. Both looked ready for a nap.

Noah motioned for his daughters to follow him.

They tiptoed out and Tess took up the rear. As they left the stable, Lucy piped up in her normal voice. "Daddy, did you make a movie of Baby being born?"

He smiled and wrapped an arm around her shoulders. "We did. Tess helped me edit it."

The twins fell in step on either side of Tess, reaching for her hands, as if she was their mother. A wave of sentiment rushed through her. Realizing how much she was going to miss moments like this, if things didn't work out between her and Noah, she took hold of their palms, fighting back the unprecedented ache in her throat.

Lucy pulled Noah toward the house. "Can we see the movie now?" Angelica asked.

He turned to give Tess and the twins a sweeping glance. She thought she saw a gleam of approval in his eyes. "Sure!" he said.

He already had the TV all set up and settled the girls on the sofa with him and Tess. The film was short and sweet, with everything potentially too much for three-year-olds to witness cut out.

The twins curiosity faded as quickly as it had appeared. Avery slipped off the sofa. "Daddy, can we go see our doll babies upstairs?"

"Yeah, we want to play with them," Angelica added.

"That sounds like a great idea," he said.

Able to see as well as Tess that a storm was coming on, he went to get the computer tablet they had already set up, just for the eight-year-old.

"That wasn't a very good movie, Daddy," Lucy complained, leaping to her feet.

Tess felt a meltdown coming on.

Accepting his daughter's disappointed criticism with a nod, Noah sat on the sofa, leaving a cozy space between him and Tess. He patted the empty cushion between them. "It was perfect for the twins, Lucy. But you're right, you do need something geared for an eight-year-old." He beckoned her with a kind, loving glance that melted Tess's heart.

"So come and sit with us on the sofa, and we will show you the more grown-up version on the computer tablet, that Tess and I worked on, just for you."

The home movie was still cut to avoid anything too

gross or scary. But it did show Baby coming out in full diving position, blinking and looking around for the first time, then being dried off with a towel. The footage also included Noah feeding her colostrum from a baby bottle, and Baby's faltering first attempts to stand and then nurse. Relaxing music, suitable for a kid's nature movie, filled the background on this version, too.

As Tess had expected, Lucy had a lot of questions. Tess answered them one by one.

When she had finished, his daughter wrapped her arms fiercely around Tess and said, "Thank you for taking care of Miss Coco and Baby and helping Daddy make the movie for me."

Her heart filling with gratitude—that Noah and his beautiful children had come into her life—Tess fought the emotion rising in her throat. The sudden impulse to burst into tears. A wave of fierce maternal love sifting through her, Tess hugged Lucy back.

"I was happy to do it," she murmured thickly. She leaned back so she could look into the vulnerable little girl's eyes. "And just so you know, our work with Miss Coco and Baby is just beginning. They are going to need a lot of care. You can help with that—as long as there is a grown-up nearby."

Lucy looked at Noah for confirmation.

"I'm fully on board with that," he said, giving Tess a grateful look.

Was this what it would feel like to co-parent with him? To step into the mother's role in this adorable family?

Tess only knew she liked the feeling, very much.

"I don't know what's wrong with her," Noah murmured to Tess several hours later.

Lucy was outside by herself, desolately sitting on a

swing, rhythmically kicking the ground beneath her feet. Upset that she couldn't play with Baby, for hours on end, the way she had played with Tank when he was a puppy? And instead was relegated to just visiting twice a day? She had gone into a funk she showed no signs of relinquishing.

Tess joined him at the window. Their arms brushed briefly. As always, she had endless patience for his emotionally volatile eldest daughter. She moved closer and gave him a soothing smile. "I think she is just overtired."

He remained where he was, the warmth of her body transmitting to his. Then swiveled slightly, making no effort to hide his worry. "Then why won't she consent to taking a nap like her little sisters?" Who had fallen asleep, shortly after they had gotten home, on the upstairs playroom floor. And were napping still.

Tess gave him an appreciative grin, letting him know in that instant just how much she had learned about his kids since living at the ranch. "Because she's eight. And third graders don't take naps on purpose."

He exhaled. "I still feel like there is something else bugging her." Something he needed to further investigate. If his daughter would ever let him.

Tess touched his forearm gently. Her voice was as commiserating as her gaze. "Well, here is your chance, cowboy. She's stomping our way."

The back door opened and shut, more loudly than needed. Lucy took off her jacket and dropped it on the mudroom floor. Noah lifted his eyebrows. The child sighed, picked it up and put it on the hook, then came all the way into the kitchen. She slapped her hands on her hips, frustration bubbling up. "Daddy, I'm bored!"

"Well, you could read a book," Noah offered calmly. "Or watch one of your favorite programs on TV."

Lucy vetoed both with a shake of her head.

Suddenly, he had the sudden sense this was all working up to something. "Is there something you'd like to do?" he asked mildly.

"Well…" Lucy tensed nervously, then sent a hopeful look Tess's way. She inhaled deeply. "Maybe Tess could teach me to bake something."

The last thing he wanted to do was put Tess on the spot. He was about to interject when Tess lifted a staying palm, and smiled at Lucy so warmly his moody daughter smiled back in return.

"Baking sounds fun." Tess sat down at the kitchen island and gestured for the youngster to join her. "In fact, that is one of the things I like to do to relax. What would you like to learn to make?"

Lucy slid onto the stool next to Tess, then announced decisively, "*Not* scones. You taught all my aunts to make those."

Tess tilted her head, giving admirable weight to his eldest daughter's need to feel special. "Good point."

Encouraged, Lucy continued, "Maybe something I could put in my lunchbox and take to school. But it can't be cookies or brownies or cake. My teacher said we have to eat healthy at lunchtime."

Tess absorbed that statement with the importance in which it had been delivered. "Is banana bread okay?"

Lucy's smile faded. "That's what Bethany takes to school. She makes it with her mom. But I don't like banana bread."

Was this where this was coming from? She was in competition from a classmate? Or maybe just feeling left out because she no longer had a mom? Noah's heart went out to her.

Judging from the kind way Tess was looking at Lucy, she was feeling the same way he was. Like all she wanted to do was ease his little girl's pain. Make her life as care-free as a kid's life should be.

Tess's eyes lit up. Her cheeks took on a gorgeous pink. "I might have an idea." She whipped out her cell phone. "Have you ever had apple-fritter bread?"

Lucy shook her head.

Noah had no idea what it was, either.

Tess typed something into her phone. She pulled up a recipe with a photo. "Feel up to trying this? It's got chunks of apple and applesauce, and cinnamon in it. And a light apple glaze on top."

Lucy lit up, the way she used to when Shelby included her in the kitchen. "That looks yummy," she said sincerely.

Tess returned her enthusiasm. "Then we'll try it!"

"I used to bake stuff with my mom," Lucy told Tess, as they got the dry ingredients out of the pantry and set them on the kitchen island.

"Me, too." Tess's smile was a little sad. She gently touched Lucy's shoulder, then helped his daughter put on an apron. "You must miss doing that."

"I do." Lucy turned back to Tess, looking like she wanted to give her another hug, but was a little too shy to try. "But sometimes my grandma lets me cook with her at the Circle L. It's fun. But…" She sighed. "It's not re-ally the same as being with my mom and making stuff."

Tess tied an apron on, too, looking so at home in his kitchen Noah wasn't sure how he was going to feel when she eventually left.

Maybe Lucy wasn't the only one in trouble…

"I get that," Tess returned candidly. "My mom died al-most ten years ago, and I still miss her. But I have a lot of good memories and I try to concentrate on those, and hold them here," she said, placing a hand over her heart.

Lucy nodded seriously. "That's what I do, too."

Which meant, Noah mused in relief, Lucy had retained a lot of what she had learned in her grief-support group for kids, back in California.

Noah brewed a cup of coffee while they went to the fridge, and got out those ingredients, too.

"How come you don't have kids?" Lucy blurted.

So much for things going smoothly, Noah thought with a wince. "Lucy!" he interjected. "You know better than to ask a grown-up something personal like that."

Tess turned to Noah. "I don't mind."

He could see she didn't. Another plus in her favor.

She focused on Lucy. "The reason I don't have kids of my own is because I haven't been lucky enough to have any."

Tess's answer came easily.

Which meant she had thought about it.

At least in the last few weeks.

"But do you want some?" Lucy asked.

Did she? Not too long ago, when she had first arrived in Laramie, and been so standoffish initially, and careful not to intrude in his family life, Noah would have said probably not. Even though she was very good with kids.

Tess paused thoughtfully, this time not looking at Noah at all. "I'm beginning to think I might want to be a mom someday, after all," she said softly.

AT EIGHT THAT EVENING, Tess had just picked up the remote and settled on the sofa, when Noah came into the living room. Flashing her a lazy grin and sporting a day's worth of stubble, he was the picture of rugged masculinity. As he sat down beside her, she felt her heart give a little jolt. Why did he have to be so darn attractive? And why couldn't she stop wanting to be naked with him again, even though she knew that kind of intimacy made her emotionally vulnerable.

His gaze drifted over her, taking in her flannel-lined jeans and red wool sweater. His voice dropped to a tantalizing rumble. "You made Lucy's week, cooking with her this afternoon."

She stopped scrolling through the channels long enough to spare him a flirtatious glance. "You saw us slicing up and wrapping the individual pieces of apple-fritter bread for her lunches?"

"Yep," he said in open admiration. "Luckily there was some left for everyone to have with dinner." He covered her hand with his. "Anyway, thank you for doing that."

She loved the fact he took anything related to his kids' happiness so seriously. Aware this was the kind of thing they would be doing if they were married—hanging out together after the kids were in bed—she confessed, "It was good for me, too, you know."

As she turned to him, she inadvertently brushed up against him even more. Their hips were touching. He didn't move away, and neither did she. "I haven't done anything mother-daughter like that for a very long time. Not that she and I are mother and daughter," Tess corrected awkwardly, catching a whiff of his masculine scent. "But…"

He chuckled at her self-conscious manner. "I know what you mean."

They exchanged glances.

He squinted at her affectionately. "Lucy's not the only one who was a little spoiled with attention this weekend, though."

She tried not to think how intimate it felt, sitting here together, with the evening stretching endlessly out ahead of them.

Pretending not to know whom he was really referring to, she said playfully, "Miss Coco?"

He wrapped his arm around her and tucked her into the curve of his body. "Me." He pressed a kiss on the top of her head, then his dark eyebrows knit in frustration. "I don't know how I'm going to get by not having any alone time with you."

Tess pursed her lips. Their eyes met and held. "Well, I am usually off Wednesday mornings," she reminded him.

He rubbed the inside of her wrist with the pad of his thumb. And regarded her in a way that left no doubt they would be making love again very soon. "Brunch here after the kids are in school?"

She loved the romantic turn their conversation was taking. The fact he was trying to nail down the next time they were together, instead of just letting things happen at will. She splayed her hand across the hardness of his denim-covered thigh. A melting sensation started deep inside her. "Brunch sounds nice."

"To me, too." He flashed her a warm smile, similar to the one he gave her when he was about to ravish her. "But what really sounds good is an actual date." He put his hand over hers, trapping it against his muscular thigh. "Will you let me take you out?"

Telling herself this was not the time or place to indulge in her most tantalizing fantasies, not when his three kids were sleeping right upstairs, she replied in her most matter-of-fact tone, "Yes. But not until I move into my own place."

He leaned closer and brushed his lips against hers. "And when will that be?"

"My furniture is supposed to be delivered somewhere between the thirteenth of February and the sixteenth. I'll know more as the time gets closer. Kind of depends on what else is on the moving truck, and where it has to be delivered."

"Gotcha. So—" eyes crinkling at the corners, he paused to calculate "—you'll still be here for around twelve more days?" He seemed as pleased about that as she was.

She turned, gliding her hands across the sinewy warmth of his chest. "Mmm-hmm. I'm not sure whether to wish for the thirteenth for delivery, though," she added wryly.

He chuckled with undisguised affection. "Why not?"

Trying not to wonder if he was becoming as serious about her as she was about him, she said, "It's a Friday." She wrinkled her nose. "So maybe it'd be good if it wasn't delivered on February the thirteenth."

He shook his head, drawing her closer still. "Ha ha. I'm not superstitious."

"Good to know," Tess said, flirting back as he stroked a hand lovingly through her hair. "And all joking aside, neither am I."

She laid her head on his shoulder, sighing contentedly. He kissed her temple, the curve of her cheek, the shell of her ear. "Well, however it works out, *whenever* it works out," he told her huskily, looking deep into her eyes, "I can't wait for our first date."

CHAPTER FOURTEEN

IT FELT LIKE Tess had just gone to sleep, late Sunday evening, when she felt a light tap on her shoulder. She opened her eyes to find Lucy standing next to her bed, in the dark guest room.

Tess sat up against the pillows and turned on her bedside lamp. The bedroom was diffused with soft light.

Lucy's lower lip trembled. Panicked, she told Tess, "Something is wrong with Tank. He's crying and he won't get up."

That did *not* sound good. Wide-awake now, Tess tossed back the covers. "Where is he?"

"My room." Lucy took her hand and led her there.

Tank was curled up on the pink polka-dot dog cushion next to Lucy's bed. Tess could tell by the way the chocolate Lab was panting he was definitely in pain. She wondered if this was why he had been so quiet and lethargic all day, rarely venturing from the house even when everyone else went out to the stable.

She touched Lucy's shoulder gently. "Let me go get my vet bag. I'll be right back."

The child nodded, and sat down next to Tank, petting his back gently. "I'll stay here," she promised.

When Tess returned, she got out her stethoscope. Tank's heart rate was a little fast, given he was reclining, but his lungs were fine. She examined him, finding nothing amiss, until she went to touch his ears and he winced and let out a little whine of pain.

Tess got out her otoscope. His ears were definitely inflamed, with a funky smell and discharge inside the ear canal. "He's got an ear infection, honey." She got two swabs out of her bag, gently sampled the gunk in each ear and then slid each test into a plastic bag that she sealed for examination later.

Lucy watched, mesmerized. She continued petting Tank soothingly. Comforted, he curled into her touch. The young girl looked at Tess anxiously. "Can you give him some medicine or something?"

Tess nodded. "Absolutely." She got what she needed out of her vet bag and showed it all to Lucy. "But before we do that," she said as she twisted the application cap on the bottle, to open, "we're going to clean his ears with this solution." Tess held up his ear flap and squirted some in. She lowered the flap, and Tank immediately shook his head.

"He's trying to get it out!" Lucy protested.

Tess smiled reassuringly. "He's also spreading it around inside the ear canal, and pushing out the gunk in there, along with the liquid cleaner I just put in. So that's a good thing." When he had settled, Tess wiped the inside of his ear with some cotton balls. Her heart went out to Tank as he winced and whimpered a little in pain.

Lucy teared up. "He's hurting," she said, her lower lip trembling again.

"Not to worry." Tess did his other ear, and then showed Lucy the tube of medicine she had pulled out of her bag. "This ointment I'm going to put in has a numbing agent as well as antibacterial and antifungal medicine. So he'll be better in no time."

Quickly, she applied seven drops of medicine to the inside of each ear. Finished, she rubbed the medication in by gently massaging his ear flaps. She urged Lucy to do the same.

Tank stopped whining and panting, and within another minute or two, completely relaxed.

Lucy smiled at her chocolate Lab then grinned up at Tess. "You did it! You made him all better."

"Yes," a low masculine voice murmured, breaking the middle-of-the-night silence, "she sure did."

They both turned to look.

Tess caught her breath. Noah was lounging in the open doorway, his hair rumpled, looking sexy as all get-out in a pair of pajama pants and a cotton T-shirt. It was clear he had been there for a while.

He strolled into the room. Then hunkered down next to Lucy and Tank. Hugging her, while petting their dog, he looked at his daughter soberly. "But you probably should have come to get me, instead of Tess, sweetheart."

Lucy turned back to Tess, immediately contrite. It was clear the thought hadn't even occurred to her. Which made sense since Tess was the animal doc, not Noah. The distressed expression was back on her young face. "I'm sorry I waked you up in the middle of the night," Lucy told her sincerely.

Knowing this was one thing the child did not need to worry about, Tess took her into her arms and embraced her tenderly. "Oh, honey, it's okay." She stroked her hair lightly, before letting her go and sitting back on her heels. "I'm glad I was here to take care of Tank. And even if I hadn't been here at the ranch, you could have called me, and I would have come out to see what was wrong."

"Really?" Lucy's face lit up with surprise and delight.

"Really," she said, meaning it with all her heart.

Noah sent her a questioning look she didn't quite understand. Then he turned back to his daughter, and reminded gently, "Tomorrow's a school day, Lucy. You need to go back to sleep."

Lucy made a face. "But I'm not sleepy now, Daddy."

Tank sat up on his cushion, looking concerned.

Like the family pet, Tess sensed an argument coming on.

In an effort to help Noah, she told Lucy, "I understand where you're coming from, honey. I feel pretty wide-awake now, too. But the thing is… Tank needs his sleep, so he can get better. And he will settle down faster, if he thinks you are going back to sleep, too."

"I'll bring you some warm milk," Noah offered.

Lucy lit up. "With vanilla and sugar like Mommy used to make?"

Noah hugged his daughter and helped her climb back into bed. "Exactly like she used to make," he promised.

Leaving them to talk privately, Tess eased out of the room. She was happy Shelby was still so much a part of their lives. That was a very good, very comforting thing. She just wasn't sure there would ever truly be room for anyone else in the family, especially if that person was seen to be taking Shelby's place.

NOAH WASN'T SURPRISED that Tess excused herself and slipped out. She had a great sense of knowing when to give someone space, or privacy. He just didn't expect her to leave the house and go down to the stable, at two in the morning.

"Everything okay?" Noah asked when she came back in.

Lucy had barely had a few sips of her milk before she was fast asleep again. As was Tank.

Now, only he and Tess were fully awake.

Problem was, they were no longer alone in the house, so

he couldn't do what he really wanted. Which was to take her back to his bed and make love to her, and sleep with her wrapped in his arms all night long.

Tess's hair was in gorgeous disarray, her cheeks pink from the cold. Still in her pajamas, she slipped off her coat and rubber boots, and left both in the mudroom. Only her vet bag came into the kitchen with her. She answered his question quietly, with her usual cheerfulness. "Yeah, I just figured as long as I was up…that I'd go out and see how Miss Coco and Baby were doing. And they are both fine."

He searched her face. Aware that sometimes, like now, he had a little trouble reading her. One thing he did know—she seemed to have her guard up again. "You weren't irritated with Lucy's middle-of-the-night house call?"

Tess blinked, looking confused by his query. "No, of course not. Why would you…oh—" She splayed a hand across the center of her chest. Recognition lit her pretty eyes.

"You said it was one of your pet peeves in your previous job."

She slid onto a stool opposite where he was standing. Sighed. "That's true."

He took the saucepan off the stove and poured warm vanilla milk into two mugs. Thinking he might have unintentionally embarrassed her, he continued, "Which is understandable if people were deeming a nothing burger an emergency, and just calling you out, for the sake of calling you out."

Tess sighed ruefully. "Because they were rich and they could? Yeah—" she let out a little breath as their hands touched when he handed her the mug "—that part still rankles and always will. But," she admitted, her voice laced with joy, "I just realized tonight that things are different here. I love the people in Laramie County, and how much they love their pets. The way no one ever throws their weight around. But instead, is helpful and considerate to the max. And, best of all…" She took a long sip of her vanilla milk. "Lucy's a sweetheart."

Aware Tess really seemed to mean that, Noah chuckled. "Are we talking about my moodiest, most demanding child?"

"That would be the one. And actually, I kind of like how she shows her emotions so readily." She flashed him a grin. "You never have to worry where you stand with her. She lets you know, flat-out."

All of a sudden, he felt a little choked up. "She does love you, you know."

"I love her, too." Tess stopped, as if realizing what she had said. She averted her eyes and sipped her milk again. "You know…" She lifted her hand in an airy wave, still not looking at him. "As a family friend."

Funny, he had been thinking, *hoping*, it was more than that. But sensing she needed reassurance things weren't moving too fast, or getting too serious, he said, "Same for Lucy." Even though the intuitive-dad part of him felt like it might be getting to be more than that. A wanting-a-mom-again kind of more.

An introspective silence fell.

He waited for a signal from her. Did she want to head on up to the guest suite? Stay there and talk? He noted with relief it was the latter.

"Anyway," Tess said, turning the conversation back to the subject at hand, "what happened tonight made me realize that what seemed like a pain to me in my old practice was now something I really want to do."

He walked around the island and took the stool next to her. "And that troubles you?"

She shifted to face him. "A little. I thought my stance

on that had been in response to my old clients' narcissistic attitudes, but maybe I have my own bit of reckoning to do. Maybe…because of the way I was hurting over the whole Carlton thing…and the really disappointing way it ended… the fact that I knew deep down all along I shouldn't have been letting him make all the decisions but instead should of just stood up for what I wanted and needed, too—I let the situation at work become too much of a battle of control, instead of what was best for the pets and the people who loved them."

Noah could see that. He hadn't been the easiest person to be around when Shelby'd passed, either.

Still, he didn't want Tess to be too hard on herself. Their knees were touching. He could feel the warmth of her legs through her flannel pajama pants. "You are so sweet, you know?"

"But I know I can be aloof, too, especially when I am hurting."

"We all can. And that's okay, too," he continued gruffly.

She gave him a faint half-smile, as if guessing where he was going with this. "Because we're human."

He nodded. "And not perfect. Nor do we have to be."

She took a moment to consider that. Seeming to not quite agree. He took both her hands in his, wondering if their romance was going to take fire as much as he hoped, when she moved into her own place and they finally had the opportunity to really pursue each other.

For a moment, it seemed like she wanted to kiss him as much as he wanted to kiss her. But then he felt something shift inside of her and he caught the look of wariness filling her eyes.

She was still afraid he would hurt her in the end.

When that was the last thing he would ever want to do.

She slipped off the stool and moved away predictably,

her guard up once again. "You're a pretty good guy, too," she returned casually, turning her back on him and picking up her vet bag. "But—" she hitched in a breath "—as you told Lucy, tomorrow's a school day, and a workday, and we all need to get some shut-eye."

Leaving him to ruminate on that, she headed up the stairs and to the guest room.

"LOOKING AT SLIDES ALREADY?" Sara asked Tess, early Monday morning.

It was barely seven o'clock, and they were the first two in.

Tess adjusted the microscope, zooming in on the samples she had taken from Tank's ears. "Yep," she said, passing up the chance to admit it was her unwillingness to see Noah that had her here this early.

He might not know it, but she had come very close to making love with him again last night. And while maybe initially, their intimacy had been a physical release, and a cure for the ever-present loneliness she had felt for some time, now it was getting to be much more than that.

The fact that her heart was involved—with him and his kids—made her way too vulnerable.

And it scared her.

Sara slipped on her white lab coat over the dark blue clinic scrubs the entire staff wore. "What are you seeing?" She sat down at one of the computers and logged in.

Tess frowned. "Just what I thought. Bacteria and yeast in both ears." She grabbed her laptop and added the results to his chart.

Her eyes still on the computer screen in front of her, Sara asked mildly. "Those from Tank Lockhart?"

Tess swiveled around in her chair, curious. "How did you know?"

Sara got out her cell phone. "I got a text from Noah this morning. It said—" she paused to bring the message up, then read "'—go easy on Tess this morning. Tank and Lucy gave her a rough night.'"

Actually, it had been the way Noah had been looking at her, like he wanted to get way more involved with her, that had kept her awake. She wasn't surprised by their physical attraction to each other. But she was a little shocked, and let's face it, thrilled, by the increasing emotional bond developing between them.

A closeness that now had spread to his children. Angelica, Avery and Lucy were not only coming to rely on her, but they also seemed to love spending time with her as much as she adored spending time with them.

Briefly, Tess explained how Lucy had come to her in concern over her pet. "Although why Noah would think you would need to know about that baffles me." She exhaled and shook her head.

Sara chuckled. "He's just being protective of you, in that gallant way all men are when they are interested in a woman. Which—" Sara's eyes sparkled with hope "—is nice to see."

If it were to last, yes. Which they did not know yet if it would. "Let's not get ahead of ourselves here," Tess said, sensing even more matchmaking to come.

"And let's not lag too far behind, either," her boss teased.

Luckily, several more members of the clinic staff walked in. As well as a client whose cat had gotten into a fight with a possibly rabid raccoon. The rest of the day was packed with a similar mix of appointments and emergencies that kept her thoroughly challenged and busy.

She was happy and exhausted at day's end, when Noah called via FaceTime.

She picked up her cell, unable to stop herself from smiling when she saw his face. Tingles of awareness swept through her. "What's up?"

"The kids want to come into town and have dinner at the Dairy Barn. We were all hoping we could talk you into joining us. See?" He turned the phone and the girls all giggled and pressed their palms together.

"Please!" they yelled in unison.

Tess couldn't help but grin. "You're sure I won't be intruding?"

"Actually," Noah said, turning the camera back to him, "I think it's the other way around. But seriously, they have the best fast food in town."

She returned his confident grin. "So I've heard."

"Problem is…all they have is counter service there."

Like she cared where they ate if she got to spend more time with him and his three adorable daughters. Feigning shock, she splayed a hand across the center of her chest and joked, "Are you telling me I'd have to wait on myself *and you-all, too*?"

He waggled his eyebrows in a way that promised fun, and more fun. "I'm saying I'll pay," he corrected wryly, before he sobered and said, "But you would be required to be an extra hand. Because, well…let's just say when they carry their own trays—" his voice dropped a confidential notch "—it isn't pretty!"

"Daddy!" Lucy chided in the background.

Noah chuckled again. "What do you say, Tess? The kids love it there, and it'll be fun."

The fatigue from a long day faded. She smiled warmly. "Then count me in."

NOAH AND THE girls were waiting for her when she arrived. They ordered burgers, milkshakes and fries. The kids all ate a surprising amount. Tess and Noah polished off their meals, too. "Do you love it here, too?" Angelica asked, looking around at the old-fashioned ice-cream-shop vibe. The five of them were sitting in a cozy corner booth, centered by a round table.

"'Cause we all do," Avery chimed in.

"I do." Tess smiled.

She frowned as her phone chimed. "Sorry, I have to get this. I'm on-call tonight." She eased away from the table. When she returned, her emotions were crazily awhirl. Noah lifted a questioning eyebrow at her. "Got to go?"

Not quite yet. But soon, she would definitely be leaving her current arrangement. Tess shook her head. "That was the rep from the moving company. She wanted to let me know that the truck will be loaded tomorrow, and here in approximately eleven to thirteen days, depending on the weather."

Clearly, Noah didn't see what the problem was. And Tess knew she shouldn't see one, either.

His mouth quirked. "That's what you wanted, right? For your stuff to get here weekend after next? Right around the time your house is going to be finished and ready to move in?"

Tess nodded. He was right. This was happy news. Then why did she feel so sad?

"Tess is moving?" Avery looked confused. So did her twin.

"Yes, we told you that, remember?" Noah gathered up the trash and began stacking it on trays. "That she was only going to stay with us until her place was ready and her stuff got here."

His matter-of-fact pronouncement was as practical as he was. So how come, Tess wondered, did it leave her feeling disappointed?

"*Where* is your house?" Lucy asked, her brow furrowed.

Grateful for the activity, Tess got up to help clean up, too. She pushed aside her unprecedented emotions. "About five minutes from here. About ten blocks from downtown. On Spring Street."

"Can we go see it? Please?"

Noah looked torn. Their glances meshed. She knew by the way he delayed answering that he was leaving the decision up to her and would back her, either way.

The girls still looked confused and off-kilter. So maybe what they all needed here was a reality check, Tess mused. She forced a brilliant smile. "Yes, of course, we can all go over and take a peek. But we will have to be careful when we walk through it because it's not finished yet."

Scowling, Lucy walked through the downstairs, then the upstairs. Counting rooms under her breath and muttering insults as she went. "It's too small. There is only one bathroom up here."

"We have a powder room downstairs," Tess said.

"And three bedrooms." One of which was going to be a study.

The eight-year-old pivoted, hands planted defiantly on her hips. "It needs to be bigger, like at the Welcome Ranch, where everyone has their own bedroom and bathroom. So," she proclaimed, lifting her chin autocratically, "you need to sell this house and continue staying at our house, with us."

Her suggestion obviously pleased her younger sisters. Angelica yanked on Noah's arm. She smiled hopefully. "We have room, don't we, Daddy?"

With an enthusiastic nod, Avery chimed in, "Yes. Tess can stay with us some more."

For a moment, Noah's expression was inscrutable.

Tess realized this was what he had feared all along. That

his daughters wouldn't be able to handle it if they got too close to her, and then she left.

Guiltily, she realized she and Noah never should have lost sight of this. But they had, so…

He hunkered down to face his kids. "Tess knows she is always welcome to stay with us, whenever, however long she wants," he told them all gently.

And Tess knew he meant it. That he would never kick her out or ask her to leave.

Noah gestured at their half-finished surroundings. "But this is her house and she wants to live here with all her stuff. As her friends, we need to all be supportive of that."

Friends…

Was that all she and he were?

Somehow, it had felt like more.

Much *more.*

"Well, I still don't like the house!" Lucy said, fuming.

Avery and Angelica looked at Tess, then their dad, and back at Tess. "It's very pretty," Angelica said. Then the twins came forward to give Tess a group hug, which she returned.

"We love it," Avery added diplomatically even though it still wasn't finished, and Tess doubted the three-year-olds could envision what it would look like when it was.

The twins gazed up at Tess hopefully. "Can we come and visit you here?" Avery asked.

Tess could feel Noah's eyes on her. His emotions were as deliberately contained as her own.

He gave a slight nod, granting permission.

She ignored the wrenching of her heart, and said, "Anytime it is okay with your daddy, yes, you can."

THE REST OF the evening and the next day passed swiftly. Tess was called out to a ranch on the other side of the county to care for a pair of calves who'd gotten wound up in a barbed-wire fence and needed stitches. By the time she got home Tuesday evening, everyone was in bed except Noah. He took one look at her exhausted state, and handed her the sandwich and icy cold beer he had waiting for her. She inhaled both, then pointed in the direction of the stairs. "I'm sorry. I don't mean to be rude, but if I don't shower and go to bed soon, I'll never make it up those stairs."

He grinned. "In which case, I would have to carry you. But…unless there is something else you need, we'll say good night now, and meet for brunch in the morning. That's still on, isn't it?"

Even though she knew it might not last, she lived for their Wednesday mornings alone. "It is."

"Then my advice to you," he said, bringing her close for a warm, welcoming hug, before brushing his lips tenderly across her temple, and ever so reluctantly, letting her go, and stepping back, "is sleep in."

Tess tried to, but the girls got in a fight over hair elastics and bows, and the wrong kind of braids, before school. Hearing the ruckus, she felt obliged to go out and help.

Lucy used the time with Tess to lobby. Which, although not surprising, was not the best way to start off a morning.

Luckily, they were already running late. With an exasperated look sent her way, Noah ushered them out the door.

Tess had barely enough time to gulp a quick cup of coffee and get dressed. She had just finished doing her hair and makeup when Noah returned from dropping them off at school.

He lounged in the doorway to her suite. "I'm sorry. Lucy is still campaigning for you not to move out."

Tess moved toward him, not sure this was the best place to have a serious conversation. He closed the remaining distance between them in two steps. Tess could feel his body heat and breathed in the fragrance of mint and man. Wistfully, she let her gaze rove over his solidly built frame and powerful shoulders.

Ignoring the shimmer of sexual attraction between them, she touched his arm sympathetically. "You don't have to apologize, Noah. I know Lucy is at an age where she wants what she wants when she wants it."

The way I am beginning to...

"She's not old enough to have figured out life doesn't always work that way," she added.

Noah looked down at her, his expression still shuttered. "She will."

Another thoughtful moment ensued. She slipped her hand in his.

He brought her arm up, and for a moment she thought he was going to kiss the inside of her wrist, but then he dropped it back down to her side. A surprising jolt of disappointment went through her.

He shook his head in silent remonstration, looking even more somber now. "It's deeper than that."

Her pulse pounding, Tess waited.

Noah put his arms around her waist and settled her against him. He inhaled sharply. "As you know, we haven't had a woman in the house with us, the way you've been in the house with us, since Shelby died. Honestly, I had gotten so used to being a single parent I didn't think I missed it. But then," he murmured in a tone that seemed to come from the depths of his soul, "you came along, made me see..." He sifted his hands through her hair, lifting her face to his. "That I did."

He kissed her again, as if the need to make her his, not just now, but forever, was stronger than ever. Passion swept through Tess, along with the realization that this need they felt, the connection they'd forged, was something to be treasured.

So what if there were no guarantees where any of this would end, once she moved out, and into her own place in town? He touched and kissed her as if he never wanted their mutual affection to end. And the truth was, neither did she.

Skin heating, desire running riot inside her, she guided him backward to the still rumpled covers on the guest-room bed.

"I want you naked," he growled, taking off her shirt, then her bra and jeans. She kicked off her panties, and he bent her backward, her weight braced against his arm. His lips toured her throat, the curve of her shoulder. The jutting arousal of her nipples, the curves of her breasts and the valley in between.

She watched languidly as his lips closed over the aching crowns. Suckled her gently, lovingly, as if this chance might never come again.

Tenderly caressing her stomach with the flat of his hand, his palm moved lower. She caught her breath as he found her there. She had never felt this beautiful, sensual. Ready.

Moaning softly, she kissed him back while silken brushes of his fingertips alternated with the erotic rubbing of his palm.

Her knees weakened.

She swayed.

Before she knew it, she was coming apart in his arms.

His breath hot and rough against her mouth, he held her until the quaking stopped.

Tess smiled. "My turn, cowboy…"

She undressed him wantonly. A minute later, he joined her naked on the bed.

Indulging in her most secret fantasies, she traced every

sinewy inch of him. Lingering over his strong, masculine heat, she kissed her way down the treasure trail, finding him just as hard and ready as she wanted him. Over and over, she kissed and caressed him, taking her time, guiding him deeper and deeper into a vortex of pleasure, until he could take it no more.

Together, they rolled on a condom.

He shifted over her, cupping her hips, lifting them, making them one. Possessing her with a slow, sensual rhythm, he merged their bodies as intimately as they had already begun merging their lives. Until there was nothing but this wild yearning, this incredible passion, this overwhelmingly tender connection.

And this incredible moment in time.

Afterward, they clung together. Their bodies tangled in the covers, neither of them wanted to move.

Noah left a string of kisses in her hair. "I can't believe we just have a little more than a week and a half now, where we'll both be here…under the same roof," he said on a regretful sigh.

Which meant, if they were lucky, one more Wednesday morning just like this.

"Me, either," Tess murmured, cuddling closer. She shut her eyes, drinking in the essence that was him.

But she also knew they had better get used to it. The end date of their arrangement was getting here fast. And like it or not, they were going to have to deal with it.

And then figure out how to move on.

Hopefully, *together*…

CHAPTER FIFTEEN

"WELL, WHAT DO you think?" Molly asked late Thursday afternoon, in full contractor mode.

It had been eleven days since Tess had given Noah and his daughters the tour. A lot had been in-flux that day, the interior only partially done. Now, the entire house was gorgeous, from floor to ceiling.

"I love it." Tess paused to survey the kitchen with the new island, which would provide the culinary prep space she needed, without taking up too much floor space. Unfortunately, it was only big enough for three stools. Which was likely something else Lucy would complain about.

She smiled, thinking how much she enjoyed coaxing Noah's eldest out of her mercurial moods. Helping her feel upbeat and positive again.

Hopefully, the sensitive little girl would come to see Tess's moving out as something that would not affect their closeness in any way.

"Everything looks magnificent. You and Chance have truly outdone yourselves." She got out her checkbook and paid the balance due upon completion.

Molly pocketed it with thanks. "When will your belongings get here?"

"It's guaranteed to be here anywhere between the thirteen and the sixteenth. Although, right now they are expecting the truck to be here Saturday morning."

"The fourteenth."

Valentine's Day.

Hoping the other woman wouldn't make something of that, Tess nodded. "Yep."

Molly smiled, politely avoiding that minefield. "I bet you'll be glad to get your things so you can finally begin really settling in."

The only problem was she was *already* settled in. At the Welcome Ranch. Not that she hadn't known this day was coming. By Saturday, this house would be her new home. Her reason for staying with Noah and the girls, Tank, Miss Coco and Baby would be gone.

Her heart ached already. She was going to miss them all so much.

And while she would see them as much as she could, it just wouldn't be the same.

Oblivious to Tess's ambivalence, Molly handed over the instruction booklets and warranties for the new HVAC, gas fireplace inset, water heater and kitchen appliances. "Let us know if you have any issues."

"Will do," Tess promised.

Molly left and Tess headed out shortly thereafter. It was nearly dinnertime when she arrived at the ranch. The girls were all seated at the kitchen table, making out their cards for the Valentine's party the next day at school. The twins could each write their own names, on the card, along with little hand-drawn hearts, but needed help addressing the envelopes, so Tess sat down to help with that.

"Where are the candy hearts, Daddy?" Lucy asked.

Noah produced a bowl of pastel candies, with sweet, sentimental sayings on them. The girls began adding them to the cards they had already put in the envelopes.

With a smile, he brought Tess a glass of her favorite

blackberry lemonade on ice. Their fingers brushed briefly as he handed it to her. Her stomach vibrated with butterflies. His gaze drifted over her face, lingering on her lips before returning to her eyes.

Warmth crept from the center of her chest, to her cheeks. How much longer were they going to keep their mutual attraction private?

Neither of them was any good at pretending.

Luckily, the girls were so busy finishing up their cards, they did not notice the free-flowing intimacy between them.

"Is there anything I can do to help with meal prep?" Tess asked.

Noah got the salad out of the fridge. "Thanks. I've got it." He dressed the salad with the light lemony vinaigrette his daughters liked.

Tess turned her attention back to addressing envelopes for the twins. A brief silence fell, then Avery said, "Daddy says they don't give out valentines at his work."

Angelica squinted thoughtfully. "Do you have a party at your work, Tess?"

Good question. Luckily, she knew the answer. "Actually, we kind of do. We have been giving out valentine refrigerator magnets to all the pet owners and heart shaped treats to the pets who have come into the animal clinic this week. So that has been kind of fun."

The girls liked that. "Can we get some, too?" Lucy asked hopefully.

Funny, the things little kids got excited about. "I'll bring some home tomorrow," Tess promised.

Noah opened the oven door. A delicious aroma escaped. "Pizza is ready, everyone!" He set a large half-cheese, half-pepperoni pizza on the stove. It was from the take-

and-bake section of the supermarket. But today instead of being round, it was shaped like a heart.

The girls grinned. "Isn't it romantic?" Lucy asked dreamily.

Being there, with all of them, *was* romantic, Tess thought. Blissfully so.

She would hold this memory close.

"SOMETHING ON YOUR MIND?" Noah asked, several hours later, after the girls were in bed, fast asleep.

Acutely aware she had less than two days left at the Welcome Ranch, Tess pushed aside the melancholy that had been surreptitiously plaguing her and walked into the laundry room. She opened the washing machine, forcing herself to be matter-of-fact. "What do you mean?"

Arms folded across his brawny chest, he lounged in the doorway and watched her transfer her scrubs to the dryer. "You were awfully quiet during dinner and our nightly trip down to the stable to visit Miss Coco and Baby."

She set the dial for casuals and turned it on. Turning, she let her gaze rove over him. It was amazing how handsome he was, even with his hair rumpled and a shadow of beard lining his jaw. The problem was, she was too used to hanging out like this, after the kids were in bed. Feeling so much a part of him and his family. So...*included*.

She really was going to miss it.

Miss him.

Miss them all.

Aware he was waiting for an explanation, she swallowed around the parched feeling in her throat, and feigned an acceptance she couldn't really feel. "I was just soaking it all in."

She reached into her laundry bag and pulled out the next load.

"The kids love having you here."

But what about you, Noah? Are you starting to feel it's time for me to move on? Before the kids get any more dependent on me?

She dropped lingerie into the machine. Some of which he had seen her in. Memories of their lovemaking flooded in, overwhelming her. Her face heating, she turned to face him, hoping he would ignore the slight catch in her breath. "I've loved being here."

He came all the way into the laundry room, soundlessly shutting the door behind him. He clasped her shoulders, gazing down at her.

She cocked her head at him, sensing a building emotion in him, too.

He lifted a hand to her face and rubbed his thumb across the curve of her cheek. "I'm not sure how we're going to get along without you."

She savored the warmth of his touch. His nearness sent her pulse racing. She splayed her hands across the hardness of his chest. "I'm sure you will manage."

He stroked a hand through her hair. With a hand on her spine, he brought her in even closer. He chided softly, "Being *able* to do something and *wanting* to do something are two different things."

How well she knew that! She forced herself to be as practical as they all needed her to be. "True, but Noah... we knew this day was coming. And I really do need to get back in my own place."

"I know." He brushed his lips across her temple. Straightening, his eyes solemn, he assessed her, and in that moment, was full of the same need she harbored. With a sexy half smile, he reminded her, "We also promised each other a real grown-up dinner date when that did happen."

She knew. Boy, did she ever know. She'd been day-dreaming about it ever since he first brought it up.

He shrugged offhandedly. "Given that your stuff is being delivered on Saturday morning…"

Valentine's Day.

She put up a hand before he could continue. She knew from work that everyone had big plans with their love interests or spouses. Here in Laramie County, and San Angelo as well. "We can't go out on the evening of Valentine's Day. Not without attracting a whole lot of unwelcome attention and risking that it would somehow get back to the girls at school."

His lips thinned. "I know," he told her soberly. "I don't want that, either. *When* they hear it, they need to hear it from us."

When, not if…

A thrill surged through her.

Maybe like her, he was beginning to be more serious than either of them had so far admitted.

Serious enough that this relationship could really go somewhere.

"Which is why I was thinking," he continued, taking her by the hand and walking with her out into the kitchen, "maybe we could push our celebration up a day. Go out tomorrow night, after the kids are asleep. Jillian has already agreed to babysit for us."

"So your sister knows?"

"That I want this to go somewhere? Yes, she does. And she is delighted for both of us. Although—" he paused to exhale and roll his eyes "—she had a few choice remarks to make…about me asking you out for a first real date on Friday the thirteenth."

Tess couldn't help but laugh. She hadn't considered that, either. "Good thing I'm not superstitious."

"Me, either." He reached into a bowl of valentine candy and handed her a pink heart that said *Crazy 4 U*. And then another classic that she recalled from when she was a kid. *Be Mine*.

He gazed over at her, his eyes sparkling with sexy mischief. "So what do you say?"

Tess knew she was putting her heart on the line here. She also knew there was only one decision that would not come with immediate regret. Easing away from him with a wink, she murmured, "I'll let you figure it out." She plucked two candies out of the bowl on the table. Handed the first to him.

"*UR Cute*," he read. "Awww. I like that."

She gave him a second candy.

"*XOXO*. Like that even better," he teased in the gruff but sexy voice she loved so much.

They gazed at each other with pleasure, aware they were definitely at some sort of tipping point. "So your answer is…?" he countered softly.

She stood on tiptoe, wreathed her arms around his neck and brushed her lips against his. "Yes."

"WHERE IS TESS?" Avery asked the next morning, when she came down for breakfast.

"Did she already go down to the stable?" Angelica queried.

It had been their routine to go down for a quick visit together every morning. And a longer one every evening.

"She had to go to work so she checked in on Miss Coco and Baby on her way out."

"But it's so early!"

Noah handed the girls their farm jackets and rubber boots. He grabbed his own, too. "I know. Sometimes animals get sick in the middle of the night." Together, they headed out. "This time it was the alpacas on the Primrose Ranch. A couple animals were sick and they needed to get a handle on it quickly so the entire herd of them wouldn't become ill."

The twins readily accepted Tess's absence as necessary. Caring for ill animals was her job, after all. Lucy, however, was sanguine about it. Maybe because she'd come to depend on her cheerful interaction with Tess, at the start and end of most days.

His eldest daughter was still in a little bit of a funk when he dropped her sisters off at preschool. Concerned, Noah headed for the elementary school, a mile away. "Something on your mind, sweetheart?" he asked.

Lucy caught his glance in the rearview mirror. "Yes, Daddy." She sat up straight in her seat. "I want to talk. So can you pull over for a minute?"

Better here, on a side street, than in the drop-off line in front of the school. He did as requested, put the SUV in Park, then took off his seat belt and turned around to face her. It was a little awkward, given the confines of the driver's seat, but since she wasn't big enough to sit in the front passenger seat yet, it was the best they could do. He draped an arm across the front seats. "What's on your mind?"

Their eyes met, but only for a moment. "Are you going to ask Tess to be your valentine?"

Whoa. What? He kept his expression inscrutable. "Why would you think that?"

"Because!" Lucy rolled her eyes in exasperation. "She *wants* you to ask her."

He sort of had, with those candy hearts, and the invitation for their first real date tonight. But Lucy didn't know that. And shouldn't, for now. With Tess's belongings arriving tomorrow, and her moving out, after a fantastic, fun, way-too-short month at the Welcome Ranch, they faced too much change as it was. "No, I did not do that, honey."

Lucy squinted her displeasure. "Well, then," she retorted, "Tess will get mad at you, just like Mommy used to do when she didn't get what she wanted and then she will leave us."

Just like that, bad memories came flooding back. His heart going out to his eldest daughter, because she had witnessed and experienced far too much pain and misery in her first eight years of life, he reached over the seat and reminded gently, "Mommy didn't leave us. Not like that. She went to heaven. You know that."

Refusing to clasp his outstretched hand, Lucy harrumphed loudly and clamped her arms across her chest. "But Mommy said she was going to, lots of times, when she got mad at you, Daddy. I *heard* her talk about divorce!"

More guilt flooded Noah's heart. He withdrew his palm, letting his little girl have her space. "That was just in the heat of the moment. She never meant it."

She made another frustrated sound in her throat. "But she did leave, Daddy." She turned her glare toward the window, as another car drove by.

Knowing Lucy needed a reassuring hug whether she wanted one or not, Noah got out of the SUV, and opened the back passenger door. He slid in beside her, wrapping his arms around his daughter. She tensed at first, but he didn't relent in his expression of love, and after a moment, she sagged against him.

He dropped a kiss on the top of her head. "Mommy didn't leave us on purpose. She had an accident, Luce. She fell and hit her head when she was out on a run with her friends. She didn't plan that. And I can assure you that she did not want that. She loved all of us very much and wanted to be here with you and your sisters to see you grow up."

Regardless of the flaws in his marriage, he would always wish that, too.

Looking so much older than her years, and wiser and sadder, too, Lucy unclasped her seat belt. She scooted away from him, still radiating a ton of frustration. "The point is, Daddy, Mommy isn't here. She is in heaven. But Tess is here. And *she* could be our new mommy if you would just ask her to be."

The ironic thing was that deep down Noah wanted to ask her. But after everything they'd both been through, a part of him was hesitant. He also knew it wouldn't be wise to hurry things. Or push Tess, who was already a little skeptical that what they had was just a convenient fling.

He knew it was more.

That it had always been more.

From the very first moment they had kissed, and made love.

He also knew Tess deserved the kind of romantic courtship he had never given any woman, including his late wife. Which meant if he wanted their relationship to get off on the right footing, and become as serious and lasting as he wanted, he couldn't act impulsively.

"Lucy," he said gently, trying again. "We just met Tess. I know it kind of feels like she is already part of our family…"

His little girl exhaled with increasing annoyance. "Daddy, Tess is a part of our family! Or she could be if you would just stop being so hardheaded and ask her!"

Hardheaded was what Shelby used to accuse him of being when she didn't get what she wanted.

It hurt to hear his daughter say it, and worried him, too. It was yet more proof he hadn't done enough as a parent, to show her better, more positive ways to resolve conflict.

He would have to get on that. Sooner, rather than later.

"It's a lot more complicated than that," Noah reiterated gently but firmly.

Lucy sighed and turned away.

He knew nothing further was going to be gained right now, so he opened the door and said, "We can talk about this more this weekend, if you want."

Lucy just huffed out another breath and shook her head.

Hoping she would cool down, with time, he put the SUV back in gear and drove her to school.

"GOOD NEWS!" LISA, the clinic receptionist, told Tess at four that afternoon. "Your movers are here!"

Tess put down the chart of the patient she had just seen. The cute Border collie and his owner were now checking out.

"That sounds promising!" Mrs. Brantley said.

Trying not to think about the secret first date she was supposed to have with Noah a few hours from now, Tess smiled back. "It does. Except..." She paused and tried not to frown. "The driver and the guy that's supposed to help him unload weren't supposed to arrive until tomorrow morning."

"That's what they said!" Lisa handed over the message slip she had written out, with the driver's name and number. "But they got here early."

A good seventeen hours early. Which was coincidentally all the time she had left at the Welcome Ranch. "Where are they now?" Tess asked. "Did they say?" She wondered if they would be amenable to taking the evening off. Not that she should even be thinking such a thing. Where were her priorities? With the man of her dreams, of course...

"They did say!" Lisa beamed. "The truck is parked in front of your house. And here is the very best part! They can start unloading for you as soon as you get over there to unlock the door and show them where everything goes."

Sara walked up and joined in the conversation. She began to shoo Tess toward the door. "Go."

"But…" Tess protested.

"We all know how long you have been waiting to get your things. Really, it's no problem. We will handle the last couple of patients of the day."

It didn't seem like she had a choice but to go.

Maybe this would ultimately end up giving her more time to spend with Noah and the girls, over the weekend. Especially if she invited the four of them over to help her unpack…

Unfortunately, it was going to totally screw up the evening she and Noah had planned for themselves as sort of an early Valentine's Day celebration.

Leaving the reception area with a wave goodbye, Tess went to get her things and slipped out the service door. Still trying not to feel too overwhelmed, she called Noah on the way out to her car.

Catching him just as she slid behind the wheel, she explained what had transpired. "So I guess our plans to drive to San Angelo for dinner are kaput."

"That's okay, darlin'. We'll have a rain check as soon as we can work it in next week," he said affably. "It'll be easier to go out clandestinely then, anyway."

Tess closed her eyes and took a deep breath. "Thanks for being so understanding."

"Always," he said in the deep, gruff voice she loved. The one that warmed her through and through. "Listen, I can still come over later tonight, after Jillian gets here, if you want."

Just like that, the clouds began to part, and she felt the sunshine coming in once again.

She could feel Noah smiling in the silence.

"In the meantime, what can I do to help?" he asked gently.

She was going to need something other than scrubs and a white veterinary doctor's coat to wear this evening. Plus her toiletries, makeup and perfume, all of which were already packed up, ready to go, too.

"I was wondering if you could bring the two suitcases from the guest-room closet into town, when you pick up the girls from school and drop them off."

There was a significant pause. Then he asked, "Sure you don't want to stay here one more night?"

She did. That was the problem. She also knew she needed a reality check before she let her dreams get the best of her.

This was the way things were going to be. She needed to get used to it.

Like it or not, so did Noah.

She forced herself to stay positive. "Um. No. I really need to start unpacking."

There was another silence, a little longer this time. "I understand," he said. Even though he kind of sounded like he didn't. "I'll be there within the hour," he promised.

"Thanks." Trying to tell herself this was indeed no big deal, and she and Noah would adjust to being under separate roofs, as readily as they adjusted to being under the same one, Tess hung up and headed for her home.

The big truck was indeed parked out front. As she stepped out of her Tahoe, she saw the two movers were seated on her front porch, ready to get going.

Tess unlocked the front door. There were papers to be signed, and then they got started.

Slightly more than an hour later, her queen-size bed and dresser, white sectional sofa and pastel wool rug had all been unloaded when Noah parked his SUV in front of her neighbor's home. He had just started up the sidewalk, a suitcase in each hand, when his rear car door, the one closest to the curb, opened up behind him.

Lucy slipped out, her expression mutinous.

The twins were right behind their big sister.

Tess's jaw dropped.

She had assumed he would drop her stuff off before getting the girls at school. Not *after*.

Noah caught the stunned expression on her face, then turned to look behind him just as all three girls dashed past him straight for Tess.

Exasperated did not begin to describe the look on his handsome face. But with both hands full of her heavy bags, there wasn't much he could do except verbally reprimand them. "Girls!" he called after them. "I told you to wait in the SUV!"

Normally, they would have immediately stopped in their tracks and obeyed that deep, paternal tone.

Not this afternoon.

"I want to see what's going on!" Lucy shouted back, purposely disobeying her dad. She reached the house first and raced up the front steps, right past Tess, and stormed inside.

The twins followed a little less swiftly. "We want to see Tess, Daddy!" Avery explained. Angelica nodded her agreement. Unlike their elder sister, they were more in awe of the big moving truck and all the accompanying activity than upset.

Noah caught up with them as they stopped to gaze around in wonder. Knowing he had them under his supervision, Tess went into the house.

Lucy was stomping around the downstairs in full temper. Tess had never seen her look more miserable. Or scared. And in that moment, she understood as only an orphan could. Lucy had lost her mother. Tess had moved in—temporarily—and started to fill up that void.

Now Tess was leaving, too.

And even though Lucy had known that was the plan all along, she still wasn't ready for the reality of it.

None of them were.

That was abundantly clear when Noah set down her two bags, in the living room, out of the way.

He came toward her, a mixture of sorrow and apology on his face. Like he was hurting, too.

Sensing drama, the movers headed out to the truck.

The twins went to the L-shaped white sofa and sat down, gleefully testing out the cushions, and finding them "very comfy."

Well, at least someone was happy, Tess thought.

Lucy glared at the boxes piled up in the kitchen. Her face started to crumple. Tess thought she was going to burst into tears. Yet, somehow, she managed to stop her small chin from quavering. "This is all your fault, Daddy!" she said accusingly, crossing her arms in front of her. Her angry eyes filled with tears. "Tess, you need to stop this right now and come back to the ranch!"

"Lucy," Noah warned, his tone stern. "You know better than to be rude. Apologize right now for speaking to Tess like that!"

Lucy shook her head defiantly, still shooting daggers at Tess like she had betrayed them all in the worst way. And maybe she had, she thought miserably. If she'd let the kids think, even for a minute, she could ever fill their mom's place. Never mind know what to do in a volatile situation like this.

Work, animals…she understood.

Family dynamics with multiple kids? Not so much.

"Say you'll come home with us," Lucy demanded again.

Tess knew the child wanted and needed reassurance. But she honestly wasn't sure what to say. Especially since she and Noah were still trying to work things out on their end.

Suddenly, the movers were standing on the porch, ready to bring in Tess's big desk and chair.

Looking exhausted, the taller one asked, "Where do you want this?"

Knowing this was no time for family drama, Tess asked them to put it in the smallest bedroom, upstairs.

Noah ushered his daughters out of the way.

"Tess!" Lucy cried again, plaintively now. The twins slid off the sofa and came to stand beside their big sister. Then, their dad. Their expressions sober and confused, they each hung on to one of Noah's legs, as if abruptly afraid he might go away, too.

"We'll talk about it later," Noah said.

Lucy's distress escalated tenfold.

Tess kneeled down, held out her arms and looked Noah's eldest child straight in the eye. "We will," she promised. But when she tried to give Lucy a commiserating hug, the little girl would have none of it. And she knew when Noah gathered up his girls and shepherded them out of there, that he was every bit as worried as she was.

THE MOVERS FINISHED and left at eight thirty on Friday evening. Needing to know how Lucy was doing, Tess texted Noah.

Is Lucy okay?

He wrote back. That's what we need to talk about.

Tess wanted to talk, too, so they could figure out how to handle this together.

I know it's late. Can I come over?

She smiled in relief. Absolutely.

Have you had a chance to eat anything?

That was just like him. So thoughtful. Not yet.

I'll bring something, then.

Thanks. See you soon.

Figuring she had just enough time, Tess opened up her suitcase and got what she needed to freshen up. She had just changed out of her work clothes and into jeans and a sweater when the doorbell rang.

Noah was on the other side of the portal, with a picnic basket full of wine, cheese, gourmet crackers, a loaf of crusty bread and fruit.

He handed over the basket, then went back out to his SUV, returning with a large shopping bag. Inside was a satin heart filled with chocolate candy, a funny Valentine card, asking her to be his forevermore, and a beautiful bouquet of antique red roses from his sister Jillian's ranch.

Stunned, Tess looked at the array of gifts. She was touched by the grand romantic gesture, but wasn't used to being spoiled. And none of this was part of their agreement. She sat back, not sure what to say, except the truth. "You didn't have to do all this, Noah. Especially tonight. Especially after what happened with Lucy."

"I wanted to." He brought her close, kissing her sweetly, deeply.

She curled against him, soaking up his warmth and his strength.

But, eventually, he drew back. "But you're right," he murmured, tenderly stroking a hand through her hair. He kissed her cheek, then their gazes met and held. "We do need to talk."

Tess could tell by the careful way he was looking at her this wasn't going to be good.

She also knew there was nothing they couldn't handle as long as they approached it as a team.

Still held safe in his arms, she drew on every ounce of courage she had. She reminded him, "You never answered my text about Lucy."

Sadness came and went in his deep blue eyes. An interminable pause ensued. Finally, he admitted thickly, "She was still upset when I tucked her in."

Tess took in the grim set of his sensual lips. "How upset?"

He eased away, his every step crackling with deliberately suppressed emotion. "She pretty much cried herself to sleep." Shoulders slumping, he turned to look at the flames licking at the gas-log inset. He shook his head in regret, then swung back around. "I did my best to comfort her, but she wasn't having any of it."

Guilt mixed with shame, that she had somehow made such a mess of things with his sweet, sensitive, passionate-to-a-fault, eldest child. "I'm sorry." She took a seat on the sofa and motioned for him to do the same. "I never meant for this to happen."

Accepting her rueful look with a nod, Noah exhaled. He took a seat beside her, opened up the bottle of pinot noir and poured two glasses.

Maybe eating something would help them both feel better.

Using the plates and utensils he had provided, she sliced

cheddar, gruyere and gouda. Spread out an array of crackers, too.

Tess admitted sadly, "If I'd had any idea that she would react to my leaving, the way she did today…"

"I know that." Broad shoulders tensing, he sipped his wine. "Which doesn't mean that I shouldn't have seen it coming." He gripped his glass with both hands, staring down into the liquid. "I knew Lucy was still struggling with her grief over losing her mom. I thought moving back here, spending time with her cousins and aunts and uncles, and living on a ranch, would help her move on."

Sensing he needed his physical space, more than a hug, Tess sipped her wine, too. "But she hasn't."

Noah swung to face Tess, his bent knee bumping up against hers. "I thought she was. Especially by the way she had started to accept you—i.e., another woman who wasn't her mom—in our lives."

Tess held back a frustrated sigh. "But now she thinks I—we—betrayed her."

Noah's expression grew even bleaker. "She really did not want you to leave."

Tess really hadn't wanted to leave, either. But she also knew she and Noah couldn't just jump into a long-term, lifelong relationship the way he had with his ex, on the spur of the moment, and expect everything to magically work out. Not when his kids and their emotions were involved. Because he was right—he and his girls had already lost too much.

She could see he was struggling with the complexity of the situation. "So what do you think we should do?" she asked gently. Because like it or not, this involved both of them.

He put aside his glass of wine and stared at the food as if he had zero appetite. "Not entirely sure."

Nor was she.

"But," he said, picking up a slice of cheese and a cracker, and holding it like it was kryptonite, "I am going to put Lucy back in a grief group for kids, like the one she was in back in California. And maybe go to counseling with her, too."

That sounded like a positive step. Encouraged, Tess smiled, "Do you want me to go to that, too?"

"No." He put the cheese and cracker on a napkin, next to his barely touched pinot noir. He kept his glance averted. "I don't think that will be necessary."

Tess couldn't say why exactly. Maybe it was his cool, pragmatic tone, or the fact he wouldn't look her in the eye, but it felt like she had just been shoved to the side and had a door slammed in her face.

"Is that because I'm the problem? That, or the way I've dealt with things? Letting Lucy and I get too close, too soon?" *Letting us feel like we could be mother and daughter one day?* Heart aching, Tess pushed on deliberately, "Or is it because you don't want to give her the mistaken idea that I'm ever going to be there for her again, the way I have been recently?" *Because you are not really sure that I will be? Especially if my presence makes your life more complicated, instead of just easier.* There was no way to tell for sure. She only knew he suddenly had reservations, about them moving forward as the tight knit team they had become over the last weeks. And that reaction made her think of her ex. The small but deliberate ways Carlton had started extricating himself from her, before they split up for good. She didn't think she could bear that kind of pain again. Noah didn't look as if he wanted to suffer that way, either, which was why he was probably starting to put up a wall around his heart, again.

The silence drew out, even more painfully. Clearly still

struggling emotionally with all this, Noah let out a long breath. He turned to her once again. "I'm not trying to hurt you, Tess."

But he was nevertheless, she thought miserably.

He swallowed. "I don't want you to be part of our counseling process, because I feel like this is a problem that Lucy and I have to solve separately, apart from you."

And just like that, Tess was inundated with memories of other times when she had been excluded, and pushed aside, only to ultimately end up alone. Now, she *really* felt like crying.

"But that doesn't mean you and I still don't have work to do to provide a solid foundation for what happens next," he told her soberly.

Now he had really lost her. She bit her lip. Sensing he was about to say something he really wished he did not have to say, she said, in return, "I don't understand."

He leaned a fraction closer, inundating her with his heady masculine essence. "I know it might seem like it is too soon for me to ask you this, given everything that has gone on today." He took her hand in his, stroking the palm of her hand with the pad of his thumb.

Delicious sensations swept through her.

The kind that usually preceded making love.

His eyes turned a molten blue. "And I don't want you to be pressured into saying yes." He gripped her hand tighter. "But—"

The last thing Tess wanted was any kind of proposal born out of despair. Panicked, she withdrew her hand from his. Stood and went over to adjust the flame on the gas fireplace.

She knew she shouldn't have interrupted him at that crucial moment. But she couldn't help it. She didn't want them going down another path they never should have begun. She swung back to him. "If you're having this much reservation, then maybe we really shouldn't talk about it yet." Just like maybe they shouldn't have rushed into acting on their fierce physical attraction to each other and making love.

Her plea for caution fell on deaf ears.

No less determined, he walked over to stand next to her, coming right up to her face. "I want us to be together, Tess." He clasped her shoulders, the tenderness of his hands sending warmth swirling through her. Making her want to forget the talk and simply kiss him. Lose herself completely in the two of them. Worry about all the problems facing them, later.

He leaned forward, too, his expression so earnest and sincere. "But…"

And here it came. The break-up.

Lips tightening, he continued, with obvious regret, "It can't happen the way things are right now." His gaze shifted lovingly over her face. In a way that suddenly seemed to indicate he was as committed to her, as he had been. In a way that said, he still wanted to move forward. As long as she gave him exactly what he asked for…

"Unless we take steps to *really* change things in a positive, permanent sense."

Tess blinked. Was he really about to ask her to forego any kind of courtship and just run off and get married, the way he had with his late wife?

While it might provide the constancy the kids yearned for, as well as the deeply romantic relationship and longevity she had always wanted, a hasty act like that would also add to the overall confusion. Not just for the kids, but for her, too! Because the only reason she had ever wanted to marry was for deep, abiding love and commitment, and that did not happen overnight. It took time.

She thought of Lucy's despair earlier. Knew for all their sakes' she had to get Noah to slow down and take a step back. She lifted a hand in stop-sign fashion. "I agree. The kids need stability. Permanence. And if we can't give that to them right now…" *Or ever, maybe, she worried unhappily, if you're going to start setting conditions for us to be together…*

"Then we have to make adjustments," he agreed.

Reassured they were on the same page, she began to relax. Maybe the thing to do was not pretend she and he didn't feel anything for each other when they did. Wouldn't it be better to just be honest with the kids, at least as far as they were able, and let them know that she and Noah cared about each other. *Deeply.* And build very, very slowly from there.

"Because I don't want to end up in the same situation I did with Shelby."

Not a comparison she wanted made. Especially by him. Beginning to feel like the rug was being pulled out from under her again, she asked warily, "What do you mean?"

His dark eyebrows drew together. "Well, my late wife and I couldn't always get along."

So he had mentioned previously.

"And when we did disagree, we would usually end up arguing." He exhaled, unhappy again, then shoved a hand through his hair. "I'm only now beginning to see just how much those quarrels affected Lucy."

Who was a very sensitive, often introspective little girl who tended to keep her feelings bottled up until they exploded. "But not the twins?"

"They were infants when we lost Shelby. They don't recall anything about her other than what they hear others, mostly Lucy, talk about. And even that, they don't really understand. So none of this is an issue for them. At least not right now. If it becomes one, I'll get them into a grief group, too."

"So what are you trying to ask me, that you can't quite bring yourself to actually say?" she said finally, feeling even more confused. Clearly, this wasn't any kind of a proposal, Tess thought. Surprised to realize that for a moment she had thought—hoped—maybe it was. Even though the supposed rationale behind it and the timing would have been all wrong.

He opened his mouth and shut it. "I want to know if you will hold off on the two of us taking our relationship public indefinitely. And go to couples counseling with me instead."

COUPLES COUNSELING. THE phrase reverberated in Tess's head. Again and again…

Noah watched her react, as if she was a time bomb that could go off at any second. "You look upset."

Duh. Did he think? Deciding this evening had to come to an end, she marched over and turned off the gas fireplace. "I am."

His expression showed his astonishment, and he watched the flame dwindle to nothing. "Why?"

Tess rubbed her forehead, feeling a headache coming on. "Because I've been down this road before, with my ex. He had doubts about whether we belonged together or not from the very beginning, but he couldn't admit that. So every time we got close to taking our relationship to the next level, he put in some new caveat that we would have to abide by."

Noah frowned, impatient. "Like you could spend the night together, but only once a week, so you wouldn't be distracted from your vet-school studies. Stuff like that," he said, recalling what she'd told him.

She nodded. "And always doing what we each needed to do for ourselves first, like take post residency jobs in other states."

"You think if you hadn't done that the two of you would still be together?"

"No." Tess grimaced, the pain she felt over their failed romance long gone. "I don't. Because all that did was show how wrong we were for each other." The ache in her chest grew, and she gestured helplessly. "Kind of like where you and I are now."

He went still. "Now I'm the one who really doesn't get it."

Her body felt locked up tight. "Then let me spell it out for you, cowboy. If this is where our fling is headed," she warned him, her heart breaking, "I wish you would just have the guts to make a clean break."

"I don't want to end this fling, Tess. I'm here tonight because I want it to work! And I especially want it to work for the kids."

She could see that.

And yet…

Tess's heart ached as she thought how utterly miserable Lucy had been. How unwilling to accept comfort. Much like she felt right now. Maybe she and Noah's eldest daughter were more alike than he knew.

Maybe it was time to be realistic and do what was best for each and every one of them.

Especially his children.

Wearily, she said, "The chivalrous side of you probably does want everything to work out with fairy-tale precision. Because otherwise you would have been using me for sex and vet care and part-time nanny work, just like I apparently inadvertently used you for lodging and sex and the cure to the kind of loneliness you feel when you move to a place where you don't know a soul.

"And you don't want to think of yourself as that kind of guy, any more than I want to think of myself as that kind of woman. As someone who would trade intimacy for tangible goods and services. Yet, here we are." She shook her head ruefully. "With you trying the most creative way ever to let me down easy. In a way that will ultimately absolve you of any kind of blame."

A muscle ticking in his jaw, he gave her an incredulous look. "What are you saying? That you think I'm going to lure you into couples therapy, so someone else can tell us we are incompatible? And use that as an excuse to end this?"

Well, he *had* said the first night they met he didn't want to date or be married again, that his life was too full as it was. She had told him the same thing. And she had meant it with all her heart, at the time.

Trouble was, living with him and his girls had changed all that for her. She did want a husband and kids. She wanted a *life* with him.

And he, apparently, still wanted a life without a wife. A life on his ranch, with just him, and his girls and their pets.

Which was what made this all hurt so bad. Knowing that he did not need to be with her to be happy.

She shrugged, her emotions getting the better of her once again. "Stranger things have happened."

"Do you really think I would use someone else to break up with you?" He rubbed a hand across the scruff on his jaw and continued harshly, "I'm not that kind of man, Tess. I thought you knew me better than that."

Her heart aching in a way she had never imagined it could, she told him coolly, "I thought I did, but your actions tonight say otherwise." She walked stiffly to the front door, and opened it. "We need to end this," she said. Cold air came streaming in, adding to the discomfort between them. "And you need to leave."

He stared at her in disbelief as she picked up his jacket and shoved it into his hands. His jaw tautened. "So that's a *no* to counseling?"

"A *no* to that," she confirmed sadly, "and anything else you ever ask!"

He put his hands on her shoulders, his touch as soft and compelling as his low voice. "Tess. Please. Don't do this." His voice caught as her heart wrenched in her chest. "You're making a terrible mistake."

Was she? Or was he? Were they both? She only knew one thing.

If he continued holding her, if she surrendered to his warmth and strength, they would end up kissing again, and if they kissed, they'd make love, and she would be in deeper still.

And that, she feared, would destroy her if, in the end, this didn't work out.

"I can't talk about this anymore." She wrenched herself from his grasp.

For a moment, she thought he was going to try and persuade her again.

Then something changed in his face. Went cold and still.

He stared at her a second longer, then turned without a word, and walked right out the door.

CHAPTER SIXTEEN

TWENTY MINUTES LATER, feeling more hurt, and numb, and disappointed than he ever had in his life, Noah walked into his home. His sister was curled on the sofa, reading a book. "Thanks for babysitting," he told Jillian. With the kids asleep, and Tess not there, it had never seemed quieter. Although he supposed in defeat, without Tess there going forward, it would likely feel even more desolate to him. Especially during the times he'd come to depend on spending with her. Early mornings, late nights. Their Wednesday morning lovefests.

He'd been a fool to let himself fall for her.

To think she would ever be able to really let her guard down and open up her heart enough to let him in. Or think that he would be any better at man-woman relationships this time around.

Oblivious to the anger still simmering inside him, Jillian continued surveying him in surprise. "That must have been the shortest date on record. You've only been gone an hour and a half!"

"Good to know." Not up for a heart-to-heart, Noah got his sister's coat. He walked over to hand it to her. "Thanks again for babysitting."

Seemingly aware there was reason for concern, she put up a hand, refusing to be escorted out. "Uh-uh, buddy. I am not leaving until I find out why you have *that look* on your face."

Oh, boy, here they went. "What look?" he asked wearily. As far as emotions went, after his quarrel with Tess, he was all tapped out. Not that this would satisfy his incredibly romantic sister.

She made room for him on the sofa. "The look that says the world has ended. What happened?"

Equally empathetic, Tank got up from his place on the hearth and came over to sit next to Noah, cuddling against him.

He reached down and petted his dog's head. Robotically, he explained, "Tess's furniture arrived today. She has a house full of moving boxes. She wanted it to be an early night, so we cut it short. It's no big deal."

Jillian tilted her head. No doubt thinking about the beautiful bouquet of antique roses she had brought over for him to take to Tess. She'd also seen the wicker basket and shopping bag full of gifts he'd walked out with. And knew a romantic evening had been planned. "Except it looks very much like it *is* a big deal to you," she noted gently. "Did you reschedule?"

He shook his head.

She surveyed him intently. "Why not?"

Tank turned to look at him, too. "Because Tess never wants to see me again."

"Ah, now the rub… What did you do?"

Her accusing tone rankled. "Why do you assume it's me?" he asked heatedly.

"Because I've spent time with Tess and I know she is not the type of person who overreacts at the slightest thing. Plus, I've seen the way she looks at you when she doesn't realize anyone else is watching. She's in love with you, dude. She's *been* in love with you from that first weekend."

Hope rose only to be immediately quashed. He knew better than anyone that love didn't solve everything. Sometimes passion made it worse. And tonight had definitely been the pits.

"She and I never said anything about love," he said, biting out the words.

"But you were close."

More than that. *Inseparable.* To the point he hadn't been able to imagine his future without her in it. His gut knotted. "I thought so."

Silence.

"What was supposed to happen tonight?" she asked.

"We were going to have our first real date. But we were going to do it on the down-low."

"Because the two of you are still in that private stage of your relationship?"

Was it a relationship? He had thought so. Hell, he had thought it was even more than that. Which just showed how much he knew.

"Yeah, we didn't want anything getting back to the girls until things were more settled. You know how people, especially in our family, can jump to conclusions when it comes to romance."

Jillian shut her book and set it aside. "But you thought things would be more settled soon, so you could start openly dating and tell everyone you were seeing each other, even the kids?"

"That was the plan. At least—" Noah exhaled his frustration "—until Lucy became upset, when she found out Tess was moving out of our guest room, and into her home in town today." Briefly, he told his sister about the conversations he had had with his eldest daughter both before and after school.

Jillian gave a slow, pensive shake of her head. "And that worried you because she is such a sensitive kid."

"Right. Which is why I told Tess that I would be enrolling Lucy in a grief-support group for kids again, and taking Lucy to counseling to help her get through this new wave of grief."

Jillian leaned forward. "Did you ask Tess to be part of that?"

He shook his head, still firm in his decision. "No. I didn't think it was a good idea."

She gave him a baleful stare. "Why not?"

"Because," Noah explained sourly, "if ultimately it didn't work out between Tess and I, then Lucy would suffer *yet another loss*."

"Lucy… Or you?"

Man, his sister didn't pull any punches. "Both of us," he retorted tersely. "But it's Lucy I am mainly concerned about here."

"Uh-huh."

Jillian didn't believe him.

Noah wasn't sure he believed himself.

Because the truth was, he was now in as much pain and distress as his eldest child had been earlier. As hopeless that things would ever work out again, too.

He grimaced in renewed defeat. Then made himself focus on what he hopefully could fix with love and time. "Back to Lucy…and the loss she could suffer…"

"Could?" Jillian harrumphed. "You don't think she is suffering one now?"

"Not as much as she would be, if she gets her hopes raised only to have them dashed again."

His sister looked at him with perceptive eyes. He could tell she was holding back a whole lot of what she wanted to say. Finally, asking only, in a cool, calm voice, "How did Tess react to this plan of yours?"

"She was okay…"

A raised eyebrow.

"Sort of…" Noah amended. "Until I asked her to hold off on telling anyone we were seeing each other indefinitely, while we went to couples counseling."

This time Jillian was so shocked she nearly fell off the sofa. "You…*what*?"

Noah was getting really tired of defending his plan. Why couldn't Tess and Jillian see he was trying to protect everyone here? Keep them from getting hurt? He met his sister's gaze equably. "I wanted to head off any problems before they arose so we wouldn't make the same mistakes that Shelby and I made."

"So Tess wouldn't make the same errors?" Jillian persisted. "Or *you* wouldn't?"

Noah blinked.

Jillian heaved an exasperated sigh. She looked like she wanted to throttle him. "Tess isn't Shelby, Noah."

"I know that," he said, defending himself stiffly.

Jillian studied him. "Funny thing is, I think you do. So why did you do something that you had to know on some level would end this whatever-it-is with Tess almost before it began?"

Why indeed?

Could it be, Noah wondered, that Tess wasn't the only one with barbed wire around her heart, that he was running from his feelings, and putting up roadblocks to protect himself, too? Had he unconsciously used Lucy's issues as a cover to keep from really acknowledging his own true fear—that he would never be able to love and protect and care for Tess, the way she wanted, needed, and deserved? Was that what was holding them back, and keeping him from going all in with Tess right now?

TESS WAS STILL in a major funk the next afternoon, when Sara stopped by to bring a housewarming gift and see how things were going. "I'm surprised I don't see a whole crew of Lockharts here helping you put everything in order, posthaste."

"Yeah, well, those days are over." Tess accepted the Sugar Love bakery basket with a thanks. "Noah and I probably aren't going to be good friends after all."

Sara followed her into the kitchen. Then watched as Tess set down the present. "I was hoping you were more than that."

So was I, Tess thought, recalling the Valentine's Day presents Noah had brought over—flowers, candy and funny card.

"Did he do something?" Sara asked gently. "Because it doesn't look to me like you wanted to end things."

"I didn't." Briefly, she explained about how close she had gotten to Noah and his kids, while staying at the Welcome Ranch. Plus, Lucy's meltdown the previous day.

Sara sympathized. "I'm sure that was tough on all of you. But Lucy and the twins know they will still see you, right?"

"That was the plan, initially." Tess folded her arms over her chest, over her heart.

"And now?" Sara lounged against the new granite counter.

Tess got out two bottles of sparkling water and handed one to Sara. "Noah wants to take Lucy to a grief-support group and counseling, and deal with that himself." Together, they walked into the living room and sat on the sofa.

Sara took off her winter jacket and set it beside her. "Even though you are part of the reason she is so upset."

Tess ran her fingertips over the knee of her jeans. "Yes."

"But you accepted that."

The depth of her hurt made her tense. "I did. After all,

he is the parent and maybe I shouldn't be involved in this crisis with his daughter." *At least not right now.* "But when he asked me to hold off on telling people we were going to start dating and instead go to couples counseling first, to be sure we were going to be compatible, it became clear to me we weren't on the same page after all."

To Tess's surprise, her boss didn't look at all surprised by Noah's plan.

"The request felt like it came out of left field?" Sara guessed.

"And then some," Tess confirmed, feeling more unsettled than ever.

Sara tilted her head. "And you're opposed to going because you don't like therapy in general? Or because you don't want to go to couples counseling with *him*?"

"I'm opposed because I think his even asking me to do that sends a strong signal that he's gotten more involved with me than he ever wanted to be, or planned on being, and now he doesn't know how to get out of it, with his self-esteem and character intact." She released a long, labored breath. "So he's going to let someone else do the heavy lifting and tell us kindly that we are not a good match after all. And then he won't have to feel guilty or like he led me on when we do split up."

"That's a lot of work just to say he's not ready to date after losing his wife. Which has clearly been the case up to now. Usually, he just tells a woman outright. Politely and directly, so there are no misunderstandings. Which is one of the things that has made it very hard to match him up with anyone."

Tess hadn't been ready or willing to date anyone either, when they had first met. They had both been up front about that.

"But if that were the case," Sara continued, "you are not

the kind of woman who would hold his continued grief and unwillingness to move on against him. And I know that he knows that. So he could have just ended it, without all the extra confusion and drama, if that was what he wanted."

Tess buried her face in her hands. Had she been wrong comparing him to Carlton? Thinking he was taking the coward's way out, or putting up roadblocks to prevent them from getting closer? She swallowed. "Then why did he ask me to go to couples therapy with him before we really even had our first official date?"

Sarah flashed a gentle, understanding smile. "The same reason I joined a support group for spouses and asked Matt to get counseling at the West Texas Warriors Association for his PTSD, when the two of us first got emotionally involved. Because I knew without some outside help, our chances to have a healthy family were never going to be as good as we both wanted them to be."

Tess took a moment to think about that.

"There are a few other reasons he would have come up with this solution. First, his mother is a social worker and she is very good friends with Kate Marten McCabe, who runs the grief-counseling services at Laramie Community Hospital. So I am sure she has been wanting him to do this, anyway. Plus, Noah and his family went through a lot of trauma, both when Shelby was in cancer treatment and after she died, and Noah and Lucy both did grief counseling in California that first year."

"He mentioned that," Tess admitted. "He told me that's why they moved back to Texas. So he and the girls could be close to his parents and all his siblings, for the familial support."

"Right." Sara filled in some more gaps in Tess's knowledge. "And although Lucy has continued to struggle from time to time, mostly from sibling rivalry these days, it has seemed like they were all finally moving on. Especially by how they all welcomed you into their lives this last month."

Sara's hopeful analysis made sense. And yet... Tess had behaved foolishly once. She did not want to jump to erroneous conclusions again. "I still think he is looking for a way out, now that I'm no longer going to be living with them," Tess admitted stubbornly.

"Is he?" Sara asked kindly. "Or are you?"

TESS SPENT THE rest of the day unpacking and thinking. Was Sara right?

Was *she* the one who was scared?

By the following afternoon, she knew what she had to do. She developed a plan. Her heart feeling like it was lodged in her throat, she texted Noah.

Are you free tonight? I'd really like to talk.

She saw the little bubbles that indicated he was responding.

What time? he texted back.

Her knees sagged in relief. Seven? My place?

I'll be there.

The next few hours passed with a flurry of activity and anxiety. When the doorbell finally rang, Tess's pulse was racing. Smoothing the folds of her skirt, she went to answer it. Noah stood on the other side, in a cashmere sweater and slacks, looking as handsome as could be.

Her heart took another leap. She ushered him in.

"Wow..." He looked around at the perfectly put-together living room and kitchen. His voice was a sexy rumble in his chest. "Who helped?"

She thought about all the boxes she had emptied and collapsed and carried out to the garage, for recycling. "Just me."

"If you weren't a veterinarian, you could hire out for this." He caught her wry look. "Sorry." He sobered. "When I'm nervous I make jokes. The place really does look nice."

Pride and contentment radiated within her. "Thank you." She took him by the hand and led him over to the sofa, trying hard not to notice how warm and solid and enticingly masculine he felt. Or how good he smelled, like soap and cologne. They settled side by side. "And for the record, I'm nervous, too."

He gazed at her hopefully. "So..."

"First, I'd like to apologize for kicking you out Friday evening and peremptorily ending our date. I should have had you stay and let us work through this."

He studied her closely, still on edge. "Which means you're willing to do so now?" he asked in a low voice, husky with emotion.

Tess nodded. "I talked to Sara about what the WTWA counseling services had done for her and Matt, how it had made their love so much stronger and better. And I know now I completely overreacted when you asked me to consider counseling."

He threaded his hand through hers. "Why did you?" he asked gently.

She moved closer. "That took a while to figure out, but eventually I began to put it all together." Their gazes locked. "You remember when I told you that a lot of different family friends cared for me while my mom worked nights at the restaurant?"

"Mmm-hmm." He shifted her over onto his lap and wrapped his arms around her.

"Well, there was always a point when my welcome kind

of got worn out. But everyone who cared for me was so kind, no one wanted to see me go without care, and they knew especially in the early days for my mom and me, finances were tight. So the person or family would soldier on, thinking they could do it. Until it became just too hard or inconvenient to have me there."

His gaze remained on hers, as steady and strong as his presence. "And then they would tell you and your mom to find other arrangements?"

Tess sighed ruefully. "If only they had been able to be that direct, maybe it would have been easier. Instead, they started making up excuses as to why they couldn't care for me."

"That you were able to see through."

She nodded, sadness drifting over her. "It was pretty obvious, even at an early age." She released a deep, shuddering breath. His rapt attention encouraged her to go on. "Anyway—" she hitched in another breath "—when you brought up the idea of going to counseling, I thought that was what it was. Again."

His expression remained serious, even as his welcoming smile broadened. "Oh, darlin', the last thing I ever wanted was to push you away," he confessed huskily. His gaze roved her face, lingering on her eyes. "I was just so afraid of making the kinds of mistakes I made in my first marriage." He threaded his hands through her hair, and gazed down at her. Repentantly. Somberly.

"Of hurting the kids again. Hurting you. And I couldn't bear the thought of that," he confessed raggedly.

She splayed her hands over the steady thrumming of his heart. "The only thing we ended up hurting was each other."

"Agreed."

"I want to go to couples counseling with you, Noah. I

want to learn how to be the best partner and mother figure possible."

He studied her intently. "You're sure?"

Tess noted with relief, it was no longer a condition for moving forward. "Very." She offered a tremulous smile. "I'm coming late to this party. I want to get started off on the right foot." She caught the happy gleam in his eyes and murmured mischievously, "We'll consider it a kind of imprint training for…us."

Beaming, he took her face in his hands. "I think I could go for that."

"Me, too." She kissed him fiercely.

He kissed her back until they were both breathless and then rested his forehead against hers.

"Oh, Tess, I love you," he told her in a low, rusty sounding voice. "I love you so much…"

They shared another sweet, evocative kiss. Tess wreathed her arms about his neck. "I love you, too, Noah." Bliss filled her heart. For a long moment, all they could do was drink each other in.

He flashed her a sexy smile. "So we're back on track?"

She met his coaxing look with one of her own. "To a future together? Absolutely."

EPILOGUE

Fifteen months later

LUCY PROPPED HER hands on her hips, as her little sisters gathered around. "Well, what do you think, Daddy?" She tossed her long hair triumphantly. "Are we beautiful or what?"

Noah stepped back to admire the family in his life on their beloved Welcome Ranch. Tess and the girls had matching spring dresses on. The rose pattern of the fabric was carried over into the wreaths they wore in their hair, and the ribbons attached to the donkeys' halters, as well as to Tank's collar.

They looked so damn fine and were so happy it brought tears to his eyes. The support groups and therapy had provided them with the skills needed to weather any problem, big or small. His and Tess's marriage six months before had provided a testament to their faith in the future, and a solid foundation for their lively family. He surveyed them all in turn, his heart filling with love and pride. "You all are gorgeous!" he told them in a low, gravelly voice. His gaze swept gratefully over Tank, Miss Coco and Baby, too.

They were all so damn lucky to have what they did.

Looking a little choked up as well, by their incredible family, Tess grinned. "We can't forget what Aunt Jillian brought over for you, too, cowboy." She pulled out a matching pale pink-rose boutonniere and pinned it to the lapel of his linen sport coat. She patted his chest while gazing lovingly into his eyes. "You're going to be our master of ceremonies today—" her gaze scanned his open-throated white shirt, jeans and boots "—so you've got to be as dressed up as the rest of us. Right, girls?"

"Right, Mommy!" the three of them declared in return.

Tess beamed, the way she always did when the girls honored her as their new mother. Which wasn't surprising, since she loved them just as fiercely in return. Things hadn't been perfect, of course. They'd all had their ups and downs. But they'd all weathered the storms together, and come out, closer than ever, every time.

Angelica clapped her hands while Avery squealed in excitement. "The Pet Palooza at the fairgrounds is going to be so much fun!"

Noah imagined it would be.

The first annual event had been organized by his wife. All the kids would walk with their parents and leashed pets around the fairground track. Then retire to the pens in the various barns, after the low-key parade, to await their turn on stage, as they introduced their pets and told all about their care.

Everyone who participated would get a trophy for their pet. And there were going to be lots of them.

"Are there going to be any other miniature donkeys?" Lucy asked.

Tess shook her head as they shepherded Miss Coco and Baby to the waiting horse trailer, which had been lined with soft, clean hay. "No, but there will be two Shetland ponies, a lot of lambs and sheep and goats, a few alpacas, a chicken and a rooster, and even some full-sized horses."

Thanks to carefully ordered placement, the parade went

great. The time in the pens gave them all an opportunity to relax. When it was their turn on stage, Noah held the microphone and asked the questions of his daughters, about their pets' care and personalities. Tess fielded the veterinary-level inquiries. And Miss Coco, Baby and Tank showed off their charm.

All three were given superior ratings. And, to their delight, the girls each received an award for being such good pet owners.

By the time they all got back to the ranch, they all partook in the picnic dinner they had prepared before they left. It had been a long exhausting, fun-filled day for everyone, and before they knew it, the girls were ready for sleep, all the animals bedded down for the night.

Tess and Noah retired to the newly installed porch swing on the back deck, in time to watch the sunset. He'd thought Tess might want to open a bottle of wine, but instead she had an icy cold beer for him, and a raspberry lemonade for herself.

She settled down into the curve of his arm and clinked her glass with his. "Great job today, Daddy."

"Great job to you, too, Mommy," he teased right back.

They exchanged smiles.

His thoughts turned to the conversation they hadn't had time to have that morning. "Any ideas about what you want to do about the offer on your house?"

She sipped her lemonade serenely. "I'm going to accept it."

He knew the bid had been over asking price. Still... "Are you sure?"

She nodded. "I know I honored my family by returning the property to its former glory, but Lucy was right the first time she did a walk-through with us. It is too small. And we have the home here, on the Welcome Ranch."

He wrapped his arm about her shoulders, drawing her into his body. "It still has sentimental value to you, though."

She rested her head in the curve of his neck. "You're right." She took his hand and pressed it to her lips. Remembering. "It's the place we first met, the thing that brought us together initially, and the place where a lot of our courtship occurred. Where we occasionally have hosted sleepovers for the girls and their friends and or cousins. And had the occasional staycation as well."

All were wonderful memories. His heart swelling with love, he kissed her temple. "It's also where they were the first time they called you Mom."

"I know." Her eyes misted over.

He pushed on, wanting to make sure she would not make a decision that would later lead to regret. "And there's no mortgage on it. Just a small amount of property tax to be paid every year, which is offset by the increase in value. So if you wanted to keep it as an investment, or even a hang-out place for us when the girls are busy in town, I would understand. I mean, who knows, maybe one of the girls would want to live in it one day."

Tess turned to face him, her expression sober. "I thought about that. But that would be years from now, Noah, and the house needs to be occupied now by a loving family, like the one who made the offer. Besides—" she grinned impishly "—when I said the house is too small for us, I really meant it, cowboy."

For a second, he wasn't sure where she was going with this. When she took his hand and put it on her tummy, he began to get the idea. Suddenly, he felt like he'd been picked up by a tornado and set down so hard all the wind was knocked out of him. Yet, somehow, he was still upright. Feelings bubbling up inside of him—joy, love surprise, wonder—and he rasped, "You're...?"

"Pregnant." Her smile was as dazzling as her beauty. "Yes, I am."

He paused to take it all in. "How far along?"

She set aside her glass. He moved his, too. "Three months. The pregnancy calculator says the baby will be here in November."

Happier than he could ever remember being, he pulled her over onto his lap. They shared a tender, celebratory kiss. When it finally ended he held her close, soaking in her warmth, gentleness and strength. The joy between them was as strong as their love.

"In case you haven't noticed, I'm thrilled," he said, finally managing to get the words out.

She returned his smile cheerfully. "I'm over the moon, too. About this. And the fact I finally have a family of my own. And the Welcome Ranch to call home." She hitched in an emotional breath. Tears of bliss suddenly shimmered in her green eyes. "Because it has been that to me, you know."

From the first moment she had set foot on it.

"And it always will be our home," he promised, kissing her again, sweetly and thoroughly this time. "Not just now, but forever."

* * * * *

Grace And The Cowboy
Mary Anne Wilson

MILLS & BOON

Mary Anne Wilson is a Canadian transplanted to California, where her life changed dramatically. She found her happily-ever-after with her husband, Tom, and their family. She always loved writing, reading and has a passion for anything Jane Austen. She's had over fifty novels published with Harlequin, been nominated for a RITA® Award, won Reviewers' Choice Awards and received RWA's Career Achievement Award in Romantic Suspense.

Visit the Author Profile page
at millsandboon.com.au for more titles.

Dear Reader,

Two broken people, Grace Bennet and Max Donovan, have been hurt by life, and both have decided to do whatever it takes to never be hurt again. Then Grace gets a notification that the uncle she never knew existed has passed and left her land and a lodge near the small Wyoming town of Eclipse. Fate brings Grace, a city girl raised in Las Vegas, and Max, the county sheriff and one of the famous sons in the Donovan rodeo family, together in Eclipse. Instant attraction between them is strong, but neither one wants to go beyond friendship. They can't take that chance. But sometimes taking a leap of faith can be the safest thing to help you find where you really belong.

Writing *Grace and the Cowboy*, the last book in the Flaming Sky Ranch series, was a joy for me, and I hope that you enjoy reading it.

Mary Anne

DEDICATION

For Deborah Leisher:

My dear friend who's willingly tackled
the impossible for me and made it
a win for both of us.

I love you.

CHAPTER ONE

ON A BRIGHT mid-November day, Grace Bennet stood alone by a private hangar at the airport outside of Tucson, Arizona, scanning the northern sky. Finally, a sleek private jet came into view and started its descent toward the main landing strip. As it touched down, Grace shielded her eyes with her hand to block the noon-hour sun and tried to ignore the knots in her stomach. She hadn't seen her father, Walter Bennet, founder and CEO of the Las Vegas–based Golden Mountain Corporation, for at least six months. After her mother had passed a year ago, what had always been a tenuous link between father and daughter had almost ceased to exist.

Now her father was begrudgingly making a brief stopover on his way to Japan on corporate business. She hadn't actually begged him to meet her prior to leaving, but she'd come close before he'd finally agreed to it. Grace needed a legitimate face-to-face moment with him, not a phone call or a video call. She needed to ask him one question that no one else could answer for her. She really needed the truth.

Walter Bennet might be a lot of things, including domineering, controlling and a bully at times, but he wasn't a liar. He was brutally frank, never editing his words to spare anyone's feelings, not even hers.

The plane with the glittering Golden Mountain logo on its tail section slowed and taxied over to a stop about thirty feet from where she stood. The cabin door lifted up, the steps dropped down to the tarmac, then Sawyer Bakker, her father's executive assistant, motioned for her to come on board.

"Come on, Grace," he shouted over the whine of the idling engines.

The man was dressed in an immaculate three-piece navy suit, and he was smiling at her. He was fifty-eight to her father's sixty but looked ten years younger. Grace figured that might be because Sawyer was given to freely passing out genuine smiles, making up for the profound lack of warmth from her father.

"You're going with Walter to Japan?" she asked as she took the steps up into the plane. She'd called her father Walter all of her life. He'd insisted on it. Her mother had always been Marianna. No Mommy and Daddy.

"He wants me there for the investors' meeting in Brussels after we finalize the expansion plans in Tokyo." He motioned her past him into the cabin. "Sorry to rush you, but we're on a tight schedule."

"How is he?" Grace asked in a lower voice.

"Impatient. I'd say you're looking at a ten-minute window before he gives takeoff orders."

"Got it," she murmured and went farther into the eight-passenger cabin, a space that looked like a well-appointed study with its rich dark woods and leather finishes. Walter was sitting at a round table by the closed door to his sleeping quarters in the back. A crystal decanter that she knew held his special whiskey blend was to his right. Some of the amber liquid was in the glass in front of him.

Walter didn't stand and greet his only child as she approached him but motioned her to a captain's chair directly across the table from him. "Sit," he said abruptly before he pointedly glanced at his wristwatch. He looked at her and his ice blue eyes narrowed. "You said you were in a hurry for this, so let's get to it."

He tossed back his drink while Grace took her seat, feeling as uncomfortable as she always did around him. When she finally met his gaze again, she was taken back to see how much older he looked at that moment. What had once been thick brown hair was thinning and streaked with gray. The lines at his eyes and the brackets at his mouth seemed deeper. It looked as if the last year hadn't been kind to him. Clasping her hands in her lap, she tried to focus past a sudden sadness that came out of nowhere.

Quickly she said, "I need you to answer a question. That's all."

He shrugged. "If it's not about you coming to work with me, I'm just losing time and money sitting here."

He hadn't changed. His time was valuable to him, and he rationed it out to the last minute. He poured more whiskey. "So, *are* you coming to claim your spot at the Mountain?" Walter had called his corporate headquarters in Las Vegas "the Mountain" for as long as she could remember. His eyes narrowed when she didn't answer. "Why do I sense you're going to disappoint me again, Grace?"

She wouldn't be baited to go down that rabbit hole and let him control the conversation. She kept eye contact and said simply, "That's not my plan."

His exhale of air was a low hiss. "You really are Marianna's daughter. She was beautiful and passed her looks down to you, along with her ability to make me miserable without even trying."

Her parents had met when Marianna had been a top international runway model, and Walter had already made a name for himself and a lot of money in his business ventures. Grace had inherited her mother's height at five-ten, the same ebony black hair and striking violet eyes. But her mother had drawn attention wherever she went and loved it immensely. Grace hated being noticed unless she wanted to be. She hadn't been born to be a model, not any more than she'd been born to take over her father's empire when the time came.

"Marianna was always beautiful," she half whispered.

"She never looked like some thrift store reject," Walter said before he downed his drink.

Her outfit—a gold silk blouse, black leather pants and black wedge sandals—had been a real find in the consignment shop she ran with her former college roommate near their apartment in Tucson. She liked the style and the fact she hadn't had to spend a week's pay for it. Walter would have preferred she wear sharp business suits—the female version of his style—with her hair styled in a short bob and brushed sleekly back from her face. She'd never dressed like that and preferred to wear her natural curls loose, falling just past her shoulders from a center part. She didn't respond to his critique.

"There was just one Marianna," Walter finally murmured as he stared down at the now empty glass in his hand.

Grace felt her throat tightening, thinking about her mother. Taking a breath, she swallowed hard, then tried to steer their conversation back on track. "The question I need answered is—"

He abruptly cut her off. "Is this where you ask for money?"

She looked right at him. "No. I don't need your money."

His sarcasm grew sharper. "Did some guy with tattoos and a Harley get you in some trouble, and you need a lawyer?"

"What? No," she said more sharply than she'd meant

to. "I'm here about a letter I received from an attorney in Wyoming."

That caught his interest. "Was it a job offer?"

"No," she said again. "I have a job I'm happy with."

"Of course you are. Who wouldn't want to spend their life selling used clothes and coffee after getting an expensive degree in business and marketing?" He sat back, looking so in control that it made Grace feel slightly nauseous. She braced herself for what she knew was coming in his attempt to intimidate her. He didn't disappoint.

"Obviously you don't appreciate the life my work has made possible for you. I've indulged you at every step, letting you take your time settling down, leaving it up to you to tell me when you were ready to become part of the company. You're going to be twenty-seven years old in a few months. I was twenty-one when I bought into my first investment. You've had a lot of time to do nothing except indulge your need to be some ridiculous free spirit."

His words hurt, but she tried to at least give the appearance that they didn't. "I did what you asked me to do, including carrying a 4.0 GPA all throughout college. While doing that, I was working, and I haven't asked for anything from you since my freshman year." Her tone became more defensive than she'd wanted it to be, so she made herself finish as evenly as she could. "I have friends and a life that I like in Tucson. That's all that matters to me right now."

"Do you want me to applaud you?" He chuckled roughly. "You're a fool, Grace."

She'd had enough, and she'd end this now on her terms. She got right to the point. "The letter from the attorney in Wyoming was about him settling the will of a man from a small town in the northern part of the state. I was named as his sole heir."

Walter looked surprised. "Who is this guy?"

This was it, and she spoke carefully to get it out before he cut her off. "Martin Roberts. His will says I'm his niece. All I want from you is to tell me if this Martin Roberts really was my uncle."

Her father's expression hardened. The only sound in the cabin was the muted whine of the plane's engines idling until he said, "Martin Roberts used to be Martin Robert Bennet, my older brother."

She hardly knew how to process what he'd admitted so easily. "Your…your brother? I had an uncle and you never told me about him. Why?"

That brought a scoffing exhale from Walter. "Martin was a waste and not worth anything." He waved his hand dismissively. "Now you know. Forget about that letter and a man who doesn't deserve to be remembered."

Grace was stunned. "Your brother—my uncle—is dead."

He shook his head. "He's been dead to me for almost thirty years. You contact the attorney for a full monetary assessment of the inheritance. No, don't bother with that. I'll make this all go away. Leave it to me."

Walter was throwing out orders that he expected her to follow without question, and for most of her life, she had done as he'd told her to do. But after she'd left to go to college, she'd realized she was capable of making her own decisions. "No, this is my inheritance and I'll handle it."

It seemed to take a second for her answer to sink in with him. When it did, he didn't explode. She remembered his rules for winning: *Get your adversary angry and when they get emotional and start yelling, you keep control and make them look like a fool, then you win.* He stared at her, holding eye contact, another tip he'd given her: *Never look away.* "I'm offering to help so you don't get tangled up with some yahoo who calls himself an attorney."

"I have what I came for, so I'll leave and let you go to Tokyo," she said. She wasn't going to play his game.

"Listen to me," he said, his voice tight. "Uncle or not, Martin was a no-good born loser."

"But he *was* your brother," she allowed herself to say.

"It was his choice to walk away and give up the Bennet name." He smiled at her, a totally humorless expression that he used to keep an adversary off balance. It only made her more determined to not back down. "In hindsight, it was probably the only good thing Martin ever did, to get out of here and leave us alone."

Grace flinched inside, and she had to fight to keep her tone calm when she responded. "He's dead, Walter, and I never even knew he existed. How could you keep that from me?"

"It wasn't any of your business," he said without hesitation as if that justified and explained everything.

"He was part of my family, and I deserved to know him. Why did he walk away? What did you do to him?"

"Nothing." His single word was hard and flat.

Grace almost sagged from the weight of sadness she felt. "I can't believe you don't care your own brother died."

He shrugged. "Martin's whole life was a mess and it's over. We won't talk about this again. Ever. I'll make it go away. Am I making myself clear?"

What was clear to her was Martin Roberts had been her uncle. He'd been family, and his own brother didn't care about what happened to him. She'd stepped inside the corporate jet expecting one of two possible outcomes: either the attorney had the wrong person, or by some twist of fate, the man really had been her uncle. Maybe she'd been naive enough to think that she and Walter could share the shock and grief of his loss if the attorney had been right.

"Yes, I understand," she murmured. But she wouldn't

agree to anything with him. Her world had changed. Instead of what Walter wanted, she would go to the place her uncle had called home, and she'd find out the truth for herself.

She stood abruptly to end the meeting. "You can bill me for your time, Walter. I'll leave you to mourn Uncle Martin." She turned away as Sawyer appeared from the cockpit and went to raise the door and lower the stairs for her.

Before she could get outside, her father called after her, "I don't need you to tell me to mourn anyone. You call the attorney, or, trust me, I will!"

She looked back at him. "Don't you dare. It's not your business."

For a moment she thought he was going to break his own rules and yell at her, but he didn't. He kept his voice level, but he spoke slowly, enunciating each word clearly. "Listen to me—if you decide to head out to the Wild West, you are on your own." A smugness entered his tone. "You'd probably fit right in at some run-down motel in some jerk-water town in the middle of nowhere."

She bit her lip hard to keep from saying something that would only make things worse. She settled for, "Whatever it is, it's my life and my choice. It's got nothing to do with you."

He waved her away with a dismissive motion of his big hand. "Go and do whatever you want to do, but if you fall on your face, I won't help you get up. If you need money, get a second job. See how that works out for you."

Grace knew if she left then, she'd pay a price. Maybe banishment from Walter Bennet's world. If so, she'd pay it. "Go to Japan. I'm heading to Wyoming!" she called back to him as she took the first step down.

He threw out one last verbal volley. "Regrettably, it looks as if you've inherited some of Martin's stupidity."

She didn't look back this time as she hurried down onto the tarmac and over to where she'd been allowed to park by the hangar. She tried to let go of a wild mixture of pain, anger and disbelief as she slipped behind the steering wheel of her old green Jeep. She didn't drive away immediately but stayed to watch the corporate jet taxi back onto the main runway. When its wheels lifted off the ground and the plane climbed into the heavens, she finally felt as if she could breathe again.

It was done. She was going alone to Wyoming to see where her uncle had lived and find out all she could about a man she'd never heard of until two days ago, a man she'd never be able to meet.

CHAPTER TWO

One week later, Wyoming

IT WAS ALMOST MIDNIGHT, and Sheriff Max Donovan was worn-out. He was on his way home after spending twelve hours driving around the southern section of Clayton County, trying to track down thieves who'd been stealing irrigation system components. He was frustrated that he'd come up empty-handed again. He was heading north toward the town of Eclipse and debating if he should sleep in the back room of the sheriff's substation in town or tough out the extra twenty miles to make it to the Flaming Sky Ranch his family owned and ran.

But when he drove onto the main street of the town, Clayton Way, he remembered he did have another option just over two miles north of the town limit: Split Creek Lodge. A couch there was more comfortable than the cot that was too short to accommodate his full six feet two inches. The Lodge had been shut down since the owner had passed away, a man who had been a good friend to Max. Marty Roberts was a quiet man who'd shown an uncanny understanding of what Max had gone through during a low point in his life three years earlier.

He drove past the station and kept going, envisioning the huge sectional couch in front of the double-sided firebox in the rock fireplace in the great room of the Lodge. He could stretch out there and not worry about his feet hanging off the end. He only wished that Marty could've been there to greet him, grinning and offering great coffee and a game of chess.

As he drove, he rotated his head to try to loosen his neck and shoulder muscles. Other vehicles were few and far between at this time of night. He slowed when he caught sight of the Lodge sign ahead. The only part of the ten-foot-tall electric sign that was still lit up was a two-word advisory: "No Vacancy." The Lodge was empty, but at least no unsuspecting traveler would pull in and try to get a room.

Max pulled up to the double gate. A sign above the keypad set in a rocky pillar read "Welcome to Split Creek Lodge." He put in the security code, and once the gates opened, he drove through and onto a packed dirt drive half-buried under the dead leaves from the trees that formed a canopy overhead. He'd only driven halfway up to the Lodge itself when he stopped the truck abruptly and flipped off the headlights. The lights were on inside the reception area and the great room to the right of it. He'd locked up tight two days ago when he'd made his last security check.

He cautiously drove forward in the shadows until he was able to make out the sprawling log-and-stone single-story structure with its central peaked roof. Suddenly the light in the great room went out. With it being a moonless night, Max couldn't make out much from the top of the drive where it merged into the cobbled parking area that ran along the front of the Lodge.

Only one parking slot was occupied. An old canvas-topped Jeep sat in front of the steps leading up to the porch. Taking his night vision binoculars from the console, he focused them on the back of the lone vehicle. Its license had been issued in Arizona.

He entered the number in his dash computer and kept

watching the Lodge as he waited for a response. He wasn't going inside without some clue about what he might be facing, especially without any backup. A high-pitched beep signaled that the data was loading, and he watched the information on the Jeep come up on the screen.

The 1982 Jeep was registered to a Marianna Grace Bennet in Tucson. She was twenty-six with blue eyes, black hair and was five feet ten inches tall. She had valid insurance and two speeding tickets that had been settled with a fine. Most people hated their pictures on their driving license, but Ms. Bennet had no reason to complain. By any standard, she was strikingly attractive. If he ended up having to arrest her, she'd definitely be the best-looking criminal he'd ever handcuffed.

He called the dispatcher covering the northern section of the county overnight and when Lillian Shaw picked up the call, he was surprised. She'd worked at the substation in town for the past twenty years, and her time off the clock began at nine in the evening. "Lillian, what are you doing there?"

"You were gone and there wasn't anyone to cover until Denton takes over at two. Now, cowboy, what's your 911?"

The tiny middle-aged lady had more energy than a kid. She'd been a real plus for Max when he'd taken over as sheriff six years ago. Thankfully, she wasn't showing any signs of winding down to retirement. "I'm at Marty's place. Someone's inside and I'm going to check it out. Give me fifteen?"

She responded briskly. "You got it, cowboy. Be safe."

He eased the truck slowly forward, rolling to a stop behind the Jeep to block anyone leaving in a hurry. He wasn't in the mood or the condition for a car chase tonight. Killing the engine, he tossed his hat onto the passenger seat, then undid the front of his brown suede jacket.

He got out as quietly as possible and approached the Jeep, trying to see inside. All that was visible was a wrapper from a candy bar on the passenger seat and a take-out coffee cup sitting in what had probably been meant to be an ashtray. He stepped back and took the stairs up to the wraparound porch in two strides, then ducked down as he moved closer to the door to keep from being seen through the windows. Once he was at the wall between the last window and the doorjamb, he straightened up and inched closer to the heavy wooden doors with frosted glass inserts. One thin strip of glass was clear, but as the lights in the reception area flashed on, all he could see was a narrow section of the long check-in desk directly across from the door. Nothing moved.

He pushed back the right side of his jacket to have access to his radio and his weapon in its hip holster, unsnapped the guard, then rested his hand on the butt of the gun. He listened for movement inside. He was tired but angry that someone had broken into the Lodge, and he wouldn't let it go any further, no matter who was in there.

A dragging sound suddenly came from within, then a jarring crash that he could feel vibrate in the wooden floor of the porch. He reached for the door latch, felt it disengage, then kicked the barrier back hard enough to hear it impact against the interior wall.

"Police!" he yelled with his gun half-drawn as he rushed inside. He barely managed to stop before he'd trip over a woman sitting on the hard floor with a heavy metal display rack overturned by her side. The brochures that had been in its pockets were scattered all over the dusty wooden floor.

Her hands were up in surrender, and she looked horrified. "Stop! Stop! Don't shoot, please."

"Don't move," he ordered. "Who else is in here?"

"No one. I'm alone. I swear."

He wasn't about to trust her and quickly scanned the area but saw nothing and heard nothing except her rapid breathing. As he secured his gun, he stared down at her. Dark shoulder-length curls tangled around her face as she sat there, awkwardly on the floor with her hands up. Dressed in a well-worn black leather motorcycle jacket, jeans with rips at the knees and totally out of place black-strapped sandals, she watched him with eyes that were more lavender than the blue her driver's license had claimed. They were wide from the shock and fear of someone bursting into the Lodge with a gun and screaming at her.

Her pale lips worked silently before she actually spoke in a breathless voice. "Are…are you really the police?"

He pushed back his jacket again to expose his badge and gun. "Yes, ma'am."

She frowned up at him. "You could have bought that stuff online."

"Ma'am, I'm the sheriff of Clayton County. Who are you?"

"Marianna Grace Bennet, but… I go by Grace."

"Okay, Grace. Now I need to know why you broke in here."

"I did not break in here," she said quickly.

Pretty or not, she was in the wrong place at midnight and lying to him on top of that. He hunkered down in front of her to make serious eye contact. "The gates by the highway were locked when I left here after my last security check two days ago. Inside lights were off. The entry door was locked." He reached behind himself to feel for the door, then swung it shut as the wind began to grow outside. "The back door was locked, and the cellar doors were double locked. How do you explain that? And please don't lie to me. I'm not in a good mood."

She surprised him when she sat up a bit straighter. "I want my one phone call a prisoner's entitled to."

This wasn't going to be easy. "Ma'am, you aren't my prisoner, not yet."

"Then I want to call 911 to make sure you are who you say you are."

"Okay," he said. "Call 911, but the thing is, at this time of night, I *am* 911. Your call will go to central dispatch at headquarters in Two Horns, where they'll track the call then contact the closest substation and it's sent to the officer on patrol to respond. Your call will be forwarded to *my* cell that's in *my* jacket pocket since I'm the only one on duty around here. Believe it or not, even with all the rerouting, it only takes a minute to get to my phone."

She looked up at him with narrowed eyes, and he could tell whatever shock and fear he'd generated in her with his sudden appearance was almost gone. Unfortunately, his adrenaline was waning, too, and his weariness was making a comeback. "I'm not saying you're lying, but I'm alone out here in the middle of nowhere and you broke in, slamming that door into the wall, not to mention the gun, and I can't take your word for anything."

She was right, and he wanted to get this over with. "Okay, do what you need to do, but the landline phones here are shut off."

"I have a cell phone," she said and fumbled getting it out of her jacket pocket. When she held it up so he could see it, her hand was slightly unsteady.

"Okay. Go for it."

Max watched Grace Bennet put in the call and a minute later, his phone rang in his jacket pocket. He guessed the main unit had bypassed Lillian completely. He took it out and held it up so she could see the screen. "My phone, your call." He put in the code that stood for "no episode," then looked at Grace.

With a roll of her eyes, she exhaled, then said, "So, you really are 911, huh?"

"Yes, ma'am, and I'm at the end of a very long day." He stood up. "I want to go home, but I can't leave until you answer my questions so I can sort this all out."

"Okay. I'll make this as clear as I can. I got here fifteen minutes before you showed up and scared me almost to death."

"How did you get on the property?"

"Through the gates, once I put in the code, and I shut them behind me. Then I drove up that long drive. I thought when I got inside I could warm up." That admission was followed by a scoffing sound. "Sure, get in here, warm up. It's probably colder in here than it is outside." She extended her hand to him. "Speaking of cold, this floor is freezing. Can you help me get up?"

He reached to grasp her hand and helped leverage her to her feet. Once she was standing, she pulled free of his hold, but that didn't keep him from feeling how cold her hand had been. He was very aware of her height, not quite eye to eye with him, but a lot closer to it than most women he knew.

"Now, let me get this straight," he said. "You had access to the gate code somehow, and you came up here to break in?"

"I told you I didn't break in. I have the gate code, but I used the keys to open the door. I put them down somewhere and I was looking for them. I thought they might have fallen under that stupid rack that I tried to move and knocked over. The owner's attorney left the keys behind a pot on the porch, and he sent me a text with the gate code."

That took him back. "What attorney?"

"Mr. Burris Addison. He's the executor for my uncle's will, and he said that my uncle left this place to me. This lodge is mine…which, I guess, makes you the trespasser here."

So, the possible heir Burr had mentioned to him weeks ago had been found, and he was looking right at her. He couldn't see much of Marty in her beyond her height, but he knew Burr would have had her thoroughly vetted before giving her the key.

"Marty was your uncle?"

"His name was Martin Robert Bennet, but it seems he went by Martin Roberts around here."

"He went by Marty, not Martin, and although he was a good friend of mine, he never mentioned having any family."

She exhaled. "Then we're even. I never knew I had an uncle until a week ago."

His cell phone sounded again, and with one glance at the screen, he knew that Lillian had counted down the fifteen minutes from his last call. When he connected, she immediately asked, "What do you need to tell me, cowboy?"

He rattled off his army serial number to let her know he was in a safe situation. "I'm inside here and everything's under control."

That wasn't enough of an explanation for her. "Who or what did you find in there?"

He kept his eyes on Marianna Grace Bennet, who never looked away from him. "I found Marty's heir, a niece."

"Oh, my goodness," Lillian said. "So, he did have family?"

"It looks that way."

"Tell me you didn't draw your gun on her."

"We're both in one piece. Burr apparently forgot to mention he'd found her and—"

Grace cut him off. "He wasn't expecting me until the beginning of next week. I'm early."

Lillian obviously heard that explanation. "I'll give him a call and let him know she's already at the Lodge."

"Aces," Max said.

"Are you coming here or heading home when you finish?" Lillian asked.

It looked like he was going to be sleeping on the cot at the substation since Ms. Bennet appeared to be staying at the Lodge overnight. "I'll be going to the station," he said.

"Okay, just one last question. There was a rerouted emergency call from an unknown number that was cleared. What was that about?"

"That was a mistake."

"Okay. Safe ride, cowboy," she said and hung up.

Max put his phone away and found a smile for the woman in front of him. "Ms. Bennet, I want to officially welcome you to Eclipse and the Split Creek Lodge. People around here just call it the Lodge—capital *L*—or Marty's place."

GRACE NEVER LOOKED away from the sheriff, a tall man who didn't look much like the law, except for what she saw when his jacket was open. His deep brown hair was trimmed and combed straight back from strong features and dark hazel eyes. His black jeans were faded, and his Western boots were scuffed and dusty. She caught the cowboy vibe he gave off, even if there was no fancy Stetson in sight.

"Thank you," she said and looked down at the messy floor. "I went into town first to see about a hotel or a room of some sort. Everything was pretty much shut down except a place called the Golden Fleece Saloon. I figured there wouldn't be any rooms available there."

"You figured right. Everything shuts down early around here."

"I guess I'm stuck here at least for tonight." Even keeping her jacket on hadn't made her a speck warmer. Her sandals were the worst; her feet were so cold she expected them to turn blue any second.

The sheriff's phone rang again, and he pulled it back out. "What now, Lil?" He nodded, said, "I'll pass it on to her," then put his phone away. "Lillian called Burr, and he'd like you to come into town in the morning and meet up with him at his office. He'll be there from nine until noon."

"Good grief. This Lillian person called the attorney at midnight to tell him I was here?"

He shrugged. "Burr's up late all the time. The man never sleeps. I'm going to leave and get off your property, but I'd like to ask you something first."

"Of course."

"Why didn't you know about your uncle?"

She spontaneously shivered and wrapped her arms around herself. "My parents never told me my father had a brother who left before I was born." She shrugged, bitterness she couldn't shake caught in those words. "I don't even know why Uncle Martin walked away from the family. I sure can't ask him now, so it is what it is."

He nodded. "It sure is. So, you're okay staying here for the night?"

Finally, he'd asked exactly what she needed to talk about. "I will be, but it's freezing and the heaters I tried don't work. On top of that, a lot of the light bulbs are burned-out." She glanced up at the deer antler chandelier hanging from the high, heavily beamed ceiling over the desk. Only five bulbs out of a dozen were lit. "I like both light and heat."

He smiled ruefully. "Marty had a thing about not replacing light bulbs until he had no choice, and the heaters are useless without fuel. The propane tanks were shut down a few months ago, and the earliest you can get a propane delivery is tomorrow, if you're lucky. The water pipes are wrapped, so you should have water."

She glanced through the archway into the shadowy room beyond it, where she could make out a massive see-through fireplace in the middle of the space. If it was safe to use, it could be her answer for heat. Before she could ask the sheriff if it worked, he made her an unexpected offer.

"Listen, I live just north of here, and we have plenty of room at the family ranch. You're welcome to stay there for a couple of nights until you can get this place livable."

That had come out of the blue. She'd been brought up in Las Vegas in a penthouse on the top floor of the first hotel and casino her father had built, and this was way too small-town for her. The man seemed nice enough now that he knew she wasn't a burglar, but going to his house wasn't an option. He was still a stranger, sheriff or not, and she couldn't trust him like that.

"Don't take this personally, but I don't know you and you don't know me, so I'll stay here and hope the fireplace in that big room works. You go home to your family. I'll be just fine here."

"I guess there isn't any point in telling you that Marty and I were close friends and he'd vouch for me, since you know nothing about your uncle."

She sure didn't. "Yeah, that wouldn't impress me," she said with bit of a smile. "The fireplace does work, doesn't it?"

"Yep, it does, and it gives off good heat. But it won't heat more than one room."

That was good news. "That's all I need. I can sleep in there, and even if half the bulbs are burned-out, there'll be light. I'd imagine there's a couch in there somewhere under those dust sheets."

"There are big sectionals in there that face either side of the hearth."

"That's great," she said. "And thank you for the offer. I'm kind of surprised with you being a cop and all, that you'd take a stranger into your home with a wife and kids there."

He shook his head. "I'm not—"

She cut him off. "I'm sorry. I didn't think that through before I said it out loud."

He shrugged. "No problem."

She had a thought, maybe a better idea for where she'd spend the night. "Did Uncle Martin live in this building, or did he have a place off-site? Maybe a house close by?"

"Marty lived behind the desk."

"He what?"

"In his living quarters, a room behind the desk at the back," the sheriff said, gesturing. "That way he would always be close by to greet guests when they came in, especially those who showed up well beyond check-in time. He never wanted guests to feel they were imposing on him."

Grace turned to look past the desk that butted up against the side wall by the archway and stopped at a wide hallway on the other side of it. A large-faced clock that had stopped at three o'clock sometime in the past was hung beside an old-fashioned cubbyhole structure with room keys dangling under the room numbers. A closed door to the right of that had a brass plaque on it: "Office. Ring

Bell for Assistance." She hadn't noticed that before. "He lived in his office?"

"Technically, I guess you could say that, but the office is only part of what's back there. It's more like a studio apartment with a kitchenette, sleeping area and double doors that lead out onto a raised deck." As if he knew she was thinking about staying in there, he said, "There's lights in there, but no fuel for the heater."

She shrugged that away. "Then I'll stick with the couch for tonight."

"Come on and I'll get the fire going for you before I leave," he said as he turned and started toward the archway. Grace hurried after him, forgetting all about the brochures scattered on the floor until her foot slipped on one. She frantically reached out and managed to grab the edge of the desk with one hand—relieved until her grip failed and she lost her footing completely. In a blur she was falling until she wasn't because the sheriff had caught her under her arms before she hit the floor. As she found her footing, he let her go and they stood facing each other.

"Wow, I didn't expect that," she said. "Thank you. I don't fall, not usually, but…" She frowned at the brochures under their feet. "Those pamphlets are slippery."

"Are you okay?"

She was embarrassed and tired. Her right wrist stung from hitting something, most likely the edge of the desk, but for some reason she found herself able to smile ruefully at the big man. "I'm fine, unless embarrassment's fatal. It isn't, is it?"

His expression morphed into a crooked grin. "Not that I know of."

"That's a relief." She crouched down and started picking up the leaflets as quickly as she could while the sheriff righted the metal rack. Then he hunkered down by her and started gathering up the scattered travel brochures along with her.

"You don't need to do that," Grace said. "This is all my fault. I can do it myself."

"It's not a problem," he murmured as he slipped the brochures he'd already picked up into one of the empty rack pockets.

Grace put those she'd retrieved in another pocket as she asked, "What do people call you besides Sheriff?"

He was starting to make another stack. "My name's Max."

"Okay, Max, can you describe Mr. Burris Addison for me?"

He kept clearing the floor. "Well, he's about five-ten or eleven, midsixties, partial to flannel shirts, jeans and boots. Got a full head of hair that's been gray for as long as I've known him."

She liked what he was telling her, but that wasn't what she really needed to know. "What about his character?"

"He's exceptionally good at what he does. He genuinely likes people, and he makes himself available at any time." More brochures went into another pocket. "You can trust him to do right by you."

"He sounds almost too good to be true. Most attorneys I've known I wouldn't trust with anything except to do whatever it takes to win." She really disliked her father's head counsel, Fredrick Moore. The man reveled in reducing his opponents to rubble.

"Well, Burr's for real. An honest man who chooses his battles, in and out of court," Max said as he straightened and put the last of the brochures where they belonged. He towered over her. "I'll put the rack back."

As he pushed the now full rack into the corner where the desk met the sidewall, Grace said, "Thank you."

He turned, headed to the archway and disappeared into the shadowy space beyond. A moment later, lights flashed on overhead, and what bulbs hadn't burned out in the massive wagon-wheel fixtures hanging from the ceiling gave off enough light for her to be fine.

When she stepped into the great room, Max was standing in front of the massive stone fireplace. Crouching down to open the screen on their side, he said, "Marty always kept split logs and kindling in here, so you're in luck. You've got fuel for more than a few fires."

Grace saw what he meant. A large square niche cut into the rock face was stacked neatly with logs and kindling. "Please, Max, I'll do that. I'm really good at making a fire, and you need to get home. You said you were tired."

He glanced up at her and motioned to the covered furniture beside her. "That's the couch under there. It's good for sleeping on—I've done it before." He turned back to the hearth as if he hadn't heard what she said about the fire-making and reached for two logs.

She didn't like that, him taking over and telling her how things would be. It reminded her too much of the way her father played at being a father: telling her what she needed, what she wanted and how he'd make it happen. "Honestly, I can make the fire."

"Of course you can. It's not brain surgery," he said without looking back at her.

Well, I guess that's that, then. Short of being rude and telling him to leave, he'd be making the fire. She moved to reach for the dust cover and tugged on the corner, and the sheet slid off onto the floor exposing a black leather sectional couch. It wasn't old and saggy as she had expected it to be, and the long center section looked as if she'd be able to stretch out on it comfortably. It was definitely do-able for the night with the fire to keep her cozy.

Max spoke while he laid the logs in the hearth along with kindling. "If you didn't already bring your things inside, why don't you go and get them while I try to get it warmed up in here."

The man was just trying to be helpful, but he was getting on her nerves issuing orders. She wished she wasn't getting edgy from it. She picked up the dust sheet and tossed it to the far end of the couch. "I'm glad Uncle Martin kept wood in here for the fire. I would have hated to have to break apart the furniture to burn for heat."

Grace was surprised when Max stood abruptly and turned to her, frowning. "You were going to chop up the furniture?"

"Oh, no. I was kidding, just kidding," she assured him quickly. "Sorry."

He shrugged it off. "Forget it. It's been a long day."

"I guess breaking up any of this furniture and burning it would be a felony."

"No. This is all yours, so legally you could grind it up into sawdust if you wanted to, but that'd be a real shame. Most of the wood furniture in here and in the rest of the Lodge was handmade by Marty. This building isn't the only thing he left to you. It's everything he had in his world, really."

The impact of that statement blindsided Grace. She'd been so wound up from the meeting with her father and the decision to come to Wyoming on her own, that it overrode everything else. Now she faced the reality that the man who had left her everything he'd valued in his life hadn't tried to contact her while he was still alive. "He was a furniture maker?"

"Among his many gifts," Max said as he turned and crouched by the hearth. He struck a match, and moments later there was a pop and the first flame leapt to life. "He made my dad a chess table, a duplicate of the one he'd made for himself."

She didn't think her dad had ever made anything with his own hands. All he did was sign contracts and boost his bottom line. The fire was obviously all the sheriff's, so she headed toward the door. "I'll get my things," she said.

By the time Grace brought her luggage inside, Max had the fire roaring, its heat starting to defeat the cold. He was staring down into the leaping flames with his back to her. Grace moved over beside him to hold her hands out to the lovely warmth and sighed with pleasure. "That feels wonderful."

He seemed startled when she spoke, as if he'd forgotten she was even there. "What?" he asked as he turned toward her.

"I just said the heat feels so good. Thank you for making the fire even if I could have done it myself."

"So you said, and you're welcome," he said, then went to the far end of the fireplace and disappeared for a moment.

Grace heard a dragging sound then a solid click before Max came back into sight. "I closed the other side to send the heat in this direction." He went past her around the couch to a low bank of cabinets under the windows that took up the entire front length of the room. He opened up the first door and pulled out a couple of blue blankets and two pillows. He set them on the end section of the couch by the crumpled dust sheet. "There's more in there if you need them."

"Thanks," she said.

He pointed to a door on the other side of the room. "There's a bathroom through there to the left. It's small, but it's functional. Is there anything else I can do before I take off?"

When the fire flared and shot embers up into the chimney, Grace was close enough to see the tiredness in Max's eyes. She figured he really was a nice guy, probably with a beautiful wife and adorable kids and that's where he should be, not here doing what she could have done for herself. "I'm all set, thanks to you," she said. "I do have one more question. If I take a shower, will there be hot water?"

He grimaced slightly at that. "There won't be any hot water until you get the propane tanks filled. That can't happen until you call the propane company. Put that at the top of your list of things to do in the morning."

This man wasn't like any cop who had ever crossed her path before. "Is it part of your job description to aid and abet total strangers you come across in abandoned lodges while you're obviously dead tired?"

Max grinned. "I am tired, for sure, but you're one hundred percent within your rights to be here, and I'm being hospitable to an old friend's niece. You can get a long way in this town on the goodwill Marty Roberts built up here over the years."

She'd never heard her father spoken about like that. "I wish I'd met him, even just once." She bit her lip to stop saying any more. Her problems weren't his.

"He was worth knowing. In a way you'll get to know him by just being here and seeing the life he lived." He motioned vaguely around the space. "He loved this place, and when he got too sick, he had to shut it down and it broke his heart." He hesitated before he said, "I guess I should warn you that the same people who cared about Marty are expecting you to bring the Lodge back to life."

She'd assumed she'd sell once she found out what she wanted to know about her uncle. "You mean, they'll be angry with me if I sell it?"

"No, just disappointed. The Lodge has been a home of sorts for out-of-towners, even a few locals over the years.

There was an old-timer in town who lived in one of the rooms here after his wife passed. His name was Laz, and he was here for six years. It's a special place and sort of a landmark, too. I guess it's only natural to expect that they'd want Marty's only relative to pick up where he left off."

"I'm glad you warned me, but I'm here to take care of the estate before I head back to Tucson, where I live. I'm not here to take over this place and run it." When he frowned at her words, she quickly tried to explain it to him. "I mean, I inherited it out of the blue. I can't live here." She was still building her new life in Tucson piece by piece. "I'm sorry if that's not what you and the others would want from me, but I'll only be here for as long as it takes to put this up for sale."

He surprised her by passing that off with a shrug. "Well, you do what you need to do." Max pushed his hands into the pockets of his jacket. "When I was a kid the LeRoy-Toney family ran it. Then I came back from the army and Marty was here catering to new families and helping people who needed a break. This place was solid and peaceful, the same way Marty was."

There was no suggestion from the sheriff that her uncle had been any bit the "loser" her dad had claimed he was. That eased something in Grace, and she decided to ask Max a question that had come to her while he'd been talking. "Why don't you buy it and bring it back to its old glory? You obviously care about it so much."

She could tell she'd surprised him, but he didn't hesitate too long before he gave her his answer. "Maybe in another life I would have done just that, but my reality is working around the clock as sheriff. I'm up for reelection soon, and that's going to take up whatever downtime I might have had. Then there's my family and our ranch. There's always something that needs doing or some event to plan for. So, if anyone wants to resurrect this place, I'll help in any way I can, but it can't be me taking it over."

Grace knew it had been a long shot, but she was still disappointed. "I understand. Of course you have your life and family. It was just a thought."

"Okay, then," Max said. "Sleep well and stay warm."

Grace followed him to the front door and as he reached for the latch, she said, "It was nice meeting you, despite the way it happened."

He glanced back at her. "Nice meeting you, Ms. Bennet," he said.

"Please, call me Grace."

"Grace. You sure you don't need anything else?"

"Do you think Uncle Martin was happy here?"

He didn't look annoyed, but she didn't miss the slight sigh that came before his response. "Maybe *satisfied* is more the operative word. He took life as it came, you know, one day at a time, and it worked for him." He was doing up his jacket while he spoke. "Marty said once that he'd found the real Marty out here, the one who finally understood who he wanted to be—the man who rode the Split Creek land to ease his heart, and he said his past was what had made him appreciate what he'd found here."

The more she heard about her uncle, the more her regrets grew. "Thank you for telling me that," she said softly.

Max narrowed his eyes on her. "The propane," he said, totally out of context for her.

"Pardon?"

"Sorry, but as soon as you get up in the morning, call Van Duren Propane Services. Try to set up something for tomorrow. Don't forget," he said before he opened the door and stepped outside and closed it behind him.

The fact that he had to get in one last order before he left irritated her, but it was done. Max was heading back to his family, and as she heard his truck start up, she looked around at a strange place that seemed sad in its emptiness. The least she could do was leave it more welcoming to strangers. Kind of a tip of her hat to her uncle and how he'd welcomed strangers every day. The thought made her smile.

CHAPTER THREE

MAX WOKE IN his office at the substation just after dawn, a bit stiff from sleeping on the cot. Grace Bennet had been an unexpected midnight surprise, a woman who looked as if she could have been a model, tall and slender, and she'd be called beautiful by anyone with functional eyes—man or woman.

So, Marty hadn't been alone after all but apparently chose to make no contact with what family he'd had. Max didn't understand that, but then again, he didn't have to. Marty had to have had his reasons. All that mattered now was that Grace had shown up, even though Max held little to no hope she'd stick around.

He stood, stretched his arms over his head, then grabbed fresh clothes out of his locker and went into the small bathroom to shower. He needed to get ready for a planned meeting at the mayor's office, and he hoped a shower might just take the edge off him having only five hours of sleep. When he stepped out of the shower, feeling vaguely restored, there was a knock on the office door.

"Hey, cowboy," Lillian called through the barrier.

He was startled to hear Lillian was there after working so late the night before. "What are you doing here?"

"I forgot my wallet last night and came back to get it before making Clint's breakfast. Are you decent?"

"Nope, haven't been for a long time." Lillian laughed at his answer to the same question she always asked him when he was in the shower. It never got old for her. "Did you find your wallet?" he called back.

"Yep, but I was wondering how it went with Marty's niece."

He briskly dried off while he talked. "His niece slept over there last night. That's why I'm here trying to get my mind working again." He glanced in the small mirror over the sink and decided not to bother shaving.

"And?" Lillian nudged him for more information.

"She's going to see Burr this morning." He ran a towel roughly over his hair, then reached for his clean clothes and dressed quickly in black jeans along with a fresh beige uniform shirt. Lillian was standing not two feet from him when he opened the door.

"What does she look like? Is she nice? Does she have someone with her, a husband or kids or anything?"

"Hey, slow down. She's tall, black hair, violet eyes and I have no idea if she has a husband or kids. She came alone and didn't mention anyone joining her."

"Did you say *violet* eyes?"

"Her license says blue eyes, but they're a shade of violet."

"Call me surprised that you're making a distinction between a woman's eye color."

"They were just unique," he said.

Lillian, dressed in the beige shirt and black slacks she wore every day, crossed her arms over her ample chest. "Pretty?"

"This is not the time for this discussion. I'm due at Leo's office soon, and I'm foggy enough from sleep deprivation. But, yes, she's very pretty."

"Hmm, interesting," she said and kept asking questions. "How did she explain not being here for poor Marty all these years, especially toward the end?"

"Because she never knew she had an uncle," he said. "Seems her parents kept that from her for some reason."

"You tell her she'd better ask them why. Marty didn't deserve to be alone at the end when he had family."

"That's her business, not ours."

"What about the Lodge. Did she say what she plans to do with it?"

Max sat on the single chair in front of the corner desk to pull on his boots. "She indicated to me that she's only going to be here long enough to get the conditions of the will settled. When that's done, she'll head back to Arizona, where she came from."

"Oh, no," Lillian said on a groan. "We'll have to figure this out."

"There's nothing for us to figure out. It's all up to her, no matter what we'd like to see happen."

"I guess you're right, Max. But it wouldn't hurt to make her feel real welcome and let her see how much the Lodge means to people around here. If she's Marty's flesh and blood, she might just come around and stay."

He was almost certain—niece or no niece—Grace was going to leave sooner rather than later. "Who knows?" he said, barely covering a yawn. "I'm getting too old for double shifts and always being shorthanded."

"Nonsense, you're a kid," she said.

"On what planet does a thirty-seven-year-old pass for a kid?"

"You need time off, cowboy," she said. "You also need to have a life away from here."

He had a life, and after the election at the end of the month, that life would change completely if he lost. For now, he did what he needed to do and was thankful for his job. "You're starting to sound like my mom," he said.

"You ought to listen to your mother." He put on his

belt and holster before he walked with Lillian up to the front to get his hat and jacket and see her out to get back to her husband.

A call came in on the nonemergency line and Lillian took it. He was doing up his jacket when she finished the call. "Forget the meeting. Leo's youngest had a fall and broke his wrist. He'll reschedule for later this week."

So he got up at the crack of dawn for nothing. "Okay," he said, putting on his hat. "I'll head home, then. I'm craving Mom's huevos rancheros."

"Lucky you. Maybe drop in on Marty's niece today to make sure she's doing okay." The phone rang again, and Lillian took it. She smiled, then simply said, "On my way." She turned to Max. "Clint's hungry," she explained. "I'll be back around nine." Then she left.

ONCE MAX WAS in the pickup heading home with the heater blasting full force, he considered Lillian's suggestion. He would check in on Grace on his way back from the ranch before he went down to Two Horns for his shift. When he was barely a mile from town, his attention was caught by someone walking on the gravel shoulder of the highway with their back to the traffic. Not a smart move, even on a highway that wasn't usually busy. A car could be coming right at them, and they wouldn't know it until it was too late.

He slowed, then realized the not-so-smart pedestrian was Grace Bennet, her dark hair blowing back in the breeze. She was wearing her motorcycle jacket and jeans and was seemingly staring at her feet as she walked briskly. Thankfully, she had on bright red running shoes instead of sandals today.

He eased onto the shoulder, checked that it was safe to do a U-turn and pulled up behind her, then tapped his horn to get her attention. She stopped abruptly about a car's length from the truck and turned. He motioned her toward the passenger door to keep her away from the passing vehicles.

She jogged over as he slid down the window. "What's going on?" he asked.

She smiled in at him, her cheeks rosy from the cold. "I'm walking as fast as I can to get to town. It's freezing outside!"

"Is there something wrong with your Jeep?" he asked.

She groaned. "I hate to admit this, but after you left I went back out to the Jeep to get the charger for my cell phone, and I couldn't find it. So, I went inside, and the charger was in my bag, but my phone wasn't in my pocket or anywhere I looked for it, but eventually I just gave up. Anyway, I accidentally left the key in the ignition after I'd used the interior light to hunt for my charger. My Jeep doesn't warn you when the door's open and the key's still in the ignition." She turned both hands palms up. "So, no car. I knew the town couldn't be too far and I could walk to it, then get a burner phone and call a taxi or use Uber to get back to the Lodge after I met with Burris Addison. I didn't want to be late."

She jumped when a bright red muscle car zoomed by, shaking the truck in its wake. "The town is 2.1 miles from the Lodge," Max told her.

Her shrug was breezy. "Not a problem. I do more than that in the gym most days." She shivered. "I have to admit, though—it's a lot balmier in the gym than it is out here!"

"Climb in and get warmed up," he said.

She shook her head. "Oh, no, I can't keep you from your appointed rounds. The walk will do me good."

"That's the Postal Service motto. But I'm not asking, I'm *telling* you to get in here."

Her smile died at his tone. "Is this, like, a police order?"

"I protect and serve, and I'm protecting you. We not only don't want people walking on the side of the highway unless it's an emergency, but there are laws against performing dangerous actions while walking on a major thoroughfare."

"Dangerous… What are you talking about? I was doing fine."

"You were walking with your back to oncoming traffic, so you'll never know a car's coming at you until it hits you."

"So, what's the penalty?"

"No penalty. Just please get in."

She still didn't move as he unlocked the passenger door for her. Then she finally said, "Okay, fine," as she opened the door, stepped up into the cab and settled back to do up her seat belt.

Before he drove back onto the highway, he took his phone out of the charging slot on the console. "There's a local mechanic who's really great with cars, Henry Lodge. Let me call him and put him on speaker."

"Can't you give me a jump start?" she asked.

"That Jeep of yours is pretty old, isn't it?"

"It's a 1982 Renegade."

"I gave an old truck a jump start last year and totally fried the wiring. I really don't want to be sued for killing your Jeep."

"I wouldn't sue you, but I'd be pretty ticked off," she said on a soft laugh that he found he liked a lot more than the frown she'd given him moments before.

"We don't want that," he said. "If Henry says I can jump start it safely, problem solved."

Max put in the call, and Henry Lodge's deep voice came

over the speaker. "Max, I'm on a job by the mill, so if you need help, you'll have to check in with Donny Boudreaux."

"I don't need that, Henry. This is about a dead battery, but it's in an older vehicle, and I'm worried about trying to jump it in case I fry the wiring the way I did with Kenny's old truck."

"What's the year, make and model?"

"The owner's on this call. She can give you the details."

Grace gave him the information and explained the situation.

"I don't think you should take the risk of trying to jump it," Henry replied.

"So how soon can you get over to the Lodge to figure it out for Grace?"

"I could maybe meet up with her around two."

Max glanced at Grace, who nodded her approval. "Okay, two it is."

After Max put his phone back in the charging slot, he pulled back onto the highway. "So, I said I wasn't going to issue you a ticket, but I was serious when I told you it was against the law to be hitchhiking on the side of the highway."

"Hitchhiking? I wasn't hitchhiking," she said. "I didn't have my thumb out, and I didn't ask you to stop."

"No, but you had no idea if any cars were coming that could have easily swerved and hit you. Protect and serve. I swore to do that six years ago."

"Okay, I get that, and I won't do it again. Just drop me here," she said at the town limits. "I have to point out that there are no cars around us." She twisted to look behind them. "Just one truck waaaaaaaaaay back in the other lane."

He kept driving. Burr's office was five blocks ahead on the left side. "Okay, point taken."

"So, can you stop and let me out now?" she asked, her gaze burning a hole into the side of his face.

"Of course," he conceded and slowed, and kind of wished there were at least a few cars coming toward them. But the street was almost empty as he cut across and slipped nose first into a parking space right in front of the attorney's office.

He left the truck idling and turned to Grace halfway. "You're here. There's no ticket and I apologize for lecturing you. If you ever have to walk on the highway again, face the traffic."

SHERIFF MAX DONOVAN sure knew how to annoy Grace, but she found she couldn't work up any anger toward him. "Oh, I'll remember. I guess I should thank you for bringing me here."

"You don't have to thank me," he said when she looked over at him. His expression had softened and there was a teasing glint in his hazel eyes. "But it's nice to be appreciated once in a while."

He certainly didn't resemble any of the police she'd dealt with over the years. And for whatever reason, she was having trouble holding on to being annoyed by him. Instead, she found herself almost smiling. She'd been nervous about facing the attorney, actually hoping the hike into town would help settle her. But Max had distracted her to the point that she'd forgotten about the meeting.

"Then, thank you again," she said as she looked at him, realizing his cowboy image was complete now that he was wearing a real Western hat, black with a band of braided leather around the crown, along with black jeans and his jacket. "I won't bother you again. I can figure things out from here."

All he said was, "It's no bother."

Grace looked around at the town from where she sat comfortably in the warmth coming out of the truck's vents. The stores lining the main street were eclectic, from a gourmet chocolate shop to one that specialized in Western wear. There were only a few cars around, along with a man on a horse coming from the opposite direction toward them.

She was delaying going inside, and she realized why. She was worried about the reaction she'd get when the attorney found out she wanted to sell the Lodge. Hopefully he wouldn't hate her.

Just when she was about to open the door, Max spoke up. "You obviously couldn't have called for propane this morning, so you really should do that now." He picked up his cell phone and scrolled through his contacts before he handed it over to her. "That's the number for the propane company. Make sure you let whoever you talk to know that you're Marty's niece."

"I… I… Yes, of course," she said, and took the phone from Max. She looked down at the screen and the name that went with the contact's phone number. "Little Albert?" she asked. "Is he tiny? Or just short? Or really skinny or really fat?"

"He's big and strong and irritating as heck. He's little because he's the son of Albert Van Duren Sr., who's called Big Albert. The truth is I beat out Big Albert for sheriff six years ago, and he's running against me this election. He's serious about kicking me out. So, don't mention me when you call, just Marty."

"Okay," she said, her head swimming a bit from all the information. She made the call and by the time she got through and dropped her uncle Martin's name, Little Albert had given her a slot for line maintenance and tank servicing at four o'clock. When she ended the call, she looked at Max. "Okay, four o'clock sharp. Little Albert said and I quote, 'I'd do anything for Marty's family.' So I'm all set as long as I'm back at the Lodge by two for the mechanic, then four to meet Little Albert."

"Please, forget you ever heard that nickname from me," Max said while the truck still idled.

"Of course. What's said in this truck, stays in this truck."

He grinned at her. "You bet."

"Cool," Grace said as she opened the door and got out. She swung it shut, but not before she heard Max's quiet chuckle behind her.

MAX HAD BEEN right about Burr Addison being good at what he did. But he'd failed to mention the attorney was a bear of a man with an impressive mustache that he slowly stroked with his forefinger as he listened to her. His office had a set of steer horns on the wall behind where he sat and a golden horseshoe lying on top of a stack of folders in front of him. After he'd gone over the section of the will that mentioned Grace, he settled back in his chair, a touch of sadness in his blue eyes.

"Marty did things his own way, so I can't give you your copy of the will until I take care of some loose ends. When that's done, I'll give you the full version and get the grant deed finalized in your name. I'm sorry for any delay."

"That's okay," she said. "You knew my uncle well?"

"He was a good friend. I met him just after I came down from Montana and set up this office. He'd been here three or four months and was just starting on renovating the Lodge."

"I don't know much about my uncle. Actually, I just know what the sheriff's told me."

Burr smiled at her. "Let me contribute a totally ran-

dom story about Marty. Ten years ago he won a contest to
rename Tipsy's Pool Emporium. They wanted to change
the name of their business and held a contest to see who
could come up with the best one. Marty won with One Q-
Ball. Clever, huh?"

"That's a great name. What did he win?" she asked.

"A custom pool cue complete with a leather case. Also,
a free game every day for a year and no entry fees for tournaments in perpetuity."

She was fascinated by what he was telling her. "Was he
a pool shark or something?"

There was a twinkle in Burr's blue eyes now as he
stroked his mustache. "With all due respect to Marty, honestly, he was horrible, the worst. I can't tell you how many
times he'd sink the cue ball on the break." Burr looked almost wistful. "But he loved playing. No matter what Marty
did, he had fun."

The more she heard about her uncle, the more she knew
he and his brother had to have been polar opposites. Walter
Bennet's definition of fun was making money and spar-
ring with his opponents in the business world. "He sounds
like a great guy."

"He was indeed." Burr sat back. "You come on up to the
diner sometime and we'll talk some more about Marty."

Grace had no idea she was tearing up until Burr passed
a box of tissues over to her. Grateful, she took a couple
and wiped her eyes. "I wish that I could have helped him
when he needed it."

"If wishes were horses…" Burr said on a deep sigh.
"But you're here now, and you're getting to see where he
lived and where he built a good life."

"Do you know why he left the Lodge to me and not to
someone else, like Max?"

"I don't try to second-guess my clients. Besides, Max

has his own life. He's doing well as sheriff, and he has his family and the ranch to consider. He couldn't run the Lodge, too. Logic says he left it to you because you were all the family Marty had. Now, you take all the time you need to decide what you're going to do with the Lodge. Whatever you decide, whether you decide to keep it or sell it, I'll be there to help."

Max had been right. Burr Addison was making the whole process as easy on her as possible. She definitely felt that she could trust him. "Thank you so much."

A rap sounded on the door and Burr called out, "Come in!"

The door swung open, and Max was there. "Hey, Burr, I don't mean to break up your meeting," he said from the doorway, "but Anna called and told me you wanted to talk to me. I'll just wait outside until you're done." He looked at Grace. "Sorry for intruding."

"Hold on there, Max," Burr said. "We're pretty much done here, and I won't keep you more than a few minutes."

Grace stood. "I'll leave and let you and the sheriff do your business."

She hitched the strap of her purse over her shoulder, ready to leave, but Burr stopped her. "I actually need to talk to the both of you together."

She slowly sat back down, glancing at Max, who hadn't moved. "What's this about, Burr?" he asked.

Burr leaned forward and picked up two blue envelopes that were beside his folders, then stood and came around the desk and held out an envelope to each of them. "Marty left directions that after you two had the chance to meet, I was to hand these to you."

Grace took hers and looked down at her first name written on it by an unsteady hand. "Thank you," she said and pushed it into her purse before turning to Max, who was staring down at his.

He took a breath, then asked, "Do you know what this is?"

Burr shook his head. "I don't. Marty just stipulated when I was to give them to you. Why don't you two go down to the diner and grab an early lunch and maybe figure this out between the two of you? My treat. Just tell Elaine I sent you."

Max turned to Grace. "If you want to go, we should get there before the noon rush takes over."

The lure of the blue envelope and Max maybe being able to clear up why they each had one made her agree. Besides, she was starving.

"Okay," she said and watched him push his envelope into his jacket pocket.

When they were outside, Max started down the stairs toward his truck and Grace followed, then climbed in on the passenger side. As they pulled onto the main street, she looked over at him. "You don't have a guess as to what the letters are about?"

He exhaled. "Not any more than you do. I don't want to open mine at the restaurant, but you can open yours if you want when we get there, and we can discuss it, I guess."

She didn't particularly want to open it with people around. "No, I think I'll wait, too."

Within minutes, they were pulling into a parking space in front of the Over the Moon Diner. After he shut down the engine, Max turned to Grace. "You need to know that Marty never did anything without a clear reason behind it."

"Did he like to meddle?"

"Not really. He was always up for a good conversation and liked to debate things. He talked me through something around three years ago, but not by meddling—he was just helping me."

He stopped her from asking any questions she might have wanted to ask him by saying, "I'll make this easy. If you don't want to go to lunch, just say so."

Oddly, she didn't want to be alone right then. And there was little to no food back at the Lodge. "I'm starving."

"Then you're at the right place. Their food truly is over the moon," he said.

"Cool," she said as she opened her door and stepped out, then went around to meet Max at the front of the truck. His hazel eyes met hers, and he gave a crooked grin. "Way cool," he said then started up the stairs. Grace smiled to herself as she followed him.

CHAPTER FOUR

MAX HAD BEEN eating at the Over the Moon Diner for as long as he could remember. When he was around seven, he helped his mom deliver handmade tamales and salsa to the original owner, Elaine's father. Even though that had been thirty years ago, when he stepped inside with Grace by his side, he almost felt as if it was his first time setting foot in the place.

The red-and-white-checked tablecloths matched the uniform shirts worn by the servers. The booths that lined most of the walls had red Formica tops and black faux leather seats. A photo wall opposite the front windows included black-and-whites of lunar and solar eclipses, along with stunning color photographs of meteor showers labeled "Flaming Skies." The place had the vibe of a 1950s diner and Burr's wife, Elaine, ran it with friendly ease.

When she spotted them, the petite woman with silver curls came over and greeted them with a bright smile. "Welcome, welcome! Burr just called and told me to expect y'all." She looked at Grace, her smile fading as sympathy showed in her eyes. "I'm deeply sorry Marty's gone. He's really missed around here in so many ways."

"Thank you," Grace said. "It makes me feel better to know that he wasn't alone here."

"Oh, he sure wasn't," she said. "That man was a real people person." She glanced at Max, then said, "You two sit wherever you want."

The diner was about half-full and country music played in the background. "Table or booth?" Max asked Grace.

She scanned the room, then turned to Max. "Whatever you prefer."

Elaine pointed to the booth by the door. "Your regular booth is available, Max, if y'all want to sit there."

"Sounds good to me," Grace said and crossed to slide in with her back to the door. Max sat across from her. "You can watch the world go by out the window and catch any lawbreakers," she teased.

Elaine smiled at that. "Now, I already know what the good sheriff wants, but what can I get you to drink?" she asked Grace.

Grace ordered tea, and after Elaine disappeared back into the kitchen, she reached for the menu. "What's good here?" she asked Max.

"Honestly, everything," Max said. "I usually just get the breakfast special."

"'Two eggs, bacon or sausage, a side of home fries and toast'?" Grace read out loud. "Sounds delicious," she said, then put the menu back in its metal stand.

"How did it go with Burr?" Max asked her.

"Great," Grace said. When Max raised his eyebrows, she amended, "I really like Burr. He's pretty awesome, actually."

"Never tell him that," Max said, shaking his head, a smile playing at the corner of his lips.

Elaine returned with Max's coffee and Grace's tea. "Never tell who what?" she asked.

"Never tell your husband that he's awesome," Max said.

"Oh, I tell him that he's awesome all the time," Elaine said, chuckling.

"Oh, you two are married?" Grace asked.

"Yes we are, and Burr is well aware of his awesomeness. Now, have you two decided what you'd like to order?"

After they'd relayed their breakfast special preferences, Grace studied the wall opposite their booth. "Are those photographs of meteor showers from around here? They look incredible."

"Yeah. I've learned to love them, but dang, they sure used to scare me when I was little," Max said.

Grace leaned back to look across the table at him. "It could be scary, I guess. All I've seen are a few shooting stars, but nothing close to that kind of a show."

"Up at the original Donovan ranch my grandpa built in the high foothills before the family moved down to the bigger property in the valley, we used to watch them all the time. The old ranch is still the place to watch meteor showers. You feel as if you're in the middle of a firestorm, or the most amazing pyrotechnic display ever. Back when I was in my teens, that was *the* place for a guy to take a date."

Elaine came with their food, and Grace ignored the heaping plate of scrambled eggs, bacon and potatoes as she cocked her head and eyed Max. "So, who did you take to watch the meteor showers?"

"A girl I was dating in high school. I just remember it being freezing cold. Meteor showers are at their best from December to January. Although sometimes they show up earlier or later."

"But was it romantic?"

He shrugged, not much wanting to talk about those nights. "Yeah, some, but it was hard to do anything when all of my family and neighbors were right there."

She smiled. "I bet that was awkward."

He hadn't thought about those nights for a very long time. The world had been so different back then. He'd been so different. "Yeah, it sure was," he said and nodded toward her food. "I thought you were starving."

"Yes, yes, I am." She picked up her fork and speared a home fry. She chewed and swallowed then smiled over at him. "Good, very good."

They ate in silence for a while and then she asked Max, "Did Uncle Martin go watch the meteor showers?"

"Most of the time he viewed them from his back deck at the Lodge, but he'd come up to the old ranch, too."

"Can I ask you something a bit personal about him?"

"I guess so," he said with a touch of discomfort. There were a lot of things Marty and he talked about that they both understood would remain between them.

"Did Uncle Martin bring dates up there? I mean, was there, you know, any special woman in his life? I don't even know if he was ever married." Max watched a faint blush creep over her cheeks.

He could answer that. "He dated once in a while, but none of the women stuck around. Before I came back from the army, I heard he was dating a woman named Angie. Some thought they were serious, but I never met her."

"What happened to her?"

"I don't know. He never mentioned her to me, so I didn't ask."

"There was no one else?"

"No marriage as far as I know, but he told me he'd once found a woman he thought he could love. Unfortunately, it didn't work out."

"What did he say about his life before he came here?"

They'd joked about their talks being like therapy for both of them. For Max, there had been real truth in that, and one of those talks had led him to running for sheriff at Marty's urging. But all Max understood about Marty's past was that whatever had happened before had been painful for him, and that he'd had an alcohol problem that almost destroyed him. He never went further than admitting to that.

"Not a lot," he said in response to Grace's question. "I got the impression he had it rough, but the Marty I knew wasn't a complainer, and he wasn't a man who looked back very often. He lived in the moment."

"He…never talked about any family?"

Max knew what he could share that might help Grace. "Marty told me that about twenty years ago, he was driving through on his way up north to Montana and stopped at the Lodge for the night. When he woke the next morning and saw the view from the Lodge in the light of day, he knew he didn't want to leave. He loved to joke that he checked in, but he didn't check out."

"So buying the Lodge was an impulse?"

"Maybe. The owners were thinking of selling, and he made them an offer right there and then. If it helps, he told me he never once regretted coming here and staying, but he did regret past things that he couldn't fix."

Grace reached for her mug to have a drink of tea, then changed subjects abruptly. "Burr's so nice. He treated me as if I was a friend."

He smiled at that. "People around here are friendly, and they help each other."

"That's small-town stuff, isn't it?"

"It's the way it is. I remember when I was maybe ten years old and a neighbor's barn burned down. All the locals showed up to help him rebuild. The first day, they'd cleaned up and finished the framework. The next day they came back and finished the outer walls and the roof." That was the day he'd noticed Freeman Lee's daughter, Claire, for the first time. He hadn't thought about that for what seemed like forever, and he was mad at himself for remembering. "They soon had their barn fully back."

Her violet eyes widened slightly. "I've never known anyone who was at a real barn raising."

"You do now. It was fun until I started showing off my roping skills on a fence post and ended up pulling down a small section of Freeman's back perimeter fencing." Claire had hurried over to help him push the post back in the ground. Another memory. He finished his coffee, then added, "The moral of that little story is, if you need help, ask."

"Speaking of help," Grace said, "I appreciate everything you've done for me, but I'm pretty good on my own once I'm up and running. I've already taken up way too much of your time."

"Well, I needed to eat, too," he said, reluctant to just finish up eating and drop her off at the Lodge. She needed exposure to the town and its people to appreciate what Marty gave her. Maybe it wouldn't make a difference in her selling and leaving, but he had to try. He owed Marty that much. "You mentioned you wouldn't be staying here too long. How long is not too long?"

"I don't know yet. Maybe a few weeks. I'm not sure how much time I can be away from work."

He'd never asked what she did in Tucson. "Work's calling?"

"Yes and no. I work at a combined consignment and coffee shop. I'm covered for now, but I don't want to push my luck and find out I don't have a job when I get home, either."

"Can I ask why you're here alone? Aren't your parents curious to see what you've inherited?"

Grace stared at him blankly for a minute, then said, "Oh, my parents, no, no... They...they're both gone."

Max hadn't expected that and found himself apologizing for bringing them up. "I shouldn't have asked. It's a side effect of my work, and I work too much. My social skills need attention. I apologize." She was too young to be alone like that, unless there was a boyfriend she hadn't mentioned.

"No apology needed. I was an only child, and my grandparents died before I was old enough to really know them. So it was just me and my parents. Then I… I found myself on my own, building a new life in Tucson."

"There's no other family?"

"No, not that I know of. Then again, I never knew I had an uncle."

She didn't look sad, but maybe a bit lost. "I'm sorry that's the way it's worked out for you."

"Me, too," she said.

"Since we're here, and you wanted to get that burner phone, why don't I show you around town on the way to the electronics store? I'll make sure you get back in time for Henry."

She looked down at her empty plate, and he could almost see her thinking of how to refuse his offer. "Sure," she said finally. "That would be great."

Elaine showed up right then, smiling as usual. "How was everything?"

"Very good," Grace said, "thank you." As Elaine began to clear their table, Grace slid out of the booth and stood up. "I'll be right back."

Max watched as she headed toward the short hallway that led to the restrooms. Before Elaine could take off, he caught her attention. "Can I talk to you for a minute?"

"What a coincidence," she said, pausing with the plates stacked on her arm. "I wanted to talk to you, too."

"About what?"

"Grace. The word is, she's going to sell the Lodge."

"She's figuring out what to do, but she probably will. She's got her own life in Arizona."

"If she's not sure…" Elaine leaned closer toward Max. "Maybe she can be persuaded to stick around and keep the Lodge."

"I hope she'll stay, but it's not up to me. It's her choice."

Elaine grinned at him. "How about you turning on the Donovan charm?"

"That ran out a long time back," he murmured. "But her feeling comfortable here wouldn't hurt."

She looked past his shoulder and nodded. "Sure glad you stopped by!" she said as Grace approached the table. "Maybe I could run out to see you sometime and show you around the kitchen at the Lodge. I did some cooking for Marty and filled in when he was short on help."

"That would be really nice of you," Grace said. "But I wouldn't want to take up your time."

"No worries. I own this place. I can take off any time I want to, and I'd love to talk to you more about Marty and the Lodge."

"I'd like that," Grace said.

"See you soon," Elaine said, then turned to cross to a table where a couple was just sitting down.

"Nice lady. As nice as her husband, it seems," Grace said as she settled into the booth again.

"Elaine was wondering what you've decided to do about the Lodge."

She glanced down at the table, then back at Max. "I haven't even been here a full twenty-four hours, so I don't have a clue, but I appreciate her offer to come out and show me what my uncle was doing out there. If I sell, I'll need all of that information to pass on to the new buyer."

"It couldn't hurt."

"I should freshen it up, but that means more time away from Tucson. If I just sell it as is, it's going to minimize how much I can get for it. Maybe the best I can do is find someone to buy it who wants to work on it and won't just tear it down." A sad smile touched her lips. "I'm pretty certain from what I've learned about him from you and Burr, Uncle Martin wouldn't have wanted the Lodge to be torn down to make room for some new development."

It took Max back that Grace understood what some people would want to do with the land. A large ranch in the area had almost been taken away from a family that had owned it for years by an underhanded development company. They wanted it to be split into luxury ranches. The Eclipse Ridge Ranch was safe now, but that didn't mean that developers wouldn't set their sights on the land the Lodge sat on. He knew they would, but he also knew now that Grace understood what Marty had wanted, even if she didn't stay. "Did Marty put any restrictions in the will on what you could do with the Lodge?" he asked.

"Oh, no, none. Maybe he mentioned something in the letter Burr gave me." He could see her eyes glisten slightly as if she was close to tears. She reached for her napkin, and he thought she was going to dab at her eyes, but she simply held it bunched in her hand and stared down at it. "I'm sorry. I just want to do the right thing."

"Hey," Max said. "It's okay. You might not have known Marty, but he was family." He added something that he'd found out the hard way. "They say you can't miss what you never had, but that's wrong. That can hurt more than anything."

She raised her eyes to meet his. Moisture clung to her dark lashes but didn't fall on her cheeks before she swiped it away with the napkin.

Max checked his watch. They had two hours before Grace needed to be back at the Lodge. "Ready to go?"

Grace put her purse over her shoulder and stood. "Yes."

Once outside, Max walked north on the raised sidewalk, intending to do a loop at the end before coming back to where he'd parked so Grace could get an overall look at the town. She walked to his right and seemed to be enjoying looking in the display windows of the shops. As they approached the town's consignment shop, Gabby's Vintage Treasures, Grace slowed, then stopped to look at the display. "Lovely," he heard her half whisper before she glanced at him. "I'd like to go in and look around. Professional curiosity."

"Go for it. When you're ready to head back to the Lodge, you can call me."

"I don't have a phone yet."

"You said you wanted a burner, so go back by Burr's and four doors down—there's an electronics shop. Herb can set you up for now. You can also ask him to tell you where the substation is so you can go there and ask a tiny lady with a huge smile and gray hair in a tight knot to contact me. Lillian always knows where I am."

"The famous Lillian. I'd love to meet her, but I can't pull you away from your work again."

"You can't walk back on the highway, either. Just call me. If you're late getting back in time for Henry, he'll leave for his next job."

"Okay, okay," she said reluctantly. "I don't have a number for you that isn't 911."

"Have Herb put in the nonemergency number for the station."

"Okay."

Right then, Gabby Brookes, the owner, came out onto the walkway. Gabby was in her midtwenties and given to wearing jeans and fussy tops that seemed to match the character of the Grand Lady B&B she ran out of a beautifully maintained Victorian house on River View Drive. She had opened the consignment shop a few months ago.

"Sheriff Max," Gabby said as she came toward them. "You haven't been in here since… Oh, I remember." She grinned at him. "Since never."

"I'd say that's about right." He grinned back and cleared his throat. "Gabby, meet Grace Bennet. She's Marty's niece. She's staying out at the Lodge."

"Oh, my gosh," Gabby said to Grace, her smile slipping. "I'm so sorry about Marty. I just loved him."

"Thank you," Grace said. "Your store looks lovely. I work at a consignment shop in Tucson."

Gabby moved closer, seemingly studying Grace's leather jacket. "Is that an authentic Harley-Davidson?"

"Yes! Would you believe I found it in a donation bag? The owner of the store wanted to tag it for fifty dollars. I told her I'd like to buy it. I felt guilty for a hot second, then thought that I'd never sell it, so it wasn't like I was going to make a five hundred percent profit on it or anything."

"What a find," Gabby said and touched the sleeve almost reverently. "It's in great shape. It must be from the sixties or early seventies."

"You've got a good eye—1968."

Gabby and Grace hit it off right away and Max took his leave. The time he'd had to kill earlier had been filled by Grace Bennet. She was pleasant, pretty determined not to bother anyone and had repeatedly declared that she could handle things on her own. He smiled to himself as he headed to the substation to get some paperwork out of the way. He couldn't help but think that despite her insistence that she could take care of herself, she could use a helping hand for the time that she was in Eclipse.

WHEN GRACE FINALLY left Gabby's shop, Gabby walked her out. She'd enjoyed her time talking business with Gabby and had given the other woman a few ideas to increase foot traffic for her store. She was pretty sure that if she wasn't leaving, she and Gabby would become good friends.

When she turned to say goodbye, Gabby surprised Grace by hugging her. "I'm so glad you stopped by here. It's fun to talk to someone who knows the business."

After they parted ways, Grace went down to the electronics store, and she left with a basic flip phone ready to use. She had asked Herb for the nonemergency number for the station, and he had put it and Max's cell number in the phone's contacts for her. Once out on the street she almost called Max but reconsidered. In spite of Max's warning, the Lodge was an easy two-mile walk from town, and she could be back in plenty of time for the mechanic. She crossed to the other side of the street, avoiding the only traffic—a kid on horseback—then started toward the highway.

She'd barely started walking on the southbound shoulder facing the traffic when she was startled by a blaring horn. She looked up and saw Max's white pickup slow down, then make a U-turn across the vacant lanes and pull in front of her. She felt guilty for being caught but was taken back when Max opened his door and yelled at her.

"Get in! Now!"

Everything in her wanted to dig in her heels and wave him off, but she got the feeling that the insistence in his voice wasn't just about her going against his orders; something else was happening. She approached the truck and climbed inside. "I was facing the traffic and staying back from the road. It wasn't—"

"We'll deal with that later," he said abruptly. "Buckle up."

"This is ridiculous," she said, only to have her words

cut off when he pulled across both lanes to head north and put on his siren and lights.

"Seat belt," he said over the noise.

"Yes, sir," she said tightly and did it up.

"Sorry, I'm on a call and didn't expect to see you on the highway again." He quickly explained about a possible sighting of the thieves who'd been looting ranches for irrigation equipment. A ranch hand had called in about two men who could be the culprits. "I'll drop you off at the Lodge."

"Oh, okay," she said, feeling just a bit foolish for her reaction to the man who was clearly doing her a favor. She smiled wryly and spoke loud enough to be heard over the noise around them. "I've always wanted to ride in a police car or a fire truck with the siren going and lights flashing."

They were quickly approaching the Lodge when Max slowed the truck and drove off the highway then came to a sharp stop in front of the gates. "Okay, out," he said.

"Yes, sir!" she said, unsnapping her belt.

WHEN GRACE WAS out of the truck, she turned to look in the open door at Max. "That was incredible!" she exclaimed, her eyes shining.

Max wouldn't have expected her to react like a kid, but it seemed as if she was completely over being angry with him and had thoroughly enjoyed the ride.

"Thanks, Max. Seriously, that was so cool!"

She shifted emotions so quickly; he felt a bit dizzy. "Dang, I was going for awesome," he said.

"Maybe next time you'll get there," she called over the siren's screech, then her smile faltered. "Stay safe," she said just before she pushed the door shut and went to open the gates.

After searching the area around the ranch where the

flatbed truck had been spotted, Max found two men parked near a culvert close to the sign for Wolf Bridge, eating sack lunches. They were from Montana and looking for work—not irrigation systems. After he checked them out, he let them go, then drove to headquarters in Two Horns to cover for Lawson, one of his deputies.

It was nearing six o'clock when he left. When he neared the Lodge, he spotted the Van Duren propane truck near the open gates, and he kept going. As he approached the town limits, he slowed and pulled off into the empty dirt parking lot adjacent to the Grange Hall, which had closed down months ago for renovation. Positioning himself where he had a clear view in both directions of the highway, he let the truck idle.

He took Marty's letter out of his pocket and stared at his name written on the front of it. Blowing out a breath, he carefully worked his forefinger under the sealed flap to get the letter out: a single sheet of lined paper with unsteady writing on both sides. As he read the note, he could almost hear Marty saying the words.

Max, my dear friend,
If you're reading this, I'm gone, but I couldn't leave without thanking you for being such a special part of my life and for all your help and support over the years. You always understood how important the Lodge was to me, giving me a life I never dared hoped for before arriving in Eclipse. A simple stop to rest from my wanderings for one night and I found my home.

You've done more for me than I could have ever have imagined, yet I find myself in the position of needing to ask one last favor of you. If a girl named Grace Bennet comes to town to see about the Lodge sometime in the future, I would appreciate it if you would do for her what you did for me and be her friend. If Grace does come, you'll understand why I'm asking you to be there when she needs you, to watch out for her and make sure she's on the right track with a friend by her side.

One thing I leave up to your discretion: Rebel. If Grace does show up and sticks around, I want her to have Rebel, but only if you think she'll really care for him. If not, please keep him at the Flaming Sky and tell him I miss him. You make that call.

If Grace never gets there, which is very possible, I've left Burr contingent instructions for the disposition of the land and buildings.

Have a wonderful life, my friend, and never live in the past. Face your life head-on and know the best is yet to come. Find your easy heart, and don't doubt yourself. I have never doubted you.
Marty

A sigh caught in his throat as he put the letter back in his pocket. "I'll do what I can for Grace and for you, Marty," he whispered into the space around him. He hoped against hope that Grace could be the right person to keep Marty's dreams alive one way or another.

His phone rang and a glance down at the screen showed a number that wasn't local. He answered it. "Sheriff Donovan."

"Hello, Sheriff Donovan. This is Grace Bennet."

CHAPTER FIVE

MAX HAD BEEN thinking about Grace since he dropped her off at the Lodge, and now she was calling him. He sat back, his eyes on the few cars passing by on the highway. "Is this a 911 call?"

"Well, no, I didn't dial 911. I got a phone and Herb put your cell number in it for me."

"Good. What can I do for you?"

"First, did everything work out okay on your emergency?"

"False alarm." He closed his eyes. "Did Henry get there?"

"Yes, right on time, but he couldn't fix it. He needed some parts he'll have to hunt down because the Jeep's older. He needs to rewire it and he said he'll be back tomorrow as soon as he has the parts."

"What about the propane?"

"Albert tested the tanks, filled them, got the furnace going, and I now have hot water and a stove that works. You won't believe what else he did." She didn't give him a chance to even guess. "He found my phone caught in a broken part of the desk's kick plate in reception. It must have flown out of my pocket and lodged there when I almost fell the second time. He also mentioned something about a dance celebrating the grand opening of the Grange Hall, and I thought he was going to ask me to go with him.

I don't even know what a Grange Hall is, and I sure as heck don't know him."

"Did he ask?"

Grace made a scoffing sound over the phone. "No, not directly. He just said something like he thought I'd have a great time there."

Max opened his eyes and glanced in the rearview mirror at the newly painted building some thirty feet behind him.

"He also talked about Uncle Martin and how he was a really nice guy. That made me happy—that and having heat and getting my phone back."

Max knew the truth about most people in the small town: the good, the bad and the ugly. He knew a lot about the ugly side of Albert Jr. as a kid in school, and about his marriage that he'd destroyed by cheating. Now he was going through a bad divorce. "I'm glad he got you heat in the Lodge."

"Me, too, and Henry said that the wiring only takes a couple of hours, so I should have transportation tomorrow. That's kind of what I called you for."

"What's that?"

"I totally forgot about needing food out here. Could you give me the number of a store that delivers groceries?"

Max could almost hear Marty's words from the letter. *I would appreciate it if you would do for her what you did for me and be her friend.* A friend would make sure Grace had food at the Lodge, even if there never had been an official food delivery service in town.

"Sorry, there isn't much of that around here, but tell you what, if you send me a list of what you need, I can go by the general store, get it filled and drop your order off on my way up to the ranch."

"Oh, gosh, no. I can't have the sheriff delivering my food when he's supposed to be out keeping the town safe. I have some cashew nuts, and there's hot water for a shower. I can survive until tomorrow."

"I'll have you know that I'm capable of doing more than just going after the bad guys. I can also catch runaway steers, help old ladies cross our busy streets, start fires when I need to, and I can deliver food."

Her laugh over the phone eased something in him that had felt heavy since reading Marty's letter.

"Wow, skills, huh?" Grace said.

"Unbelievable skills." He stopped that patter right there. "I wanted to come by there anyway, so I can kill two birds with one stone."

"Why?"

"To talk to you about that stunt you pulled today. So, text me what you need, and I'll see to it that you get it within an hour. How's that?"

She didn't like the idea of them "having a talk." She hesitated. "Okay. Can I give you my credit card number to pay for the food? I have a bit of cash, so if I keep the list short, I should have enough for a day or two until I can get to the bank."

"Don't worry about it. You can pay me then," he said.

He could tell she didn't want to do that or have him lecture her about her being back on the highway, but she finally caved.

"Okay, but I'll pay you as soon as I can get to town."

"Of course, and I know where you live so I can do a collection if I have to."

"I guess I can run, but I can't hide?"

"Nope. I'll see you soon."

AN HOUR LATER when Grace opened the front door, Max stood there, taller than she remembered, wearing his leather coat and black Stetson, and holding two full bags of groceries in his arms. He went past her to set the bags on the desk. "Farley didn't have those small jellybeans you wanted, so he put regular ones in the order, and he saw you wanted a coffee grind he's temporarily out of, so he substituted the grind Marty used to get. He didn't put it on the bill," he said as he handed her the receipt. "He said it's a housewarming gift, and if you don't like it, take it back and he'll find you one you'll love."

"That's sure nice of him," she said. "And thank you for making the delivery."

"No problem," he said.

"So, what do I do with the huge can of roasted cashews I found on top of the fridge?"

"Eat them. Marty loved them. His idea of the perfect afternoon was relaxing with a coffee and a bowl of cashews."

She loved learning that about her uncle, but her nerves were making her uncomfortable as she waited for Max to lecture her about walking on the highway after his firm warning not to do it again.

"I'll try that," she said, then found herself blurting out, "Max, I'll make this easier for both of us."

"Make what easier?"

"I owe you an apology for what I did today. I shouldn't have even thought about walking back here after you warned me not to, but I didn't want to take up more of your time, and it's not a long walk. I stayed well over on the shoulder and walked facing traffic."

He studied her, then shrugged. "I don't remember the last time someone apologized to me for doing something as utterly foolish as walking on the side of a highway and endangering themselves *and* the lives of others. I told you that the only time you should ever be doing that is in an emergency."

This was worse than she thought it would be. "For Pete's

sake, I wasn't robbing a bank. I just didn't want to bother you again and take you away from your work. Now I'm foolish?" she asked, accompanied by an eye roll.

Max took off his hat, laid it crown down on the desktop by the groceries, then instead of being mad at her, he picked up the bags. He looked at her then said in a very even voice, "If you're done confessing to your wrongdoing, how about we put these things away before the mint-chocolate-chip ice cream melts?"

"I apologized to you. I didn't confess anything," she said.

"Oh, I thought that's what you did. I was going to go easy on you because I didn't want to have to lock you up for ten days."

"What?" she gasped. "No, no, no, no. You can't do that. I apologized even though I don't believe that there's any law against trying to get home."

"Yes, you apologized, and I appreciate it. I don't get apologized to that often, you know. I'll just forget your confession and keep it between us, then you'll only get a ticket."

"That's not legal, is it?"

"No, it's not, and I wouldn't do it anyway. The truth is, you were stranded and refused to take my offer of a ride, which you ended up having to accept anyway. Being stubborn isn't breaking any law."

She exhaled. "Then why did you tell me all that in the first place?"

He broke out in a huge grin. "I'm sorry for making you sweat."

She reluctantly smiled back at him. "I don't sweat," she said, "I glow, and for what it's worth I only apologized so you wouldn't scold me first. You're so mean."

"That hurts something awful," he said, then laughed.

Grace stared at Max, knowing her face had to be beet red. He was teasing, and she fell for it. "That was all a joke, wasn't it?"

"Yeah, but a bad one. I apologize, really I do. I was going to talk to you about being stubborn and about not taking help from people. But I wanted to see how far you'd go apologizing. I let the rope out too far," he said, still holding the grocery bags. "Now that's over with, let's put this stuff away."

She followed him into the kitchen, which had surprised her when she'd seen it for the first time that morning. The appliances were all stainless steel and the refrigerator was huge. The dishwasher was a double—something she'd never seen before—and the stove had six burners and a central double grill. Max crossed to the counter by the fridge and pantry and put the contents of the bags away, then washed his hands in the extra wide farmhouse sink. An old microwave by the sink was the only thing that wasn't restaurant quality.

The rest was simple: white cupboards, dark wood floors and six windows along the back wall that overlooked the large deck and the land beyond. The dining room shared the same view from a table that looked as if it could seat sixteen people at least.

Max closed the fridge and turned to Grace. "If you're up for it, as a way of making up for my unfortunately horrible sense of humor, how about I make us breakfast for dinner, and add a cup of Uncle Martin's coffee?"

Before she could answer, his phone rang. "Hold on." He retrieved his cell from his pocket and glanced at the screen then took the call. "Hi there," he said, looking out the window over the sink at the view. "I'm in the middle of something."

He listened, then shrugged. "No, I'm off unless they really need me."

More listening before he said, "Okay, okay, I'll be there. Give me half an hour. Love you, too," he murmured, then stopped the call and put his phone away before he looked back at Grace. "I'll have to pass on dinner. I'm supposed to be back at the ranch, and I…" He exhaled. "I'm sorry."

Of course. She'd thought he was married, probably with kids, but even so, she was disappointed to find out it really was true. "It's got to be hard having a family and doing the job you do."

"Yes, it is," he said on a sigh. "You enjoy your dinner, and I'll head out." He grabbed his hat off the desktop on his way out.

She followed him back into the lobby. "I've told you I'm sorry for taking up your time. Would you please tell your wife that I won't do it again?"

That stopped him and he turned, his eyes narrowed on her. "What?"

"Your wife, or your significant other. I'm sorry I had you delivering my food when you were supposed to be at home."

He stared at her for a long moment, then he actually chuckled. "You're on the wrong end of that lasso."

"What does that mean?"

"I'm not married. My mom and dad are waiting for me."

"You aren't married?"

For some reason he frowned at that. "No."

She was surprised and a part of her was kind of pleased. "Oh, I assumed… I'm sorry. So, you live with your parents?"

He grimaced at her words. "Now that sounds bad, doesn't it, living with Mommy and Daddy at my age?"

"I didn't say that." She spoke quickly. "I was just asking."

He cut her off, holding up his hand as he said, "Whoa, there!"

She knew she was blushing. "I wasn't making fun of you."

He moved closer to her, the frown gone, but he wasn't smiling. "Grace, please. I'm kidding."

It took her a second to get what he said. "Really?"

"Really," he repeated as he tipped his hat slightly back with a forefinger to the brim. "This is my 'I'm kidding' face. Okay?"

"Okay," she breathed. "I guess I'm feeling a little over-whelmed by everything that's happened in the last twenty-four hours. I'm sorry, I'm not usually like this. That was foolish." She stopped talking the moment she realized she was reacting to Max the way she used to with her father when she'd make a mistake. From what she'd seen so far, no man could be more different from her dad than Max, except for his penchant for telling her what to do.

"You've gone through a lot, and I promise to tell you when I'm joking from now on. Okay?"

She exhaled. "Yes, please."

"For your information, my parents live in the main house on the ranch, and when I came back from the army, I didn't want to be around a lot of people. The foreman's house was empty, so I took it over." She noticed a vague tightness in his expression as he explained that to her.

"You live alone out there?"

"When I'm there, I'm alone." He abruptly changed the course of their discussion. "Have you had time to check out Marty's apartment yet?"

"No, I haven't. I wanted to take my time and…" She shrugged, at a loss for words to describe why she hadn't walked through the door to see where he'd lived. "Maybe tomorrow after the Jeep's fixed."

"I just think you'd be more comfortable in there than on the couch."

Maybe she would be, but she was staying on the couch for now. "The couch is comfortable and now that I have heat, I'll be just fine wherever I choose to sleep."

"Okay, good, then I'll be going. By the way, I never would have lived in my parents' basement…if they'd had one."

She smiled. "That's a joke, isn't it? You're funny."

"Good, you're a fast learner. I won't have to raise my hand every time and say, 'Just kidding.' That makes life simpler."

She promised herself that she'd do better around Max. She didn't want him getting tired of Grace Bennet, the new girl in town with no sense of humor. "You said before that Uncle Martin liked life to be simple. I believe I do, too."

He nodded. "That makes three of us. Sleep well," he said, then left.

Her phone chimed as the sound of his truck engine faded away and she glanced at the screen. It was from the sheriff's office.

Checking in to make sure all is well at Marty's. Hope grocery delivery was successful.
Lillian Shaw, dispatcher, Clayton County Sheriff's Office.

A well-being check on her from the sheriff's dispatcher. That must be a small-town thing, too. She typed back:

Delivery perfect. Great service. Thanks. Have a good evening!

She went into the great room to set up the couch for her bed again. No fire was needed tonight with the heaters doing their job, but she missed the snap, crackle, pop and the smell of the wood burning. She made herself a dinner of tomato soup and a grilled cheese sandwich and ate it alone sitting on the couch. She kind of wished Max had been able to stay. She wasn't used to being alone so much. In Tucson, her roommate, Zoey, was always around, and before that, there were people paid to tend to her every need by Walter.

Her eyes fell on the square blue envelope she'd put on the coffee table when she'd arrived back at the Lodge after her siren-and-lights ride. She was almost afraid to read it. "Just do it," she muttered to herself as she reached to pick it up. She made herself open it and found a single sheet of lined paper inside it. She tossed the envelope onto the coffee table, then opened the note with shaky writing on both sides.

My dearest Grace:
I'm not sure you even know who I am, so let me in-troduce myself. I am Martin Robert Bennet, your uncle. Even though I never met you, you've been on my mind ever since I found out about you on your sixth birthday. I don't regret much of my life, but one thing that hurts to think about is the loss of you ever being in my life. But that was never possible.

Since you're reading this letter, I know you came to see the Lodge. If you want to sell it, that's your de-cision. But if you keep it, a good friend of mine, Max Donovan, the county sheriff, can tell you all about it and why it's been so dear to me. I hope you will stay, at least for a while, to get to know the Lodge and people in the town of Eclipse. They have been my lifeline, friends that I never expected to make. I came to love the people and this place.

I can say I love you because I know I would have under different circumstances, but I think it's more that I've loved the idea of you, something good coming from Walter and Marianna. I promise you, if you stay, you'll never regret it. But I understand that you have your own life to live, the way I chose to live mine on my own terms. I do have a wish for you, that you find an easy heart. I found mine on a piece of land that called to me, a building that wrapped around me, and a town that accepted me. I wish for you to find your easy heart, too.
Love,
Uncle Martin

At first, Grace couldn't even figure out how to react to the letter, then tears came—tears for lost years and time that could never be reclaimed. She'd never been a crier, but she curled up on the couch and cried until she couldn't anymore. Exhausted and overwhelmed, she closed her eyes. *An easy heart.* She had a vague idea what that could mean, but she had no idea how a person found it.

IT SEEMED NO time had passed when Grace woke up to a hard pounding sound, and she realized someone was at the front door. Shifting on the couch, she glanced out the window and saw the thin light of dawn creeping into the room. She'd slept all night. Scrambling to her feet, she hurried to the door so the pounding would stop. When she pulled it open, she found herself face-to-face with Henry Lodge, the mechanic she'd met the day before.

He was a short man, wearing a heavy jacket and black rubber boots, his dark hair in a braid that hung halfway down his back. The cold air flooding in cut through the sweater and jeans she'd slept in.

"Good morning, Miss Grace. I'm sorry for being so early, but I can't get the piece I need until later this morning. Just wanted you to know."

"Thank you."

"Just be here at noon. My time's real tight today."

"I'll be here," she said.

After Henry left, Grace went into the washroom and made herself presentable. She brushed her hair, then dressed in a vintage red sweatshirt, one of her finds at the consignment shop. The logo on the front was for a college she'd never heard of. Putting on her jeans along with her red running shoes, she looked around for cleaning materials, but there were none. So she grabbed a towel and started dusting in the lobby, making her way to the great room after she found a broom to clear the dust that had accumulated on the fireplace stones.

When she looked at the time on her phone, she was surprised it was almost eleven o'clock. She needed warm clothes, but she couldn't get them until the Jeep was fixed. Dropping down on the couch to relax for a few minutes, she looked around the room that she'd freed of the dustcovers earlier. Now she could appreciate the size of the space and the way her uncle had laid out the furniture.

Along the front wall were the couch and easy chairs where guests could sit and visit, read the books that were stacked neatly on a bookshelf, or just rest. The back area was totally different. The space in the far corner held several small, round tables. Board games and toys sat among them in wicker baskets, and a large chalkboard took up most of the end wall. No TV, but there were speakers in the corners. The remaining part of the room was taken up by a few tables that she figured were meant for guests to sit at while they drank coffee or hot cocoa and enjoyed the beautiful view out the back windows. It was family oriented, and she liked that. She also loved the view out the back windows.

She moved to pick up the dustcovers she'd left by the archway but hesitated when she spotted something white between the black cushions of the sofa she'd slept on. When she tugged it out, she found herself holding a small photograph that she recognized immediately, even if she'd never seen it before.

She remembered the day it was taken twenty years ago at the exclusive restaurant on the top floor of the first hotel/casino her dad had built in Las Vegas. She sat across from her father at a private table, her mother sitting to the side between them. Marianna had always seemed to hover between father and daughter. A Mylar balloon was attached to her chair back with an oversize pink bow, and a fancy pink cake sat in the middle of the table with a large silver number-six candle on top of it.

Her sixth birthday. She'd asked for a pony again, something most kids asked for during their younger years, and she'd received a plethora of presents that circled the cake and hadn't been opened when the photo had been taken. There had been no horse, not even a stuffed version. But she did get a charm bracelet from Tiffany's that she'd lost the next day. The clothes she got had some big-name designer labels that thrilled her mother, at least.

The only toy among those presents had been a fashion-model doll in her mother's image from when Marianna had been at the height of her career. Grace had never opened the box the doll came in because she wasn't allowed. "It's a collector's item and worth a lot of money," her father had told her. So she'd been afraid to even touch it.

She turned the photo over and saw "Grace, 6TH BP"

scrawled on the back and she recognized a stronger version of Uncle Martin's handwriting. She stared at the picture of three people at a celebration and none of them smiling. The photograph had either fallen in between the couch cushions sometime in the past or it had slipped out of the envelope without her noticing it last night. Frowning, she put it in with the letter from her uncle and laid the blue envelope back on the table. She wished she knew the story about how that picture had ended up with Uncle Martin. Just one more thing no one was left to explain to her.

She stood and decided that it was time she checked out Uncle Martin's private quarters, a place she figured would put her as close as she'd ever get to him. Before she could overthink it, she reached for the brass doorknob and let herself into the apartment.

She wasn't sure what she'd expected, but the room could have been anyone's. It had been stripped, the way the rest of the Lodge had been, and she didn't know if she was disappointed or relieved that she didn't see anything that would tell her more about her uncle. It was exactly as Max had told her. It amounted to a studio apartment with an office area near the door, a wrought iron bed, a kitchenette and an easy chair placed near the back wall in front of a set of sliding glass doors. The brown corduroy chair was turned toward the view and looked well used.

She breathed in the musty air tinged with a faint lemon scent, then crossed to stand in the center of the space, not certain what to do first. Then the view caught her eye: the land beyond the raised deck seemed to go on forever toward distant mountains. No wonder the corduroy chair was so worn; what a view to wake up to and to go to sleep by. It would be the perfect place to watch eclipses and meteor showers.

There was a straight line of trees running north and

south, off in the distance past a sea of dried grass and scrub brush. Beyond that were the foothills, then the mountains that rose into the true blue Wyoming sky.

She walked over to the chair and sat down. She'd been wrong. Uncle Martin had left his stamp on the room in the form of an easy chair turned to the view he'd loved. She had no doubt that what she saw was what had drawn him to stay and never leave.

She was startled when someone called out, "Miss Grace?"

Henry was back. "Yes, yes, I'm coming!" she called as she got up and hurried out of the room. Henry stood in the open doorway.

"I'm so glad you're here," she said. "Did you get the part?"

"Yep. I'll get right on it. It shouldn't take more than a couple of hours."

"I have coffee made. Would you like some?"

"Thanks, I sure would," he said, then headed down to the Jeep.

After she'd delivered the coffee to Henry, Grace went back inside and into her uncle's room. Before she'd actually been in the room, she'd thought it might be smart to repurpose the space and turn it into a business office. Now she knew she wouldn't do that. In fact, she'd do as little as she could so she could stay in it while she was at the Lodge. Just standing there, she finally felt a connection with her uncle that she didn't want to lose.

In exactly two hours, Henry was at the door with the good news that the Jeep was fixed. "She's ready to go," he said. "Come on out and I'll show you."

After bundling up, Grace followed him out and he got in behind the wheel. When he turned the key, the car started right away. "That's terrific!"

"She's all yours," he said, and he slipped out, leaving the Jeep idling. As she slid behind the wheel, she heard Henry say, "Ah, the good sheriff."

Grace turned to see Max pulling up to park beside Henry's tow truck. She hadn't heard the pickup arriving because the Jeep was pretty noisy.

Max got out and strode toward them, his black hat pulled low against the glare of the afternoon sun. "Howdy, there," he said, his smile welcoming.

"I heard about the steer that's jamming traffic down south on the highway, and I'm surprised that you aren't roping the critter." Henry's tone was edged with teasing. "I mean, that situation had Max Donovan written all over it."

Max shook his head. "I do enough of that on the ranch. Lawson owed me, so he's down there taking care of the steer." He looked over at Grace. "It sounds as if Henry worked his magic."

"He sure did."

The mechanic crossed to his truck, reached inside and took out a clipboard. He wrote on it and tore off the top sheet of paper before he came back to hand it to Grace. "Here you go. All new wiring, a new fuse box and I hooked up your heater. It had been disconnected. It's perfectly good now—no frayed wires or any possibility of a fire."

"A fire?" Grace asked as she looked up from the paper in her hand.

"The wiring was frayed, and you could have had an engine fire."

That kind of unnerved her. "I guess the battery going dead was a good thing."

"It was great timing," Henry said as she looked down at the bill again.

The price on the invoice seemed reasonable to Grace for all the work he'd done. "You do take credit cards, right?"

"Usually," he said. "But the thing is my handheld card reader isn't working today for some reason. I take checks or cash."

Grace grimaced. She hadn't brought much cash on the trip, didn't use checks and had depended on her credit cards. All the cash she had was barely a hundred dollars. "Would it be okay if I came to your shop today after I go to the bank and get cash?"

"The yard's shut down. I'm running up to Big Horn territory to watch my boys compete in a roping contest. I'll be there a few days. I'm running short and I need to get on the road."

"Call me when you're back, and I'll bring the money," she said.

Max had been quiet up until then. "Why not simplify this, Henry?" he said. "Grace has an awful lot to do around here, so how about I settle with you now, and she can settle with me when she gets the money?" He looked at Grace, waiting for her to agree.

She could see that Henry was anxious to leave, but she didn't want Max to pay for her, even if it was a short-term loan. There was that horrible feeling of her control slipping away, and she didn't want that. But she didn't want to make things harder for the mechanic. "How about I wire the money to your account when I get it from the bank?"

"You know, don't worry about it. When I get back, I'll let Max know and we can take care of it," Henry suggested.

He didn't know her except that she was Uncle Martin's niece, yet he'd let her pay when she could. "If you're okay with that," she said.

"No problem. Now, I need to get out of here and head north. Great to meet you, Miss Grace. And Max, safe ride."

"You too and tell your boys I can't wait to see them at the rodeo."

"Will do," Henry said, then got in the tow truck and headed off with a wave.

"I'll get the money out of the bank today, so I have it ready when Henry comes back," she said.

"If you're going to do that today, why don't I meet you at the bank and introduce you to the manager?"

That wouldn't hurt. "Oh, sure," she said.

"How about I meet you there in an hour?"

She found herself saying, "Two hours," just to feel she had some control over the situation. Petty, but it made her feel a bit better.

Max didn't blink or try to talk her into meeting sooner but said, "Deal," and headed toward his pickup.

"Max," she called after him. "I went into Uncle Martin's room earlier and sat in his old chair by the window just looking at my land." She'd actually called it *her* land. She kind of liked the sound of that.

He stopped and looked back at her. "What do you think about it?"

"It's breathtaking. I think Wyoming was showing off for me."

He smiled over at her. "That's been known to happen."

"I'll see you at the bank."

"Call me if you're there before I am," he said, then got in behind the wheel of the truck and drove off.

As she watched him pull onto the highway and drive in the direction of town, she wanted to kick herself. Why had she pushed for another hour just to make sure she had the last word? That was a knee-jerk reaction, courtesy of her dad. She was letting him affect her even when he was nowhere around.

She sighed and went back inside to her uncle's room. She went directly to the chair and sank down in it, rubbing her temples with her fingers.

She barely knew Max Donovan, but she called his motives wrong every time. The poor man couldn't win with her, but she'd change that. He wasn't Walter. She had a gut feeling that Uncle Martin was a very good judge of people, and he and Max were close friends. That ought to be good enough for her. She closed her eyes and breathed deeply, feeling her muscles relax. This wasn't Las Vegas, and she wasn't known as Walter Bennet's daughter anymore. She was Marty's niece, which suited her just fine.

CHAPTER SIX

GRACE FINISHED AT the general store with ten minutes to spare to get to the bank across the street. She put her bags in the Jeep, grateful for the fleece-lined denim jacket she'd found at Gabby's, which had been her first stop in town. She'd also bought a new pair of thermal boots from Farley's, and she had worn them out of the store. They looked cute on her feet, and she already felt warmer.

After locking up the Jeep, she took the stairs back up onto the walkway. As she turned in the direction of the bank, she spotted Max talking to an older man with a short gray beard. He was using a cane to lean on as he engaged in what looked like a serious conversation with Max.

She didn't want to interrupt, so she walked slowly, taking her time approaching the two men. As she got closer, she caught a few words from the older man: "…should know about it."

"People are people, even in Eclipse…not fighting them," she heard Max say.

"Dang it, someone's gotta…ain't right…take him on."

Max shook his head, and now she could clearly hear what he was saying. "It's one man who's got a burr under his saddle."

Grace didn't go any closer, pretending to admire the window display in the bakery next to her. But she heard the older man because his voice was rising.

"He's runnin' around like a chicken with its head

chopped off, but his voice is reaching ears out there." He leaned in toward Max. "I'd be right happy to have a little come-to-Pappy meeting with Big Albert, if ya want. There ain't nothing to lose, and it might turn out aces for ya. I'm old and slow, but I got a lot stored up about Al in my thick head that he'd never want to see the light of day."

"Freeman, no, don't. That would just be fuel for his fire. If I lose the vote, then I'll step away. I could go back to the ranch and be okay."

The old man chuckled roughly. "I know. You're a good man. Ain't no meanness in you. I'm right proud of ya. Now, I gotta hitch up and get back before Beulah comes hunting for me."

He moved back and looked surprised to see Grace standing there. "Oh, ma'am, are we blockin' your way?"

"No, not at all. I saw Max…and I… I don't mean to intrude," she said as Max turned. For a moment, his expression appeared blank, but then he smiled.

"Right on time," he said and flicked his eyes over her. "New jacket and boots?"

"The jacket's from Gabby's place, and Mr. Garret had the boots."

The older man was smiling at Grace. "Max, don't you have no manners? Introduce me to your friend."

"Freeman, meet Grace Bennet, Marty's niece. Grace, Freeman Lee."

"It's downright wonderful to meet you, Miss Grace." His voice was raspy, but his blue eyes were bright. "I'm glad the Lodge ain't empty no more. Marty'd be pure happy about that. If you need help, ya'll tell Max to round me up."

"I appreciate your offer, Mr. Lee. Thank you so much."

"Yes, ma'am," he said, touching the brim of his hat.

Then he turned to Max. "Hang on, son. It's going to only get rougher the nearer you get to the end of this ride."

"I know. Tell Beulah I'll be by to visit soon."

Freeman nodded, then limped off down the walkway, using his cane.

"He seems very nice," she said to Max.

"It was his barn that I told you about being burned down then being rebuilt by the town. It's still standing."

"If I'm out of line asking, just tell me, no hard feelings, but I couldn't help overhearing. What's going on with Big Albert?"

He ran his hand roughly over his face. "It's no secret around here. I told you Big Albert never forgave me for beating him at the ballot box last election. He's a talker, and a lot of his cronies are still around and want the good old days back when Al did favors for people around here that were right on the border of being illegal. Freeman's ready for a showdown, but I don't want that. If I'm the one knocked off when the voting comes along, it is what it is. If I'm not doing a good enough job for the majority, I'll walk away."

"Do you think Freeman would really do anything?"

That brought a rueful smile to his face. "Freeman might look old and slow, but if you get him started, he'll tan a hide or two."

"Maybe the cane would come in handy if he did decide to do something."

He shook his head. "I want to pull the reins in on that visual. Freeman's protective of the people he cares about, and he's lived here all his life. He's protective of the town, too."

"Is he family?"

"Close enough." He glanced down the street. "The bank?"

"Oh, yes," she said and as he started off, she fell in step

beside him "Maybe if the bank gets robbed while we're in there, you can catch the robber and save the day. You'd be a real hero. That would certainly help you get reelected."

He laughed, an easy sound as they kept going. "There's only been one bank robbery while I've been sheriff. Lyndon Briggs was drunk and thought he was breaking into his brother's store not the bank. So, I guess technically it wouldn't be considered a robbery."

"What happened to him?"

"Jackie Sykes, the bank manager, didn't press charges, but he did make Lyndon pay for repairs and banished him from the bank forever. That ban ended up lasting for all of two months before Jackie lifted it, but Lyndon got the idea."

"No Old West justice, huh?"

"Not on my watch, pardner," he said, then stopped just before Gabby's store and pointed out a brick-and-wood structure directly across from them. The sign by the door read "Eclipse Community Bank." A smaller sign on the door read "Closed."

"But it's only four o'clock."

"Jackie also does real estate and sometimes he has to shut down temporarily to show a prospective client property."

Grace could wait a day. "Okay, I'll get it tomorrow."

He nodded. "Are you heading back out to the Lodge?"

She'd forgotten one of the things she wanted to buy. "I need to get some new linens for the bed in Uncle Martin's room."

He pointed back the way they'd come. "Two stores past Burr's office is a shop called Heavenly Dreams. Laurel May, the mayor's wife, owns it."

"Okay, I'll try there."

"You need to hunt down a hat, too," he said out of the blue.

"Excuse me?"

"You've got the boots and jacket, but if you don't get a good hat, you're going to be cold no matter what you do."

She swallowed the impulse to tell him she'd get a hat if she wanted to, but she'd promised herself that she would chill out when it came to Max and his bossiness. She was being petty, and she cringed inside, thinking of her reaction to his innocent comment. "I'll get one. Anything to stay warm."

"I need to get to the station. Safe ride," he said and touched the brim of his hat with his forefinger. He took the steps down to the street, stopping at the bottom to look up at her. "Don't forget the hat."

WHEN GRACE DROVE back into town three days later, she was more than ready to take Max's "suggestion" and find a warm hat. She'd tried going outside to explore the property around the Lodge and get a better feel for her surroundings, but all she got was cold—very cold. She only managed to get as far as an old stable set back from the Lodge to the south. Its wooden walls and roof were silvered from age, and the stalls were all empty. Outside, two holding pens held nothing but dried grass and weeds.

She drove to Gabby's store, but it was closed, so she continued on to the general store, where she hoped they'd have a warm hat and maybe a scarf she could pull up over her chin and mouth.

The bell that tinkled when the door opened got Farley's attention and he came out from the back area to greet her.

"Well, howdy there, Miss Grace!"

It kind of tickled her that the older men she'd met called her "Miss Grace." She liked it a lot better than "ma'am."

His voice rose over the country music that played in the background. "What are you searching for today?" he asked. The silver-haired shop owner was wearing an orange-colored Western shirt with fringes, white jeans, a belt with a horseshoe-shaped gold buckle and dark green studded boots with two-inch heels. She liked him. He was good entertainment when he showed her around the store, and a bit of a gossip about what was going on in town.

"I'm looking for a warm hat."

"Oh, my. Well, come on with me. I've got the best hats in town." He winked at her. "The best everything in town."

His hat section had a rack devoted to Flaming Coop D merchandise. Farley caught her looking at a poster on the wall beside it. "That's Coop Donovan. I watched that boy grow up to be the best of the best on the rodeo circuit."

She saw the price tag on a beautiful women's hat that was branded with the Flaming Coop D logo on the inside liner. It was pricey. "He's a local hero?"

"You bet. All the Donovan boys used to be on the rodeo circuit, just like their dad, Dash Donovan. Coop's the one who stuck it out and made it big."

That was interesting. "Quite a family," she said. "So, the sheriff was in the rodeo?"

"For a while, then he left to enlist in the army and got into one of them special units. A few years ago he came back here and took over as sheriff. Hope he gets reelected."

She saw a chance to ask something she wanted to know. "I'd think him getting elected again would be a slam dunk."

"It probably is, but you never know when you have someone running against you, someone willing to do whatever it takes. Sometimes it's not about character—it's about greed and politics. Even around here it can get messy."

"That's too bad."

"Sure is," he said. Then he asked her, "What kind of hat did you have in mind?"

"A warm one."

Grace walked out of Farley's wearing her new hat—a soft gray knit beanie with earflaps—and carrying a bag with a scarf, some flannel shirts, thermals to wear under her clothes and a jar of jellybeans. A second bag had some cleaning supplies in it. She went down to her Jeep and put the bags on the passenger seat, then her cell phone rang. Max was calling.

"Hello, stranger," she said when she answered.

"I like your new hat, and the earflaps were a good idea, but turn your collar up. That helps keep you warmer, too."

He liked the hat? How could he…? "Where are you?"

"Turn around, then come on over."

She turned, and there he was standing on the walkway in front of the leather-tooling store across the street. She pushed her phone into her jacket pocket, then crossed the empty street. As she got closer to him and he flashed a smile, it struck her that she'd actually missed him the last three days, a man she barely knew.

"I haven't seen you for a while," she said, her voice slightly breathless even though she hadn't exactly hurried across to him.

"I've been chained to a desk." He didn't look very happy about that. "Did you ever get to the bank?"

"No, I was just heading over there now. I've been busy at the Lodge, cleaning and trying to explore the property without freezing to death."

"The hat should help, but putting up your collar will keep your neck warm."

It was surprisingly easy for her to say, "Thanks for the suggestion. I actually bought a matching scarf, too."

"Good. I'm going down to the bank to make a deposit

for Lillian. You want to come with me, and I'll introduce you to Jackie this time?"

The bank manager. "Sure," she said.

"How's the Jeep?" Max asked as they walked side by side down the walkway.

"It starts right up, and the heater works. Not as well as the one in your truck, but it's nice. So, are you done sitting at your desk?"

"I hope so. It's the worst part of my job. I was actually down at headquarters in Two Horns working. A new hire screwed up big-time, and I had to fix his mess before it got out of hand."

"What did he do?"

"I really can't tell you, but it's over and done with, and I'm short a deputy for a week." He hesitated, then added, "Do me a favor and keep this between us. I don't need it to get around, especially not now."

"Of course." Grace grimaced. "I'm sorry it happened."

"Me, too, but it's part of the job—the messy part. Marty always said that if you go through the mess, pain and all, you'll appreciate the peace at the end of the road."

Grace knew all about the messy parts of life. She was just crawling out of one, finally putting it behind her, and she would embrace the peace when or if it came.

"My uncle was pretty smart, huh?"

"Marty was smart about a lot of things," Max said. He still felt the loss of his friend. As they approached the bank, he realized how much ease there was between him and Grace. It wouldn't be a chore for him to be her friend. Marty had asked him to be there for her and he would be.

Before he could reach for the door to pull it open, a local teen, Oscar Warring, the oldest of five Warring kids, slowly passed by riding an old quarter horse and holding up a car stuck behind him.

"Hey, Sheriff Max!" Oscar called out,

The kid was strong looking in his scruffy clothes that weren't keeping up with the growth spurt he'd obviously had.

"How's your mom doing, Oscar?" he called back to him.

The boy pulled his horse to a stop in the street, seemingly unaware of the car right behind him. "She's doing lots better and was pure happy with the cord of wood you sent over last week. It'll help a lot until Pa's back on his feet."

"You tell her to let me know if you get low again, or if you need help with grains and hay."

"I sure will."

Oscar nudged his horse to get going at the same time the driver behind him sounded his horn. The old horse reared at the sound, and Oscar barely kept in the saddle.

Max jumped off the walkway and landed between the luxury SUV and the horse. Seeing Oscar had regained control of his ride, Max headed directly to the vehicle before the driver did something else reckless.

He rapped on the window and the glass slid down to expose a middle-aged man who was wearing Western-styled clothing that Max knew set the guy back a good amount of money.

"What in blazes were you thinking doing that?" he demanded, trying very hard to keep his anger at a minimum.

"The kid's riding as if he owns the street and blocking everyone else on the road. Then he stops traffic completely." The man's face was flushed with anger. "This is none of your business, buddy. Get out of my way."

Max undid the front of his jacket and pushed back the right side to make sure the driver saw his badge and his gun. "Wrong. It is my business as sheriff in these parts. But I'm feeling charitable today and I won't cite you for reckless endangerment, if you head out of town and keep going."

The driver looked like he wanted to say something else but had the good sense to keep it to himself and rolled up the window.

Max went over to Oscar. "You okay?"

"Yeah, I'm okay, Sheriff."

Max looked back at the SUV, then up at Oscar again. "Where're you going?"

"Up to the blacksmith to get a halter he fixed for us."

"Okay, get going but don't rush."

The boy understood. "If you say so."

Max patted the horse's rump. "Safe ride," he said, then went back to where Grace was still standing by the door to the bank.

"You really do love this town, don't you?" she said with a soft smile.

"It's my home," he said as he reached to open the door for her. Grace stepped past him into a small room with only one of three teller cages open. There was a jarringly modern-looking ATM to the left of the door.

She reached into her jacket pocket and took out a red wallet, from which she retrieved a black credit card. "This won't take a minute," she said, crossing to insert her card in the flashing green slot on the face of the machine. Max turned to talk to the teller to make Lillian's deposit.

"Hi, Rose," he said to the bank manager's daughter. "Lillian's account for deposit." He handed the envelope over to the girl with the short brown hair and pierced nose, ears and eyebrows. "Is your dad in today?"

"No, he's out looking at a ranch for someone from the Jackson Hole area who wants a quieter location."

The transaction was simple, and as Rose handed him back the receipt for Lillian he was surprised to see Grace was still at the machine taking a silver credit card out of the slot this time. The machine beeped as "Card Declined" flashed on the screen.

"I don't believe this," Grace murmured.

"Problem?" Max asked.

She stared at the machine. "Yes…no, um, I must be getting my PIN numbers mixed up." She rubbed the silver card on the side of her jacket, then inserted it one more time. It beeped and flashed "Card Declined." She took her card back, then tried a gold card. That card was declined, too.

Max could see she was embarrassed and avoided looking at him. "I don't know why it's doing that. I just bought stuff at the general store with my black card."

Rose spoke up. "Those cards mess up all the time. Bring it over here and let me slide it for you."

Max moved back to give Grace access to the teller cage. She passed her gold card to Rose. "I don't understand what's wrong."

He hadn't read Grace as wealthy; nothing about her shouted it. "Maybe the machine's too low on cash," he said, a perfectly logical reason that could have happened with any card.

Rose smiled reassuringly at the two of them. "Don't worry, it happens. Let me run it again." She slid Grace's gold card through the machine in front of her and turned the pad toward Grace so she could put in her PIN. Rose's smile turned to a frown. "Can you put in your PIN again, please?"

Grace did, and even before the woman looked up, Max knew it hadn't worked.

"I'm sorry," Rose said. "I've never seen one of these

cards refused unless it's stolen." Almost immediately, the girl realized whom she was talking to. Color flooded her face. "Of course, it's not. The screen would have alerted me." Quickly, she asked, "Do you want me to call it in and see if there's a hold on it or something?"

Grace nodded, her cheeks pink. "Yes, if you would, please."

Rose made the call, listened, then hung up. "I'm sorry. The card's been canceled by the company it was issued to at their request." She read the name off the monitor. "Golden Mountain Corporation. Maybe they went out of business, or their account was hacked?" Rose suggested.

"It didn't go out of business," Grace muttered tightly. She took the card back. "Thank you for trying," she said as she slipped the card into her purse.

"I'm sorry, ma'am," Rose said.

Grace nodded. "Me, too." She looked anxious to leave as she glanced at Max. "I'll be outside."

She hurried to the door and out. Max thanked Rose, then went after Grace.

When Max stepped outside, Grace was waiting there. "I never expected this, but maybe I should have. Whatever, I'll get Henry's money."

"You should have expected someone to cancel your card?"

"No, I... It's just, it should have occurred to me that he'd pull the cards."

"Who pulled your card?" he asked.

She looked around, then finally back up at him. "The CEO, the founder and all-around dictator of the company. He was upset with me the last time we talked, and he has his ways of making a point. He's particularly good at making a point with the greatest impact possible."

"He didn't ask for the card back when you left, or quit, or whatever happened?"

"No, he didn't, but I can imagine him enjoying it when he finds out I tried to get money and was denied."

She didn't give a name to the man, so he asked, "This person, was he just your boss?"

She looked down and her shoulders sagged. "No, he wasn't, and he wasn't what you're thinking he was, either."

She'd read his mind, because he'd thought the guy was someone she'd been involved with romantically, someone who had decided he was done with her, or maybe she'd walked out on him, and what better way to get his revenge?

Max touched her arm to get her attention, startling her. "Listen to me. Don't even think about rushing to pay Henry. I can take care of him."

"No, you won't. I'll take care of it."

Her tone wasn't angry, but hurt and sad.

"Okay, but don't go smashing any piggy banks."

PIGGY BANKS? As Max said the words, Grace realized she had what could be called a piggy bank of sorts. Her father had set up a bank account in her name when she'd gone off to college, with automatic quarterly deposits as long as she kept a 4.0 GPA in her business and marketing courses. She'd only used the money in the account to buy her textbooks the first semester and to set up her dorm room. She'd left it alone after she'd started working at the college and had all but forgotten about it until right then.

It was *her* money, not her father's. She'd earned every cent of it. What was in the account wouldn't be a fortune, but it would help her right now when she needed it.

"I don't mean to be abrupt, but I need to go," she stated.

He looked down at her, his eyes shadowed by his hat,

but she could see the concern in his expression. "I don't care about the money," he said.

"But I do. I'll call you soon, okay?" She hurried off to get back to where she'd left the Jeep. She didn't realize Max was right by her until she stopped to cross the street. There was no traffic in either direction and she hurried over to where her Jeep was parked. Max stayed beside her until she had climbed into the Jeep and started the engine.

"Max, I need to go," she said.

"Sure, of course." He took a step back. "Go and do what you have to do. We'll talk later."

"Yes, later." She put the Jeep in reverse and eased back out onto street. When she neared the highway access, she knew she had to stop before she threw up. Just the two miles to the Lodge seemed impossible for her to drive right then. Turning off onto a side street named Longbow Trail, she pulled to the curb and took out her phone.

She looked up a number and held the phone to her ear, her hand shaking. There was one ring before an automated voice gave her options regarding her bank account in Henderson. She pressed the number to hear her balance and barely breathed until she was given an answer. There was more in her account than she'd thought there would be. Relieved, she sank back into the seat. Walter hadn't gotten to it yet.

When given the option of hanging up or staying on the line to speak to a representative, she chose the human being. Half an hour later, she had arranged to have the account put on hold until she could personally sign for an electronic transfer of the remaining funds to an associated bank in Cody. She agreed to be there at ten thirty the next morning. Things would be okay. She'd beaten Walter to the punch. It wasn't a victory for her, but it was the final cut of her connection with Walter Bennet.

CHAPTER SEVEN

MAX WOKE IN his house on the ranch at the crack of dawn. He'd had scattered dreams throughout the night that he really didn't remember beyond being left with the sense that they were sad. It was probably better he didn't remember, especially if they were anything like the dreams he'd had when he first got back from the army.

He quickly got out of bed, showered and dressed, then left to go check in at the substation. As he drove down the highway, the sadness from the forgotten dreams dogged him. Then he thought of Grace Bennet. It had bothered him more than he liked to admit, thinking about what some guy had done to her. She was alone. No parents, no uncle and apparently no other family. Maybe that had filtered into his dreams.

His stop at the substation lasted longer than he'd anticipated, and he didn't get out of there until eight forty-five. As he drove along Clayton Way nearing the bank, Rose stepped down off the raised walkway and waved at him to stop. He pulled over and she hurried up to the driver's window. As the glass slid down, she smiled up at him.

"I'm glad I spotted you. I was just on the way over to the station to give this to Lillian."

He saw her hold out what he recognized as Grace's red wallet.

"Marty's niece left this on the shelf by the ATM and forgot to take it with her. Maybe you can get it to her."

He took the wallet and laid it on the console. "Sure, I'll drop in and give it to her."

"That's great, Max. Thanks."

"No problem," he said.

"Have a good day."

As Rose headed back toward the bank, he took out his cell to call Grace to let her know he had her wallet, but an incoming call stopped him. "Hey, Lillian. What's going on?"

"You're free for the day. That second recruit passed the firing range with flying colors, so he's eligible for duty. He'll be with Jimmy Jay in the cruiser. You don't have to worry about covering the eastern border."

He almost didn't know what he'd do with himself for a whole day. Taking the wallet back to Grace was a start, but after that he figured he'd play it by ear. He drove away in the direction of the Lodge. When he went through the gates and up to park, he found Grace's Jeep idling, the exhaust rising up into the cold air. It looked as if Grace was getting ready to go somewhere. He got out and found the door to the Lodge was open, so he stepped inside.

The place seemed fresh again: the dust was gone, and the front desk had been polished to a mellow sheen. Sitting on top of it was an older landline phone and an old-fashioned cash register. They'd been stored in the cabinet under the desk after Marty had computerized everything and stopped using them.

"Grace?" he called out as he closed the door behind him. "You here?"

"Coming," he heard her say from somewhere in the back.

Then he saw her hurrying over from the direction of the kitchen, and she looked different. Her dark hair was slicked back from her face and tucked behind her ears, and she'd traded her jeans and flannel shirt for tailored black slacks and a white cable-knit sweater.

"Don't stare," she said with a slight grimace as she did up the front of her leather jacket. "I was trying to look more professional, but I think the motorcycle jacket ruins that impression. I'm not good at dressing up."

He thought she looked incredibly attractive. "Why are you dressed up?"

"I'm on my way to meet with a banker in Cody to sign some paperwork." She crossed to the door. "I don't want to be late." She stopped before pulling it open. "I'm sorry, Max. Did you need something?"

Could she be going to sign sales papers for the Lodge already? His stomach sank. "Something to do with the Lodge?" he asked as casually as he could manage.

"No. Burr's taking care of all of that. This is personal business for me." She gave him a rueful smile. "I'm sorry. I need to make sure I'm not late for my appointment."

She opened the door and motioned for him to go ahead of her, and then she locked up and took the stairs down to the drive. Max walked beside her, over to where he'd parked by her Jeep. She turned to him before she opened the Jeep door. A light breeze teased her hair where a few errant strands had already started to curl at her cheekbones.

"What time's your appointment?" he asked.

"Ten thirty."

He suddenly knew exactly what he'd like to do on his free day. "Strange coincidence, but I'm on my way to Cody, too."

"You aren't working?"

"No. I came by to give you something you might have been missing."

"What?"

He took her wallet out of his pocket and held it out to her.

"Rose found it by the ATM machine. You must have left it there by accident."

Her eyes widened with surprise. "Oh, gosh, I didn't even know it wasn't in my purse." She took it from him. "I can't believe I did that. Thank you so much for bringing it out here."

"Which bank are you going to up there?"

"The Reliance Community Bank."

"My brother's business, CD's Place, is only two blocks from there. I don't have to work today, so I'm going to see Caleb and have lunch." She looked impatient now, and he quickly finished with, "How about we go together, you do your bank business and meet me at Caleb's place for lunch afterward? The food's great and it's on the house." He smiled at her. "I promise to get you there by ten thirty."

"You must have something better to do than hang out with me on your day off."

He'd told himself he was doing it to help Grace because of Marty, but in fact, he realized he wanted to spend time with her. "I am painfully available for the day. How about we flip to see who drives, then get moving so you aren't late? I'm not supposed to use the truck for personal reasons when I'm not on duty, so I'd just have to stop by the ranch on the way and pick up my own truck there."

"No, we can take the Jeep," she said. "But could you drive? You know where we're going, and I can't be late."

"Sure thing," he said. While Grace went around to climb into the passenger seat, he got behind the wheel. The Jeep was old, but it ran well, and they were soon heading up to Cody on the highway. "Don't worry. We'll be there on time. Trust me."

She nodded and said, "I slept in Uncle Martin's room for the first time last night."

"How was it?"

"It was nice. I had been contemplating turning that whole space into a big office, but I'm not going to. I worry that if I change things too much, I'll lose that sense of Uncle Martin that I feel in there, especially when I sit in his old chair by the windows. It's not like a ghost thing or anything, but he's there."

He smiled to himself, grateful Marty was becoming more real to her. And who knew? Maybe she would change her mind about selling after all. "How long do you think you'll be at the bank?" he asked.

"I just have to sign some papers to close out a savings account I'd forgotten about until yesterday. It's not a lot of money, but I'm kind of lucky you're coming along so I'll have a bodyguard."

Max cast a quick sideways glance at Grace. "My rates aren't cheap for private work."

"How much?" she asked.

"I'll accept your company on this trip as partial payment."

"What about the rest?"

"That's where things get iffy."

She seemed puzzled when he looked quickly over at her. "Iffy? Why?"

"I'll introduce you to Caleb when I go by there, and you have to promise me you'll ignore anything he says about me unless it's good."

She chuckled softly at that. "I never had siblings, but I made up an imaginary younger sister who was sweet and fun and always wanted to do whatever I was doing. I called her Poppy, for no reason I can remember, but she kept me company…sort of."

"Caleb's very real, and he can be fun. He's a genuine people person and very social. He's never boring, but he's only recently become what you could call 'sweet.' And that's because he has a wife now, Harmony, and a little girl named Joy."

"I'm looking forward to meeting him, and I bet he'll only say good things about you."

He laughed ruefully. "Easy to say when you don't know him."

When her phone chimed, she took it out of the leather shoulder bag resting in her lap. "Just a minute," she said to Max and took the call. "Hello. This is Grace Bennet." She listened silently while Max kept driving. Then he heard her inhale softly before she spoke in a slightly panicked voice. "No, no, no, no, no. That's my account. Mine. I was promised the money would be there when I got to the bank today."

Max glanced at her. She was nervously rubbing at her slacks with the flat of her free hand. Her eyes were closed tightly. Something was very wrong. "Yes, please, call me right back."

The call ended, but Grace didn't say anything. Finally, Max flat out asked her, "Is there a problem?"

"Just something I thought was settled." She cleared her throat and said, "I'll figure it out."

His promise to Marty mixed with the tension he could feel radiating from Grace wouldn't let him give up easily. "Talking it over with someone can help, and if you want, I'll listen. It won't go any further than your Jeep. I promise."

She didn't answer for what seemed an eternity, then he sensed her turning toward him. "I thought I had things settled with the bank, but it looks as if it's falling apart. The man said he'd call me back, but I'm not sure he's going to be able to help me. I think you should probably take me back to the Lodge."

Maybe she'd been trying to do more than just close an account. Perhaps she'd been looking to borrow money and been denied. A sheriff didn't make much, but Max and his brothers all owned part of the ranch that had been incorporated years ago, and they received quarterly payments. Last time he looked, he wasn't wealthy, but he was well-to-do. "How about you tell me exactly what happened, then if you still want to go back, I'll take you." He slowed, pulled over to the side of the road and turned toward her to give her his full attention.

She looked down at the phone she clenched in her hand. "There's a demand that's going to be filed against the account—like a lien, I think. If that happens, the funds will be unavailable with no time frame for them to be released to me, or else seized by the person filing against it."

"This person doing it, is he the same one you mentioned yesterday?"

She was silent for a long moment, then nodded and spoke in a low voice. "Yes, and I don't know what he'll do. I gave up trying to figure him out. For a long time I thought he did what he did because he knew best and I trusted him. But it's always been about him, and he doesn't care about anything or anybody else." He saw her bite her bottom lip, then say, "I won't let him do this to me now."

Max couldn't stand the thought of someone out there trying to hurt Grace. There was no way to get the guy, but he would do whatever he could to keep him from taking what seemed like the last of her money. "Who just called you from the bank?"

When she looked at him, there were no tears in her eyes, but that lost expression he'd seen at the diner. "Norbert Brown, the manager."

"Good, good," he said. "I've known Bert for years, and he's a reasonable man."

Before he could suggest she call Bert back, her phone rang and she jumped at the sound, dropping the phone to the floor by her feet. She reached down to retrieve it and looked at the screen. "It's the bank," she said.

"Let me talk." He held out his hand for her phone.

"I can do—"

"Please, allow me."

She shivered slightly, then dropped the phone in his hand. He answered it. "Hello?"

"I'm calling for Ms. Bennet."

He recognized the voice. "Bert, you're talking to Max Donovan."

"Max. What's going on?"

He didn't want Grace to hear their conversation. "Hold on, Bert." He hit the mute button on the phone and told a small lie. "The reception's not good in here. Be right back." He got out and walked to the rear of the Jeep, then went another ten feet just to make sure Grace wouldn't hear him. He unmuted the call. "Bert, why is Ms. Bennet's money not available for her?"

"I received a notification of intent to file a lien against the full funds held in the account."

"We're on our way to see you. When we walk out of the bank, I want her to have the money that's in her account with her. If you can't make that happen, tell me how much money's involved and I'll cover it."

"Max, you know I can't give you that information, not

without her permission. Put her on the line, and I'll ask for it."

"No, forget I said that." He knew she wouldn't go for that, but it had been worth a try. He glanced back over his shoulder and saw Grace watching him. "Bert, she's Marty Roberts's niece, and she needs help. She's inherited the Lodge and she came up here alone and is trying to deal with everything by herself. I'm not asking you to break the rules. I'm just asking if there's any way you can help her to get her own money legally."

Bert was silent for a long moment then said, "Hypothetically?"

"She needs real currency, but if your answer has to be hypothetical, go ahead."

"If a hypothetical account is to be closed, but a hypothetical lien was going to be put against it, the demand wouldn't be legal and binding until the documents for said lien had been wired to the target bank and they'd been accepted. The manager would have to sign off on it. If that happens before the owner of the account can close it, the action is irreversible."

Max frowned. "In this hypothetical situation, how long does it take between the notification about the coming lien and the actual filing?"

"If the notification of intent to file came across the bank manager's desk from an out-of-state bank, it could take around fifteen minutes to be approved and finalized." Bert cleared his throat. "However, if this hypothetical bank manager at a small regional bank is in an important meeting when it arrives, that could push the time it would take up to half an hour, but not any longer. Remember, this is all hypothetical, but if the legal owner of the account is there before that time, they'd get the payout."

Max checked his watch. Twenty minutes to get to Cody if there was no traffic. "Okay, Bert, we're on our way now." Bert was willing to do what he could within his means and that was all Max could ask for.

He got back in the Jeep and gave Grace her phone. "We need to get there as soon as possible. There's a good chance that you can get your money."

She just stared at him for a moment before she asked, "What do you mean?"

Max knew he couldn't make any promises, but as he drove back onto the highway he explained some of it to Grace. "Bert knew Marty, and you're benefiting from that. It's still a fifty-fifty chance you'll get the money, but that's better than no chance at all." He reached out to touch her hand, which was clenching her phone. "Relax, Grace. It'll be okay. Trust me."

Unexpectedly, she laid her free hand over his. "I'm really glad you showed up this morning," she said just above a whisper.

He felt her touch on him tighten for a fleeting second, and then she drew back. He wanted nothing more in that moment than to see her get her money and be smiling when they left the bank.

GRACE SILENTLY WATCHED Max on the drive to Cody, wondering where his suit of shining armor was stored. He was always coming to her rescue, and even if she couldn't access the money in her account, she knew he'd done his best to help her.

"I'm sorry I got so upset. I've had a lot of stuff happen lately, and I'm trying to figure things out. Finding out about Uncle Martin and the Lodge came completely out of the blue, and since then other things have kind of, gone sideways."

"That's all we can do in this life…adjust," he murmured.

As the miles slipped past, her nerves started to get to her. Finally Max pulled off the highway and onto Cody's main street. His phone rang and he handed it to Grace. He didn't want to stop again. "Could you put it on speaker for me?"

She took it and did as he asked. "Lillian, I'm not working today," Max said.

"God bless you, I know, but I have a message for you from the bank manager in Cody. Bert said that you have fifteen minutes to walk through the door."

"Got it," he said, then motioned Grace to end the call.

"What does that mean?" she asked as he took his phone back and put it in the slot on the dash.

"We have to be there in under fifteen minutes, or you won't be leaving with the money."

"Can we make it?"

"We'll be early," he said and turned off the street into a parking spot in front of a brick structure that had "Reliance Community Bank" written in blue letters on the facade.

Grace grabbed his right arm. "I can't believe we made it! You're wonderful!" She hadn't meant to say that last sentence, but it was true. The man had taken away a weight she wasn't sure she could have carried much longer.

His hazel eyes were touched with teasing. "Dang, I was going for awesome!"

She let go of him and laughed. "Well, surprise, Sheriff, you've officially achieved awesomeness."

Too late, Walter, too late, she thought but without any real sense of joy. She was just thankful that she had at least some money to keep her afloat.

CHAPTER EIGHT

HALF AN HOUR LATER, Grace and Max were back in the Jeep, the papers signed, the account closed and her money in a plastic bank pouch she'd put in her purse on her lap. They were waiting for an opening to get out on the street into traffic that moved at little more than a snail's pace. Grace felt as if her world had steadied again.

"If you hadn't brought my wallet back when you did, and if you didn't know Mr. Brown, I don't think I'd have the money now."

"Bert really came through."

Max came through, too. "How long have you known him?"

"We went to high school together."

"I would have thought he was older than you."

Max glanced at her. "I guess you're so young that anyone over thirty seems really old."

She chuckled at that. "No, of course not. I just meant Mr. Brown seemed more like he was in his forties than his thirties."

Max answered his cell phone when it rang. "Hey there. I'm close by and I need a table for two for lunch. I also got the background checks on the band members." As he listened, Grace saw a frown emerge on his face.

"Nah, if you aren't there we'll head back, but I can read off the background checks if you need me to." He tapped the screen on his cell and read through some data. "The backgrounds came back clear except for a Randy Lawrence from Slater's Yahoo Four. A drunk took a swing at him when he was playing at Overboard in Cheyenne, and he decked the guy. Claimed self-defense. He was released with no charges." He listened. "No problem there... No, we're fine." He put his phone in the slot on the dash.

"No free lunch?" she asked.

"No Caleb—he's visiting friends up near Sheridan. Are you real hungry?"

She hadn't eaten anything because of her nerves and was starting to feel vague hunger pangs. "I'm in no rush for food."

"Well, I do need to eat, and I know just the place."

"Where's that?"

He didn't reply but put in another call on his cell. "It's me. I have a friend with me, we're heading back from Cody and we're hungry. We should be driving by you in thirty or forty minutes. I was hoping we could stop by, if that's okay. Text me back."

"Who's going to get back to you?" Grace asked.

"Oh, my mother," he said as he finally found a gap to pull into traffic and drive toward the highway. He glanced at her and that crooked smile that he had lit up his face. "She'll be incredibly pleased to meet you once I explain to her about your connection to Marty and the Lodge. Marty had an open-ended invitation to our family meals. He loved my mom's cooking, especially her tamales."

Family meals were foreign to her—at least meals made in her home by her parents. On the rare occasion that they ate together, it was always at some fancy restaurant. Most of the time, they just ordered room service from the hotel where they lived in the penthouse.

Max's phone chimed, announcing a text. He opened it and handed the phone to Grace. "Read it to me, please."

"'I'm sorry, Max,'" Grace read. "'But Dad and I are on our way to meet up with Lance Burke and his family. He was hurt on a ride in Arizona, and he's decided to retire. You go ahead and stop at the house and help yourself to some chicken and tamales in the fridge. Just reheat them. They taste even better on the second day. Let Lawson take some with him so Evelyn won't have to figure out how to feed him and take care of the new baby. Stay safe. Love you lots.'"

Grace handed the phone back to him and he slipped it into his jacket pocket. "Who's Lawson?" she asked.

"A deputy and a friend of mine. We ride double off and on, so Mom must have assumed that's who was with me." He chuckled to himself. "Maybe it's better she doesn't know."

"Why?"

"Both of my brothers are married or engaged, and she sees me as a bit of a lost cause. Frankly, she tries to set me up with available women she comes across every chance she gets."

She kept her eyes on Max's profile and decided that the man had to be single by choice, because he had no bad side. He'd be a magnet for single women wherever he went, even while doing his job. "You poor thing. You have a mom who cares. Must be tough," she said, with deliberate sarcasm in her voice.

He glanced over at her, and she hoped she hadn't been too harsh. "You're right. She cares, a bit too much most of the time, but she does care, and I appreciate that. She raised us boys, and we didn't make it easy for her. My dad's an easygoing guy, the kind who rarely got angry, and then you only knew it when he called you by your full name. A normal dad. Together, he and my mom were—and are—a formidable duo, and very happily married. So, she thinks that's what I need. She sees that kind of life as normal."

"That's lovely, but marriages can also be cold and indifferent and end up with no one being happy."

He glanced at her and their eyes met for a brief moment before they both turned away, him to focus on driving, and her to wish she hadn't opened the door to any personal discussion.

MAX'S FIRST THOUGHT was that she had been married and it had ended badly with her ex-husband, the card canceler. "You sound as if you're speaking from experience."

She didn't respond right away, and he waited. Then she finally said, "Yes, it's personal. My parents' marriage was…just a relationship, at least what I remember about it. It sure wasn't a good marriage, maybe a passable one at best." She actually chuckled at that, but there was no humor in it. "You know, it made me mad, and the way I showed it indirectly was by choosing the worst men to date."

He hadn't expected that, but reconsidered the credit card man and decided he probably was her last bad relationship, in spite of her implying that he wasn't. "How did that work out for you?"

"Not very well. My parents were so busy with their lives, I'm not sure they even knew about my dates. They definitely didn't show much interest in Bubba."

That caught his attention. "Bubba?"

"An old boyfriend who was, let's say, less than perfect. Bubba Ralston. Big mistake. Big, big mistake."

He wanted so badly to ask why it had been a mistake but didn't want to push too hard. "Not a nice guy?"

"He was pretty boring, actually, but he had a massive Harley, and we went on some great rides. He was a tattoo artist and really good at what he did. Basically, he was the kind of guy who would have really bugged my dad, but my dad was never home when Bubba was there. My mom met Bubba once—but she was headed to New York for a shopping spree, so she didn't say more than two words to him."

"So, it was all for nothing?"

"I learned I'd rather ride a horse than be on a Harley with a man who tattooed his own name on his chest in big black letters and showed it off to everyone."

"What happened to Bubba?"

"Last I heard he opened up a tattoo parlor just off the Las Vegas Strip and had most every part of his body covered in ink."

"One question?"

"Sure."

"Did he tattoo you?"

"Now that's personal, Sheriff," she teased.

"Oh, so he did…"

"No, but he wanted to. I'm not into pain, and tattoos are pretty much there forever. I didn't want that. Since you asked me, I'll ask you. You were in the army, right?"

"For eight years, most of them in Special Ops."

"So, what tattoos do you have?"

He glanced at her. "I have no tattoos."

"Come on, you have to have tattoos."

"No, I don't," he said. "I couldn't think of one thing I wanted to carry around with me for the rest of my life."

"You could have had your name tattooed somewhere on your body. I mean, you'll always be that person."

He kept his eyes on the highway. "I sure will be me."

"If you had your full name tattooed, what would it say?"

"Maxim—after my dad—Little-Hawk—after my grandmother's maiden name—Donovan."

"Little-Hawk. That's a pretty cool name, isn't it?"

"It means a lot to Mom."

"Okay, so since you won't admit to having a tattoo, I'm going to change the subject," she said. "Do you know anything about legal things? I've heard a lot of police want to be lawyers."

"I never have, but I can see it might help—and I don't have a tattoo."

"Yeah, okay," she said. He was about to protest, but she cut him off. "I'm just wondering, if I get a safety deposit box, and I put my money in it, can anyone else find out I have one and what it contains?"

"I don't think so, with privacy laws and that sort of protection. But anything's possible in this day and age, I suppose."

She sank back in the seat. "Maybe I should just stuff the money under my mattress," she muttered.

"Why not simply put it in a private safe?"

"Just assume that I don't have a safe, okay? Because I don't."

He cast her a look. "How about I assume that you do?"

She turned to face him more directly. "You can assume what you want, but I still won't have a safe."

"You do. Marty put in a safe at the Lodge."

"You're serious?"

"I told you I'd let you know when I'm joking by saying, 'I'm joking,' so we can both laugh. I'm not joking."

"Wow, I'd have thought Burr would have told me."

"I thought he had, and the safe isn't in sight. Marty made sure of that. When we get back to the Lodge, I can show you where it is."

"It's behind that meteor-night-sky painting over the bed, isn't it?"

"Nope."

"I guess I've watched too many movies where the rich

guy exposes his safe behind a Rembrandt or a Picasso. So, where is it?"

"In the tall wall cabinet that's between the desk area and the kitchen."

"I opened that, and it was empty. Are you sure?"

"Very sure."

"Okay, then all I have to do is call Burr and ask for the combination."

Max glanced at her; her expression now was nothing like it had been on the drive up. Now, she looked relaxed, her features soft. He liked that. "No, I can tell you what it is. He gave it to me and made me memorize it."

GRACE DIDN'T ASK why her uncle trusted Max Donovan so much. She—who basically trusted no man—was getting closer to trusting Max. He seemed to be a good person. It was that simple. She'd trusted Walter for a while when she was young but found out the hard way that he was the very kind of person he'd warned her about, someone always with a self-serving agenda. It had been painful for her to realize that it was all about him, all the time.

"We're here," Max said. The entryway to the ranch came into view. It was fancy, set off the road and surrounded by white rail fencing. A carved gold-lettered sign swung from the massive brick archway above a wooden gate. It announced, "Flaming Sky Ranch—Welcome!" Under that was the logo of a black horse with its mane and tail fanning out behind it and a burst of red-and-yellow flames shooting out of its hooves. Under that sign was a smaller one that swung in the light breeze: "Everything Rodeo."

"They just had the arch built and installed a new calling system." Max entered a code in a keypad by the gate and it slowly swung back, giving access to a broad driveway with a rise ahead that blocked whatever lay beyond it.

They drove past more rail fencing until they reached another sign carved to look like a huge golden saddle. It held a list of several locations with arrows pointing visitors in the right directions. The list included everything from the ranch offices to a rodeo arena, food sales, deliveries and even a first aid station. It almost reminded her of a sign at an amusement park.

"This is it," Max said as they crested the rise, and Grace saw Flaming Sky Ranch appear in front of her: a mix of buildings and livestock enclosures dotted the landscape, and rolling pastures stretched into the far distance, up toward the foothills.

"Wow, I thought a ranch would be a…a ranch, but this looks like a resort of some sort or a Western theme park."

"It is a ranch, but it's grown a lot over the years. My grandparents started with cattle, then horses, then my dad took over and he kept expanding it." Max drove slowly ahead. "When he had sons who fell in love with the rodeo, he decided to give us and other kids around here a real rodeo experience. We hold junior rodeos three times a year. The next one is in a week, over the Thanksgiving weekend. My dad has been building the ranch piece by piece—it's been his main focus since he retired from the rodeo. It's been an ongoing project for as long as I can remember."

Grace blinked, taking it all in. The view ahead of her almost rivaled the one from the Lodge deck. Among the buildings, one stood out: a long white structure with a weather vane on top of a steepled roof and holding pens out front. It had to be a stable. Not far from it was a big parking area next to an impressive outdoor arena. She could see men inside painting the bleacher seats.

"That's where the kids have their rodeos and where my

brothers and I learned to rope and ride," Max said as he pointed to the arena. "It's used a lot." He slowed and turned onto a dirt road just before they would have passed the stable. Massive trees arched over the road, their fallen leaves making a crunching sound as the Jeep drove over them. A tenacious few still clung to the mostly naked branches.

"Both houses down here can't be seen from the highway and are out of sight from any of the public areas."

They drove past a scattering of outbuildings—one looked like a much smaller version of the big stable, painted the same in white with black trim. A couple of paddocks were situated by double barn doors.

As the dirt road changed to inset brick, Grace asked, "How big is this ranch?"

"Just under four thousand acres, mostly flat land 'til you hit the foothills."

"That's huge. How many horses are here?"

"That varies so much that I couldn't make a good guess. The stable up here is for our horses. There's seven in there now."

"I saw an old stable at the Lodge, but it was empty. Did Uncle Martin have horses?"

"He did, a couple, but after he got weaker, working hands from here took care of them. Do you ride?"

"I did one summer when my parents sent me to camp while they went to Florida for some business thing. They didn't know it was a riding camp, and I was in hog heaven for ten days. I never got to do it again."

"So, I take it that if you were staying here, you'd want that stable at the Lodge to have at least one horse in it?"

"Maybe two or three, if that were the case."

"Let's get some food, and then I have someone I want to introduce you to. Rebel was a real close friend of Marty's, and I think it would do you both good to get to know each other."

"Who is he?"

"That's a surprise for after lunch. As for now, we're here," he said as he pulled into a semicircular driveway that led to an impressive portico framing the doorway of a sprawling, single-story house that blended perfectly with the land. From the aged clay tile roof to the sandy adobe block walls, arched windows and dark wood trim, the Spanish-style structure wasn't what she'd expected at all.

Max got out and came around to her side of the Jeep, opened her door and smiled in at her. "You're going to have the best tamales and salsa you've ever tasted."

For a day that had started with Grace being so nervous, even upset for a while, she now found that she couldn't stop smiling. "Wow, this is beautiful," she said as she stepped out of the Jeep. "You grew up in this house?"

"The one I live in now. We lived there while Dad had this house built for my mother after the ranch started really taking off. My dad had just retired from the rodeo. I was ten or eleven when we moved in just before Christmas one year." Max touched the small of her back. "Let's go inside."

He leaned around her to push open the unlocked door, and as she stepped into the foyer, she half whispered, "Wow!"

HE LOOKED AT HER, at the smile and wide violet eyes, and he thought *Wow*, too. But even *wow* didn't adequately describe Grace Bennet in that moment. He felt some spark in him, and he almost laughed, but couldn't understand it. What he did know was he was kind of relieved his mother wasn't there to read whatever expression was on his face right then. She was way too good at that and inevitably jumped to conclusions.

"I'll start the food," he said, walking through to the great room, which had views of the ranch through a series of sliding glass windows. He led the way to the kitchen, which was the room in the house that got the most use. He'd get their lunch together, then take Grace down to meet Rebel, and concentrate on that and not on his reaction to the woman smiling at him.

"This is quite a setup," Grace said.

He exhaled, figuring it might take time to stop having that reaction when he was looking at Grace. It made no sense. She'd be gone soon, and he'd always be here. That was a deal-breaker. That was reality. His reality.

CHAPTER NINE

GRACE ENJOYED THE food that they heated up, and the company. Max told wonderful stories about the three brothers who wreaked chaos on the ranch. He told her about the pond at the original house in the foothills, about hot summer days spent swimming and exploring. Rodeos held for kids that were as exciting as any professional rodeo. His dad retiring so he could be with his family, and how that had been one of the best days of his life.

As Max gathered up the dirty dishes, he asked Grace, "What was one of the best days of your life so far?"

She had to think, then finally said, "I'm not sure. Those tamales were the best I've ever had, though."

Max loaded the dishwasher, then came back to the table. "Dessert? There are a couple of pieces of my mom's apple pie left."

"No, thanks. I'm stuffed, but happy. So, who is this Rebel person?"

"Let's go find out," he said.

"I want you to know your refusal to give me instant gratification amounts to cruel and unusual punishment."

"Ma'am, I know the law, and I don't agree. It builds character to have to wait for something rather than getting it right away."

"Okay, Sheriff," she said with a smile and went with him back into the foyer to retrieve her jacket and purse.

When they stepped outside, Grace quickly pulled her

hat out of her jacket pocket and put it on with the earflaps down, then flipped up her collar. When she looked at Max, he had a smug expression on his face.

"Okay, so you were right about the hat and the collar thing," she said.

"I appreciate you saying that I'm right. In my business I don't hear that very often from the people I'm dealing with."

"I bet you don't. No apologies and no admission that you're right."

He grinned at her, then crossed to the Jeep and opened the passenger door. She followed, expecting to get in and go and meet her uncle's friend, but that wasn't the case.

Max said, "Let's leave your purse here. We're gonna walk."

She hesitated. It held literally all the money she had in the world. If it disappeared, she'd be lost. "I don't know…" she said.

"It'll be there when we get back. If it isn't, I'll give you the money you lost. How about that?"

It wasn't easy for her to just trust what he said, but she could try because it made sense. When it came to Max, she was gradually seeing the man he was, and that included a man with a deep need to help people, and a man who seemed real, not as if he was playing a part like a lot of the men she knew.

She pushed her purse under the seat. Standing back, she said, "I'm anxious to meet Rebel."

"I think you two will get along great. He knew Marty very well. They spent a lot of time together at the Lodge. I promised Marty that I'd find a place for him when Marty was gone. He likes it here, but losing Marty was hard on him."

"They were that close?"

"For almost ten years. We're going to take a shortcut. The ground's rough but it's a lot faster to get to the stable this way."

"I'm open for a walk. It's beautiful."

She was surprised when Max reached out to take her hand and firmly hold it in his. He met her eyes with that twinkle in them that she was beginning to notice gave away when he was joking or teasing.

"I don't want you to fall again," he explained.

She almost made a joke about no brochures and no wooden floors, but instead she let him hold her hand. She kept pace with him as they started across a mown grassy area toward a stand of trees. They walked in silence to the tree line, a mixture of old pines and deciduous growth. Soon, Max veered off to the left where there was a clear path through the stand.

He never let go of her, and she thought that it had been a long time since anyone had held her hand protectively. She liked the connection as they walked together over the ground that was spongy with layers of fallen needles and leaves.

When they cleared the trees, they stepped out into a wide open area. About a hundred feet ahead, she saw the smaller stable they'd passed on the way to the house. Two other buildings looked like double garages and a fourth was more of a lean-to with hay stacked under it. A man was pitching hay from a side pen into the bed of an old truck. When he saw Max and Grace coming toward him, he waved.

"Howdy there!"

His skin was weathered and lined, and she could see snow-white hair poking out from beneath a beat-up old brown Western hat. The hair matched a full beard. His clothes were familiar: boots, jeans and a heavy coat. He could be sixty or eighty, but he looked pretty spry.

Max let go of her hand as he moved closer to the older man. She thought she might be looking at Rebel, until Max said, "Chappy, I thought you were going to visit your brother in California."

So, he wasn't Rebel. With a pitchfork in one hand and the other on the side of the truck bed, he shook his head. "Naw, he's heading down to Mexico to look at some breeding stock, and I had no hankering to go with him."

Max turned and motioned Grace closer to him. "I want you to meet Marty Roberts's niece, Grace Bennet. She's staying out at the Lodge."

The man smiled. "Oh, real nice to meet you, ma'am. I sure was worryin' some idiot would tear it down or let it rot away. My heart'll rest easier knowin' it's not empty no longer."

Grace wasn't going to say anything about selling the Lodge; she couldn't do it. "I really like the Lodge. The setting is just beautiful."

"Marty loved it. He rode around his place all the time." He looked at Max. "What're y'all up to?"

"I wanted Grace to meet Rebel."

He pointed a thumb back over his shoulder. "He's inside being lazy." He shook his head. "He's missing Marty somethin' fierce. We all are, but work don't wait."

"That's for sure." Max motioned Grace toward the open stable doors. Grace walked with him into a ten-stall stable replete with the fragrance of leather and fresh hay in the cold air. Max kept walking to the last stall, which housed a beautiful pinto. The brown-and-black markings on its pure white coat were stunning, and a midnight-black mane and tail set off the coloring.

The horse crossed to the half gate. "Rebel, I brought a visitor. Grace Bennet, Marty's niece."

Grace stared at the man, then the horse. "Rebel?"

As if the animal understood, he tossed his head and whinnied.

Max reached out and stroked his neck. "Yes, this here's Rebel. This guy knows all of Marty's secrets and where he liked to ride. He's a living encyclopedia of knowledge when it comes to Marty Roberts."

A horse was the last thing she'd expected. She stepped closer. "I thought..." She shook her head, then cautiously reached to touch the horse's muzzle. It felt soft and his exhaled breath was warm on her hand. "Uncle Martin gave him to you?"

"I just promised to make sure Rebel always had a good home and was appreciated and treated well. I think, legally, you're his new owner since Marty left everything he had to you."

Rebel moved closer and pressed into her hand. "He's mine?"

"Yep, and he seems to like you." Max moved back a step to give her more room against the stall's wooden rails.

"Oh, my gosh," she breathed as she looked into his soft brown eyes. "I've wished for my own horse for years and years. I mean, since I was old enough to know how to wish."

"He's all yours if you promise to do what Marty wanted for him, give him a good home and treat him well."

She looked at him and the thought came to her that Max had made her wish come true. After some twenty years, she finally had a horse, a beautiful horse. She'd figure out how to best take care of him back in Tucson. "I promise I'll give him a good home and treat him well."

"Then he's yours."

She was so happy and excited, she had to resist hugging Max. "Thank you," she said. "I wish I could take him with me to the Lodge."

"Why not? The stable there was his home for ten years or more. I'll have it checked out to make sure it and the hay barn are safe to use. The weight of snow can be destructive to old wood. Once we know it's solid, you can take Rebel down there whenever you want to."

This only got better and better. "How long will it take to check it out?"

"A couple of days. But if there's a problem it could be longer before you can take him back there, maybe a week or more. While you wait, you can come up here and ride him around the ranch. Get to know each other."

Now Max was offering his ranch for her to ride on. "That makes sense, but I wouldn't know where to go for a ride around here."

"Don't worry. Someone'll ride with you at first."

"Would it be okay with you if I came back tomorrow for a short ride just to make sure I remember how to do it? Although I've heard that riding a horse is like riding a bicycle—you never forget after you've learned."

"I guess you'll know if that's true tomorrow. Early morning's best for riding."

What a day, Grace thought as she reluctantly left Rebel with Chappy while she and Max walked back to the house. Max took her hand when they got to the trees, and she cast him a sidelong look. Holding his hand could be addictive, and trusting him was becoming easier and easier. Yet, she barely knew him.

When they got closer to the house, she was prepared to ease out of Max's hold on her, but he beat her to it by abruptly letting go and waving to someone ahead of them. A lady was standing in front of the house, and Grace was pretty sure she was going to meet Max's mother. She was tall and slender, her dark hair streaked with gray and confined in a long braid. She hurried over to them and pulled Max into a hug.

"I'm glad I got back in time to see you today," she said, then turned to Grace.

"Grace, my mom, Ruby Donovan," Max said. "Mom, Grace Bennet, Marty's niece. She's staying at the Lodge."

"Yes, I know. Not that *you* told me about it, Max, but Elaine was by a few days ago and filled me in." Her dark brown eyes went from looking pleased to being touched by sadness. "Grace, I am so sorry about Marty's passing. He was a dear friend of our family. One of the nicest men I've ever met. I'm thankful he had family after all, and you're at the Lodge now."

Grace felt so good at what Ruby Donovan said about her uncle. "I'm glad I came," Grace said truthfully. She never would have known anything about the man who had lived here for so long, and who had made so many dear friends, if she'd done what Walter had ordered her to do that day on the jet.

"Elaine said you weren't sure if you're staying or selling."

"I need to settle my uncle's estate, then I'll figure it out, one way or the other. But even if I do leave, I won't forget where Uncle Martin called home or all the great people I've met."

"I was hoping you'd stay on and possibly reopen the Lodge, but you have to do what's best for you in the end."

"All I know right now is I want to honor Uncle Martin no matter what I end up doing."

"Thank you for that," Ruby said.

"Oh, and by the way, your tamales are fantastic."

Ruby smiled. "I'm glad you liked them."

Max spoke up. "Mom, Grace is coming over tomorrow to ride Rebel and get used to him before she takes him back with her to the Lodge."

"Well, you come over anytime you want to ride here. You're always welcome, and Rebel needs love," Ruby said.

"I was thinking, when Grace comes to ride, how about you ride with her on Jiggers?" Max suggested. "He could use the exercise, and you could get away from work for a while."

Ruby started to say something but seemed to think better of it. "I would love to," she finally said. "But I can't right now—I'm in the middle of getting the tax papers organized. I'm sure one of the boys would be glad to get a reprieve from painting the grandstand seats."

Ruby walked over with them to the Jeep and Grace decided to ask her something. Stopping by the passenger door, Grace turned to Ruby, very aware of Max standing close by. "Can I ask you something about your son?"

Ruby nodded. "Sure."

Grace leaned closer and whispered, "Did Max get a tattoo while he was in the army?"

Ruby looked surprised before she said, "I don't know. I don't think so... Why?"

"Oh, we were just talking about tattoos, and I didn't quite believe him when he said he didn't have any."

"What are you whispering about?" Max asked as he came closer.

Grace glanced at him. "Does he always hide things?" she asked Ruby, smiling.

He shook his head, a grin teasing his lips. "What things?"

"Tell me honestly, with your mother as a witness. Sheriff 911, do you or do you not have a tattoo?"

Ruby folded her arms and looked at her son. "Well, cows and horses."

Max shook his head. "Oh, no, you don't. I plead the Fifth."

"What's that mean, 'cows and horses'?" Grace asked.

"It's something we did with the kids when we wanted the truth. If we called cows and horses, they had to tell the truth. If they lied, their punishment was to not get to ride for a week or longer. They had to work the cattle for a week instead."

"Oh, interesting," Grace said.

"No, it's not." Max was smiling. "We're leaving."

"Thank you, Mrs. Donovan. And thanks again for the tamales."

Ruby hugged her again and whispered in her ear so only Grace could hear this time. "Thank you for making my Max smile."

That touched her heart. She couldn't imagine a Max who didn't have a smile for people. "Thank *you* for everything," she said, then got into the Jeep. She reached under the seat and the purse was still there. She tugged it out and put it in her lap, then looked at Max as he settled behind the wheel. "You were right again."

He glanced over at her, then down at her purse. "I'm on a roll," he said and with a wave to his mother, he drove around the semicircular drive and back onto the dirt road the way they'd come. At the main gates while they waited for the barriers to swing open, Max asked, "What did Mom say when she hugged you?"

Grace shifted to see him better. She liked the smiling Max. "Tell me the truth about your tattoos. Cows and horses. Now you have to tell me."

"You have that wrong. That's only between my brothers and my parents. Not just anyone can use it."

She waved dismissively. "I'm kidding. Your tattoos are none of my business. I don't care if you have a full-color picture of Santa Claus on your stomach."

"Sure you don't," he murmured and pulled through the gates and headed toward the highway.

"I really don't, but I'd love to hear the story behind your middle names. I remember you told me your full name is Maxim Little-Hawk Donovan."

"Little-Hawk was my grandma Eagan's maiden name. She taught at a rez school south of here. Grandpa was helping repair their small schoolhouse when they met. Her full name was Martha Ray Little-Hawk, and her family was Eastern Shoshone. My mom wanted to keep the names of her ancestors alive, so she gave one to each of us as a middle name."

Now she saw where Max's looks came from, the high cheekbones, the tan skin, and Ruby was tall and slender, so maybe his height came from her, too. "That's a wonderful thing to do for her family."

"At first I hated it," he said as he stopped at the highway. "But I'm pretty proud of it now."

"Proud enough to get tattooed with it?"

He gave a low chuckle and shook his head. "You're relentless, you know that?"

She grinned back at him.

"Now what did Mom say to you back there?" he asked.

"If she wanted you to know, she wouldn't have whispered it to me."

"I'll remember this," he murmured with fake gravity in his tone. "That means I'll never tell you if I have tattoos or not."

They both laughed at that, and as they drove south, Grace couldn't remember any man in her life who was so easy to talk to and laugh with. When the Lodge finally came into sight, she was still smiling. Today had been pretty great, and she owed most of it to Maxim Little-Hawk Donovan.

WHEN THEY ARRIVED at the Lodge, Grace went straight to the office and opened the tall cabinet where the safe was stored. She had to stand on her tiptoes to see the top shelves, and even then she wasn't quite tall enough.

"Barely warm," Max said, going across to her.

Grace looked over her shoulder at him. "It's nice and warm in here."

"But you are barely warm looking for the safe way up there. Clue—it's at eye level, or at least, Marty's eye level."

"I looked there. It's empty."

Max hadn't been in the room since Marty passed, and it seemed almost the same except for the bed, which was decidedly more feminine-looking now with a comforter in shades of blue and lavender. One other thing was the windows were sparkling clean now; all the dust and grime were gone.

Grace said, "This cabinet is empty."

"It's there."

She turned to Max. "It's not. Look for yourself."

"Let me show you how something can disappear then be there again."

"Please do," she said and stepped to one side to give him room.

He could feel her eyes on him as he peered into the cabinet. Marty had done a good job making something that was there appear almost invisible. But he could see it beyond the shelf: a very fine gap existed between the wood at the back and the edges around it.

When he reached in, Grace leaned toward him. "There's

nothing there," she said, so close to him now that he felt the heat of her breath brush his cheek.

He pressed a small spot at the back close to the right side where the white paint had been worn away. There was a soft click right before a twelve-by-twelve piece of painted wood swung silently forward to expose a wall safe that looked like an antique. Its burnished brass front had a heavy leverage handle and a combination lock.

Now Grace was leaning against him to get a better look. "I never would have found that." She moved back, put her purse on the kitchen table, and he got out of her way so she could have access to the safe. She reached inside, and he could see her running her fingers over the dial.

Grace turned to him. "I'm almost certain I can open this."

"What are you, a safecracker?" he asked, liking the way she blinked at his ridiculous question.

"Like I'd tell you if I was," she said with an expressive roll of her violet eyes. "I've only opened one before. I was nine years old and with my father at one of his offices. I hated being there and Sawyer knew it, so he gave me a challenge. He said if I could open the safe with one number missing from the combination, he'd give me a prize.

"I did it, after around thirty failed attempts and two clues from Sawyer. Inside it, Sawyer, who obviously knew how to open it, had left me a 1935 first edition of *National Velvet*." Her expression was almost wistful. "He knew I'd love it. I mean, I was obsessed with horses."

"Who was this Sawyer?"

"He was my father's assistant back then, and part of Sawyer's job was to keep me from annoying my father and the rest of the staff."

"That book must have cost a lot of money."

"I never even thought about the money until I was told

the book had to be put in some protective display box and not touched by human hands because it was so valuable."

A nine-year-old had a book she was obviously thrilled with, and someone told her not to touch it, to keep it in some sort of protective case? "So you never got to read it?"

"Sawyer told me he'd take care of it for me, but he winked when Walter wasn't looking." That brought an almost mischievous glint in her eyes. "So, he put it in the box it came in and left with it. When I went to my room, I found it under my pillow and the box was on the top shelf of my bookcase." She giggled at that. "I read all night under my blankets with a flashlight, and most nights from then on. It was wonderful, and I cried and…" She shrugged. "The ending was so bittersweet."

"Who's Walter?"

Her expression changed in a flash from the softness in her eyes at the memory to a faint frown. "Excuse me?"

"You mentioned someone named Walter."

Grace looked away from Max and back to the safe. "Oh, yeah…my father. He was hard to be around." She cut off any other questions he might have asked. "Let me see if I can open this safe." She moved closer and spun the combination dial. Taking a breath, she aligned the mark at the top of the dial with the start arrow, then exhaled. "First number?"

"Twelve," Max said.

She turned the old dial three rotations past the top point and stopped on twelve. "Next?"

"Twenty-two."

For the second number, she went two full turns left and stopped on twenty-two. When Max gave her the third number, she went one full rotation right and stopped at the number. "Okay, here it goes," she murmured.

Her hand was a bit unsteady as she reached for the brass lever by the dial and pulled it down. Nothing happened.

"Shoot," she muttered and spun the dial.

She tried again, and she echoed each number under her breath as she lined them up. The lever didn't move.

"You're sure that's the right combination?" she asked over her shoulder, her eyes fixed on the dial as she repeated the number Max had told her.

"I'm sure."

"Okay, old dials can shift from use. Let me try it one more time." She repeated the combination out loud as she turned the dial, then whispered when she stopped at the last number, "It can't be."

It had hit her suddenly: the combination was the same as her birth date. She didn't believe much in coincidences, but it had to be a coincidence in this case. Her uncle wouldn't know her birthday. Then she knew he had known. "The picture."

Max was quiet, probably thinking she was losing it, and maybe she was. She touched the lever, then tugged down on it hard. There was a click, then the safe silently swung open. Just three tries, but she didn't feel victorious. Uncle Martin had known her birthday, used it for the combination yet never tried to contact her. She felt as empty as the safe looked inside.

When she turned to Max he seemed uncertain. "I thought you'd be happy you conquered the safe," he said.

"Oh, I am. I'm just overwhelmed. I want to lock the money up and figure things out from there."

Max leaned over, picked up her purse and held it out to her. "Here you go."

She took it, reached in for the bank pouch, then dropped her purse to the floor. She opened the pouch to remove a thin stack of bills that she'd had Bert separate from the other thicker stacks. She handed it to Max.

"That's Henry's money and your money." Then she turned and closed the pouch with the rest of the money and put it in the safe.

She almost closed the door but stopped when she realized something was already there, lying at the bottom almost out of sight. She took out a single blue envelope that was identical to the other two Burr had passed out. The same unsteady hand that had written her name on the first envelope had written *"Leave in safe for Grace"* on this one. She shut the door, then spun the dial before she held her find up for Max to see.

"Just one this time," she said, then reached to lay the envelope on the table. "Thanks again for all you've done for me, Max, and thanks for taking me to meet Rebel and trusting me with him." She knew she was starting to babble, and she stopped herself then added, "Let me know when I can get him down here."

"Of course."

She moved past him toward the door. She didn't want to be in the room any longer. She needed to breathe and digest what had just happened.

When she'd passed through the reception space, she went into the great room and sank down onto the couch. Max came to stand between her and the fireplace. She looked up at him when he spoke. "I wasn't going to say anything, but... I need to."

She hoped it wasn't about the new letter she'd found. "What is it?"

He sat down next to her and shifted to meet her eyes. "What happened in there when you were opening the safe?"

She wasn't actually surprised that he'd noticed the moment she'd recognized the combination. She wanted to tell him nothing had happened, but she couldn't because he might have answers for her. "You're too good at your work, Sheriff," she said.

"What does that mean?"

She shrugged. "I'd hoped you didn't notice, but you obviously picked up on the fact that something surprised me or bothered me."

"So what surprised you or bothered you?" he asked patiently.

"The combination to the safe. I recognized it." She reached for the original envelope she'd received from Burr that she'd left on the coffee table. Fumbling, she took out the small picture and, ignoring the unsteadiness in her hand, offered it to Max. "Look on the back," she said once he took it.

He turned it over, and she caught the moment he realized what the numbers on the back were. He took another look at the picture, then his eyes lifted to hers. "It's your birth date?"

"It is. He knew it when he set the safe's combination." She bit her lip, then said, "You knew him. Tell me why he'd do that and never try to meet me in person."

"I honestly don't know." He looked more closely at the picture. "These are your parents?"

"Yes, at my sixth birthday party when I'd wished for a horse, and I got a fashion doll modeled after my mother."

When he lowered his gaze again to the picture, she knew what he was probably thinking: that no one was smiling, especially not the birthday girl.

"Where was it taken?"

"At a restaurant on the top level of…a hotel in Las Vegas."

He handed the picture back to her and she slipped it

into the envelope. "I want to show you a picture I have," he said and undid his jacket to get to his jeans back pocket. He took out a tooled leather wallet, flipped it open and handed it to Grace. "It's from five years ago, the day we finished the extension on the back deck. Chappy took it."

Grace looked down at a five-years-younger version of Max in the photo, with longer hair and a grin on his face. Then she saw Uncle Martin, who looked very much like Walter, but more tanned, with more gray hair. Where Walter was very refined, his brother was rougher look-ing wearing a red plaid shirt and jeans, and he was grin-ning like Max. Only five years ago he'd looked healthy and strong. Then she realized she'd never asked what ill-ness he had.

"What did he die from? No one's said."

Max hesitated, then exhaled as he took off his hat and laid it between them. "Kidney failure. He'd had problems off and on, then it got worse."

"He wasn't…you know…alone, was he?"

"No, I was with him, and Burr and Elaine were there. Most of the town had visited him over his last week. He knew he was loved, and he was peaceful."

She closed her eyes. "I should have been there," she said.

She was startled when she felt Max touch her cheek for a fleeting moment. "Don't do that to yourself. That's a black hole that is hard to climb out of. Marty had an easy heart."

"An easy heart," she whispered, wishing her heart didn't ache. She felt overwhelmed by everything. The world was unpredictable, and she was exhausted. She had to open the second letter, but she had to do it alone in case she bawled like she had after she read the first one. She cleared her throat with a soft cough, then looked at Max. "Thanks for showing me that picture. He…he looks a lot like his brother. Now, you should go and take what's left of your day off to do something for yourself for a change."

He glanced at his watch, then said, "I need to check in with Lillian before I head home."

"Don't waste any more of your free time."

He stayed seated. "One thing you'll learn about me is I only waste my time when I want to."

She felt drained. "I'm just really tired."

He put his wallet in his jacket pocket. "I wish I had answers for you about Marty. But just know that he always had a reason for what he did."

By that logic, Grace felt even worse. Then she remembered the anger in Walter when he'd spoken about his brother. Maybe he didn't make any contact because he wouldn't face his brother again. No matter why he did what he did, it was over.

"Even if I had answers, it wouldn't change the past," she said softly.

CHAPTER TEN

MAX KNEW HOW true her words were. The past was done. It never changed. There was no way to edit anything. And he could see how much it bothered Grace to not understand why Marty had done what he'd done. He couldn't give her answers to her questions, just guesses.

"If you'd like, I can change the combination on the safe or find someone to do it."

"No, thanks. It is what it is."

"Maybe an early night will help."

"Maybe so," she said on a heavy sigh.

He almost told her he'd make tea, but he knew she wanted him to leave. She was too polite to tell him to go away. He'd promised Marty to help Grace, not smother her. He eased to his feet and put his hat back on. "I'll be heading out."

Grace stayed sitting as she crooked her neck to look up at him. "Max? Can I ask you something? If it's too personal, I understand completely, but I was wondering if Uncle Martin mentioned me at all in the letter he left for you."

He didn't know what answer she wanted: that he'd mentioned her, or that he didn't mention her at all. Then he thought of one mention that he should have told her on the way back from the ranch. "Yes, he did. He wanted me to make sure you got Rebel, if you really wanted him. A cowboy always takes better care of his horse than himself, and he always took great care of Rebel."

That seemed to distract her. "Cowboy? Uncle Martin?"

He liked the idea that her emotions were so easy to read. Happiness when she found out about Rebel. Surprise, happiness, a bit of sadness having to leave him there, and now, disbelief that her uncle would be considered a cowboy.

"You didn't think Marty was a cowboy out here?"

"I thought he did all of this. I never thought he'd have time to do cowboy things."

He chuckled at that. "What do you consider cowboy things?"

"You know, taking care of cows and horses and plowing."

"He didn't own any cows, but he plowed and cleared land, and he rode Rebel every chance he got. He loved riding."

"I've always loved the idea of a horse, and when you're young anything seems possible. It didn't matter that I lived in a hotel suite." Thankfully, she was almost smiling now, even if her voice was tinged with sarcasm when she said, "I would have settled for a stuffed horse."

"You finally have a horse."

She stood slowly and looked up at him. "Because of you," she said and unexpectedly reached out and hugged him.

He froze for a second, and when he finally realized he wanted to hug her back, she was moving away. "What was that for?"

She actually blushed. "I'm just happy and you made it happen. I can't wait for tomorrow to go to your ranch to ride him."

What he needed right then was to leave, to go out into the cold air and think straight. To be a friend to Grace was his goal, but he wasn't stepping over the line. He was there to try to show her the Lodge as Marty saw it; with the hope she'd end up staying. He knew the odds of that happening were low to nonexistent.

"Get some rest and come by in the morning when you're ready to ride."

Grace followed him, talking quickly. "I can go down and check out the stable. I saw it, and it looks okay, I mean, old and weathered, but it's not tipping to one side, and I didn't notice any holes in the roof."

He got to the front door and reached for the handle but paused before he opened it. "I'll be in touch as soon as Chappy checks it out."

"I just don't want to be a bother," she said.

She wasn't a bother—only when she hesitated every time he offered to help and called herself a bother. He wouldn't do that again, unless it was really important. He'd figured out that she didn't like feeling as if she wasn't in control. "You have my number," he said.

"Max, I finally have an answer to your question about the best day of my life."

"What was it?"

"Today was the best day of my life."

He was speechless. "Good…good, I'm glad," he said, feeling as awkward as a teenager. He quickly opened the door and headed out to his truck.

Between the hug and what she'd just told him, he felt confused as he took deep breaths, then got behind the wheel of the pickup. He figured Grace was kind of a spontaneous person, and that was why she'd hugged him. It was that simple. What wasn't so simple was his confusion when she'd smiled at him and said she'd just had the best day of her life. What stunned him even more was the day he'd spent with her was now in the running to be the best day of his life, also.

GRACE WAS UP most of the night thinking about the second letter. As dawn broke, she sat in the big chair looking out at the coming day. Finally, she retrieved the envelope and opened it when she sat down in the chair again. It contained a single sheet of paper with only one side written on.

She took a couple of breaths, then read the unsteady script.

Dear Grace,
You have found the safe and been given the combi-
nation. Hopefully Max gave it to you. I wanted to let
you know that every time I opened it, I thought of you
and I smiled. Life sorts out in odd ways, but there
is always a plan, a reason for everything. I found
that out the hard way, but I hope you're a better stu-
dent of patience and fate than I've ever been. But
at the end, all fell into place, and I saw how perfect
a life I'd had, that the peace I'd hoped for became
a reality. Don't give up, never stop, and know that
you became a very important person in my life even
though I couldn't be with you. I hope you'll forgive
me for my choices if they hurt you but know that I
always loved you.

The tears were soft and not harsh and cutting, the way they'd been after the first note.

"I could have loved you, Uncle Martin," she whispered into the air. "I could have been with you when you needed me." She blew out air and swiped at her eyes. All she could do for her uncle was to make sure nothing he left was destroyed. This wasn't about her anymore, but all about Martin Robert Bennet's legacy.

She stood and hurried to get dressed for the ride. As she pulled on her new thermal boots, she looked up at the ceiling and said, "Thank you for Rebel, Uncle Martin. I love him." For some reason she felt her uncle would know that, and she actually smiled.

Dressed for the cold, she pulled on her hat and felt almost giddy, like her nine-year-old self had felt when she'd conquered her fear and found that being high in the saddle on an old brown horse at the camp was about the best thing she'd ever known back then.

She stepped outside into a deep chill in the air. Hurrying down the steps to the Jeep, she stopped when she saw a red pickup truck coming up the driveway. She couldn't see the driver until the truck slowed at the curve and came to stop at the foot of the steps. The window slid down and Chappy smiled out at her.

"Mornin', Miss Grace. I come to check out the stable and hay barn for Max."

"Oh, thank you so much."

"No need for thanks. Are you taking off?"

"I was going to drive up to Flaming Sky and ride Rebel so he can get used to me."

"That's aces. I'll take care of everything here."

"Is Max still there?"

"I don't think he got back last night. But Ruby's there. She'll let you in. We'll get Rebel back home as soon as we can." With that, he drove off toward the gravel access road beyond the end of the Lodge and headed down to the stables.

Grace climbed in the Jeep and went in the opposite direction to the gates.

When she arrived at the entrance for Flaming Sky,

someone buzzed her in, and she continued to drive up to the main house. She parked in the driveway in the same spot Max had parked the day before; no other vehicles were in sight. Before she even got out of her Jeep, she heard an engine getting louder. Then the county sheriff's truck came into view. She had been excited before, but now she felt downright elated.

Max pulled up beside her Jeep and the passenger window slid down.

"Come on, get in," he called out to her.

She did as he said, closing the truck door before she turned to look at him. "I didn't expect to see you here. I thought you'd be on your way to work."

"I have to go down to headquarters at Two Horns to have a one-on-one with the fiscal adviser for the county about expanding the size of the substations. But I have some time before I need to leave. I thought I'd go with you for a short ride and see how you and Rebel do together, then head south."

That was perfect. She'd been worried about riding with a stranger when she didn't even know if she could get up in the saddle by herself. "If you can, that would be great."

"Aces," he said and drove around the top of the half circle and back onto the dirt road. When they neared the smaller family stable, he kept going. Before she could point out the obvious, Max said, "Rebel's down at the main stables being checked out. He had a tender foot when he came up here from Marty's. He's been fine, but I figured checking it before we left wouldn't hurt."

"He's okay, though, right?"

"Sure, he's good. Chappy asked one of the hired hands to saddle him and Thunder up since I don't have a great amount of time."

She sank back in the seat. "Thunder?"

"My horse. I've had him going on six years. When Marty and I rode, he and Rebel got along just fine."

"Friends, huh?"

"I don't know if that's what you'd call them, but they never got snippy with each other or acted up when they were together."

They came to the main drive and Max turned left toward the busy part of the ranch, where all kinds of activity were taking place around the stable. Horses were being led toward the arena, and several trucks were parked in the area.

Max came to a stop near the open double doors and glanced over at Grace, who was trying to take everything in. Red, white and blue bunting hung from the fascia of the stable, giving it a festive feel. "We'll leave the truck here for now."

No sooner had they stepped out than a man called out, "Max! Perfect timing."

Grace looked in the direction of the voice to see a tall man with longish graying dark brown hair showing under a white Western hat striding toward them from the stable doors. His broad shoulders tested the fringed suede jacket he was wearing, and he looked as if he was used to hard work. When he smiled, Grace knew without Max having to introduce him to her that the man was his father. They were so much alike, from the long strides to the strong build and sharp features. Then as he came closer, she saw hazel eyes that mirrored Max's. She figured she was seeing how Max would look in thirty-plus years.

Max moved over to Grace by the truck. "Hey, Dad, I want you to meet Marty's niece, Grace Bennet, all the way from Arizona. Grace, my dad, Dash Donovan."

He stopped in front of them, touched the brim of his hat

and his smile really did remind her of Max. "Right pleased to meet you, Grace."

"Nice to meet you, Mr. Donovan," she said.

"Around here, I'm either Dad to my three sons, or recently Papa to my new granddaughter. I'm Dash to everyone else. No formalities, okay?"

"Dash it is."

"I thought you were going back up to Cody, Dad."

"The contracts are signed. Burgess was generous this year and signed right away."

"Good for you." Max seemed impressed. "We're going riding. Do you have time to come along?"

"Oh, son, I wish I could, but I've got a lot of prep to do for the rodeo," he said on a rough chuckle, then nodded to the two of them. "Ride safe," he said before heading off.

Max touched Grace's arm to urge her toward the stable doors. When they stepped inside, Grace realized it wasn't just a stable. There was a large indoor training ring that took up one full half of the space, with seating on the outside of the low wall that ran around it. The other half of the structure was taken up by stalls.

Grace spotted Rebel right away, saddled and ready to ride, standing with a second horse at the hitching rail by the training ring gates. The other horse was waiting patiently. Its coat was unique, at least to her—a pale gold color set off by a deep brown mane and tail, along with identical stockings on all four legs.

"Hey, Chance," Max said to the man standing beside Rebel. "Thanks for saddling them up for us."

Chance was short and stocky with smears of white paint on his jeans, khaki jacket and worn work boots. "Chappy asked me to do it, and I was stoked to get a break from painting the bleacher seats." He glanced at Grace and smiled. "Howdy, ma'am," he said.

Max made the introductions. "Chance, Grace Bennet, Marty Roberts's niece from the Lodge."

"My, my, my," the man said. "I'm right honored to finally meet Marty's family and know Rebel can go back home. He's been grieving hard over Marty's passin'."

Grace turned toward Rebel, her eyes starting to burn with tears that she didn't want to show up right then. "Can I take him now?" she asked, thankful her voice didn't betray the crushing sadness she was feeling. She thought it was Max who handed her the reins, but she didn't turn toward him. "Thank you," she said and led the horse toward the open doors to get outside.

Max followed with Thunder and stopped beside her. "Do you need help getting in the saddle?"

"No," she said as she turned to Rebel.

Grab the saddle horn, then get my left foot in the stirrup and pull hard and push with my right foot.

In her thoughts that sounded so simple, but when she was actually positioned for what she hoped would be a successful mount, it eluded her. She pulled but couldn't find the leverage to get even close to sitting on the horse's back. Rebel was patient, and Max wasn't rushing in to boost her into position.

All he said was, "Grip the saddle horn with your left hand, the back of the saddle with your right, then push off with your right leg." After two attempts, she was safely on Rebel's back. She exhaled with relief. "This is higher than I remembered."

"Don't worry about that. Look up and around and enjoy the view. You'll do just fine."

Grace looked away when a slow smile touched his lips. Max Donovan was a man she was starting to like being in her life, a man who she figured would make a very good friend. She could use that while she was here. But she knew that depending on others had cost her with her father, maybe even with her mother. She took a deep breath of cold air and tried to clear her mind so she could concentrate on riding.

IT WAS A peaceful ride for Max, enjoying Grace taking it all in and talking to Rebel as if he was going to answer her. That further cemented in him the feeling that he'd done the right thing by giving the horse to Grace. As they neared the foot of the switchback that led up to the original ranch house on Donovan land, his cell rang to let him know he was needed at headquarters as soon as possible. They rode at a faster pace coming back to the stables, and Grace was able to keep up.

After asking Chance to look after the horses, he drove Grace back to the house so she could get her Jeep, and Max let the truck idle while Grace was getting out.

She turned to look back in at him. "I can't believe how much I remembered once I was up in the saddle."

"You did a good job with Rebel," he said. "I'll see you later."

"Okay," she said, then reached to close the door, but stopped. "Max?" He glanced back at Grace who met his gaze. When she spoke again, he almost lost his breath. "I think I'm falling in love."

That blindsided him, and he tried to figure out what to say, but Grace threw him a lifeline.

"I just feel as if I've known Rebel forever. Silly, I know, but he's so great. I can't tell you how much I wish… I'd come here before. I wish…" She shook her head. "I wish I could tell Uncle Martin that I love Rebel."

She was talking about the horse, and he'd immediately thought she was talking about him. That was ridiculous. He managed to say, "I think it's mutual."

She smiled at him. "I hope so."

She swung the door shut and he drove off around the curve in the drive to get back onto the road to the gates.

CHAPTER ELEVEN

WHEN GRACE GOT near to the Lodge, she didn't slow down, but kept going to town. The day had been perfect so far, and she'd meant it about loving Rebel. Without a thought, she'd told Max the truth; a man she barely knew was the one person who would understand her instantaneous connection with the horse. He'd looked surprised when she'd said it out loud, and then he'd hurried away to get to his meeting. She understood: he was in work mode. But she was glad he'd been there for her first ride even though it was cut short.

She wanted some really great riding boots and remembered a pair she'd passed over the first time at Farley's. They were a deep mahogany leather with silver studs and images of shooting stars tooled into the sides. Farley had told her they were about the best boots she could buy for warmth and riding. She was going back to try them on and hoped they'd fit.

After she'd parked in front of the general store, she hurried inside. Farley was right there to greet her, talking nonstop while she tried on the boots. She left the store wearing them and had to admit they were incredibly comfortable. Her other boots were in a bag along with a couple of flannel shirts and more heavy socks. As she was putting the bag inside her Jeep, her phone chimed, but she didn't recognize the number except for the area code being local.

She answered and a lady's voice asked, "Ms. Bennet?"

"Yes, this is Grace Bennet."

She was surprised when the caller introduced herself. "Lillian Shaw. I work at the substation in Eclipse with Sheriff Donovan. Would it be all right if I came up to the Lodge to talk to you about something important?"

"Sure, of course." Her imagination went to the worst reason the woman would want to talk to her, that Max had been hurt or… She stopped right there. "I'm in town now at the general store."

"Perfect. Do you know where the substation is?"

"Yes, I do."

"Do you want to just meet me there instead?"

"Sure," Grace said. "I'll be there in ten."

Grace left the Jeep by the store and walked to the station. When she stepped inside the door, she came face-to-face with Lillian Shaw. From what she'd heard about Lillian, she'd expected a bigger woman, stern and firm in her duty. Instead, the lady who stood behind a large desk was barely five feet tall, with graying brown hair in a tight knot, wearing a neat uniform shirt and sharply creased black slacks. She smiled warmly at Grace, motioning her to a wooden chair in front of a section of the front desk that formed an L-shaped workspace.

"Thank you so much for coming here. Please sit down."

Grace fumbled with her jacket buttons, feeling a bit warm after the brisk walk to get there, then took off her hat and pushed it into her pocket. She didn't wait to ask, "Is something wrong with Max… Sheriff Donovan?"

"Oh, no! I'm sorry, I guess it might have sounded like that. I apologize, dear. He's in Two Horns at a meeting."

She didn't try to hide her relief while she wished her

imagination didn't always go to the worst scenario first. "That's great," she said. "Now, why *am* I here?"

"I need to ask you one thing before I explain that to you."

"What thing?"

"I know the sheriff trusted your uncle implicitly and from what he's told me about you, you're a lot like Marty. I need to trust you to keep what I'm going to say between the two of us."

She had no idea what this was about, but if Max trusted Lillian so much, she would, too. "You have my word."

"Thank you," Lillian said. "This is the thing. That so-called meeting at headquarters turned out to be a meeting with internal affairs at the request of one of the citizens in town. They sucker punched Max with a complaint against him brought by a concerned citizen." She put air quotes around *concerned citizen*. "The man claimed Max was repeatedly squandering county money during work hours on personal business. He requested an investigation. He never mentioned you by name, but insinuated enough so anyone would assume his personal business was with you."

Grace was dumbfounded. "Was the man serious? I've been here mere days, and all I've seen is Max working all the time and helping people. Why would the man do that to Max?"

"Bluntly put, Albert Van Duren is running against Max to be sheriff, and he's trying to stir the pot any way he can to beat Max in the vote."

She understood why Lillian was speaking to her about it. "Max told me about Mr. Van Duren being sheriff for a long time and how he wanted to be back in office."

"Albert is what I call a snake in these parts, a truly low human being even if he was sheriff once. He wants to win,

and the trend around here leans toward Max. I guess he's
going into full gear now there's only a few weeks left before the election. It's two Tuesdays after Thanksgiving,
you know. Albert's claiming Max is tarnishing the office
and that he's making overworked deputies cover his shifts
while he's off having fun with a new resident."

"Wow," she whispered.

"Yes, that's how I felt when I got the call from a friend
who was there. Albert knows Max is relatively young, and
there are pretty women around. Some men can get lost that
way, but he's not on the prowl. He almost got married a few
years ago but it blew up in his face and he's pretty much
all about his family and work now. And he's darn good at
what he does. But if people get the wrong idea, they can
go after you. We have our jerks around here, and Albert
seems to cultivate that circle of townsfolk."

"That's horrible. There's nothing between…" She
stopped herself when it occurred to her that someone
thinking that something was going on between her and
Max wouldn't be that far off the mark. "I'm so sorry. I
knew he was helping me, but it took time away from his
family, not his job. That's garbage. What can I do to stop
this?"

"Be careful if you're approached by some good old boy
who tries to pump you for information. These people tend
to show up at a few town locations—the diner, the general store, any rodeo-linked event, the Golden Fleece Saloon, the One Q-Ball Pool Hall. If you're ever at one of
those places and someone starts talking about politics,
don't take the bait."

"Everyone around here seems so kind and neighborly.
I could tell them how great Max is, and how kind he's
been to me, but I won't even say that, if you don't think
I should."

Lillian smiled. "You shouldn't. Thank you so much for coming over and understanding the situation. Max didn't seem to think it was going to be an issue, but I'm afraid he's wrong. The truth is Max has been kind of like a son for me and Clint, my husband. I've seen him graduate from high school, go on the rodeo circuit, then to the army. He came back home six years ago and fit right in with this job. He's had a few rough patches here over the years, but he's solid."

"I know how solid he is. Thank you so much for the warning."

Lillian glanced past her, then said quickly, "Max is coming. He can't know we had this talk. He'd be embarrassed."

"I don't know what you're speaking about, Ms. Shaw."

The older woman smiled conspiratorially. "Call me Lillian, please."

Max pushed the door open and stepped inside, turned, and saw the two women. "Is this business?" he asked. "Grace, you didn't have trouble, did you?"

She could smile easily about that question. "No, I... I came to meet this Lillian person you talk about so much, and we got to chatting, and..." She glanced back at Lillian. "I'm sorry I took up so much of your time, but I'm glad I got the chance to meet you. Well, I should get on the road."

When she looked back at Max, he had his jacket off and had hung it on a hook on the wall by the door. His hat, too.

She would have loved to have lunch with Max if he asked. She was starving, but she figured the diner wasn't a good place for her to be seen with him right now.

"How did your meeting go?" she asked.

"It went. They refused our request for funding to expand the space in county substations. It was my third try, but I don't give up easily."

She looked around the long narrow space that served as

the sheriff's office in the town. From what she could see over a half wall that separated the reception area from the business area, they could have doubled its square footage and it still wouldn't be enough.

"Can you put it on the ballot?"

He shrugged. "I think that's my next step, but I wanted to save the expense of a special election."

"Yes, of course," she said. "I should get back. Chappy was there when I left for the ride."

"Maybe I'll stop by and see what he's done."

"You don't have to. I know you're busy."

He narrowed his eyes slightly but didn't answer.

Lillian stepped in. "Not so fast, cowboy. For now you're needed at the Grange Hall to talk about security. They're opening soon and need things to be signed off." She looked at Grace. "You come on back anytime, Miss Grace."

"I will," she said, pleased to find another resident who called her Miss Grace as if she actually belonged. She liked it. Then, as she stepped back to leave, she saw a stack of election signs leaning against the wall. Her first impulse was to ask for a few to put up at the Lodge entry, but that probably wasn't a good idea, either.

With a glance at Max, she left and walked back to the Jeep. Just when she was getting used to him and was actually starting to trust him and his motives, she had to stop being seen with him in public. Maybe the Lodge would be safe ground, and the Flaming Sky would be safe, too. But even then someone could pull up and see his truck parked at the Lodge or her Jeep at the ranch.

She smiled ruefully at the way things had to be from now on. Clandestine meetings between the newcomer and the handsome sheriff, planned impeccably to never be seen together. At any other time she would have laughed out loud at her thoughts, but not then. She'd just left Max at his office, and she already hated the thought of eating lunch alone.

She had just parked in front of the Lodge when a text came in. After turning the Jeep off, she got out her phone and saw it was from Max.

Chappy says weak cross beams need to be reinforced before heavy snow. Water line needs replacing and insulation. A couple of days if supplies are available locally. Could be a week, possibly two, if they have to be brought in.

She had enough to do around the Lodge, so a couple of weeks wouldn't be lost time. She sent a text back.

Thank Chappy for me. I'll be at Flaming Sky early tomorrow to ride Rebel again. Thanks for going with me today.

She waited for a response, but as the Jeep got colder and no text came back, she gave up and went inside. Max was probably at the Grange Hall, whatever and wherever that was, doing his job.

MAX WAS IN no mood to see Big and Little Albert at the Grange putting in their two cents on how security at the event hall should be set up. He looked down the long expanse of the narrow building, which had all recently been redone, from the newly painted dark beams overhead to the wood plank flooring underfoot. A food area was off to one side, a bar to the other, and in between were tables arranged in a ring around a greatly expanded dancing area. With a stage for live bands and caged lamps providing the lighting, it looked nothing like the old building had before.

The new owners were overseeing the final touches and

doing potential employee interviews. Max was stuck at a large table by the bar across from the two Van Durens, Big and Little Albert. There were no overt mentions of that morning's meeting, just sly digs here and there at Max.

"A little late for this meeting, too," Big Albert said when he arrived.

His laboriously irritating son nodded in agreement. "Time's money, you know."

Yeah, Max knew, and he wasn't going to rise to the bait dangled in front of him. He turned to the owner, Preston Clayton, the great-great-grandson of the first Clayton to have settled in the area. The middle-aged man had the build of a former bull rider and the patience of a saint, until he was crossed. Max had suggested that they didn't need heavy security every minute they were open if Preston was around. He was a deterrent just by his size.

"Yeah, you're right. I'll be dogging people," Pres said.

"The only other thing is you might want to have someone monitoring the cameras during your busiest hours to stop things before they can escalate."

"I'd say that's a good idea."

"Maybe rethink that, Pres," Big Albert interjected. "I've done a lot of security layouts, and it's wasting money paying someone to sit for hours watching the cameras."

Max shrugged. "That's up to you, Pres. You're smart and I'm leaving. If you need anything else, you know where to find me."

"Where would that be, Max?" Big Albert asked and Little Albert smirked. "Just north of town?"

He'd have to be foolish not to catch the meaning in that jab, but he simply stood, held out his hand to Pres to shake, then with a touch to the brim of his hat, headed to the door and outside. The sky was gray, and he could almost smell snow in the air. Once he was in his truck, he drove to town. He didn't know where he was going until he passed the substation and kept driving until he was out of Eclipse and approaching the Lodge.

He turned off the highway onto the cobbled area that led up to the gates. After putting in the code, he drove to park by Grace's Jeep. Once out, he took the steps two at time onto the porch, then crossed to knock on the door. There was no reply and he rapped again. Finally he heard something inside and the door swung back to show Grace facing him.

"Oh, Max, I didn't expect you to come here. Is there a problem?"

"Does there have to be trouble for me to stop by?"

"No, of course not," she said, but he sensed she was uncomfortable with him showing up unannounced.

"Are you okay?"

"Sure, just a bit sore from riding today. But I'm going to stand under a hot shower before bed and hope my muscles relax."

There was something different about Grace that hadn't been there that morning. He'd noticed it at the substation, and now he really felt her backing off for some reason.

"Good. Keep riding and that should clear up pretty soon. You just have to get through it."

"I had no idea that I'd have to suffer to ride, but I'll do it."

"You're a real champ."

She chuckled at that. "No, but now that I finally have my own horse, I'm not going to let anything stop me from riding. Did you need something?"

"Can I come in for minute?"

She hesitated, but said, "Of course. I'm sorry."

She closed the door after Max stepped inside. He took off his jacket, tossed it on the desk, then did the same with his hat. When he turned, Grace was close and the ease he'd felt with her, riding or driving or just talking, seemed to be fading.

"Do…do you want to sit by the fire and warm up?"

"I could use the heat," he said, and she led the way.

They settled on the couch and the fire did feel good. "I was on my way home and stopped to tell you there's a storm coming soon. The clouds are dark and angry and the air smells of snow."

She curled her legs under herself and sank back into the soft leather. "You can *smell* snow?"

"The air's different and the cold's sharper. Just wanted to make sure you're prepared for it."

"If it snows, can I still ride Rebel?"

"You shouldn't until you're more seasoned with him. If you went off alone, it could be a mistake."

His phone rang in the pocket of his jacket out in the reception area. "I'll be right back," he said, then went to answer the call.

GRACE KNEW SHE shouldn't have asked him in, but she wanted to. And it was a safe space. No one would know he was here. Maybe she could ask him to stay for a late lunch or an early dinner, so she wouldn't be eating alone. She glanced through the archway and saw him leaning back against the desk, intent on his conversation, then he stopped the call and came back into the great room.

"That was Lillian. Her husband Clint's sick with food poisoning. He ate something on a trip out of town and barely made it home. She needs to be with him, so I've got to get to the substation as soon as possible to cover for her until nine."

There was no point in asking if he wanted to eat with her. "Seems like you work all the time," she said.

"It feels that way to me, too, sometimes."

He went back to get his jacket and hat, then turned at the door before he left. "I'll see you when I see you," he said, then was gone.

As soon as the sound of the truck engine had faded into the distance, Grace felt the emptiness settle around her.

CHAPTER TWELVE

AFTER MAX LEFT, Grace started reading through ledgers that she'd found in her uncle's office space. She learned that the Lodge had brought in some good capital over the years, until eighteen months ago when the money began to dwindle down until the entries stopped.

She glanced out the back windows and decided she didn't want to eat her dinner alone in front of the hearth. Eclipse might be a small town, but she was almost sure that it wouldn't be a scandal for a single lady to be seen eating by herself at the diner. She bundled up, then grabbed her shoulder bag and car keys, and hurried out to the Jeep.

When she walked into the diner, the door had barely shut behind her before Elaine called out, "Hey there, Miss Grace!" and hurried over to meet her at the end of the counter. The diner was half-full, with people talking and laughing and country music playing in the background. The effect was very welcoming.

"Any special seat that you'd like?" Elaine asked.

Grace glanced at the booth she'd shared with Max, but a couple with a baby were seated there. "How about the counter, if that's okay?"

"Sure thing. Choose your stool," Elaine said.

Grace took one close to the door and swiveled to face Elaine, who had gone behind the red Formica counter and offered her a menu. The minute she saw the picture of the French dip sandwich, she knew what she wanted. But before she could order, a phone rang and Elaine went to pick it up at the end of the counter.

Grace smiled to herself when Elaine answered with, "It's a beautiful evening at the Over the Moon Diner. How can I make you smile?" She liked Elaine.

Then she heard the restaurant owner say, "Oh, I can't. I'm short-staffed. Maybe if it slows down in a bit, the cook could run something over for you." She paused. "I'll make it happen," she said and put the phone down before she came back to Grace. "Poor Max is covering for Lillian. Her husband got awful food poisoning and Lillian's at the clinic with him. Max is stuck at the station and starving, apparently."

Grace changed her idea about dinner right then. Max had brought her groceries when she was hungry, and she'd bring him dinner tonight. She owed him that much. "What's Max's favorite thing to order here?" she asked, leaning closer and lowering her voice some.

"That's easy. My beef stew, fresh rolls, cookies and coffee."

She lowered her voice more. "Okay. I'd like to order that and a French dip with fries for me. I'll deliver Max's dinner to him, but this has to stay between us."

That moment might have been the first time Grace had seen Elaine frown. "Oh, no. You heard about the meeting, didn't you? I swear that Albert is a miserable excuse for a human being. He thinks he's so smooth, but I heard he insinuated that you were involved with Max."

She nodded. "I don't know much about it, but I think Max deserves a good meal. I just don't want to make things worse for him in any way. He's been nothing but good to me."

Elaine leaned a bit closer, and her voice was only loud enough for Grace to hear. "I understand. Don't say any more. So, when you deliver Max's meal, park in the back lot off the side street, not in front. Use the back door. I'll let Max know he'll have a delivery soon, but I won't mention who's doing it."

This was getting really clandestine.

"Thank you so much."

"I'll get your orders. Give me a few minutes."

When Grace pulled into the back parking lot to the substation fifteen minutes later, there was only faint light coming from two back windows on either side of a low porch at the back door. Picking up the bag for Max and one of the coffees, she quickly got out and hurried over to the porch. Taking the single step up, she knocked on the door. At the same time a bright light came on outside, lighting up the whole area. It almost blinded her. She was tempted to leave the dinner on the porch and take off. But a bolt slid back, then the door swung open to reveal Max standing there.

"Grace. You…?"

"Delivery from the diner for Sheriff 911," she said.

He smiled at that. "You moonlighting for a delivery service now?"

"I offered to drop off food for you on my way back to the Lodge." She held out the bag and his coffee cup, anxious to get it over with and out of the light. She obviously wasn't meant to ever have a career in undercover work. "Beef stew dinner with hot coffee."

He took his order from her. "Come on in out of the cold."

"Thanks, but no. You…have a good dinner and stay warm," she said and turned to leave, but Max stopped her.

"Hey, it's warm in here, and honestly, I could use the company."

"Oh, I don't know… It's, well…" She couldn't stand

there much longer and hope not to be seen. "I... Sure, okay," she said. "I need to get my food out of the Jeep."

"You didn't eat at the diner?"

"No, I decided to do takeout."

"Great," he said and handed his order back to her. "I'll get yours from the Jeep and you put mine on Lillian's desk."

She'd hated him giving her orders when they'd first met, but now she was more than willing to take them and get inside. She stepped into a back room with a cot up against the wall on one side, shelves filled with files across from it and a credenza on top of which was a hot plate along with a coffee maker.

When Max came back with her meal, she was still standing there staring toward the front of the station at the large picture window that exposed the interior to anyone passing by. He eased past her in the limited space.

"The food smells terrific," he said. "Come on."

It had been a bad idea, unplanned and foolish. Max was at the front now, the food on the desk, turning toward her, frowning then calling to her. "What are you doing? The food's going to get cold."

She was relieved and surprised when he turned to lower a blind that covered the whole window, then snapped on a brighter light. She hurried to the desk and sat down in the wooden chair she'd used on her visit to Lillian. Putting his dinner down by hers, she waited while he went around the desk to sit in the computer chair, then reached for his bag and emptied its contents on the desk: a large container with the stew, two rolls and a small paper bag that held the cookies.

He looked up and smiled at Grace. "Wait until you taste Elaine's cookies."

She reached for her coffee and took the lid off. Taking a sip, she glanced across at him. "I've heard they're legendary, just like her coffee."

He lifted his cup, took off the lid and sipped some. "Great coffee," he said with a sigh. He seemed to study her before he said, "I'm glad you're here. I hate eating alone, especially when I'm stuck here, but at least Clint's doing okay. Poor Lillian, she does love that man."

Grace took her wrapped sandwich out of the bag and opened the container of dip. "It must be in the water around here, or in the air."

"What's that?" Max asked as he took the lid off his stew container.

"Love, I guess. It seems this town has a lot of longtime married couples who know what love's really about. You know, soulmates, that sort of thing. Like your parents, or Elaine and Burr."

He smiled ruefully. "How long do you think Burr and Elaine have been married?"

"I don't know. Maybe thirty years?"

"How about just over a year."

"I never would have guessed that."

"Well, they've known each other for years but it took a while for them to acknowledge the spark between them. Everyone else saw it way before those two realized what was right in front of them all along."

"At least they figured it out."

"My folks were different. Dad says he knew from the first time he saw Mom barrel racing that he was going to marry her. What he didn't know was that she'd already decided to accidentally-on-purpose cross paths with the infamous bull rider Dash Donovan to see if he was as charming in person as she hoped he'd be. Two months later on Christmas Eve, they were married."

She sighed softly. "Soulmates."

"If you believe in that kind of thing, yes."

She wasn't sure if she believed in that for her, but some people seemed to find that one person they could love forever. "You don't?" she asked, dunking her sandwich into the rich beef broth.

"I went on that wild ride once before and was bucked off. I'm not doing it again." He speared a chunk of beef. "I'll leave that up to my brothers."

"It was that bad for you?" she asked.

"Did you ever get hit so hard you had the wind knocked out of you and you had to fight to breathe again?"

"No. Well, maybe. I fell on a volleyball once, and it hit my stomach. For a second I couldn't catch my breath. Like that?"

"Not even close." He slowly took a drink of his coffee before looking back over at Grace without a smile this time. "It took me a long time to be able to breathe again."

"I'm sorry. Was it someone from around here?"

"Yes, right here in paradise." The sarcasm in his voice gave her goose bumps.

"Have I met her?"

"No, but you met her father, Freeman Lee."

"The man who was going to square off against Big Albert?"

"That's him. Claire is an only child, and she always wanted to do something bigger with her life—in her mind, she deserved better than the small-town ranch life. We dated in high school, then went our separate ways. She got a degree in genetic research and seldom came home after that. I didn't come back much, either. I did two tours over in the Middle East with the Army Rangers, then I came home, became sheriff, and to make a long story short, Claire showed up here three years later. Something happened at her job and she'd walked away from it. We connected again, and I thought I'd found the one I'd be able to have a good life with. We made plans, seemed to want the same things, so I bought a ring and proposed."

"She refused?"

"No, she didn't. She put the ring on and said that we'd have the biggest wedding in town. She started running around, looking for her wedding dress, getting on bridal registries and getting a write-up in the largest newspaper in the state."

"Then what happened?"

"We ended up with a hundred guests sitting in their seats waiting for the wedding ceremony to start. I was standing up in front, expecting Claire to come down the aisle at any time. But she didn't. I finally went back to see what was going on, and she was in a room by herself on the phone. She was talking to a man she'd worked with, begging him to come and get her, to stop her from making the worst mistake in her life. She couldn't be tied down to the life she'd told me repeatedly she loved. She couldn't bear it that I was a cop. I found out she had broken up with the man on the phone. That's why she came back home. But she'd never stopped loving him."

Grace was stunned. "She… I mean, she played you."

"That's one way to put it. After I could think straight again, I realized that, on some level, she'd come back here to make the guy jealous. That's why she did everything she could to let everyone know she was with me, especially him. I guess he took the bait, and she told me she was leaving."

She was almost sick listening to Max and seeing the tension in his expression. "What did you do?"

"I guess you could say I broke down. I heard myself telling her to get out. Her big problem was she didn't have a ride until Russell, the guy on the phone, got there, and it would take him two hours to show up. She started crying, and I was numb, then Dad showed up wondering where we were. He figured things out and told her he'd drive her back to her parents' ranch so she could wait there for her boyfriend to come get her."

"What about you?" she asked, the remainder of her sandwich forgotten.

"I left by the back door, took off for two weeks, then came back to figure out my new life. I worked past it, mostly thanks to Marty, who was a great sounding board for me. We played a lot of chess back then." He cocked his head slightly to one side as if sizing her up. "Sorry about all of that. I never talk about it, and now here I am ruining our meal by talking too much."

"No, it's okay." She started to wrap up her sandwich. "I'm just so sorry you and your family…and her family… had to go through all that. That's so incredibly sad and hurtful. Did she leave?"

"Yep. Freeman said she's working in Texas, doing genetic research again. She's still with Russell."

"That's it?"

"Yep, that's it. So you see, when you think you've found your soulmate, don't count on it being true. I'm not even sure there really is such a thing."

"So, that's that? It didn't work out with Claire, so there's no point looking anymore?"

He sat back in his chair. "I was dead wrong one time, and I won't go through that again."

"But—"

"No buts. I just want my life to be simple and do something I like doing. That's it." He cut off the conversation. "What do I owe you for the food?"

"Elaine said it's on her because she appreciates what you do for the town. She also hated how miserable that meeting must have been for you because of Big Albert."

He grimaced. "This town has an impressively fast gossip chain."

She put the top on her broth dip and placed it back in the bag with her wrapped half sandwich. "Was it really awful?"

"Not any more than usual when Big Albert is involved."

"What did he say?" she asked, already knowing the answer from Lillian. She'd never let him know what the lady had told her.

He shrugged. "He insinuated that I was abusing my office by passing off my work to the deputies while I went out and had a good time."

"What does he consider having a good time?" she asked.

"You know, having fun when I'm supposed to be working," he said.

"I don't know what that man would consider fun," Grace muttered.

Max looked away from her for a moment, then met her gaze again. "Albert insinuated that I was spending way too much time with you. I'm supposed to have violated the rules by having you in the truck with me during work hours. But the way he's slanting it, it's not true, at least most of it isn't."

"I was in the truck when you had the sirens and lights going on that call. But you've done nothing but help me." She shook her head. "I shouldn't be here."

He frowned at her. "No, you have every right to be here. I told the board to do what they want, but I've been doing my job."

"But you can't give him any fuel for the fire."

"Hey," he said and sat forward, putting his hands flat on the table. "He's a bully, Grace. He's politically motivated to get this job, and most people that vote around here know what he is. I'm not worried."

She was very worried for him. "I'm going to go." She drank the last of her tepid coffee, then dropped the cup in a trash container by the desk. "I'm sorry."

Max stood and came around to Grace, then reached out and cupped her chin gently in his large hand. His eyes were intent on her. "I promise this is just bluster from Albert. He's making a good show of trying to prove how dedicated he was when he was sheriff, but everyone knows he sat behind the desk most of the time. Just ignore him if you stumble across him, okay?"

"Don't underestimate him, Max."

"If anything, he's underestimating me." His fingertips skimmed along her jawline, then drew away. "You need to get home."

"I guess so," she said and put her jacket on, then picked up her bag with the leftovers in it. "When's Lillian coming back?"

"She's not. I'm covering until nine, then all calls will be rerouted. I told you how that happens. Someone will be available to take the 911 calls."

Grace nodded. She hesitated before asking him, "Can you make that light not come on outside?"

"No, I can't. Why?"

She shrugged. "For the same reason you closed the front blinds."

"Got me," he murmured, then reached around her to open the door but drew back when a beeping sound came from the front of the office. "Hey, hold on. I have to take this."

"Okay," she said, and she followed him back to the desk.

He clicked an icon on the monitor screen, then said, "Nine-one-one, what's your emergency?"

As MAX SILENTLY listened to an agitated man on the speaker, he knew he had a solid chance of solving the irrigation thefts. When he had all the information he needed, he spoke to Dutch Gates, the rancher on the phone, to verify his location. "A mile past Green Valley Dude Ranch off of Running Bear?"

"Yeah, I'm watching them now."

"Keep watching, but you stay out of sight. Do nothing until a deputy or I get there." He hung up, then put in a call, still on speaker. "Lawson, we have an incident and you're closer." He gave him the information, then said, "I'm on my way. No lights or siren after the turn. Wait for me, but if you need to move, do it carefully and keep your holster open."

With Lawson dispatched, he turned to Grace and realized she'd heard the whole thing. He hadn't thought about that. Now she was staring at him hard. "Work calls." He grabbed his jacket from a peg by the front door. "Thank you for being here and for bringing dinner." He smiled at her, hoping she'd smile back, but she didn't. "I'm sorry you heard all that. I never use the headpiece when I'm here alone."

"This is serious, really serious, isn't it?"

He wouldn't lie. "Yes, it could be the end of the irrigation equipment thefts."

"You're in real danger, aren't you?"

He didn't like this at all, especially the concern in those violet eyes. "I honestly won't know until I get there. Probably they'll be gone by then, or they'll stick around and give up."

She came closer to him and pressed her hand to his chest. "You're lying. I can feel your heart racing."

He almost joked that maybe it was her being so close that was making his heart beat faster. But that would be hokey, even if it was true. "Now you're a human lie detector?"

"I'm sorry. Just be careful," she said in a soft voice. Then she reached for the door latch, opened it and went outside. Max followed her to her Jeep. She got in behind the wheel and reached to close the door, but he grabbed it before she could shut him out.

He leaned down to look inside, not quite understanding why she was so concerned about the call. "It's my job to take care of the problem and walk away in one piece. You don't need to worry about me."

"You need to go," she said. "Good luck."

She was right. "I'll see you when I see you."

She nodded, and he let go of his hold on the door so she could close it.

He turned away and hurried to the truck, got it going, then drove across the lot to the side street, before merging with Clayton Way. He looked back and Grace was still sitting in her car, more of a shadow now without the inside light on, but he could clearly see her head was in her hands.

He forced himself to keep going, but for the first time since he'd been elected, he wasn't rushing full tilt to the scene of the possible crime. As soon as he was out of town and on the highway, he turned on his lights and siren and forced himself to focus on what he was doing. He wanted to be able to call Grace when he was done and let her know he'd walked away from it unharmed.

CHAPTER THIRTEEN

AT MIDNIGHT, GRACE was alone in the kitchen at the Lodge, thinking about possibly redoing the cabinets. She couldn't sleep and had finally given up. Now she was trying to keep her mind occupied by debating between painting everything a crisp white or staining the cabinets a dark oak. But she couldn't make that matter enough to distract her, because she kept hearing Max giving his deputy orders: *If you need to move, do it carefully and keep your holster open.*

She knew what that meant without having to be told—that he'd warned his deputy to take off the safety snap and make sure the gun was easy to get out. That made her skin crawl and she admitted to herself that she wasn't going to be able to focus on cabinet finishes, not as long as she hadn't heard from Max. As that thought formed, she turned and headed to the office.

The old chair by the window had become her favorite spot in the Lodge. She understood why her uncle had put it there and why it was so worn. She settled and stared out the window at the darkness. She knew her concern about Max was more than what it should have been, and she couldn't deny that after just a short time of knowing him, she found herself liking him more and more. It had been hard for her to hear what Claire had done. Even harder for her to know he was out there with his gun that wasn't just for show. She closed her eyes and rested her head against the back of the chair.

The sound of her phone ringing startled Grace and she scrambled off the chair to hurry to the nightstand and pick it up. She didn't recognize the number, but it was local.

On the fourth ring, she answered it. "Hello?"

When she heard Max's voice say, "Grace?" she fell back on the bed and closed her eyes. "Yes."

"I know it's late, and I hope I didn't wake you."

"I'm awake." She was very awake now. "Where are you?"

"I'm at the clinic in town."

"Are…are you okay?"

"I survived," he said calmly.

She was gripping her cell so hard that she thought she might crack the phone case. "What happened?"

"I got there and one of the suspects resisted arrest."

She squeezed her eyelids shut. "Are you sure you're okay?"

"Yeah, I'm fine. He had bad aim."

"He shot at you?"

"He was way off the mark, but it distracted him enough that Lawson could get behind him and tackle him. The other guy, who'd been cooperating until that point, took off running. I went after him, and to make a long story short, he looked back to see how close I was and ran into a cistern shed. He knocked himself out from the impact. It was hard work dragging him to the truck. Lawson has an amazing black eye, and the suspect with the rifle broke his wrist somehow."

She didn't care about them. "But you didn't get hurt?"

"No, I didn't. I'm at the clinic to make sure they get medical, then I'm taking them across the Montana border to Twin Bridges tomorrow morning. They have warrants out there that take precedence over what I can charge them with."

"How? That man tried to kill you."

"He didn't kill me, and the warrant on him is for two counts of bodily injury to a female victim and her seventy-year-old mother. That's the one he should be saddled with. He'll be gone for a long time, and it's a solid case. So, I'll step aside after I file charges for assault, theft and resisting arrest on both of them as a backup."

"I guess that's a good idea. So, your cells will be full for the night," she said.

"Actually, they can share one and beat each other up if they want, as long as they're locked up and don't annoy me."

He was so calm about it she was finally calming down herself. "Were they the ones stealing the stuff?"

"You bet. They had a big load on the truck, and the weight sank the flatbed in an irrigation ditch. They were sitting ducks."

"Ducks with a rifle," she said and loved the rough chuckle on the other end of the line.

"That's a weird visual," he murmured.

She heard someone speaking to Max, a male voice, but she couldn't make out the words. Then Max said to her, "I have to go. They're ready. I'll see you when I see you."

She put her phone on the nightstand and got into bed. She closed her eyes but opened them quickly. A duck with a rifle was a silly visual, but a criminal with a rifle had shot at Max. At least he was okay. She told herself that over and over again as she looked out the window. It finally hit her that there were no stars in the sky, not even a sliver of moonlight. The night was pitch-black. She got up again to look out and peered up at the heavens. The clouds were roiling, dark and mean, gathering over the land.

She sank down on the chair and stretched out her hand to touch the nearest windowpane. The glass was beyond cold. When she drew back she saw large white snowflakes starting to fall close to the windows. Snow! She got up and pulled open the sliding door to the deck. Impulsively, in her bare feet and pajamas, she stepped outside and looked up. A growing breeze stirred the frigid air and the flakes swirled around her.

In no time at all, her feet were so cold they were numb, and she hurried back inside. Grabbing the throw she kept at the foot of her bed along with her phone, she went back to the chair to sit with her feet tucked under her. Then she called the number Max had used before.

A woman answered, "Eclipse Medical Clinic and 24/7 Urgent Care. How can I help you?"

"Is Sheriff Donovan still there?"

"Hold on. I'll see if he left."

The line went blank, then Max came on the phone. "Hello?"

"Max? It's Grace. I didn't want to bother you, but it's snowing."

"Yes, it sure is."

"Is everything around here okay? I mean the roof of the stable won't collapse, will it?"

"No, Chappy put props in the high stress areas until he could reinforce the beams."

"Good. This might be a dumb question, but you said I probably shouldn't ride Rebel in the snow."

"Yeah. Snow hides things that you won't even know are there unless you're familiar with the lay of the land."

"Okay, I'll wait to ride. I'm sorry to bother you, and I hope you get some rest soon."

"Won't be for a while. The plan changed, so I'm going to have to take the prisoners up to Montana now in case the snow ends up closing the roads. I'll be back tomorrow sometime, hopefully." There was yelling in the background, and Max said, "I'll see you when I see you." Then he was gone, and the line went dead.

Grace didn't dream that night and when she woke, the palest of light announced the arrival of dawn through the windows, which had frosted over completely. As the clouds diminished enough for the sun to finally find a route to earth, she got up and looked outside.

The land that stretched out in front of her was a sea of white with some morning shadows falling here and there. She'd thought there'd be more snow, but the storm had left a thin blanket covering the ground. The tree boughs were heavy with ice, and the sun glinted off everything, making it look as if diamonds had fallen from the sky.

She couldn't take her eyes off it; the land that was hers was beyond anything she could have imagined she'd ever own. Her father had always bragged about his hotels and casinos, often saying, "I can't believe I made all of this." Well, she didn't make this, but it was hers. Uncle Martin's gift to her was absolutely breathtaking.

She finally left the view to bundle up and go outside so she could experience the snow firsthand. First, she put on the thermals she'd bought at Farley's store, layering them with fleece-lined jeans and a pink flannel shirt. She smiled at her reflection in the small mirror in the equally small bathroom. She combed out her loose hair and caught it in a low ponytail. After putting on her thermal boots and her jacket, along with her knit hat, she headed outside.

She pulled down the earflaps on her hat and flipped up her collar as she crossed the porch to the top step. When she breathed in the cold air as she walked down to check on the stable, she felt alive, truly alive. The building was still standing, so all was well.

After she went back inside, she settled at the old desk in the office, and started looking at the ledgers again. As she checked them, she recognized the irony that her expensive business education Walter had demanded she get was helping her to find out more about her uncle.

After she'd pored over hundreds of handwritten pages, her stomach growled. When she looked up at the wall clock, it was just before eleven. She'd been going through the books for almost five hours, and she was starving. She hadn't tried to call around to find a contractor yet because she had no idea where to start, but she was eager to figure out what she could afford to do to spruce up the Lodge. Max had said to ask him for help if she needed it, and she'd do just that. But he was busy, and she knew someone she could ask to recommend at least a handyman.

She put on her jacket and boots again, pushed her wallet into her pocket, then went outside to the Jeep. She brushed the snow off the windows before she got behind the wheel. She'd never driven in snow, and when she reached the highway, she was glad that a plow had already been by and cleared one lane in each direction. The snow had been pushed onto the shoulder.

Her trip took more time than usual but was thankfully uneventful. When she drew up in front of the general store, Farley was bundled up and clearing the walkway with a straw broom. She got out and called to him. "Hello there."

"Howdy, Miss Grace," he said with his usual enthusiasm when he turned and saw her at the foot of the steps that he'd already cleared. "What brings you out in this weather?"

"I know you know everyone around here, and I need a handyman or a contractor for a couple of weeks' work out at the Lodge."

He stopped sweeping. "Yeah, I got a guy I use, and he can repair or build anything. Name's Penn Falconer. He's one of the boys at the Falcon Ranch south of town. Do you want me to call him for ya?"

"That would be great," she said.

He started sweeping again. "Go on inside and get warm. I'll be in as soon as I finish out here and we can get Penn on the line."

By the time she got off the call with the handyman, he'd agreed to come by later in the day to give her an estimate. When Grace went back outside, the walkway was cleared as far as she could see. She went back down to the Jeep, intending to go to Elaine's for lunch. But as she arrived at the diner, she saw Max standing by the pickup, just closing the driver's door.

When he looked up and spotted her, he motioned for her to stop, and she pulled in beside him. As she put down her window, he came over and smiled in at her. "I was just thinking about you," he said. Despite what he'd gone through, he looked as handsome as ever. "Are you hungry?" he asked.

She couldn't walk into Elaine's with Max not knowing who might be inside. "I don't think that's a good idea."

"Why?"

"It's just… Not after that meeting and all. We can eat at the Lodge."

"We can eat here," he said. "I'd like you to come have lunch with me."

"I don't know, Max."

"Trust me, I do." He opened her door and stood back so she could get out. When he held out his hand to her, she hesitated, and he added, "Please, come on."

Elaine met them when they stepped into the busy diner. Grace glanced around and saw the place was almost full. Then she looked over at Max's favorite booth and her heart sank. Little Albert Van Duren was seated at the booth with a man who could only be his father. They had the same coloring, the same build and the same blond hair.

They were both big men, but the father was at least fifty pounds heavier than the son. And there they sat, scarfing down huge steaks.

She turned away, quickly putting her back to them, and stood closer to Max. She could leave right then and hope they didn't see her, or she could stay with Max and hope he'd been right.

"I'm sorry it's so busy," she heard Elaine say. "How about sitting at the counter until a booth clears for you?"

Max glanced at Grace. "Maybe we should just go to—" she started.

He reached for her hand and held it. "We can sit at the counter."

He didn't have to say *Trust me*, but it was implied.

"If you want to," she said.

"I do." Still holding her hand, he guided her to two stools about halfway down the line.

Once they were seated with their jackets off and hanging over the high backs of the stools, Grace tried to casually glance past Max to the booth by the door.

When Little Albert had started her heaters for her and filled the propane tanks, he'd been a bit flirty, more or less inviting her to the grand opening of the Grange. She'd begged off saying she had too much to do at the Lodge and that was that. Now he was here, and she just hoped he wouldn't look her way.

Thankfully, both father and son were still focused on their steaks. Elaine drew her attention as she came up behind the counter. "How about drinks while you wait, then I'll bring your food when you get a table."

Before she could say she'd gladly eat right there, Max responded, "Sounds good."

"I'll get your drinks and if I come out with your food and you aren't sitting here, I'll find you."

"I appreciate that, Elaine," he said with that slow grin.

"And I appreciate you, Max," Elaine said. "I'm glad you're here."

When Elaine was gone, Grace swiveled toward him. "Max?" He looked at her. "Did you see who's here?"

"I figure you're talking about Little and Big Albert?"

She exhaled. "Good, I didn't know if you'd spotted them."

"They're in my booth. I couldn't miss them. I'm pretty sure they're going to ignore us, but if they don't, that's okay. Don't worry about it."

Elaine came with their coffees. "Your food'll be ready in ten minutes."

"Thanks," Max said, then turned back to Grace, his eyes narrowed on her. "What do you think's going to happen if they spot us?"

She shrugged. "I don't know. I just thought it might be awkward. You know, Little Albert might invite me to go to the Grange Hall with him."

"Would you go?"

She couldn't believe he asked her that. "No. I told him I was snowed under with work."

Max chuckled. "Nice pun."

"Thanks, but I'm worried if he sees me, he might ask me." Now, if Max had asked her, she would have jumped at the chance. As soon as that thought formed, she felt awkward. That time at the substation had changed things.

"Then tell him truthfully that you're busy on that Saturday. You have a date with me."

Grace could almost feel her jaw drop. "What?"

"Don't look so shocked. Mom told me to ask you to come to the junior rodeo at the ranch that day. I'm taking you."

"You are?" she asked, definitely giving away her surprise at his statement.

"Yep. Mom told me to pick you up around eleven, so you'll see the opening ceremony."

So, his mother suggested it. Even so, she'd take it. "Okay."

"I'm the sheriff, and I'm supposed to keep people safe. I'll keep you safe from those two. Remember, protect and serve."

She loved how calm he was. "Okay, but if our booth's way in the back, promise me you won't go past their table to get to it."

Max nodded to her. "Cowboy promise," he said, his deep hazel eyes holding hers. "You're safe with me."

When Max had taken off his coat, she'd noticed he was wearing a plain chambray shirt with his star pinned on the breast pocket and the gun holstered on his hip with the clip and a two-way radio on his belt. He'd obviously changed at the ranch, then headed straight back to town to work. She hoped the town appreciated what a good man they had as sheriff.

Elaine came out of the kitchen, looked around, then went over to them. "There'll be a booth in a minute, but I wanted to thank you for yesterday, Max. The irrigation thefts were hurting a lot of good people around here. You're my hero, and you don't even need a cape."

She hadn't been talking too loudly, and with the music playing over the speakers, Grace was surprised when she heard a male voice say, "You did a great job, Max." When Grace turned, Big Albert was standing behind Max, who slowly spun his stool to face the man.

"Hey, Elaine," the man said. "Two boxes and some cookies?" She went to get them, and Big Albert added in a loud voice, "You done good, Sheriff. You got them bad guys, and you didn't even break a nail." The sarcasm in his words grated on Grace but Max just sat there. "You need a big button for that shirt that says 'Hero' on it," Big Albert continued.

Unexpectedly, the other diners broke out in applause, and someone whistled shrilly. Grace watched Max nod to them, but she could feel his embarrassment. As the clapping died out, he spoke to the diners. "Thank you all. I'm just relieved it's over."

The townspeople obviously understood what was going on and were behind Max. She loved that. They appreciated him; he truly was their hero.

Big Albert leaned closer to Max and said in a lower voice, "Enjoy it while you can, *Mr.* Donovan." He glanced at Grace. "You, too, missy." Then he turned and went back to the booth.

Max swiveled around to face the counter again and cupped his coffee mug in both hands to take a drink. As he sat it down, Elaine came over to them with a coffee-pot. Before she finished refilling his mug, Little Albert was there, laying a hand on Max's shoulder. His father remained at the table with the take-out boxes in front of him, watching his son.

"Are you okay now? No injuries?"

His voice held fake concern as Max swiveled again. "Yeah, all good. How about you, Al?"

"I'm great. But I heard that real dangerous criminal you arrested got knocked out when he ran into a cistern shack. Him crashing into it almost lifted it off its foundation… So's I heard." He laughed at his own words. "You got it easy, I guess." He slapped Max on the shoulder. "You keep safe around here."

"You, too."

But the son wasn't finished. He switched his attention

to Grace. "So, can I pick you up around six on Saturday to go to the Grange with me? Put on your best jeans and we'll make the night memorable. Let your work go and have some real fun."

Grace felt sick, but even worse when she realized Max was going to stand up and face the jerk. She put her hand on his shoulder, and that drew his attention to her so she could say, "My work's done."

"Good, then we're on for Saturday," he said with a got-cha smile.

"I still can't go. I'm busy." Before he could argue, she went for it. "Max invited me to the rodeo out at Flaming Sky." She wouldn't say sorry to him, but she wasn't finished. "It's my first rodeo, and I think it's going to be memorable."

"Go to the rodeo. The Grange celebration doesn't start until later when the rodeo's over." He looked smug. "So no problem."

"I have plans for later, too," she said.

Elaine took that moment to speak up. "Have a good day, Al. Don't forget your boxes when you leave. Those steaks are too good to go to waste."

Grace could almost feel the man's anger, and she prayed that he'd at least have enough brains to walk away quietly. It turned out he did. He silently went back to the booth, picked up the take-out boxes, then he and his father left, the older man shaking his head at his son. The door shut behind them.

"Your booth will be ready in a minute," Elaine said and took off with a cleaning rag in her hand. Max picked up both their mugs, then nodded to Grace. "Can you grab the coats?"

She did and followed Max to his favorite booth, where Elaine was finishing wiping away all traces of the Van

Durens. When she stepped back, they both slid into their seats. Grace put their jackets on the seat by her and Max put their mugs on the table and murmured, "Well played, Grace. I'm impressed."

"You two make a good team," Elaine said as she came back with their meals. "I wish I could be there when they open their take-out boxes."

Max was smiling now. "What'd you do, Elaine?"

"Nothing serious. I just gave them pumpkin cookies."

Max laughed and Grace had to ask, "Why is that so funny? Those cookies are delicious."

"Thank you, Miss Grace, but both those jerks hate the pumpkin cookies."

Grace chuckled. "Then thank you for doing that."

"You bet. If there's anything else you need, just let me know!" she said and left them alone.

Grace looked over at Max. "You're awesome," she said on a chuckle. "You didn't let yourself get baited into punching him. You stayed calm."

"I'll tell you a secret. Just between you and me, if you hadn't been there, I probably would have done something I might have come to regret, especially to Little Albert."

"But you didn't. Good grief, both of them are just awful. I can't see how the dad was ever sheriff."

Elaine came by with the coffeepot for refills. "Albert Jr. thinks he's the world's gift to women. I'm glad you brought him down a peg, Grace. Very smooth."

"I didn't think anyone in this town could be so horrible."

Max chuckled at that. "You really need to get out more. We have some doozies around here."

"Amen to that," Elaine said before she straightened up. "Nice to see the two of you here. This man eats alone way too often. I used to like it when he'd come in with Marty. Two of my best customers. Now you're here, and

I like that." She smiled at them both before she turned to move on to the next table. "Enjoy!" she called out over her shoulder.

CHAPTER FOURTEEN

MAX WATCHED GRACE and noticed her eyes were glistening. "I'm sorry," she said. "I don't mean to get emotional, but it seems I'm prone to it lately. I mean, I never even met my uncle and here I am almost crying over him." She picked up her napkin and dabbed her eyes with it. "I'm sorry," she half whispered as she balled up the napkin in her hand.

He could see a certain lost look in her eyes, then considered that maybe her emotions weren't all tied to Marty. He was trying to figure out what else to say to her when his cell rang. He held up his forefinger, signaling that he'd get back to her in a minute, before he took the call. "I'm here."

Lillian was on the line. "Where is here, cowboy?"

"The diner."

"Just got an incoming from Windy Point Arena. Jed said someone's in there riding and won't leave. He wants you to get them out."

"Tell Jed to get them out."

"He says he's not going to do anything until you're there, because it's Bobby Joe Lemon, and he's drunk, and he's got a rifle. He's barefoot and bare chested, even with the snow."

"Log me in. I'm leaving now." Sighing, he hung up and looked at Grace. He regretted having to leave her there alone. "Got a call. Bad timing." Standing, she offered his jacket to him without him having to ask. He reached for his jacket, then looked over at Elaine, who was taking an order at a nearby table. "Elaine? Gotta run. Put this on my tab."

"Max, you're not paying for anything here today," she said. "Safe ride."

"Thanks." He turned back to Grace. "Got a half-dressed drunk with a rifle riding where he shouldn't be a ways south of here."

He knew instantly he shouldn't have mentioned the rifle, but it was too late to take it back. Grace looked concerned, but she spoke evenly. "Go ahead, and stay safe."

"Trust me, I will," he said as picked up his hat and put it on. "Maybe I'll see you later."

She nodded. "I'll be at the Lodge."

He couldn't leave without saying, "It's going to be okay. Bobby Joe Lemon is probably sixty years old, arthritic and has a penchant for riding half naked. He's not dangerous, just drunk."

She didn't look fully convinced when she said, "If you say so."

He wished he had time to spare to make her feel better, but he didn't, and his main priority was getting to Bobby Joe before he froze to death. "I *do* say so," was about all he could add.

Grace watched Max leave and sat back in her seat. An armed drunk on a horse, and Max was heading off to deal with him.

"Excuse me," Elaine said as she came back to the table. "Do you mind if I sit for a moment?"

"Oh, no, please do."

Elaine took Max's place and pushed his untouched food away. "I should have boxed it for him," she muttered, mostly to herself before she looked across at Grace. "Burr and Marty were good friends over the years, and I wanted to ask if it was possible for me and Burr to be there when you scatter his ashes at the bridge over Split Creek? I know you can't do it until spring after the snow has cleared, but would it be okay if the two of us were there with you? If you don't want anyone else there, we understand." Elaine quickly added, "We don't mean to be pushy."

She hadn't thought about when she could scatter the ashes, but Elaine was right. "I'd like it very much if you two would be there with me."

"We'd be honored," Elaine said as she stood. "Please, just let us know when you'll be ready to do it. Do you want anything else to eat? I have the best cookies around, freshly baked, although I'm missing a half dozen of the pumpkin."

"So I heard," she said, and they both laughed.

GRACE KEPT HER phone with her all day, but it didn't ring until the handyman, Penn Falconer, called to arrange a later appointment to give her an estimate for the work she needed done. He couldn't get there until the following week. That was fine. She wouldn't rush it, because she wanted the Lodge to be in as good a shape as it could be before she left.

It was six o'clock, and a light snow that had been falling for the last couple of hours had deposited a fresh layer of white on the ground. There had been no word from Max, but she didn't have the nerve to call his cell. So, she sat on the couch facing the fire she'd just started and looked around. She was doing this all on her own without her dad forcing his opinions on her. It felt liberating to answer to no one and to do as she pleased. But there was a sense of loneliness in it, too.

She was surprised when headlights flashed through the front windows, then went out at the same time the sound of an engine died. She hurried to the door and opened it. Just like that, she didn't feel lonely anymore: Max was standing in front of her, wearing his suede jacket, black jeans and his ever-present black hat.

If she'd hugged him the way she wanted to right then, she knew it would have been really hard to ever let him go. "Are you okay?"

"Aces," he said. "And I'll be even better if you let me inside out of this cold."

"Oh, yes, sure," she said, stepping back for him to go past her into the warmth of the Lodge. She caught the scent of leather and freshness as his movement stirred the air around her. Then she swung the door shut and turned to him, barely a foot separating them.

"No shooting?"

He shook his head. "No, just a drunk on a horse with an empty shotgun." He was undoing his jacket. "He was so drunk he didn't know where he was."

"He's in jail now, right?"

"No, he's back home. I figured having to explain to his wife what he did and how he's going to have to pay a fine for public drunkenness and trespassing is a better punishment than a few hours in jail."

"But he didn't hurt you, right?"

"Not a scratch on me." He tossed his jacket on the desk, then laid his hat next to it. "But I had to have the truck's interior sanitized. The smell of an unwashed drunk's puke is enough to bring you to your knees. Henry has some magic potion that cleans and kills the smells that get in cars, and it seems to have worked this time."

"Oh, I'm sorry."

"Don't be. So, was lunch good?"

"I haven't eaten it yet." By the time she got home, she wasn't hungry anymore. "Elaine sent me home with our meals, and she said they can be reheated. Do you want me to turn on the oven?"

"Thanks, but no. While Henry was cleaning the truck, his wife fed me the best huevos rancheros ever, and her helpings are huge."

Before she could respond, the landline for the Lodge rang, startling her. "First call since I had the phone set up," Grace said and reached over the desk for the receiver. "It's probably the wrong number," she quipped then said into the mouthpiece, "Split Creek Lodge, how may I help you?"

There was no response for a moment, then a male voice she didn't recognize said, "Hello there, Grace. You can help me by finding Sheriff Donovan. I was told he's been spending a *lot* of time with you, and I need to speak to him about that."

It took a second for what he'd said to sink in, and she quickly covered the mouthpiece with her hand. "Max, someone's trying to find you. He said he knew you were spending a lot of time here in a kind of sleazy tone."

"Can you put it on speaker?"

"Yeah, sure," she said. She pressed the speaker button, then uncovered the mouthpiece. "I'm sorry. You're looking for the sheriff?"

"I was told that if I couldn't find the sheriff he'd be with you…if you're Grace Bennet, that is. I wanted to talk about that with him, to let him know how a lot of people feel about the way he's doing his job—or I reckon I should say, not doing it."

Max touched his lips with his forefinger, then mouthed, *I'll take it.*

She nodded and was surprised when Max said in a matter-of-fact tone of voice, "If this is a life-threatening emergency, please hang up and call 911. If not, you can contact our office during our business hours of seven a.m.

to seven p.m., Monday through Friday, and arrange for a meeting with Sheriff Donovan." When he'd barely finished speaking, the line went dead, and he put the phone back in the cradle.

"Who was that?" Grace asked.

"Sounded like Benny Mason, a good old boy who's part of the Van Duren circle. They never broke the law together, but they bent it a lot. I kind of think those good old boys are one of the reasons Marty pushed me to get on the ballot. He knew what they were and wanted them out." He narrowed his eyes on her. "Are you okay?"

She probably looked the way she felt—unsettled by what had happened. "Don't worry about me. What are you going to do about the call?"

"What I did. Let him know that what he says or does means nothing to me, except for the fact that it upset you. I'll take care of him and make sure he doesn't contact you again."

"But now he knows you were here. I should have never let you talk to him."

"You didn't let me do it—I did it."

But she was involved, and she couldn't be. "You shouldn't be here." That hurt to say, but Max was the one who would really get hurt if he lost the election.

"Hey, listen to me, Grace. I'm not going to let anyone tell me how to live, or who to have in my life."

When she went back to Tucson, she didn't want to leave Max with his life in shambles. His job meant everything to him. "You listen to *me*. You can't take the chance that they won't go even further to discredit you. Men like that never stop where power or money's involved. I lived with a man who was driven like that, and someone like you would never understand how horrible they can be and justify it every time. Money and power are their drugs, and they're not going into any rehab, believe me."

Max was stunned by the simmering anger and pain that he saw in Grace at that moment. He knew who she was talking about with such emotion: the credit card man. She lowered her eyes as she hugged herself tightly.

He touched her chin with his forefinger. "Hey," he said softly.

Finally, she looked up at him. "I'm sorry. I know I sounded extreme just there, but I only meant to say that you can't beat men like that. You can't. Good doesn't always win out." She shrugged weakly. "Believe me, it usually doesn't."

He drew his hand back as he shifted to her side and put his arm around her shoulders. He felt her stiffen, but not pull back. "Let's sit and talk about this." But she didn't move when he gently tried to urge her into the great room.

"No, no, no, no," she said and twisted to move away from his touch, leaving him standing there as she went behind the desk and headed toward the living quarters. She went inside without a glance back.

Max weighed his options and opted to go after her. Thankfully, she hadn't shut the door on him and when he stepped into the room, Grace was sitting in Marty's old chair, staring out the window. He crossed to get one of the chairs from the kitchenette and put it by her, angling it so he could look at her, before he sat down.

There was heavy silence as they both sat there until Grace sighed. "I think it's better if you leave."

"Who was the man you were talking about?"

She closed her eyes tightly. "No one important."

He couldn't let that go. "Whatever happened with that man, you can talk to me about it. It won't go any further than this room. I promise."

"I don't need to talk anymore, especially about him. You need to leave. Please."

He was used to talking to people who weren't in a good place emotionally, and he knew better than to push. So he sat there prepared to wait as long as it took for him to find out who the person was that she'd been talking about in her outburst.

She shifted and clasped her hands tightly in her lap. He couldn't stop himself from saying, "I need to know about him before we settle about me leaving or not. All I know is you look as if you're hurting, and I want to help."

GRACE CLOSED HER eyes and wished she could just sink into the chair until he couldn't see her anymore. She'd scared herself a little by being so emotional about something she kept thinking she'd left behind her. He was right about her hurting, remembering all the times Walter hurt people around him, good people he crushed.

"Talk to me, Grace," Max said. "Who is he?"

The room was silent except for the furnace starting up again. His voice was low and something in it almost broke her heart. A man who'd been nothing but good to her was only asking for the truth. She braced herself, then decided he deserved that much.

"Walter Bennet." Her voice sounded alien to her own ears, low and flat. "The founder and CEO of Las Vegas–based Golden Mountain Corporation, one of the best entertainment and hospitality businesses in the country. Or so he says."

When he didn't respond, she finally opened her eyes and glanced at him. Then she said the hardest part. "He's my father."

He stared at her, then asked, "How could he have canceled your cards or gone after your bank account when he's dead?"

She looked away and out the window. "You assumed he was dead when I told you my parents were gone and not in my life." She exhaled, then kept going. "I'm sorry I let you believe that. My mother passed, but Walter's still alive and fighting battles he almost always wins. He canceled the cards and tried to take the bank balance because he's a bully, a man who values money and power over everything else in life. He's a master of control and cutting people to their core with words and never blinking an eye."

Max stood up and went to the window. She looked up at him and saw him reflected in the glass staring at her. "I thought—" He shook his head, his face slightly distorted in the glass. "How could he do all that to you, his own daughter?"

She looked down at her hands. "I stopped taking his orders and caving in to his pressure. He finds that unforgivable, especially from his only child who turned out to be a girl when he wanted a boy to carry on his name and his empire. Then I received Burr's letter claiming I was the niece of some stranger who had left me everything he had and it was the last straw."

"The gender thing's just plain mean, but why would he cut you off because of the letter?"

"I asked him if the man was really my uncle, and he verified it but didn't care that he'd died. He wanted me to get rid of whatever he left me and forget he ever existed. No hint of grief whatsoever. He just wanted me to turn my back, tell Burr to sell it all and never think about it again. I refused. Then he told me his brother was a total loser who had walked away from the family thirty years ago. He didn't care he died, Max."

She opened her eyes and saw Max's expression reflected

back in the glass as he processed the horrible words about his friend. "When I said I was coming here, he cut me off from everything. The joke on him is, I didn't care. I don't want to be around him, or to be like him, and when I left to come here, I thought I was free of him at last."

Max exhaled heavily, his breath steaming up the glass. "What did Marty ever do to him?"

"I don't know and probably never will. When I was young, I'd wish for a sister or brother and a father who would just love me and spend time with me. I gave up on all of that and just settled for wishing I wouldn't disappoint him. Maybe I'm a coward for giving up, but the one thing I can't accept is his indifference to his older brother dying."

Max turned to her, a frown showing faint lines at the corners of his eyes. "Maybe he'll come to his senses."

She made a scoffing sound. "He lives the life he wants, and I'm building a life of my own that doesn't include him." She'd confessed her lie and that weight was off of her, but she still felt awful about what Max might be facing because of men just like Walter.

When he started a sentence with, "But, you never know—" she cut him off.

"I do know," she said far too abruptly. "I'm done with him. I'm not hoping for fairy-tale magic to take over. I'm okay. I've got my home in Arizona, and I'm learning about my uncle by living in his place, walking in his footsteps. I have a horse, a child's wish that finally came true, and new friends. It's all good."

He came closer and crouched in front of her. His eyes were soft when they met hers. "Yes, you have friends. And this friend is not walking away from you. That's ridiculous. I'm a very single man and having a woman for a friend is not against the law or in any contract I signed when I took over as sheriff. Not doing my job is the only thing that could be a problem, and that's just a lie to muddy up the waters. So, we'll stop the easiest smear first and make Big Albert and his cohorts look petty and foolish."

She looked up at him questioningly.

"I'll make this simple. I'm not walking away or pretending I don't know you when I'm out in public. I won't stop coming here or riding this land with you, and I'm sure not going to take back the invitation for the rodeo. So, forget that hogwash. Instead we'll be transparent and make it known to anyone around that we're good friends and like each other."

It couldn't be that simple. "And the Van Durens are going to give up and ride off into the sunset just like that?"

"They probably won't. But if they keep dishing swill out, the more petty and jealous they'll look. Believe me, everyone knows about the standoff at the diner between them and us, and from what Lillian's heard, we're on the good end of public opinion. So, we just keep that going while I do my job and Lillian takes care of logging my work hours and what I'm doing and where I am at all times. I think this will be as easy for us to pull off as a frog picking off a fly."

"Which one of us is the frog and which one's the fly?"

"That sounded better in my head. We, you and me, we're the frogs, and those good old boys are the flies. How's that?"

"Will I get warts?"

"No, you can only get them if you kiss a bullfrog. My dad told me that years ago. I don't intend to ever kiss a bullfrog."

"You're a wise cowboy," she said.

"I'll take that as a compliment and look forward to the rodeo, where we'll have a great time being good friends."

Grace sighed. "You're so calm about the whole election thing. I don't know how you do it, especially after that call. It hurts to see them causing trouble, trying to destroy decent people for their own agenda."

"Don't give them a second thought and get ready to have fun at the rodeo."

He seemed confident, and he was making her feel more secure. "I'm looking forward to it."

"Okay," he said, then slowly stood and looked down at her, more serious than he'd been moments ago. "You sure you want to go?"

She blinked at the question. "Would it be better if I didn't go?"

"No, I didn't mean that. I want to be sure you don't feel I'm pushing you in any way to do it if you don't want to."

She'd been pushed by Walter to do what he wanted her to do most of her life, and he'd never once asked if she was okay with it. "Yes, I really want to go."

"Then you get some rest and as soon as Chappy clears the stable, we'll take that ride for you to see your land and the bridge on Split Creek."

"I have good riding boots now and enough thermal underwear to hopefully keep the cold out. And I have my knit hat."

He moved back as she stood to walk out to the entry with him. They went around the desk and Max reached for his jacket. As he shrugged into it, he said, "I just remembered something. Wait here. I'll be right back."

He headed into the great room. He was out of her sight for a moment, and then she heard the squeak of a door or cabinet open and close. Max came back holding a hat in his hand. It was brown suede with silver threading around the crown and a star inset in a silver oval at the front.

"Where did you get that?"

"It was in the carved cabinet by the chess table on the

back wall. This is Marty's hat. I just remembered he put it away when he got sick and said he'd take it out when he could ride again. I'd forgotten all about it." He looked down at the hat and fingered the brim. "He made the band himself and he forged the star at the farrier's in town." He held it out to Grace. "Would you like it?"

She took it from him and felt the brushed softness of the suede. Her eyes burned, and she fought the tears that were close to surfacing. She honestly seldom cried. She'd learned early in her life that tears only annoyed Walter and upset Marianna, both things to be avoided at all cost. But another real connection with her uncle touched her deeply.

She looked up at Max and swallowed before she could speak. "On a list of the best gifts ever, with Uncle Martin leaving me Rebel and the Lodge being the top two, you finding this and giving it to me is a strong third."

He smiled that smile that never failed to make her heart beat a bit faster. "Being number three on that list is an honor."

When Grace carefully put the hat on, it was slightly too large, but she felt as if it was perfect for her. "I'll wear this to the rodeo and hope I look like I fit in."

"Oh, you'll fit in," he said as he reached for his own hat. "Do me a favor?" He took out his cell phone. "I want a picture of you in that hat. I know a few people who'd love to see you wearing it."

"Sure, I guess so."

She expected him to take the shot, but instead he came back behind the desk, got his phone ready, then touched her hat brim to push it back slightly. "I want to make sure you aren't hiding your face." Then he stretched an arm out in front of them, put his other arm around her shoulders and aimed the camera at them. "Smile," he said and took a picture. He checked the screen, then held it out to Grace for her to see. "You take a good picture," he said.

She had never liked being photographed, but this photo was different. Max was smiling, and she looked happy. She loved the picture. "It's nice."

"Yes, it is," he said. He put his phone in his jacket pocket, then went around to the door. He looked back at her. "Everything's good with us, right?"

When she nodded, he gave her a thumbs-up sign and then opened the door and left.

Grace stood in the entry until the sound of the pickup died away. Taking off the hat, she ran her forefinger over the silver star and felt that if she looked up right then, she'd see her uncle walking into the room to get his hat back before he went to take Rebel for a ride. Foolish thinking, but it made her feel so close to him. She was slowly seeing the kind of life this place offered the right person, and she knew when she left, she'd miss so much of what she'd found.

Slowly, she walked back to her room, placed the hat on the bed, then settled in the easy chair again. She pulled her legs up, wrapped her arms around them and rested her chin on her knees. The view was so soothing, and she felt lighter after telling Max about Walter. He'd understood, and he'd figured out how to maybe make the Van Durens back off. He was amazing, and for the first time she let herself think a what-if. What if she stayed to see where this thing with Max could go? She knew it was sliding past just being friends, but she didn't know if she let go if she'd slide off a cliff or into something like love.

Her cell announced an incoming text. Reaching for it, she found two new texts, one from Sawyer and one from Max.

She made herself pull up Sawyer's first.

I thought you should know that your father is taking you out of his will completely. I know this is none of my business, but what he's doing is wrong, and you need to come home immediately to make peace with him. I will help you any way I can. Sawyer.

If she trusted Sawyer any less than she did, she'd think Walter had pressured him to contact her. Or maybe Walter had dropped that information, hoping Sawyer would pass it along to her. She quickly texted back.

Thanks for the heads-up, but it's his money and his empire, so he can do what he wants with all of it. I won't be coming back. I wish you well and want to thank you for all you've done for me over the years. You've been a wonderful friend. I'll miss you.

Sawyer wouldn't push her—he never did—so when she sent the text back, she didn't expect a reply.

Max had sent her the picture he'd taken. Then her phone rang, and it was Max. She took it. "Thanks for the photo."

"No problem. Lillian just called to tell me I have been instructed to have my gun safety certificate renewed tomorrow down in Two Horns, or I'll be riding a desk until I do. Apparently, I'm late doing it by six months. It looks bad for me, with the election coming up—it makes me look sloppy."

"You think Van Duren said something?"

"Maybe, but I'm going to do it. I'll miss Thanksgiving but I'll be back in time for the rodeo on Saturday. Chappy will be around your place. If you need anything, let him know."

"If I get another call, what do I do?"

"Hang up and call Lillian. Don't talk to them. Better yet, unplug the landline for now."

"Okay, I'll do that." Ruby and Dash had invited her to come over for dinner, and she'd liked the idea of a real Thanksgiving meal for once. She had never experienced a traditional Thanksgiving. But she wanted Max to be there. "If you won't be there for Thanksgiving, should I still go?"

"You're more than welcome to go without me and enjoy yourself. Burr and Elaine will be there. I can't let anything slide, so I'm going to have to go down now and get the certification over with. I've worked a lot of holidays, so I'm used to it, and so are Mom and Dad."

She'd go. "Okay, you do what you have to do, and I'll eat turkey and mashed potatoes with your family." She tried to keep a light tone in her voice and not expose her disappointment.

"I guess I'll see you when I see you," he said.

He hung up before she could say, "I'll miss you."

CHAPTER FIFTEEN

ON THANKSGIVING DAY, Grace woke to a sky with dark clouds but no snow. She went to the Donovans' and had a wonderful time. Their sons weren't home for Thanksgiving: Caleb was away with his family, Coop was still in Boston with his fiancée, McKenna, and Max was tied to his desk in Two Horns even though he'd passed certification with flying colors. So she had dinner with Ruby and Dash, Elaine and Burr, and Lillian and Clint.

She was so grateful for the invitation but missed Max. The food was traditional and delicious. The experience was novel for Grace, who had never had a meal like it, with people around the table who actually liked each other and made her feel very welcome in their circle. After dinner, they all went into Eclipse to put up some of Max's election signs, posting them along the main street where they would be seen by the most people, and near the town hall, where the voting would take place.

When she got back to the Lodge, she stopped by the gates to put up a couple of signs. Then she went inside and sat in Uncle Martin's old chair as evening fell, thinking about how she felt as if she belonged. She wasn't an outsider anymore. She fit right in with the townspeople and was going to an honest-to-goodness rodeo on Saturday with the county sheriff, who she had to admit was pretty great.

For what was maybe the first time, she saw that she

had options. She could sell and go back to Tucson and her life there. Or she could start a completely new life, just like her uncle had done. There was so much here that she'd come to care about: the town, the people, the land, the Lodge…and Max.

She'd miss him most of all. A man who'd gone through misery to come out the other end with a stable, good life and had told her he wasn't looking to change that. That made her wonder if she could stay here and make a life with Max around, seeing him the way friends would see each other, and be able to pretend that was enough for her. She wasn't sure what she felt for Max, but she knew that every time she saw him her feelings got stronger. Maybe it wasn't love exactly, but probably as close as she'd get to the real thing. But it couldn't happen.

The next day she spent time helping Chappy in the morning, fixing the doors on the stalls in the stable. She enjoyed doing it with him, listening more than talking, learning how to replace rusted hinges on the stall gates with new ones that didn't squeak. When Chappy left around noon to go back to Flaming Sky to help with preparations for the rodeo the next day, she stayed down at the stable to oil the hinges. She felt a sense of pride at the job she'd done and knew how to make it even better.

Chappy had been using a black marker when he'd measured where the cuts would go in the wooden beams, and he'd left it behind. Five minutes later she'd labeled the two front stalls, one "Thunder" and the other "Rebel," in large bold letters. She stepped back to admire her handiwork and almost jumped out of her skin when she heard, "That's called vandalism, lady!"

She spun around, and Max was there smiling at her from the doorway. "You're back."

"I am for now." He came closer and looked at the new

labeling on the stalls. "I never would have taken you for a graffiti punk."

She loved his dry sense of humor now that she understood it. "First a frog, then you call me a punk?"

He cocked his head slightly to one side, his hazel eyes studying her. "I take that back. You're a sight for sore eyes."

"It was that bad in Two Horns?"

"I'll tell you all about it as soon as I have a cup or two of hot coffee."

"You're in luck. I happen to have a fresh supply of Uncle Martin's grinds."

He reached to take her hand in his. "Then what are we waiting for?"

MAX BUSIED HIMSELF making a fire while Grace brewed their coffee. When she came into the great room and handed him his mug, then settled beside him, he felt an ease between them that made his heart happy. He'd missed her during the short time he was gone, and he'd come to the Lodge before he'd even gone to the substation.

He knew he'd missed her too much, and that he'd thought about her too much and he was in a precarious point in their friendship. He was wary of where it was going, but he didn't quite know how to draw back to a safe distance when he just wanted to be right where he was.

"So, what happened in Two Horns?" she asked, diverting his thoughts.

"I got certified on my first try, but then I had a whole other mess that I had to deal with—boring stuff, nothing you'd care to hear about. That took a whole day, then a deputy accidentally discharged his firearm by dropping it in the parking lot. No one was hurt but a cruiser windshield was shattered. That triggered an internal investigation that I had to authorize and monitor for twenty-four hours."

"How can a gun go off just by dropping it?"

He knew that look on her face, the same one he'd seen when he'd left to answer the call about the irrigation thieves and again with the Bobby Joe Lemon situation.

He quickly said, "It's never happened before as far as I know. It was his fault. He'd been rushed and hadn't secured his weapon. He's on leave for ten days, which is mandatory, and he has to take a safety firearms program. That leaves me short-staffed again."

"Can you still go to the rodeo?"

"I'll be here at eleven tomorrow morning to pick you up, one way or another." He saw her shoulders drop on a sigh of relief, and it pleased him that she really did want to go with him.

"So Big and Little Albert didn't cause the certification action?"

"Oh, yeah, they did. Someone let me know as soon as I arrived that Big Albert filed a complaint that I'd deliberately avoided renewing the certification because I was off doing what I shouldn't be doing and putting the entire force in jeopardy."

"Max, that's horrible. What did you do to him?"

"Nothing. I passed the firing range with a perfect score, so it didn't do anything but make him look like a petty jerk. Score one for the good guys."

"He ruined Thanksgiving for you and took time away from you to work on your reelection."

"Yeah, but I found out how much support I have from my staff, and I had some time to think about other things."

She shook her head. "You're a cup's-half-full kind of guy, aren't you?"

"Most of the time." He finished the last of his coffee, then put the mug down by hers, which she'd barely touched. "That's Marty's influence. The man could always see the brighter side of life."

"He didn't get that from his brother," she said with no smile at all.

He wouldn't let her go in that direction so he changed the conversation. "I wanted to talk to you about something, and I'm not sure how to broach the subject." He'd known that sooner or later, he'd have to put everything on the table; he just hadn't expected it to be today. But he wanted to know her answer, no matter what it was, so he could figure out where to go from here.

HIS SERIOUS TONE made Grace a little uneasy. "Sure," she said. "What's on your mind?"

"You know Marty asked me to keep an eye on you, to be a friend to you while you're here, and I've tried to do what he asked. The thing is I'm in a spot that I honestly never expected to be in again. I promised myself I'd never go there again. I couldn't. Now, it seems, I got there without even knowing where I was, and when I realized it, it was too late to backtrack."

Max was looking right at her, but she didn't understand what he was saying. All she knew was, whatever had happened or was happening, was important to him.

"I don't know where you're going," she stated.

He sat forward, his hands on his knees. "I know we only met a short time ago, and I know how you feel about relationships, and I know that you're going back to Arizona as soon as you can. What I also know is, I have feelings for you that I can't shake. Every time I see you, they're there. It doesn't make sense, but I can't let it go. I need to know that I'm not delusional to think there might be something between us."

Grace sat absolutely still, scared by what he was saying, but also relieved and happy. She was overwhelmed by the idea that what she'd been thinking about, all the maybes, might be changing to real possibilities.

"Max, I…honestly I've been thinking the same thing, but I can't figure out how it would work. I don't want to hurt you or be hurt myself if I'm wrong. And I don't have any idea if I am or not. But I need to know."

He shifted to face her and reached for her hand. "I do, too. But I'm not sure if I can give you what you need. I'm not sure if this is solid reality or a daydream. But one thing I do know is this is about you and me. As far as anyone else knowing, I've been there, done that, and I don't want to be there again, but I won't let people stop me from seeing who I want to see."

She'd never hurt him the way Claire had. "I understand not wanting to be hurt, I really do, but I don't know how to find out what's real and what isn't by pretending to care less than I do. It would be a lie. I don't want that."

With his free hand, he touched her cheek, and whispered, "I don't either," before he leaned closer and kissed her. It was gentle and wonderful, and then he moved back, his hazel eyes holding hers before he said in a rough whisper, "So far, so good."

"Yes," she answered.

He stood still holding her hand. "I need to leave. Lillian's going to be swamped if I don't show up soon, then I'll go to the ranch and help them with last-minute details for tomorrow." He smiled at her, a soft expression that touched her heart. "I'll see you at eleven."

"Yes," she said, and he held her hand until they were in the entry, and he had to let her go to put on his jacket and hat.

They faced each other, then Max opened his arms to

her and said, "I need a hug." She went into his embrace and didn't want to let go. Max was the one to step back first to kiss her on her forehead.

"I don't want to leave, but I have to," he said with that crooked smile. "Tomorrow. Eleven." He paused, then turned and didn't look back as he went out and the door swung shut behind him.

THE NEXT MORNING, Grace heard an engine in the distance and ran into the lobby to look out the window. Max was five minutes early. She was wearing her uncle's hat along with jeans, boots, a beige long-sleeved Western shirt and her denim jacket. She was so excited to see Max again after their discussion last night that she took some deep breaths before she opened the door.

He was pulling up at the foot of the stairs, and she hurried down, getting into the truck as quickly as she could. Before she could reach to do up her seat belt, Max leaned across the console and kissed her. Then he drew back grinning and said, "A very good morning," and with that he started driving.

As soon as they were on the highway, Max touched her hand where it rested on the console and laced his fingers with hers. What had happened yesterday hadn't been a dream or hallucination, but very real. She looked at him. *Yes, very real.*

"You're a punctual man, Sheriff. I'm impressed."

"One of my many attributes," he said, and his hold tightened slightly.

She smiled as she let herself look at Max in his black hat, black jeans and black leather jacket with silver buttons that looked like shooting stars. Then she saw his boots, red with tooling of more shooting stars.

"Are you staring at me?" he asked.

She was sure grateful his attention was on his driving. That way he wouldn't see her blushing like some silly teenager being caught staring at the football quarterback. "I was trying to figure out where the sheriff had gone."

"He's still here. Just no uniform, and my belt and gun are locked up in the glove compartment. I'm just Max today, taking my girlfriend to her first rodeo." He unexpectedly chuckled at that. "Mom said my first rodeo was when I was three months old, and she brought me with her for closing night when Dad was competing. He won, and I slept through it all."

"I promise I won't fall asleep," she said. "I just hope you don't get a call before it's over."

"I'm clocked out, but if Lillian calls I'll have to leave. There's an even chance she'll call."

"She's working?"

"Clint's staying with her at the station."

"Mmm," she murmured, not wanting to bring up what was worrying her, but thinking that she should, given their conversation yesterday. "Are you sure that this is all okay?"

"What do you mean?"

"Well, for one, you're driving me here in the county truck. That could be misunderstood, couldn't it?"

"Too late. We're in it, and we're almost at the ranch. I'm on call all the time. I need the truck for that."

"Oh, okay, I understand." His lack of concern made her feel better. "What do we say if someone asks if we're together, like really together?"

"That we're really together."

She waited, then said, "Okay. The tickets today, how much do they cost?"

"Nothing. It's free, but there are donation boxes set up at the food stands, at the souvenir booth and at the main arena gates. I'm hoping it does well, because all proceeds are being split between the Simply Sanctuary Horse Rescue that Coop and McKenna are involved with and the retirement home for former rodeo performers down near Cheyenne."

They arrived at the gates where a stocky man stood under the arched sign for the ranch, which had been embellished with gold, red and white streamers along with a banner that read "Welcome Future Champions."

"Hey, Boomer," Max said, sticking his head out the window. "How's it going?"

The man named Boomer beamed. "It's going real good."

"Great. See you up there." He then drove up the driveway and toward the rise. "We'll park on the private road to the house and not get tangled up in the traffic around the arena."

More streamers looped from post to post along the white wooden pasture fencing for as far as she could see. Then they got to the rise, and the transformation was even more jaw-dropping. Red, white and gold were everywhere. Horse trailers were parked in the closest pasture on dirt cleared of snow, and the arena beyond held a huge banner hung from a partial roof over the bleachers: "Youth Rodeo's Tenth Anniversary Celebration."

"Good turnout," Max said as he slowed, then drove onto the private dirt road to the main house. He pulled over, the truck wheels crunching the snow that had been cleared to the shoulder. "Dad's going to be walking on air. Every year the attendance grows."

He sounded proud of his father, and she envied him. She wished she could be proud of hers. "I didn't expect something this grand," she said, undoing her seat belt when the truck came to a stop.

"If I'm needed to help with the kids, you come with me. If we get separated, call my cell." He looked right at her, his eyes holding hers. "I don't want to lose you," he said before he opened his door to get out, and the expression on his face told her that his words held double meaning.

Grace didn't want to lose him, either. "I won't get lost," she said when she met up with Max at the back of the truck.

Seeing no one else around by the house, she reached for his hand and squeezed it.

"What was that for?" he asked.

"I just wanted to thank you for a good time today in case I forget to tell you later."

He kissed her quickly. "You're welcome," he said.

MAX WATCHED GRACE's reactions to what was going on in the arena as much as he paid attention to the actual events. She was cheering and clapping just as much as anyone in the audience. So far, things had been easy, people saying their hellos, smiling, and talking about the weather or their stock. When the last competition was over, the presentation of awards was set up in the middle of the arena and Grace turned to him, her face glowing.

"That was great," she said. "I can see why your family's so involved in it. Do you miss being more involved?"

"Honestly, sometimes I do. If I'm not reelected, I'll get more involved with the rodeos, both professional and the juniors here and in the state."

"I can't even imagine how exciting a professional rodeo would be."

"They're incredible. If I hear of one while you're still here, I'll take you to see for yourself."

His dad went up on stage, and the awarding of ribbons to the winners began. When the last award was handed out, it went to Henry's oldest son, who took top scores in three different competitions. Everyone in the place was on their feet, cheering and clapping, and Henry was there taking pictures.

Dash announced that food and dancing were about to start in the main stable area and that the hay barn was ready for the kids.

Max leaned closer to Grace and said, "Let's sit here for a bit and let the crowd thin out." He slipped his arm around Grace's shoulders. "You're cold and I'm keeping you warm. I like that."

She looked at him, their faces so close she felt the heat of his misting breath on her cheek. "Protect and serve," she said, and he gave her a good-one expression as he pulled her closer.

When the crowd had diminished to a trickle, Grace asked, "What now?"

Max stood and held out his hand to help her up. "Food, dance, visiting with people and finding Henry to congratulate him." When she got to her feet, they started down the stairs.

BY THE TIME they arrived at the main stables, the fragrance of barbecue was in the air, and laughter and voices drifted out of the open doors. The interior had been completely transformed: a wooden dance floor had been laid out in the training ring, with a stage in the center of it where a band was already playing country music. People sat on hay bales inside the divider wall, and others sat on benches just outside the ring. Heaters strategically placed around the building kept real cold at bay.

Max leaned closer to her so she could hear what he was saying over the music, laughter and conversations. "The barbecue smells great."

Elaine brushed past them, followed by several men, all carrying what looked like large roasting pans with lids.

People were filing in behind them, and Ruby was there managing a line for food that already wound out the doors.

Max drew Grace to one side. "Let's sit down and wait for the food line to thin out now." He motioned to some benches by the short wall of the ring. "The farther from the food frenzy, the better."

They had barely been seated when Farley came over, dressed in an all-red outfit with a gold-studded belt and white tooled boots. The man never ceased to make a statement with his clothes. "You two hiding over here?"

"We're just waiting for a break in the food line," Max told him.

"Hey there, Miss Grace," Farley said, shifting his attention to her. "I wondered if I might find you here after seeing you two together lately."

Max quickly changed subjects. "Did you see Henry's oldest boy take three firsts?"

"That kid's gonna be something someday," he said, but got right back to what he was interested in. "So, are you two a…thing? I heard something along those lines from… someone. I knew the two of you would be a good match but didn't know you were sparkin', Max."

"Mom invited Grace and asked me if I'd bring her. This is all so new to her—she needs someone to explain things to her so she can enjoy it."

The man actually looked disappointed with those facts, and Max wasn't about to stick around for any follow-up questions. He just wanted to enjoy being with Grace.

"Now, we're going to go dance and have fun," Max said.

"You do that. I'm heading over to get my share of them ribs."

After Farley hurried off to get in line, Grace giggled. "Sparkin'?"

"Oh, yeah." He shook his head and stood. "How

about dancing? I won't let anyone cut in—don't worry about that."

She hesitated for a second, then took off her hat and jacket and left them on the bench. Max guided her to the dance floor and once there, took her hand with his.

"It's smart you left your hat on the bench. If you get twirled, it could fly off your head and get stomped on by the dancers."

She looked at him, and her violet eyes were smiling. "Note to sheriff. Don't twirl me."

"Okay, but you don't know what you're missing."

"How about I twirl you instead?" she said.

"I don't think I'd mind that." Max moved closer to Grace, slipping his other hand down to the small of her back, and they started to dance to a slow song. Farley had nailed what was going on between them, and he'd given it a name: they were sparkin' all right. Grace shifted to slip her arms around his neck and leaned closer.

Grace hadn't danced in a long time, and when she had, it hadn't been to a country and Western song about love against the odds. At any other time, she might have snickered at the corny lyrics, but not then. When she was in Max's arms, she didn't care about odds.

"How are you feeling?" he whispered in her hair.

Without thinking about it, she said, "As if I belong right here, with you."

His hold on her tightened. "Me, too."

She closed her eyes, just letting the moment be what it was and wishing it would go on forever. The song flowed into another, a plaintive ballad about a rodeo cowboy finding love, but walking away because he could never settle down.

"Sad songs," she said as she looked up at Max.

He met her gaze and said to her, "Come on, give me a smile."

The warmth in his eyes was breathtaking and she saw his gaze drop to her lips. "You have the most beautiful smile," he whispered. Then he started to lean down, and she wanted the kiss she knew was coming.

Before that could happen, a heavy hand touched her shoulder and a voice she knew said, "Mind if I cut in, Sheriff?"

She felt Max tense, but his voice was level. "Actually, I do, Albert." And with that he expertly maneuvered Grace into a twirl, then back into his arms.

Albert was still there. "Let the lady answer for herself."

The song ended, and Grace said, more loudly than she intended, "I can speak for myself, and I don't want to dance with you." Nervously she took a step back and looked at Max. "Can we go and get food now?"

"I'm starving," he said. Without giving another glance to the other man, he put his hand on the small of her back and lightly guided her through the remaining couples on the dance floor, leaving Little Albert standing there alone.

CHAPTER SIXTEEN

GRACE SAT DOWN with Max after getting their food and was surprised to see Freeman Lee talking to Big Albert, who had stopped at the open doors to the stable.

"What's going on?" Grace asked Max and motioned to the men.

"I don't know, but Freeman can hold his own with Al."

"But what if they get into a fight?"

He chuckled at that. "Freeman talks a good game, but he wouldn't do anything to mess up today. He'd never do that to my parents."

The next time they saw Freeman, he was coming back into the stables alone and motioned to Max to come over to him.

Max stood up. "I won't be long," he said.

When he came back five minutes later, he acted as if nothing had happened. Elaine and Burr had stopped by to chat with her, and after they left to help with the cleanup, she expected Max to say something. When he still didn't, she gave up on waiting. "What happened with Freeman?"

He stood and put on his jacket and hat. "I'll tell you later. I think it's time for us to leave."

He reached down and picked up Grace's coat and hat, handing them to her. As she put them on, she said, "I should say goodbye to your parents and thank them for everything."

Max looked around and then smiled at her. "They're dancing. Trust me, you don't want to interrupt them."

She glanced over at the dance floor and saw them moving to a slow ballad. Dash said something to Ruby that made her smile, then he leaned down and kissed her forehead. Ruby cuddled closer to him and rested her head on his chest. Grace was entranced by the connection the two of them had after so many years of marriage.

"I'll thank them later," she murmured.

They stepped out into the cold night and walked side by side toward where the truck was parked. They'd just made it to the top of the private dirt road when Big Albert approached them with his son in tow. Grace barely controlled a groan. They looked determined.

"You got a minute, Max?" the elder Albert asked.

"We're leaving."

Grace wouldn't allow herself to look down. When she'd been confronted by Walter in the past, she'd learned never to show any sign of weakness. Maintaining eye contact was maintaining control. Now the two bullies were no more than a few feet from her, and she stared at them.

"I was just telling Pa how you two embarrassed me on the dance floor." He looked at Grace. "How about you make up for it now? The band's still here, and we can ask for a good song." His expression was smarmy, and she just kept looking at him without responding. She saw uncertainty creeping into his eyes, and then he actually puffed out his chest. "I can dance with any girl here, but I'm giving you a second chance."

HIM TALKING TO Grace like that put Max over the edge, and he figured it was almost time to put his cards on the table, if he had to. But first he'd try for a quick exit. He ignored

Little Albert as if he didn't exist and repeated, "We're leaving," to Big Albert.

The older man came back with, "Sneaking off, huh? Just like you. I'd bet you aren't on the way back to work, either." His laughter was almost a cackle. "Dumb, really dumb. Seems you have no respect for the office you hold. That's going to cost you big-time."

Grace was very still, and he didn't want to resort to name-calling. "Is that a threat?"

"Naw, that's a promise."

So much for a fast exit. He wasn't going to go any further with the blowhard. "Listen to me, Al, and listen good. I went down to Two Horns on a request that I renew my certification in weapons and accuracy. I got it first try, a perfect score on the written component and for the shooting range."

Al made a scoffing sound. "Am I supposed to be impressed, Sheriff?"

He ignored that. "Someone mentioned that you'd been down to headquarters the day before with a couple of friends on a tour of the place. One of them was Benny Mason. You were in your old office, which of course is mine now, and they saw you looking through my files. Then you went up to Internal Affairs carrying some files with you and left there with no files. Fifteen minutes later they were told an anonymous complaint had been filed against me for defaulting on being recertified in… Well, you know, and I had to show up first thing the next day."

The more Max said, the tighter Al's expression became.

"You're a—"

Max cut him off. "Donovan, the name's still Donovan. Oh, I almost forgot about the cameras that will verify what I'm saying and the fact that my old certification notice, which was a copy of an original, was missing out of my files. No one seemed to know what happened to it, but that didn't matter. A look through the county records, which had been archived, found the original that expires in six months. Seems you really entertained your cronies. I bet you all went for a drink after that to laugh about how you got me."

"You can't talk to my pa like that!" Little Albert said in a sudden burst.

His father said, "Shut up," then looked directly at Max while his son was turning red from anger. "What do you want?" he asked through clenched teeth.

"All I want is for you to back off and make this a clean election where the best man wins."

"What about…the other things?"

"No one except you two will know about it unless you hurt anyone I care about. Then everything's on the table. Otherwise, this is over and done. And one more thing— stay out of my office unless you get to put your name on the door. Deal?"

Little Albert looked deflated when his father said, "Deal."

Right then the junior bully rose out of the ashes of defeat and sneered at Grace. "You ain't nothing special. I only asked you to dance because Pa made me. You're nothing but a dog."

Max took a step toward the idiot with the intent of breaking a few teeth. But his father got to him first and grabbed him by his jacket collar, jerking him back so hard that he landed on the shoulder of the road in the low pile of ice and snow.

"I told you to shut up!" Big Albert bit out, then turned to Grace. "Sorry, ma'am, I'll take care of him."

"He's all yours, Al," Max said.

As the two men walked away, Max and Grace got in the

truck. Once the heater was running, Grace looked at Max and said, "I was wrong about something I told you before."

He couldn't guess what, except for things he didn't want to hear. "What are you talking about?" he asked with some caution.

"The good guys do win sometimes."

He chuckled and leaned over the console as she did the same toward him and they kissed. When she sat back in the seat, she sighed softly.

"You're a very good guy, Max Donovan," she said. "But I did think for a moment you were going to hit Little Albert."

"Naw, I wasn't going to hit him."

"Oh, good," she said with obvious relief.

"I was going to crush him."

They both laughed as Max turned the truck around and started for the gates.

When they were on the highway heading to the Lodge, Grace said, "I need to get something straight between us."

He flashed her a look. "What's that?"

"When we first met, it was really annoying that you were always stepping in to save me in some way, as if I was helpless on my own."

"Heck, no, I never meant—"

She'd put that wrong, and she cut him off. "I know. I figured out what you were doing the more I was around you and saw how you dealt with other people, your family, your friends and now… Well, I've come to really like that about you. I appreciate that I feel safe with you, and that I can trust you. I don't feel that way often. I'm not used to it. Walter always had a security detail to watch over me no matter which one of his projects we were living in. They kept us safe, but they didn't make me *feel* safe. On top of that, I couldn't get away with anything because they always found me."

"You were a troublemaker?" he said with fake shock.

"I never did anything big. But I did slip out of the penthouse to meet one of the dealer's sons in the basement laundry room once."

"Wait—dealer's son?"

She amended that with, "Blackjack dealer."

"Ahh." He grinned. "How old were you?"

"We were both twelve, and I was sure he'd kiss me. I'd never kissed anyone before, and I didn't want to be uncool."

"No one wants to be uncool," he said.

"Right. So I managed to sneak out, he showed up and we ground our teeth against each other's for a minute. Our make-out session was cut short because Walter sicced Security on us. I cried for ages over that—I was so humiliated."

"He was just being protective," he said.

"No, he wasn't. He paid Sawyer to be protective of me. He was angry with me because he'd been embarrassed when Security found out the boy was a dealer's son. That didn't sit well with Walter at all. He never even talked to me about it. Neither did Marianna. But Riley, one of the security guys, told me that if I ever wanted to learn how to kiss, he was available. I'm not sure if he meant it, but I told Sawyer, and Riley disappeared without a trace."

"Good old Sawyer," he said, then turned off the highway and drove up to the Lodge. After he'd parked next to her Jeep, he turned to her. "I can tell you something that might make you feel better about being uncool and grinding teeth."

"You've got my attention," she said.

"I've kissed you a few times and all I can say is, you're

very good at it. No teeth problems, no nose problems trying to figure out where your nose goes."

"Where were you when I was twelve and so uncool?"

"Let's see, you were twelve, and now you're twenty-
six?"

"Yes."

"I was about twenty-two years old and had been in the
army for a year and wanted to join the Army Rangers to
go over to the Middle East."

"I guess you were really good at kissing by then," she
said, wondering why she didn't feel any age gap between
them. She'd never thought about it.

"I don't know about that," he said, grinning. "But I was
cool enough."

"Cool enough to get a tattoo?"

He chuckled at that. "I was very cool by then." He didn't
elaborate any further. "Now, I'll be cool and walk you to
the door."

"Before I get out, I have a question, if it's not too personal."

"Ask me and I'll tell you if it is or not."

"What did Freeman want with you back at the ranch?"

"Oh, he told me that Big Albert and his son were miserable people, but no one seemed to be buying into their
lies. I appreciated that, but that wasn't why he called me
over, really. He just wanted to chat."

When he didn't elaborate, she decided not to push. He
didn't look mad, but he sure didn't look happy, either.

"Oh, okay… Um, I guess I should get inside and let you
go on your way. But thank you for the best time I've had
in a very long time. It might have been my best day yet."

"I like being around on your best days," he said. She
reached for the door handle, but Max stopped her.

"Grace, wait a minute, please."

"Is something wrong?"

Max hadn't expected to say anything about his meeting with Freeman, especially not to Grace; he didn't want to discuss Claire anymore with anyone. But something nudged at him, a thought that the only person he wanted to tell about that conversation was Grace, because she was becoming more and more important to him every time he saw her.

"Freeman told me he was going to Texas. Claire works at a lab there in research, and Freeman and Beulah are flying there tonight for Claire's wedding."

"She's marrying that Russell guy?"

"No, someone named Gregory O'Brian. Freeman says he has degrees on top of degrees. They work together and are going on a research grant trip to Central America for a year. So they're having a small wedding, then leaving the week after." Max couldn't read Grace's expression in the dull blue glow from the dash light. "Apparently, he's from a very wealthy family."

Grace was very quiet until he stopped speaking, then she asked softly, "Are you all right?"

That took him back. "Me? Sure. I'm okay."

"I just mean, you loved Claire for a long time and now she's marrying some guy and going off to be with him in another part of the world."

He saw sympathy in her violet eyes, and he didn't want that from her. "You think I'm heartbroken? Devastated?"

"Are you?"

"I'm not. I'm figuring out how I feel, but it's nothing like that. Claire liked to live life on her terms, definitely not around here. I guess she found what she was looking for with this O'Brian guy after she dumped Russell."

She studied him for a moment, then sighed. "So how *do* you feel?"

He took off his hat and tossed it back onto the second seat, then met her eyes again. "I think I'm feeling good about a lot of things. Three years is a long time to get over something, and Marty helped push me on that until I was in a better place and was on the right road. I'm not stepping off of that road again."

"No one could blame you if you were upset."

"Meaning *you* wouldn't blame me for being upset?"

"Why would I blame you for anything you felt? Emotions are emotions, and you deserve to be happy, and to have a family and find love like your parents did."

He couldn't explain to her how he'd felt when he'd heard about Claire, because he really hadn't felt very much except wanting to go back and find Grace and dance again without Little Albert ruining it.

"I need to go and see what's happening with the ranch cleanup, but before I leave, I want to do something."

"What's that?" she asked, but he was already getting out and coming around to her side of the truck.

When he opened her door, he held out his hand to her. She didn't understand but let him help her down to face him. "What did you want to do?"

"This," he said, and kissed her.

When he drew back, he tapped her chin lightly. "Now I'm leaving. I'll pop by and see you tomorrow. It's going to be a busy week, but I'm hoping after the election's over we can take the horses out for a ride anywhere you want to go."

"I'd love that," she said. "*And* we can celebrate you winning the election."

"Don't jinx it," he said, then got back in the truck and drove off, grinning the whole way down the dirt road.

AFTER DROPPING GRACE off at the Lodge, Max had gone to town instead of heading back to the ranch, partly to make sure Lillian and Clint weren't still at the station covering the phones, and partly because the weather service predicted snow to start falling by midnight, driven by heavy winds. He ended up sleeping on the cot to see how bad the storm would be before he headed to the ranch.

Now he stood before the big front window at the substation, watching people dig their cars and trucks out from under the snow before the snowbanks the plow left behind buried them completely. It was barely six o'clock when the calls about electrical outages had started coming in. Max had them redirected to the power company. He couldn't go anywhere until the plows started on the highway and he needed to get to the Lodge. He'd tried calling Grace as soon as he woke up and saw the snow. But the call to her cell went directly to voice mail, and the landline just rang and rang. He was worried about her and anxious to get out there.

When the plow finally arrived, Max drove out to the Lodge and parked his truck at the gate. The front gate was frozen shut and he had to jump over it; he'd take care of that later. He was relieved to see smoke coming from the chimney. Smoke meant a fire, and that meant Grace must be okay. He knocked on the door and when there was no answer, he tried the latch and opened the door. He stepped inside and was met with cold air. No furnace sounds broke the silence, just the snap and pop of a newly laid fire. He crossed to try the light switch in the great room, but the power was clearly out.

Blankets and pillows were on the couch, and a tray with a mug and a half-eaten sandwich on the coffee table. But Grace wasn't there. He went back into the reception area and walked behind the desk and over to the closed office door. Rapping on it, he waited, called her name then heard movement right before the door opened.

Grace stood there, barefoot, her hair sleep mussed, wearing pink pajama bottoms and a white T-shirt emblazoned with "This Isn't My First Rodeo, Buckeroo!" under the silhouette of a cowgirl on a bucking horse. He read the shirt out loud and laughed. Grace crinkled her nose. "A gift from Gabby."

"Wear it to your next rodeo," he said, then switched tones. "Are you okay? I've been calling you for hours, and I got worried when you never answered."

"No signal," she said. "And it's cold in here. There's no electricity and I'm on my third fire."

"Come with me and see how awesome I am," he said, getting a grin out of her.

"I already know you're awesome," she said, "and I'm not dressed for the weather."

"We aren't going outside, but first, I need a hug. I'm so glad you're okay."

She nestled up to him and he closed his arms around her, needing to feel the realness of her against him.

"Mmm," she murmured. "Now, you were saying you can make the electricity come back?"

He shifted to brush a couple of errant curls off her forehead. "It never left," he said, then took her to the backup generator in a closet off the laundry. He hoped Little Albert had done his job right when he delivered the propane. Grace was watching when he started up the generator and a moment later the furnace hummed to life.

When they'd gone to the great room and settled on the couch, Max said, "Just say it."

"Thank you. I had no idea that there was a backup generator anywhere around the place."

He'd taken off his jacket and Grace was sitting so close to him that he could feel her heat through the denim shirt he was wearing. As much as he wanted to, he didn't put his arm around her. He'd been thinking so much about her and how everything between them now was wait-and-see. He didn't much like that now. He hadn't been enough for Claire, and he'd almost lost a part of himself in the process. He knew if things kept going the way they were, he'd either have to take a leap of faith or let Grace go.

"Do you have any idea when you'll be leaving, if you do?"

She was staring into the fire. "The only person who misses me is Zoey, my friend who owns the consignment store. I'm kind of on my own schedule for now."

He tried not to grimace at the thought that only one person would miss Grace being gone. He knew he'd miss her something awful. "Have you thought about staying here?"

She surprised him when she said, "I have. I wish you'd been there for Thanksgiving—it was magical. I felt so accepted by everyone there. I loved it."

"I heard you helped put up some election signs, too. Thank you for that."

"It was fun. Clint is so funny, and so is Burr. Gosh, I haven't laughed that much in a while. This town is pretty spectacular, and you're…" Her expression changed and she shrugged as she turned to look at him. "I can't stay to run the Lodge. My dad built his empire on buying and selling and building and destroying the past to make room for the future. I'm not like Walter—I don't want that life. It frightens me how much I don't want that.

"When I was young and didn't know anything about anything, I wished for a horse and new parents who would like me more. Then I just started wishing my dad would be proud to walk me down the aisle one day when I got married. I finally got a clue and started wishing I'd never be like Walter. So far I'm doing okay on that front."

Max did what he'd wanted to do when they first sat

down and put his arm around her shoulders, pulling her against his side. He would have liked to be able to say he understood what she was feeling, but he couldn't begin to. "Hey, your horse wish came true, too, didn't it?"

"Dumb luck," she murmured.

"Maybe, maybe not," he said and thought, *What a brilliant response.*

She rested her hand on his chest. "I'd vote for maybe not."

"So, you won't stay and bring this place back to life just because it's similar to what your dad does? You'd rather walk away from all of this than follow in your father's footsteps, even the tiniest bit?"

She twisted to look at him. "Can we not talk about it? It's… I just don't want to. Please. I'm here, I'm not back in the Bennet kingdom in Las Vegas. I'm with a man who means a lot to me, and I'm so happy."

"I am, too," he said. "The Van Durens are off my back, the snow is a blessing after the years-long drought and you're here with me."

As he looked into her eyes, he was amazed at how clearly he knew that he loved Grace. What he felt was a real love. Not a convenient love, or the kind of love he'd almost settled for with Claire—he owed her for walking out on him. This was a deep-down love that seemed to wrap around him.

She looked at him quizzically. "What are you thinking?"

He wanted to tell her, but he was afraid it was too soon, too much, so he'd bide his time and when he knew it was right, he'd tell Grace that he loved her and hope she felt the same way. If she did, they could figure out the rest together. Right then, he needed to go back to work. He stood and Grace did, too.

"I have to head back to check on the situation in town and do some wellness checks on some of our seniors, to make sure they're okay."

She walked with him out to reception, where he put on his jacket and hat he'd left on the desk. "How do you feel about a second date?"

"You're counting the rodeo as our first date?"

"Sure. We can't ride too far for a while, but I want to go someplace where I can dance with you without being interrupted this time."

"You know a place?"

"Yep, a great place. Pure Rodeo. Caleb owns and runs it. It's right by the ranch and they have great live bands."

"I'd love that," she said.

"I'll check with Caleb to see when a good time would be to go. Actually, the family's going to have dinner there in a couple of days to welcome Coop and his fiancée back from their trip to Boston and talk about their wedding and things like that. Would you want to go with me?"

She smiled. "Absolutely."

"Okay, great! But in between now and then, how about a mini-date tomorrow? If the roads stay clear, you could swing by the ranch and visit with Rebel."

"That would be wonderful," she said. "I miss him. I just hope we can ride soon."

"We will, trust me," he said. "I'll call you tomorrow and let you know when I'm free."

"Sounds good," she said, and he left to trudge back to the truck on the other side of the gate. He was warming up the truck when he thought about what Grace had said about Walter Bennet. He decided to call Lillian to get a background check on the man. As he pulled onto the highway, he realized he was ready to make a leap of faith.

When he arrived at the substation a few minutes later,

he relieved Lillian so she could go have lunch with Clint. She'd left the readout on Walter Bennet on the computer for him. He scrolled through ten pages, stunned at the empire Walter Bennet had built. Yet, he'd lost his daughter. He saw a personal contact number for the man, took a deep breath and made a call. When a male voice answered, "Walter Bennet," he almost hung up, but didn't.

"Mr. Bennet, you don't know me, but I'm calling about your daughter, Grace."

GRACE WOKE THE next morning, her arms and chest aching from clearing the snow off the porch and her Jeep. She stayed in bed longer than usual, enjoying the view from the partially frosted windows.

She didn't know why she hadn't admitted to Max that she'd almost thought of staying at the Lodge despite what Walter did or didn't do. She was her own person and the idea of letting Walter still dictate her actions made her cringe. If she stayed and reopened the Lodge, she'd keep her promise; keep her uncle's legacy alive and protect the Lodge. She'd finally have a real home, something she'd never had before. She could hardly wait to see Max again to tell him she was staying.

She tried to stay busy, feeling restless now that she knew what she wanted, and she hoped that Max would be part of her future. As the hours ticked by she only heard from Lillian, who called to let her know that they were sending a smaller plow to the Lodge to free the gate so it would open and clear the snow from the highway through the gates and up to the building.

Max had no doubt arranged for it, and she appreciated him doing so. She bundled up in layered clothes, two pairs of socks, her heavy jacket with the collar up and her uncle's hat. She was going to walk down to the stable to make

sure the roof hadn't caved in and see how far Chappy had
gotten on reinforcing the top beams. The air was bitterly
cold, but the sun reflecting off the snow made everything
look so beautiful. When she reached the stable, she was relieved to see that the roof was intact, but the snow banked
against the doors made it impossible for her to get inside.

She took her time going back. When she finally stepped
out onto the driveway, she stopped dead in her tracks. A
large SUV was parked at the foot of the porch steps and
pounding echoed through the air. She moved closer and
stopped again when she saw Walter at the entry door, bang-
ing on it with a closed fist.

"Grace!" he yelled.

She entertained the idea of just turning around and
going back to the stable, but her father spotted her before
she could make her escape. Ducking her head, she went to
the car, and saw Sawyer sitting in the driver's seat with a
pained expression on his face. This was not good at all. She
managed a smile for him that probably looked as pained
as his. Then she turned toward her father, who was standing on the top step.

"What are you doing here, Walter?" she asked.

He was in an immaculately tailored gray overcoat and
polished oxfords with snow clinging to his pant cuffs—
completely inappropriate for this weather, and she was
sure he was very cold.

"Can we take this inside?"

She didn't want him to ever go inside the Lodge, but
she couldn't block him without things getting worse than
they already were with him showing up out of the blue.
She hurried up the steps past him, opened the door and
went in. He followed her, slamming the door shut so hard
it shook the glass in the windows next to it.

She was furious he was there, and her anger only grew

when he took his time looking around before he finally turned to her. "It's a dump, as I expected. Just like Martin to let it go like this, then leave it to you." Walter looked disgusted. "I was glad when he left, and his wishy-washy way of looking at life. It was always incredibly annoying to me."

He was rambling bitterly, and she couldn't stand it. "Stop, Walter. Just tell me what you're doing here."

"Well, dear daughter," he said sarcastically. "I came to rescue you and take you home where you belong."

Her stomach roiled at his words. "I don't need you or anyone else rescuing me."

He ignored what she'd said with a dismissive flick of his large hand. "I'll send in my development team when the snow melts to get an evaluation of what this land is worth. Then we can contact the developers and make sure we get every cent of profit out of this fiasco."

Grace cut him off. "This is my place, not yours. Who do you think you are coming in here and acting as if you have any part in my decisions about the Lodge?"

"I received a call from a man who felt you could use your father's help and support to figure out what you were up against instead of throwing it all away."

Had Burr called Walter and inadvertently said something to set him off? "Who called you?"

Her father had a smug smile on his face as he undid the buttons on his long overcoat. "He seemed very worried about you, so I take it you've not been doing too well on your own here."

"Who called you, Walter?"

"He said his name was Max Donovan."

Her heart dropped and she could barely catch her breath. *Max?* "No, no, no," she said. "He wouldn't do that."

"He did."

Her world closed in on her, sucking the oxygen out of the air around her. She'd trusted Max and told him things she'd never wanted to talk about before. He knew she didn't want Walter anywhere around the Lodge to taint it with his hatred for his brother. He knew she never wanted to be in Walter's orbit again, but he'd been the one to draw Walter here. That hurt her more than anything Walter had ever done. She had to fight to keep from screaming and giving Walter the satisfaction of seeing her totally break down.

"I don't want you or need you here. You really are a horrible father."

The smile was wiped off his face. "Don't you talk to me like that."

"Just go away," she said. She could feel her world starting to crumble and the idea of making a home at the Lodge crumbled with it.

"And you can either come home and let me clean up this mess or stay here, but don't expect me to come to rescue you the next time you need it. There's no more money, no more bank accounts you can clear out and nothing for you when they read my will."

"I don't want your money. I earned every penny you paid into that bank account."

He chuckled harshly at that. "When you get ready to sell this dump, call Sawyer and he'll pass on the news to me. Then we'll talk."

She knew that she would lose all semblance of control if she said anything right then. Instead, she just stared at Walter, and kept quiet.

"Okay," he said. "If you think this place is worth breaking up our family, then you deserve whatever comes."

"There is no family," she managed to get out. The closest she'd come to having a family was here, and Max had taken it away from her. She couldn't stay. She'd leave alone the way she'd arrived.

Walter stood very still, and Grace saw the glint of hardness in his eyes. "You've been such a disappointment to me."

She didn't break under his assessment. Instead, she asked him what she'd wanted to know since she'd found out about the Lodge.

"Why did you hate Uncle Martin?"

CHAPTER SEVENTEEN

WALTER SEEMED TO age before her eyes. "I didn't come here to talk about that."

"Then how about this? Did you and Marianna ever love each other?"

He ran a hand roughly over his face, then looked right at her. "Yes, we did. I loved her until she didn't love me. I think she pretty much hated me, and that's why she stayed away as much as she could."

Grace could hardly bear to hear the words. "Why?"

Walter shrugged. "We'd been married for a year before Martin showed up in Vegas at the company offices. He was out of rehab again, and Marianna had the nerve to tell me she admired him for admitting to his failures and mistakes and doing something about it. She admired a total loser. She compared me to him, and I came up short. She called me egotistical and heartless."

"She loved him?"

"Marianna claimed she didn't, but there was something there."

"So you threw him out?"

"I let him stay in the smaller penthouse by ours, but after he admitted he wished he'd met your mother before I had, yes, I kicked him out. He told me he knew he could have given her a better life than I ever could."

His sharp bark of laughter startled Grace.

"I had him tossed and told him to get out and if he ever

came back, I'd make sure he'd be sorry. He said he was only leaving because Marianna had asked him to. She told him she was married and took that seriously. But that didn't mean she loved me.

"I thought if we had a child things would change. They didn't. Marianna left me as often as she could and passed you off to your nanny. Eventually, there was no reason for me to be around for more than the occasional photo op or holiday. So I stayed out of her way."

"What about me, though?" she asked, her eyes burning now. "I was there, but you never were. Why?"

He grimaced at that. "You're right. I was as bad at being a father as I was at being a husband. That's on me." He exhaled, then appeared to diminish as he hunched his shoulders. "I'll be going. This is all yours." With those parting words, he walked out, closing the door behind him.

Grace slowly sank to the floor and leaned her back against the desk. She hurt so much she wondered if anyone could die of a broken heart. Max had drawn her to him, saying "Trust me," over and over again, and she had. She'd felt safe with him on so many levels, only to have it all pulled out from under her.

"Trust me," she muttered to herself and started to cry.

MAX HAD BEEN tied up all day with emergencies due to the storm and the power outages, and it was seven o'clock before he could leave town and head to the Lodge. He was sorry that he hadn't been able to keep his mini-date with Grace and go spend some time with the horses, but he was excited to see her again. He was smiling when he drove up the driveway and parked by the Jeep.

His knock on the door was unanswered until he heard stirring inside. Then Grace opened the door for him. But something was terribly wrong. She looked as if she'd been crying, and her face was very pale.

"Grace? Are you all right?"

She was in stocking feet, jeans and a lavender plaid flannel shirt, looking as if she might have slept in them. Her hair was mussed, and she wasn't smiling.

"No, I'm not."

He moved to come inside, but she stood in his way. "What's going on?" he asked at a total loss about what could have happened since he'd last seen her.

"I take back everything I said about you and me," she said in a low slightly hoarse voice. "I don't want to be anything to you, and you're nothing to me."

He felt dread wash over him. "What are you talking about?"

"I trusted you enough to tell you about Walter and what he did to me. But you ruined everything."

"How?"

She held up an unsteady hand. "You lied to me. I thought you were—" She stopped abruptly, her hand slowly lowering as it closed into a fist at her side. "This can't be my home. I had this ridiculous idea that I'd stay and that we could…you and me…" She shook her head sharply. "You ruined it."

He wanted her to stop saying that. "How did I do that?"

She swallowed before she said, "You called Walter. You told him he had to come and rescue me, like I'm too foolish to take care of myself. He came here to take me back to Las Vegas."

He understood what had happened, but not how she knew about a three-minute call he'd made last night. As soon as he got off the phone with the man, he'd realized Grace was right. Walter Bennet was a class-A jerk, and his call hadn't made any bit of difference. He'd asked Max what kind of mess Grace had made, then brusquely informed him that she was on her own. That had been it—followed by a click when he'd hung up on Max.

He'd been foolish to make the call in the first place, and when her father had said she was on her own, he'd ached for Grace and vowed never to mention her father again. Now it had exploded in his face in the worst possible way.

"He actually showed up here in the snow despite the bad road conditions?"

"Yes, because *you* called him. He came to take me back with him, and he wants to raze the Lodge and develop the land. He saw dollar signs and he came to claim the money through me." She pressed the heels of her hands to her eyes, then looked right at him. "You…you knew how I felt, but you ignored me. You have some delusional idea that you know what's best for everyone… You're like some messed-up superhero running amok, trying to save everyone in your path. You—" Her voice was rising, and she stopped abruptly.

Her violet eyes looked right at him, her lashes spiked with dampness, and he saw that lost look he had before. That hurt more than her words.

"I did call him, but I—"

"Stop, please. I can't do this. You're the first person I trusted in a really long time. I wanted to trust you, to feel safe with you, and…"

He was struck dumb, the same as he'd been with Claire when she'd told him she was leaving. The difference was, he'd been hurt by Claire, his heart bruised, but not broken. With Grace an ache deep inside of him was growing, and he could barely keep eye contact when he finally spoke, trying to ignore the feeling he'd lose part of himself this time.

"I can only say I'm sorry. It was silly of me to think

I could do anything to help." He went closer to her, the cold air from the still open door settling in his bones. "I'm more sorry than you'll ever know." He made the only offer he could think of. "If you stay here, I'll leave you alone."

She exhaled with a shudder. "No, no, this can't be my home. I can't stay now."

Max could almost hear Marty speaking to him years ago. *Max, if you find a spot in life where your heart's easy, don't pass it by and throw away your chances that it's right where you belong.* He'd thought that he might finally be at that place in his life, as long as it included Grace. Now he'd never know.

"I guess there's nothing I can say to change that now, but maybe later we can talk."

She shivered and hugged herself tightly. "No, there's nothing left to talk about. Please, go."

He had no option but to leave, but before he thought it through, he stepped closer and cupped her chin before he kissed her on the forehead. He felt her flinch at the contact, and he whispered, "Goodbye, Grace," before turning and going back to his truck. He heard the door shut behind him. The world was cold and gray, and he was stuck in that world with no idea how to break out of it.

He was barely to the highway before he had to pull over. He sat in the idling pickup, trying to wrap his head around what had just happened. His cell rang and he glanced at the screen. Caleb. He ignored it. As soon as the ringing stopped, it started up again. This time it was his mother calling. He ignored it and would have turned the phone off if he could have.

He realized that what he'd had with Claire had been him settling for someone familiar, someone he'd grown up with, someone he liked. That had seemed like love to him, but with Grace it wasn't anything like that. It was complicated and layered and now it was over because of him. She'd been ready to stay at the Lodge and be with him, and he'd shattered her trust. He struck the steering wheel with the flat of his hand.

The phone rang again. It was his dad. He hesitated, then didn't answer.

Instead, he put in a call to Burr. He had to ask him a few things, then maybe he'd figure out what he was going to do from here on out.

THE MORNING OF the election, Max showed up at the town hall and was the first one to vote. After visiting with others arriving at the polling place, he headed to the station. Lillian hugged him when he walked in, something she only did on birthdays, usually.

"Good to see you, cowboy."

"Catch me up to date on things," he said and sat opposite her at the desk. He'd hardly been able to think straight over the week since he'd walked away from Grace. He tossed his hat, and it caught on the hook, then he undid his jacket. "You hear anything interesting lately?"

"No, I haven't seen Grace. She's been holed up at the Lodge most of the past week. Poor thing. She has to be so lonely."

Lillian read him like a book, and it annoyed him. "I didn't ask you about Grace. I was talking about work."

"Sure you were," she said, but he knew she meant, *And bulls give milk.*

He let out a sigh. "Okay, how's she doing?"

"Seems to be selling, leaving to go back to Arizona soon, but she's been sticking close to the Lodge in the meantime. Chappy's working on the stable. He hasn't said much about anything going on out there. How are you doing?"

He almost said he was fine but wasn't. He wouldn't lie to Lillian.

"I'm here." He sighed. "But I had everything I ever wanted, and I messed it up."

"So I heard. Have you tried simply apologizing?"

"Of course, and she cut me off at the pass. She won't answer the phone or open my texts. I was so close, Lillian."

"Then clear it up."

"Easy for you to say," he murmured. "Right now I have some business to do. Call me if you have to. Otherwise I'll see you when the polls close."

THE CELL PHONE rang and Grace rolled over in bed, tired of crying all the time and reliving Max walking out of her life. She was back to where she'd been when she'd first driven into town, alone and confused, but this time, she was also miserable. She reached for the phone, saw it was Burr calling and answered.

"Hi, Burr."

"Good morning. I have some good news, I think."

She sat up. "What good news?"

"I have a buyer for the Lodge."

Her heart sank. This made everything final, and she should have been thrilled, but she only felt more lost.

"Oh, really?"

"You don't sound too excited."

"Just woke up and I'm…wow, just surprised, that's all."

He explained the offer, and the money was right on the amount Burr had come up with when she told him to go ahead and sell.

"That's great. Do you know what they're going to do with it?" she asked.

"You'll like this. They plan on running it—living on the premises and reopening it as a family-oriented destination."

That was too good to be true. "Can you make it illegal for them to cut up the land and raze the Lodge by putting it into the purchase agreement?"

"No, I can't do that, I'm afraid. It will be their property, unless you'd rather make it a long-term commercial lease. If you did that, you could hold on to it for as long as you want. In perpetuity, if that's your preference."

In perpetuity. She remembered him using that term to describe how long Uncle Martin had no entry fees for tournaments at the pool hall he'd helped name.

"I'll have to think about that."

"Sure. Take your time. The buyer wants to come out and look around and he should be available after seven tonight, though it might be as late as nine. Is that okay?"

"Yes, I'll be here."

"Okay, I'll be around. It's election day, you know, and Elaine is hosting a celebration party for Max after the polls close."

She closed her eyes. She might never see Max again, but she hoped he'd win and that he'd be happy.

"What if he loses?"

"He won't, but if he happens to, then it'll be a support party for Max instead. Elaine wanted me to invite you. But I guess you'll be busy around that time. After you meet the buyer, if it's not too late, come by and either celebrate or commiserate."

She wouldn't be there, but she evaded a direct answer. "Thanks for the invitation, and for finding a buyer so quickly."

"You bet. I'm off to vote," Burr said.

When she'd hung up, she stared blankly at the ceiling. It was over.

GRACE WAS SO nervous about the buyer coming that she could barely sit still. In her jeans and red plaid shirt, she walked around the Lodge the same way she had the night she'd arrived. She went from guest room to guest room and turned on all the lights, thinking about the new linens she'd ordered for each room and wishing she'd be there to see how they looked when they arrived. Maybe she could ask the new owner to take pictures when it reopened for business.

She rejected that idea right away because she knew seeing it become everything she'd imagined would be too painful knowing that someone else had fulfilled her uncle's wishes. She'd failed and wasn't even sure that she'd go inside when she came to scatter his ashes. She ended up in the great room on the couch with the lights out but a fresh fire in the hearth.

Burr had told her when she'd informed him she was selling that she could leave as soon as she wanted to, and all the paperwork could be done online. Right then, she made up her mind that she'd leave the next day. Burr said he'd take care of getting Rebel to her in Tucson as soon as she had a place to keep him.

She saw the headlights approaching just before nine and was on her way to the door when the person knocked.

"Coming!" she called and opened the barrier.

Max Donovan stood in front of her, and she was thankful she was still holding on to the door handle. She literally could feel her legs weakening and she couldn't seem to catch enough of a breath to say his name.

"Good evening, Grace," he said with strange formality.

"What are... Why are you here?" She had been so close to leaving and never having to see Max again, and now he was there in front of her, close enough to see deeper lines at the corners of his hazel eyes.

"I'm here to look over the Lodge. Burr said you were expecting me. I'm sorry if I surprised you."

She took a huge chance and let go of the door handle to step back far enough to lean against the desk for support.

"You…can't be the buyer."

"Yes, I am. You asked me if I wanted to take it over when you first arrived. I've reconsidered your offer, and I'm making you one. Can I come in to check everything out?"

He was a different person, more controlled than she'd known him to be. He was serious. This wasn't a joke. When she nodded, he stepped inside and swung the door shut behind him. She just stood there, trying to get her mind around what was happening.

Max took off his black hat and laid it on the desk next to her, then placed his jacket beside the hat. *Just like he used to do*, she thought, and her heart ached. She knew it would be a long time before she could wake up in the morning and not think of Max and go to sleep not thinking about him. She wasn't sure how she'd make it through that, but she had to.

"So," Max said as he looked around, "all the light bulbs work. The place is definitely in decent shape." He slipped past Grace through the archway into the great room. "Nice fire," she heard his voice say from the shadows. Then the lights in the great room came on.

Grace didn't know what to do. Max was acting as if nothing had happened, and she was so aware of him and what could have been that she felt nauseated. She hesitated, then followed him into the other room. Max had planted himself on the couch where he always sat when he was at the Lodge. He motioned her to come over.

"Sit so we can talk about the deal."

She slowly went over and sat down, leaving space between the two of them. He looked more dressed up than usual, in a dark brown Western-style shirt with silver at the cuffs and silver stars for buttons. Along with his black jeans, he was wearing the red boots he'd worn at the rodeo. She knew she was staring, and she looked down at her hands.

"So, what do you need to know that you don't already know? You know this place better than I do." She was relieved that her voice sounded almost normal. That was a huge victory considering what was going on in her mind.

"You're right, I do. Do you have any questions about the purchase, or anything special you want to be done or not done?"

"Why are you doing this?"

He blinked at that. "I told you. You asked me and I'm willing to do it."

She stood, ready to leave him there so she could breathe again. "You can figure out everything that needs to be done with Burr. I trust him." She wanted to go anywhere that Max wasn't. But he stopped her from leaving.

"Wait. I'll tell you why I'm doing this as long as you hear me out."

She stayed standing, taking whatever advantage she might have. She felt cold even though the fire was blazing.

"Just do it and get it over with."

"Okay. I did it because I've been foolish, and it's cost me a lot, probably more than I'm figuring on in the future. I want to put this right." He looked up at her. "Sit down before I get a crick in my neck."

She didn't want to do what he told her to do, but she still felt a bit unsteady, so she took a seat making sure she didn't sit close enough to make any contact. "Okay."

"Thank you," he said and shifted to face her more directly. "When I called Walter it took me three minutes to see for myself what you told me about him. We spoke—at least, he did, then he hung up on me. I was so wrong, so arrogant that I thought I could make things okay for you. I underestimated what you'd told me about him, and I'm truly sorry for that. You knew what you were doing. You've been right most every time, and I am that superhero without a cape without any real superpowers who's just bumbling along, making a mess of everything."

He exhaled roughly. "I'll take good care of the Lodge and the land." He looked at her, then dropped his eyes to his hands pressed on his knees. "I won't ask you to trust me—just know that I'll do the best I can."

Grace didn't know what to think or what to do. She could feel the tension in him as he stood up and looked down at her with narrowed eyes.

"Grace, I wish you a great life." He shook his head, and she could see him giving up, ready to leave, and if he did, she knew he wouldn't be back.

There he stood so close to her that all she had to do was reach out and take his hand. The urge to make that contact was almost overwhelming. She knew right then what she wanted, what she'd always wanted, but she'd been too afraid to trust the man in front of her. That fear was still there, but this time she didn't tell him to leave. She couldn't. She had to finally talk to him.

"Max, I know you'll do right by Uncle Martin. I don't doubt that, but I don't want to sell to you or lease to you," she said, her heart racing so hard she thought it might leap right out of her chest because of the chance she was taking.

His hazel eyes held hers and his jaw clenched. On impulse she reached out for his hand and held on to him. He started to pull away, but she tightened her hold.

"Max, don't go."

He glanced at their connection, then at her and she saw it in his eyes, what she was feeling right up until that moment…fear, and the loneliness that was almost unbearable.

"I have to go," he murmured. "I'll tell Burr to tear up my offer."

"Yes, please tell him to do that." She didn't let go. "But you sit down and listen to me this time."

He shook his head. "I can't go through this again. I'm sorry, Grace. I regret what I did, and I always will."

She tilted her chin and looked up at him. "Cows and horses. Why did you really call Walter?" she asked barely above a whisper.

"Because I couldn't stand the thought of you being alone when Walter should have been there for you. He's your *dad*, Grace. I wanted him to know what an amazing person you are, and I didn't want you to be alone in this world, even if we couldn't be together. I called him because I really cared about you."

He cared, past tense. "You cared about me?"

"That's why I butted in when I shouldn't have. That's why I made you hate me. That's why I'm here now."

"In Uncle Martin's first letter he left for me, he said he hoped that I'd find an easy heart, that he wanted that for me. I started to feel I was getting close to it, the more I was around you and the town and the other people here. But it was mostly because of you. I loved that feeling. I wanted more, and when you said that you wanted to see where things could go with us, I was thrilled. I could have told you then…" She hesitated then said the truth. "I loved you then, but I didn't say it because I didn't know if you felt the same way."

She slowly let go of his hand, praying he wouldn't walk away. Hoping she'd been right to tell him the bare truth. She'd loved him then, and she still did.

Silently, he sat down by her. His eyes were on her, and she couldn't figure out if he was happy or terrified. Then he touched her hand, lacing his fingers with hers, and looked into her eyes. He cleared his throat, then asked, "And now you hate me?"

"Oh, Max, I got scared. I was so afraid when I thought you'd broken my trust, and I...just retreated. That's what I always did with Walter when he went too far. I never apologized to him for my actions when he was like that, but I want to apologize to you. You were caring and compassionate, and I was awful. I can't ever make that up to you, but I want to try. The second letter Uncle Martin left in the safe... He knew what I needed to hear even though we'd never met. He wrote, 'I hope you're a better student of patience and fate than I've ever been. But at the end, all fell into place, and I saw how perfect a life I'd had, that the peace I'd hoped for became a reality. Don't give up, never stop.'

"He was right. I was giving up, too afraid to try harder and maybe face more pain than peace. But I don't want to give up on you. You're the most important person who ever came into my life."

Her hold on him tightened as she said, "I never hated you. Never. The truth is, I love you. I'll always love you no matter what happens."

For a moment he just stared at her, then he smiled that smile that made her heart race. "Marianna Grace Bennet, I love you. I have since the first time I saw you, sprawled on the floor here."

She all but fell into his arms, holding on to him to make very sure she wasn't imagining the happiness he'd just given her.

"I want to be with you for the rest of my life. To make this our home and to spend every minute I can loving you." His voice was a rumble against her cheek pressed to his chest.

She eased back to look up at him. "That's what I want, too," she whispered right before he kissed her.

She met his touch and let herself get lost in a growing happiness that she'd never felt before. She never wanted to stop, but Max eased her back so his eyes held hers, eyes full of warmth and the hint of a smile.

"One hundred percent cool," he said, then leaned in to kiss her again.

Moments later, she was sitting curled up beside him, resting her head on his shoulder, her hand on his chest. His heart was racing matching hers.

"Thank you," she said.

"For what?" he asked, his warm breath brushing her skin.

"I made it to one hundred percent cool," she murmured.

"You sure did," he said. "Beyond cool."

She moved back when she remembered the election. "Oh my gosh, did you win the election?"

His low laughter was so nice. "You just kissed Sheriff Donovan version 2.0. I won and the Van Durens congratulated me. How's that for a win?"

As Max stroked her hair back from her face, he asked, "Horses and cows?"

"You said that backward," she said.

"It works either way."

"Okay. Ask me anything?"

"So, just to be clear, you do love me and want to share this place with me, and you're not going back to Arizona, right?"

"That's right, Sheriff," she said. Then she glanced past him and seemed startled.

"What's wrong?"

"Out the back! Come on," she said as she took his hand

and hurried with him out of the great room, past the desk, into the office and over to the sliding glass doors.

"There!" she said, pointing toward the night sky.

"What are you—" He stopped when a shooting star flashed across the heavens, then another one right after it.

Grace was almost bouncing with excitement. "It's beautiful."

"Beautiful," Max echoed but was looking at her. He hated to think how close he'd come to losing her.

"Is there going to be more?" she asked as she glanced at him.

"I don't know," he said as he let go of her hand to pull her closer to him. He felt every breath she took. "December's the best time for the storms. Maybe Marty's behind this, letting us know that this is what he wanted when he wrote the letters. He wanted us to be friends and figured it could lead to something even better. I told you he always had a reason for everything he did."

"I think he was awesome," she half whispered.

"Me, too," Max said, relishing her closeness and a feeling of being right where he belonged.

Grace met his gaze and smiled softly. "My turn for cows and horses." She shifted and lifted her arms up and slipped them around his neck.

"You don't have to do that. I'll tell you anything you ask and always the truth."

Grace smiled at him and repeated, "Cows and horses?"

"Go for it."

She grinned at him, and it almost took his breath away. "Tattoo or no tattoo?"

"Right now at this moment, you want to ask me that?"

"Tattoo or no tattoo?" she persisted.

"Okay, okay, if you have to know, well…" He loved how excited she looked to finally hear the truth. "The truth is I don't have a tattoo, but I'm thinking of getting one on my chest."

"What?"

"One of you."

Her eyes widened, and then she smiled. "That's a joke, right?"

"What if it isn't?"

She hesitated for a moment, then shook her head. "No… you're kidding. I can tell."

"Okay, you got me. I don't have any tattoos and I'm not planning on getting one anytime soon."

"Wow! I've learned to read you, and I'm pretty darn good at it. So, no tattoo."

"What about you? Do *you* have any tattoos?"

"Me?" She laughed at that, and he loved the sound. "No, none. Cross my heart."

He laughed, too. "Well, now that's settled—" He sighed. "I'm so relieved that you want to live here. I have to admit, I wasn't too excited about moving to Arizona."

"You would have done that?"

"I'm glad I don't have to, but honestly, I'm at a point where I don't want to spend another minute without you. So I would have made the move…for you."

When Grace whispered, "I love you," then kissed him again, he knew without a shadow of a doubt, he'd found his easy heart.

IT WAS AN unusually balmy day in May when most of the townspeople joined Max and Grace to honor Martin Robert Bennet. Grace loved her uncle, a man she'd never met, and she loved the man beside her so much she couldn't put it into words. They planned to live at the Lodge after their mid-July wedding until they could build their own home close by on their land.

As the guests eulogized their dear friend, her father—an unexpected addition to the mourners—stood to her right on the bridge, his head down, his hands clasped together.

Max looked at Grace and his smile was slow and easy. He leaned down to whisper to her. "Marty would have loved to see so many people here, especially Walter."

"He would. I can't tell you what it means to me that he's here."

Grace saw the look in Max's eyes and knew what he wanted her to do. She reached to slip her hand in the crook of her father's arm. At first, Walter didn't move, but then he shifted to be closer to her. Max squeezed her other hand, as if to say, *Well done.*

The stream below them was flowing, and the day felt fresh and sweet when Burr came over to hand the urn to Grace. Max held it for her to open it, and she put her hands over his to share the moment. Then Grace felt a hand on her shoulder—Walter's hand. It was a perfect day to say goodbye to Uncle Martin as the ashes drifted downward into the clear water.

When the urn was empty, Grace turned to Max and kissed him. "Thank you for everything," she whispered before she looked at her father.

"I have to leave, Grace," he said in a low voice. "I'm sorry. Soon Sawyer will be calling the shots."

"He's a perfect choice to take over when you leave." Walter had shown up on his own to remember his brother, and she'd let him leave on his own, but before she'd do that, she did something she could never remember doing in her life. She kissed her father on the cheek and whispered, "I'm so glad you came… Dad."

He looked at her briefly as if he didn't know what to do. Then he said, "Me, too. I'll call you soon." With that, he turned and walked off.

Grace spotted Sawyer waiting for him at the top of the trail. The man waved and she had a feeling Sawyer might have been part of her father showing up so unexpectedly.

She turned and saw Max handing the urn over to Burr to take up to the Lodge. He took Grace by her hand that bore the engagement ring that he'd given her. The ring was platinum with a beautiful amethyst gem, a soft purple color that glinted violet in the sun.

He looked around, then said loudly, "Okay, folks. Barbecue and music on the back deck. Marty would want to see you all have a fun time."

Burr spoke up. "Absolutely. Marty wouldn't have wanted it any other way."

The crowd began to disperse with Elaine and Burr leading the way. Grace held on to Max as they followed the rest. "I can't believe my dad came."

"I don't know if I should tell you this," he said as they trailed after the main group.

"What's that?"

"I called Walter a week ago, and I had a heart-to-heart with him, so different than the first time. I told him about us and said that you deserved his support doing what Marty wanted. And, I added, he was very welcome to be here. I told him that it would mean so much to you. I just didn't know if he'd show up or not."

She stopped to turn and look up at Max. He did it again, and again he'd been right. "I didn't think I could love you any more than I already do, but I was wrong. Thank you for making that call."

He smiled at her. "That's a relief. Now, about our wedding."

"I'll call him about that."

"Great idea," he murmured as they started walking again. Off in the distance, Grace could see people already on the deck and hear music coming over the outdoor speakers that Chappy had installed for them. Today had been sad and happy all at once.

Max stopped before they reached the end of the trail.

"Just a minute," he said and took out his cell phone. She watched him glance at the screen, then frown.

"What's wrong?" she asked.

"I'm not sure." He hit the icon to take the call and said, "Hello?" He listened, his hazel eyes on her as his frown turned into a smile. "Absolutely. She's right here."

She took the phone. "Who is it?" she asked in a whisper.

"Take the call," was all Max would say.

She put it to her ear. "Hello?"

"Grace, it's Dad. I wanted to ask you something before we fly out."

"Okay," she said with trepidation.

"Max mentioned your wedding in our last call, said it's in July sometime, and I want to be there."

She felt her throat tighten, and she knew she was about to cry from happiness.

"But I'll only come if I can walk you down the aisle. It's a lot to ask, I know, but would that be possible?"

Now she *was* crying and smiling at the same time. "Yes, I'd… I'd like that a lot."

"Thank you, Grace. I'll call you later and get the details, okay?"

"Yes, Dad, that's definitely okay."

She handed the phone back to Max. He took it, then hugged her to him. "You all right?"

"He wants to come to our wedding, and he wants to walk me down the aisle."

"Awesome," Max whispered in her hair. "Another wish came true for you."

She swiped at the tears on her cheeks. "This is the best day of my life," she said.

Max gathered her safely in his arms and when she looked up at him, he kissed her quickly then asked, "Any other wishes you want to make?"

She didn't have to think twice about her answer. "No, how about you?"

He smiled that smile she so loved. "Nope. I have everything I want right here with me now."

"So do I."

He shifted to take her hand and she loved the feeling of her fingers laced with his.

"Let's go up to the Lodge and celebrate Marty's life, and the beginning of our new life together. He would have loved that," Max said.

As they walked toward the celebration, Grace felt her world settle around her in the most incredible way. Everything she'd missed in her life before was now falling into place, from her father showing up at the ceremony, then asking to walk her down the aisle, to finding a real home for the first time, and finding Max, who made Uncle Martin's wish for her come true. Max was the reason she'd found her easy heart, with her loving and being loved by him, her cowboy, her hero, her everything.

* * * * *

WESTERN

Rugged men looking for love...

Available Next Month

Sweet-Talkin' Maverick Christy Jeffries
The Cowboy's Second Chance Cheryl Harper

....

Fortune's Baby Claim Michelle Major
The Cowgirl's Homecoming Jeannie Watt

....

LOVE INSPIRED
A Valentine's Day Return Brenda Minton
Their Inseparable Bond Jill Weatherholt

Larger Print

Keep reading for an excerpt of
BOYFRIEND LESSONS
by Sophia Singh Sasson — find this story
in the *Texas Cattleman's Club: Ranchers and Rivals*
anthology.

One

"So you just left?" Caitlyn Lattimore said incredulously. She was used to Alice's crazy dating experiences, but this one made her sit up in the pool lounger.

Alice slid her oversize sunglasses on top of her wavy blond hair, refilled her chardonnay glass and topped off Caitlyn, who had barely touched her first glass.

"The man ordered two appetizers, lobster for dinner and a bottle of wine from the reserve list. Then he pulls 'the left my wallet at home' crap. No, thank you. I told him I was going to the bathroom and then asked the waitress if I could escape through the kitchen door because he was a creep."

Her dating stories get scarier by the day.

Alice grabbed the bottle of suntan lotion and rubbed her arms. "I need to find a better dating site."

Caitlyn reached for the sunblock. It was early June, and the sun was strong. One touch of UV and her skin would turn shades browner. She had a number of Lattimore events to attend in the next month, and her makeup artist had just spent days perfecting the right shade of foundation for her. Alice called them rich girl problems, and Caitlyn agreed. She'd won the lottery when the Lattimores adopted her twenty-four years ago. Even now, they were sitting by the sparkling blue pool of the Lattimore ranch, their wine bottle perfectly chilled and a staff member readily available should they need anything else. Alice called it the Ritz Lattimore, but it was home for Caitlyn, one she loved not because of the luxuries, but because her family lived here.

"I wish I had your chutzpah. If that had happened to me, I'd have paid the bill and spent the night seething." Caitlyn said.

"Darlin', for that to happen to you, you'd need to actually go out on a date. To leave this gilded cage and venture into the smog and filth we mortals call the real world."

"You sound just like Alexa."

Alexa had left Royal for New York City, and then Miami, when she went to college and never looked back. She'd been home recently, though, for Victor Grandin's funeral.

Alice raised a brow. "I was sorry to hear about

Layla's grandfather dying. Victor Grandin was such a pillar in this community."

"He was. Alexa came home for the funeral and I suspect Layla would like Alexa to stay permanently, because her cutthroat lawyering skills will help our two families."

"Is this about that letter that came at the funeral? You never told me the full story."

Caitlyn's stomach roiled. "Turns out Heath Thurston is making a claim against the oil rights to the land beneath the Grandin and Lattimore ranches." It wasn't the claim that worried Caitlyn but the effect it was having on her family.

Alice leaned forward. "See, this is what happens when we don't see each other for a month—I miss all the juicy gossip."

"It's more than gossip. Those oil rights include the land that the Lattimore mansion is built on. Heath claims Daniel Grandin fathered Heath's late half-sister, Ashley, and that Daniel's dad gave Heath's mother Cynthia the oil rights. He says he found some of his mother's papers supporting the claim."

Alice's mouth hung open. Even she was speechless after that. The thought of what losing their family home would do to her siblings had consumed Caitlyn every second for the last month, since Victor Grandin's funeral.

"How did Ashley die?"

"In a car crash that also included her mother, Cynthia."

"Why did Victor Grandin Sr. give Cynthia the oil rights and not Ashley?"

"We don't know. And my grandfather signed the document, too, so he knew about it. Now he doesn't remember a thing, so Victor Grandin Jr. hired a private investigator for the two families to look into why they might have signed over the oil rights for our lands, and whether Daniel really fathered Cynthia's child."

Alice sat back, speechless once again. "Have you ever met Heath or his twin brother, Nolan?"

Caitlyn shook her head.

"I went to high school with them. They are hot. I'm talking freshly seared steak hot. I'd forgotten about Nolan, he left Royal but if he's back, that changes the dating scene." She wiggled her eyebrows at Caitlyn. "They're both single."

Caitlyn smiled. "There's enough drama in my family without me trying to date the men trying to destroy our ranch."

Caitlyn chewed on her lip. Alice was right about one thing—she needed to get a life; she was tired of her image as the quiet, shy woman who startled when a man sneezed next to her. Even though the last part was right. "Maybe I should sign up for one of these dating sites. Not all of yours have been that bad. What happened to the guy who sent you flowers and took you to meet his family?"

"He was fine, a bit boring in the sex department but I was willing to deal with that until he took a call with his mother while he was on top of me."

Caitlyn had just taken a sip of her wine, and it went flying out of her mouth, spraying all over the pool lounger. She covered her mouth in embarrassment.

Alice smiled and handed her one of the rolled hand towels from a basket on the table. Caitlyn wiped her mouth and the pool lounger. "You know not to do that to me when I'm drinking," Caitlyn said, laughing.

"Sorry, I forgot about that endearing habit of yours."

"The guy actually talked to his mom while you were in the middle of having sex?"

Alice nodded. "What's worse is he talked to her for a good two minutes, and wanted to continue on like it didn't make a difference."

"How could you not tell me about this?"

"That happened on the day of the Grandin funeral. I was so embarrassed I couldn't even think about it." Alice shook her head. "You and I need to meet men in real life. It's hard to suss out the creep factor online. It's singles' night at the Lone Star nightclub. How about we get all dressed up and go?"

I'd rather face down a pack of hungry wolves.

"You know that's not my scene. There aren't enough cocktails in the world to get me comfortable enough to talk to a strange man. It seems safer to start out with online chatting."

Alice shook her head. "Dating sites are not for you, darlin'. You need someone who's vetted, get some practice in before you go out into the world of vultures and mamas' boys."

Caitlyn nearly spit out her drink again. "I'll skip the mama's boy, but I could use someone who has the backbone to withstand the Lattimore siblings. The last time I went out on a date, Jonathan asked if he could have the guy's Social Security number to run a background check. The time before that, Jayden followed me to the restaurant where I was meeting a blind date. He didn't like the look of the guy, so he stayed parked on the street the entire time I was at dinner and followed us home."

Alice put her hand to her heart. "Your brothers are super sweet."

"No, they're overprotective. They don't pull that stuff with Alexa."

"Because she moved away." Alice took a sip of her wine. "I do have a nice, decent guy with whom you can practice your flirting skills." Alice smiled cheekily, and Caitlyn narrowed her eyes.

"There has to be something wrong with him or you would've dated him."

Alice laughed. "That would be really weird. I'm talking about Russ."

Caitlyn raised a brow. "Your brother, Russ? I thought you said he wasn't into serious dating."

Alice shifted on the lounger. "He's not, which is why he'd be the perfect person to practice your conversational skills. You two really haven't hung out, so he's like a strange man."

Caitlyn bit her lip. She didn't want to offend Alice,

but she'd never felt a spark with her brother, Russ. He was a nice enough guy, but he was just so *white*. Not that she had a problem dating white men. Her biological mother was white, but in the last couple of years she'd struggled with her identity, along with most of the country. Despite her closeness with Alice, her best friend didn't understand Caitlyn's struggle with being a woman of color. Alice had never been asked where she was from, as if her brown skin automatically meant that she was exotic or foreign. Caitlyn had struggled with that over the last two years, debating her own identity. Was she Black, white, both or neither? Whenever a form asked what her race or ethnicity was, she left it blank, because none of the categories fit her. That was the one thing she and Jax had in common. Her ex-boyfriend was also biracial, and he'd understood some of the things she'd struggled with. Yet it hadn't worked out with him, either. Maybe she really was a lost cause.

"Caitlyn, what's the harm? It's just Russ, and you could use the practice."

"I don't know.... Have you asked Russ?"

Alice shook her head reluctantly. "Look, he's coming home after months of travel. I was going to have dinner with him on Friday. Why don't you come? It'll just be the three of us. Low-key. No pressure. I'll be there to back you up and fill in if you stammer over your words or spit out your wine."

Caitlyn threw her dirty hand towel playfully at Alice. *What do I have to lose?* She was bored by the endless conversations about the fate of the Grandin and Lattimore ranches in her house and of making excuses about why she didn't date more. Ever since Layla Grandin and Josh Banks had gotten together, her family had been even more determined to see Caitlyn out and dating. She was tired of being pitied by her siblings. It was time to get over what had happened with Jax. It had been a year since they'd broken up. She'd been on a few dates since then—all failures, thanks to the scars Jax had left. She knew intellectually that Jax was just a bad dating experience, but it clung to her, haunted her thoughts at the most inappropriate times. It was time to replace those memories, even if it was with something meaningless.

"Come on, Caitlyn, what's the worst that can happen?"

She sighed. *That I'll hate Russ but you'll fall in love with the idea of me and Russ and it'll affect our friendship.*

"I'll order Italian from your favorite place," Alice said coaxingly.

"I'll come to dinner. As a friend. I'm not dating Russ."

Alice beamed. "Who said anything about dating? Think of it as a practice session."

"You've got to be kidding me." Alice glared at her phone.

"Trouble?" Caitlyn asked as she arranged the cutlery on Alice's table. Alice lived in a charming row house in the center of Royal. She had decorated it in a comfortable cottage style with soft pastel colors and wood furniture. Caitlyn had come early to help Alice with dinner preparations. She enjoyed the easy way she could make a salad in Alice's kitchen. At her house, the staff took it as an affront if she prepared her own food, feeling that they weren't meeting her standards.

"Russ is late, and he's bringing a friend to dinner."

Caitlyn smiled. While Russ was supposed to be her practice date tonight, it would serve Alice right if he brought another woman home with him. Caitlyn had suspected, but she now knew, that Alice hadn't told Russ she was setting them up.

"I'll set another place at the table," Caitlyn volunteered, her voice sugary sweet. "Don't worry, you have enough food to feed the entire block." If Russ was bringing a woman, Caitlyn could sit back and watch the two of them interact and take notes. The churning in her stomach slowed, and she opened a bottle of wine and poured two glasses. She didn't like to drink when she was anxious, but the evening was looking up.

"How dare Russ bring a woman." Alice seethed.

"Did you tell him he was here to give me boyfriend lessons?" Even as she said the words, Caitlyn realized how ridiculous the idea had been all along. There was no such thing as practicing dating skills. Was there?

She took a large sip from her glass, picturing herself taking notes as she watched Russ and his date converse during dinner as if she were sitting in a classroom. The idea made her giggle.

A half hour later, when the doorbell rang, both Alice and Caitlyn had polished off equal parts of an entire bottle of Bordeaux, and Caitlyn was looking forward to the evening.

Alice opened the door and greeted her brother. Caitlyn waited patiently on the gray leather couch, not wanting to interrupt the inevitable whispered shouting of Alice berating Russ for spoiling the date setup that he didn't know he was participating in. She felt bad for Russ and even worse for his poor date, who would have no idea what she had done to incur Alice's passive-aggressive wrath.

"I can't believe it's you!" Alice's squeals made Caitlyn sit up.

Before she could react, they all walked in, and Caitlyn nearly choked on her drink as she caught sight of the most beautiful man that she'd ever seen.